THE APPLE TREE

THE APPLE TREE

TALES FROM CARAVAN
Volume One

John Galsworthy

NONSUCH

To My Wife

First published 1926
Copyright © in this edition 2005
Nonsuch Publishing Ltd

Nonsuch Publishing Limited
The Mill, Brimscombe Port, Stroud, Gloucestershire, GL5 2QG
www.nonsuch-publishing.com

Nonsuch Publishing Ltd is an imprint of the Tempus Publishing Group

For any comments or suggestions, please email the editor of this series at:
classics@tempus-publishing.com

British Library Cataloguing in Publication Data.
A catalogue record for this book is available from the British Library.

ISBN 1-84588-013-7

Typesetting and origination by Nonsuch Publishing Limited
Printed in Great Britain by Oaklands Book Services Limited

CONTENTS

INTRODUCTION TO THE MODERN EDITION

'I do wish I had the gift of writing' wrote John Galsworthy in a letter of 1894. 'I really think that it is the nicest way of making money going', he continued, 'only it isn't really the writing so much as the thoughts that one wants, and, when you feel like a very shallow pond with no nice cool deep pools with queer and pleasant things at the bottom, what's the good. I suppose one could cultivate writing ...' By 1932, Galsworthy was judged to have cultivated his writing sufficiently well to be awarded the Nobel Prize for Literature. One can only imagine to what heights he might have reached had he been blessed with natural talent. As it is, he is remembered as one of the most prolific writers of the twentieth century, commercially successful and politically influential, and as one of English literature's best-loved sons.

The author was born on 14 August 1867, at Kingston Hill in Surrey, into a wealthy middle-class family. At the age of fourteen he began at Harrow, where he became head of his house and, fashionably, was lauded more for his sporting than his academic ability. From there he moved on to New College, Oxford, where the heady life of an affluent, monocled undergraduate did not prevent him from successfully reading law, and in 1890 he was called to the Bar. His lack of interest in this august profession soon became obvious, however, and he took to the seas. While Galsworthy's father hoped this might spark in his son an interest in maritime law, what actually resulted was a meeting with a young writer by the name of Joseph Conrad, who lit in Galsworthy a fire of an altogether different kind.

His first published work, *To the Four Winds*, was released in 1897 under the *nom de plume* John Sinjohn. It was not until *The Island Pharisees* (1904) that Galsworthy published under his own name, as he considered this to be his most important work to date. It was, however, two years later that he completed possibly the most important work of his career, *The Man of Property*. This book introduced the character of Soames Forsyte, and laid the foundation for *The Forsyte Saga*, which was to eventually bring Galsworthy the Nobel Prize.

The Apple Tree is a collection of twenty-four tales making up the first volume of *Caravan*, which is in itself the definitive collection of John Galsworthy's shorter stories. These tales, all written between 1900 and 1923, are grouped together in pairs, as the author himself explains in his own introduction, with an 'early' story being followed by a 'late' one. Each pair has also been grouped together to reflect similarities in theme, mood or technique. 'The Apple Tree' for example, the tale from which this volume takes its name, is a powerful story of tragic love; Galsworthy evokes here an almost unbearable tension, a tangible friction between action and inexorable consequence. It is twinned in this volume with 'A Man of Devon' for reasons of theme, which quickly becomes apparent as this sad and beautiful story unfolds.

Taken as a whole, Galsworthy's work constitutes a vast and wide-ranging examination of the deep divisions of social hierarchy, the vagaries and machinations of love, and the constant struggle between desire and honour. Together with the second volume, *A Long-Ago Affair*, this collection represents Galsworthy as a master storyteller. Over his career he produced some 20 novels, 27 plays, 5 collections of essays, 3 collections of poetry and 173 short stories. He died in January of 1933.

FOREWORD

L<small>IKE</small> some long caravan bearing merchandise of sorts, the tales of a writer wind through the desert of indifference towards the oasis of public favour. Whether they ever arrive, or drift to death among the shifting sands of popular taste, lies on the knees of the gods—their author has no say. When he has mustered and sent them forth, he may retire and squat afresh on the carpet of vision, having done all he can.

In assembling for this 'Caravan' all my tales falling short of the novel in length, written between the years 1900 and 1923 inclusive, I have roped them two by two, an early tale behind and a late tale in front. Taking 1914 as the dividing year, I have thus paired forty-six out of these fifty-six tales. The five remaining pairs belong entirely to the last ten years, more prolific than the first fourteen. In selecting each tandem, I have tried to find tales which have some likeness to each other in theme, or mood, so that any reader who has the curiosity can mark such difference as Time brings to technique or treatment.

Ten of the tales thus paired are what one calls "long-short," ranging from 30,000 to 8,000 words—no one of the rest exceeds, I think, 6,000.

The fiction market is supposed to require of short stories a certain pattern full of "pep" and sting in the tail. The scorpion, it is said, if sufficiently irritated, will sting itself to death. So will the short story when worried by the demands of editors. The inveterately independent will resist these blandishments, go their own ways, imitate no one. They may achieve results as little to the taste of the market as are these tales, but at least they will fail after their own hearts and probably end by getting very high prices for their merchandise.

"Ev'yone that talk about Heav'n ain't goin' there!" and those who dutifully confection the short story to the sacred pattern of the hour may well become of the company which shakes its tambourines in hell. Independence is the state best worth having in life, and such as believe they can achieve it in their later tales by servitude to fashion in their youthful efforts are doomed, I fear, to the drinking of bitter waters. If the writer of the short tale submit himself to the discipline demanded by the crisp and clear expression of his genuine fancies and his genuine moods, he has submitted to quite enough.

As the untaught spider spins his delicate rose-window and assures it against wind and rain by sheer adjustment—not a thread too many or too few—so let us writers of short tales try to spin out of our own instinct and vision the round and threaded marvel. If in it we catch some hopeful editor and hold him to ransom—all the better for us; but if we don't we have none the less fulfilled our being, and that is our real end in life.

Far be it from this writer to think that he has achieved that end, but he has tried; and in this 'Caravan' the assembly of his differing and indifferent efforts sets forth.

JOHN GALSWORTHY.
ALGERIA,
February 5, 1925.

SALVATION OF A FORSYTE

I

SWITHIN Forsyte lay in bed. The corners of his mouth under his white moustache drooped towards his double chin. He panted: "My doctor says I'm in a bad way, James."

His twin-brother placed his hand behind his ear. "I can't hear you. They tell me I ought to take a cure. There's always a cure wanted for something. Emily had a cure."

Swithin replied: "You mumble so. I hear my man, Adolph. I trained him. . . . You ought to have an ear-trumpet. You're getting very shaky, James."

There was silence; then James Forsyte, as if galvanized, remarked: "I s'pose you've made your will. I s'pose you've left your money to the family; you've nobody else to leave it to. There was Danson died the other day, and left his money to a hospital."

The hairs of Swithin's white moustache bristled. "My fool of a doctor told me to make my will," he said; "I hate a fellow who tells you to make your will. My appetite's good; I ate a partridge last night. I'm all the better for eating. He told me to leave off champagne! I eat a good breakfast. I'm not eighty. You're the same age, James. You look very shaky."

James Forsyte said: "You ought to have another opinion. Have Blank; he's the first man now. I had him for Emily; cost me two hundred guineas. He sent her to Homburg; that's the first place now. The prince was there—everybody goes there."

Swithin Forsyte answered: "I don't get any sleep at night, now I can't get out; and I've bought a new carriage—gave a pot of money for it. D'you ever have bronchitis? They tell me champagne's dangerous; it's my belief I couldn't take a better thing."

James Forsyte rose.

"You ought to have another opinion. Emily sent her love; she would have come in, but she had to go to Niagara. Everybody goes there; it's *the* place now. Rachael goes every morning; she overdoes it—she'll be laid up one of these days. There's a fancy ball there to-night; the Duke gives the prizes."

Swithin Forsyte said angrily: "I can't get things properly cooked here; at the club I get spinach decently done." The bed-clothes jerked at the tremor of his legs.

James Forsyth replied: "You must have done well with Tintos; you must have made a lot of money by them. Your ground-rents must be falling in, too. You must have any amount you don't know what to do with." He mouthed at the words, as if his lips were watering.

Swithin Forsyte glared. "Money!" he said; "my doctor's bill's enormous."

James Forsyte stretched out a cold, damp hand. "Good-bye! You ought to have another opinion. I can't keep the horses waiting: they're a new pair—stood me in three hundred. You ought to take care of yourself. I shall speak to Blank about you. You ought to have him—everybody says he's the first man. Good-bye!"

Swithin Forsyte continued to stare at the ceiling. He thought: 'A poor thing, James! a selfish beggar! Must be worth a couple of hundred thousand!' He wheezed, meditating on life . . .

He was ill and lonely. For many years he had been lonely, and for two years ill; but as he had smoked his first cigar, so he would live his life—stoutly, to its predestined end. Every day he was driven to the club; sitting forward on the spring cushions of a single brougham, his hands on his knees, swaying a little, strangely solemn. He ascended the steps into that marble hall—the folds of his chin wedged into the aperture of his collar—walking squarely with a stick. Later he would dine, eating majestically, and savouring his food, behind a bottle of champagne set in an ice-pail—his waistcoat defended by a napkin, his eyes rolling a little or glued in a stare on the waiter. Never did he suffer his head or back to droop, for it was not distinguished so to do.

Because he was old and deaf, he spoke to no one; and no one spoke to him. The club gossip, an Irishman, said to each newcomer: "Old Forsyte! Look at 'um! Must ha' had something in his life to sour 'um!" But Swithin had had nothing in his life to sour him.

For many days now he had lain in bed in a room exuding silver, crimson, and electric light, and smelling of opopanax and of cigars. The curtains were drawn, the firelight gleamed: on a table by his bed were a jug of barley-water and *The Times*. He had made an attempt to read, failed, and fell again to thinking. His face with its square chin looked like a block of pale leather bedded in the pillow. It was lonely! A woman in the room would have made all the difference! Why had he never married? He breathed hard, staring frog-like at the ceiling; a memory had come into his mind. It was a long time ago—forty odd years—but it seemed like yesterday . . .

It happened when he was thirty-eight, for the first and only time in his life travelling on the Continent, with his twin-brother James and a man named Traquair. On the way from Germany to Venice, he had found himself at the Hôtel Goldene Alp at Salzburg. It was late August, and weather for the gods: sunshine on the walls and the shadows of the vine-leaves, and at night, the moonlight, and again on the walls the shadows of the vine-leaves. Averse to the suggestions of other people, Swithin had refused to visit the Citadel; he had spent the day alone in the window of his bedroom, smoking a succession of cigars, and disparaging the appearance of the passers-by. After dinner he was driven by boredom into the streets. His chest puffed out like a pigeon's, and with something of a pigeon's cold and inquiring eye, he strutted, annoyed at the frequency of uniforms, which seemed to him both needless and offensive. His spleen rose at this crowd of foreigners who spoke an unintelligible language, wore hair on their faces, and smoked bad tobacco. 'A queer lot!' he thought. The sound of music from a *café* attracted him, he walked in, vaguely moved by a wish for the distinction of adventure, without the trouble which adventure usually brought with it; spurred too, perhaps, by an after-dinner demon. The *café* was the *bier-halle* of the 'Fifties, with a door at either end, and lighted by a large wooden lantern. On a small dais three musicians were fiddling. Solitary men, or groups, sat at some dozen tables, and the waiters hurried about replenishing glasses; the air was thick with smoke. Swithin sat down. "Wine!" he said sternly. The astonished waiter brought him wine. Swithin pointed to a beer-glass on the table. "Here!" he said, with the same ferocity. The waiter poured out the wine. 'Ah!' thought Swithin, 'they can understand if they like.' A group of officers close by were laughing; Swithin stared at them uneasily. A hollow cough sounded almost in his ear. To his left a man sat reading, with his elbows on the corners of a journal, and his gaunt shoulders raised almost to his eyes. He had a thin, long nose, broadening suddenly at the nostrils; a black-brown beard, spread in a savage fan over his chest; what was visible of the face was the colour of old parchment. A strange, wild, haughty-looking creature! Swithin observed his clothes with some displeasure—they were the clothes of a journalist or strolling actor. And yet he was impressed. This was singular. How could he be impressed by a fellow in such clothes! The man reached out a hand, covered with black hairs, and took up a tumbler that contained a dark-coloured fluid: 'Brandy!' thought Swithin. The crash of a falling chair startled him—his neighbour had risen. He was of immense height, and very thin; his great beard seemed to splash away from his mouth; he was glaring at the group of officers, and speaking. Swithin made out two words: "*Hunde! Deutsche Hunde!*" 'Hounds! German hounds!' he thought: 'Rather strong!' One of the officers had jumped up, and now drew his sword. The tall man swung his chair up, and brought it down with a thud. Everybody round started up and closed on him. The tall man cried out: "To me, Magyars!"

Swithin grinned. The tall man fighting such odds excited his unwilling admiration; he had a momentary impulse to go to his assistance. 'Only get a broken nose!' he thought, and looked for a safe corner. But at that moment a thrown lemon struck him on the jaw. He jumped out of his chair and rushed at the officers. The Hungarian, swinging his chair, threw him a look of gratitude—Swithin glowed with momentary admiration of himself. A sword blade grazed his arm: he felt a sudden dislike of the Hungarian. 'This is too much,' he thought, and, catching up a chair, flung it at the wooden lantern. There was a crash—faces and swords vanished. He struck a match, and by the light of it bolted for the door. A second later he was in the street.

II

A voice said in English, "God bless you, brother!"

Swithin looked round, and saw the tall Hungarian holding out his hand. He took it, thinking, 'What a fool I've been!' There was something in the Hungarian's gesture which said, "You are worthy of me!" It was annoying, but rather impressive. The man seemed even taller than before; there was a cut on his cheek, the blood from which was trickling down his beard. "You English!" he said. "I saw you stone Haynau—I saw you cheer Kossuth. The free blood of your people cries out to us." He looked at Swithin. "You are a big man, you have a big soul—and strong, how you flung them down! Ha!" Swithin had an impulse to take to his heels. "My name," said the Hungarian, "is Boleskey. You are my friend." His English was good.

'Bulsh-kai-ee, Burlsh-kai-ee,' thought Swithin; 'what a devil of a name!' "Mine," he said sulkily, "is Forsyte."

The Hungarian repeated it.

"You've had a nasty jab on the cheek," said Swithin; the sight of the matted beard was making him feel sick. The Hungarian put his fingers to his cheek, brought them away wet, stared at them, then with an indifferent air gathered a wisp of his beard and crammed it against the cut.

"Ugh!" said Swithin. "Here! Take my handkerchief!"

The Hungarian bowed. "Thank you!" he said; "I couldn't think of it! Thank you a thousand times!"

"Take it!" growled Swithin; it seemed to him suddenly of the first importance. He thrust the handkerchief into the Hungarian's hand, and felt a pain in his arm. 'There!' he thought, 'I've strained a muscle.'

The Hungarian kept muttering, regardless of passers-by, "Swine! How you threw them over! Two or three cracked heads, anyway—the cowardly swine!"

"Look here!" said Swithin suddenly; "which is my way to the Goldene Alp?"

The Hungarian replied, "But you are coming with me, for a glass of wine?"

Swithin looked at the ground. 'Not if I know it!' he thought.

"Ah!" said the Hungarian with dignity, "you do not wish for my friendship!"

'Touchy beggar!' thought Swithin. "Of course," he stammered, "if you put it in that way—"

The Hungarian bowed, murmuring, "Forgive me!"

They had not gone a dozen steps before a youth, with a beardless face and hollow cheeks, accosted them. "For the love of Christ, gentlemen," he said, "help me!"

"Are you a German?" asked Boleskey.

"Yes," said the youth.

"Then you may rot!"

"Master, look here!" Tearing open his coat, the youth displayed his skin, and a leather belt drawn tight round it. Again Swithin felt that desire to take to his heels. He was filled with horrid forebodings—a sense of perpending intimacy with things such as no gentleman had dealings with.

The Hungarian crossed himself. "Brother," he said to the youth, "come you in!"

Swithin looked at them askance, and followed. By a dim light they groped their way up some stairs into a large room, into which the moon was shining through a window bulging over the street. A lamp burned low; there was a smell of spirits and tobacco, with a faint, peculiar scent, as of rose leaves. In one corner stood a czymbal, in another a great pile of newspapers. On the wall hung some old-fashioned pistols, and a rosary of yellow beads. Everything was tidily arranged, but dusty. Near an open fireplace was a table with the remains of a meal. The ceiling, floor, and walls were all of dark wood. In spite of the strange disharmony, the room had a sort of refinement.

The Hungarian took a bottle out of a cupboard and, filling some glasses, handed one to Swithin. Swithin put it gingerly to his nose. 'You never know your luck! Come!' he thought, tilting it slowly into his mouth. It was thick, too sweet, but of a fine flavour.

"Brothers!" said the Hungarian, refilling, "your healths!"

The youth tossed off his wine. And Swithin this time did the same; he pitied this poor devil of a youth now. "Come round to-morrow!" he said, "I'll give you a shirt or two." When the youth was gone, however, he remembered with relief that he had not given his address.

'Better so,' he reflected. 'A humbug, no doubt.'

"What was that you said to him?" he asked of the Hungarian.

"I said," answered Boleskey, "'You have eaten and drunk and now you are my enemy!'"

"Quite right!" said Swithin, "quite right! A beggar is every man's enemy."

"You do not understand," the Hungarian replied politely. "While he was a beggar—I, too, have had to beg" (Swithin thought, 'Good God! this is awful!'), "but now that he is no longer hungry, what is he but a German? No Austrian dog soils my floors!"

His nostrils, as it seemed to Swithin, had distended in an unpleasant fashion; and a wholly unnecessary raucousness invaded his voice. "I am an exile—all of my blood are exiles. Those Godless dogs!" Swithin hurriedly assented.

As he spoke, a face peeped in at the door.

"Rozsi!" said the Hungarian. A young girl came in. She was rather short, with a deliciously round figure and a thick plait of hair. She smiled, and showed her even teeth; her little, bright, wide-set grey eyes glanced from one man to the other. Her face was round, too, high in the cheek-bones, the colour of wild roses, with brows that had a twist-up at the corners. With a gesture of alarm, she put her hand to her cheek, and called, "Margit!" An older girl appeared, taller, with fine shoulders, large eyes, a pretty mouth, and what Swithin described to himself afterwards as a "pudding" nose. Both girls, with little cooing sounds, began attending to their father's face. Swithin turned his back to them. His arm pained him.

'This is what comes of interfering,' he thought sulkily; 'I might have had my neck broken!' Suddenly a soft palm was placed in his, two eyes, half-fascinated, half-shy, looked at him; then a voice called, "Rozsi!" the door was slammed, he was alone again with the Hungarian, harassed by a sense of soft disturbance.

"Your daughter's name is Rosy?" he said; "we have it in England—from rose, a flower."

"Rozsi (Rozgi)," the Hungarian replied; "your English is a hard tongue, harder than French, German, or Czechish, harder than Russian, or Roumanian—I know no more."

"What?" said Swithin, "six languages?" Privately he thought, 'He knows how to lie, anyway.'

"If you lived in a country like mine," muttered the Hungarian, "with all men's hands against you! A free people—dying—but not dead!"

Swithin could not imagine what he was talking of. This man's face, with its linen bandage, gloomy eyes, and great black wisps of beard, his fierce mutterings, and hollow cough, were all most unpleasant. He seemed to be suffering from some kind of mental dog-bite. His emotion indeed appeared so indecent, so uncontrolled and open, that its obvious sincerity produced a sort of awe in Swithin. It was like being forced to look into a furnace. Boleskey stopped roaming up and down. "You think it's over?" he said; "I tell you, in the breast of each one of us Magyars there is a hell. What is sweeter than life? What is more sacred than each breath we draw? Ah! my country!" These words were uttered so slowly, with such intense mournfulness, that Swithin's jaw relaxed; he converted the movement to a yawn.

"Tell me," said Boleskey, "what would you do if the French conquered you?"

Swithin smiled. Then suddenly, as though something had hurt him, he grunted, "The 'Froggies'? Let 'em try!"

"Drink!" said Boleskey—"there is nothing like it"; he filled Swithin's glass. "I will tell you my story."

Swithin rose hurriedly. "It's late," he said. "This is good stuff, though; have you much of it?"

"It is the last bottle."

"What?" said Swithin; "and you gave it to a beggar?"

"My name is Boleskey-Stefan," the Hungarian said, raising his head; "of the Komorn Boleskeys." The simplicity of this phrase—as who shall say: What need of further description?—made an impression on Swithin; he stopped to listen. Boleskey's story went on and on. "There were many abuses," boomed his deep voice, "much wrong done—much cowardice. I could see clouds gathering—rolling over our plains. The Austrian wished to strangle the breath of our mouths—to take from us the shadow of our liberty—the shadow—all we had. Two years ago—the year of '48, when every man and boy answered the great voice—brother, a dog's life!—to use a pen when all of your blood are fighting, but it was decreed for me! My son was killed; my brothers taken—and myself was thrown out like a dog—I had written out my heart, I had written out all the blood that was in my body!" He seemed to tower, a gaunt shadow of a man, with gloomy, flickering eyes staring at the wall.

Swithin rose, and stammered, "Much obliged—very interesting." Boleskey made no effort to detain him, but continued staring at the wall. "Good-night!" said Swithin, and stamped heavily downstairs.

III

When at last Swithin reached the Goldene Alp, he found his brother and friend standing uneasily at the door. Traquair, a prematurely dried-up man, with whiskers and a Scotch accent, remarked, "Ye're airly, man!" Swithin growled something unintelligible, and swung up to bed. He discovered a slight cut on his arm. He was in a savage temper—the elements had conspired to show him things he did not want to see; yet now and then a memory of Rozsi, of her soft palm in his, a sense of having been stroked and flattered, came over him. During breakfast next morning his brother and Traquair announced their intention of moving on. James Forsyte, indeed, remarked that it was no place for a "collector," since all the "old" shops were in the hands of Jews or very grasping persons—he had discovered this at once. Swithin pushed his cup aside. "*You* may do what you like," he said, "*I'm* staying here."

James Forsyte replied, tumbling over his own words: "Why! what do you want to stay here for? There's nothing for you to do here—there's nothing to see here, unless you go up the Citadel, an' you won't do that."

Swithin growled, "Who says so?" Having gratified his perversity, he felt in a better temper. He had slung his arm in a silk sash, and accounted for it by saying he had slipped. Later he went out and walked on to the bridge. In the brilliant sunshine spires were glistening against the pearly background of the hills; the town had a clean, joyous air. Swithin glanced at the Citadel and thought, "Looks a strong place! Shouldn't wonder if it were impregnable!" And this for some occult reason gave him pleasure. It occurred to him suddenly to go and look for the Hungarian's house.

About noon, after a hunt of two hours, he was gazing about him blankly, pale with heat, but more obstinate than ever, when a voice above him called "Mister!" He looked up and saw Rozsi. She was leaning her round chin on her round hand, gazing down at him with her deep-set, clever eyes. When Swithin removed his hat, she clapped her hands. Again he had the sense of being admired, caressed. With a careless air, that sat grotesquely on his tall square person, he walked up to the door; both girls stood in the passage. Swithin felt a confused desire to speak in some foreign tongue. "Maam'selles," he began, "er—*bong jour*—er your father—*père, comment?*"

"We also speak English," said the elder girl; "will you come in, please?"

Swithin swallowed a misgiving and entered. The room had a worn appearance by daylight, as if it had always been the nest of tragic or vivid lives. He sat down, and his eyes said:

"I am a stranger, but don't try to get the better of me, please—that is impossible." The girls looked at him in silence. Rozsi wore a rather short skirt of black stuff, a white shirt, and across her shoulders an embroidered yoke; her sister was dressed in dark green, with a coral necklace; both girls had their hair in plaits. After a minute Rozsi touched the sleeve of his hurt arm.

"It's nothing!" muttered Swithin.

"Father fought with a chair, but you had no chair," she said in a wondering voice.

He doubled the fist of his sound arm and struck a blow at space. To his amazement she began to laugh. Nettled at this, he put his hand beneath the heavy table and lifted it. Rozsi clapped her hands. "Ah! now I see—how strong you are!" She made him a curtsey and whisked round to the window. He found the quick intelligence of her eyes confusing; sometimes they seemed to look beyond him at something invisible—this, too, confused him. From Margit he learned that they had been two years in England, where their father had made his living by teaching languages; they had now been a year in Salzburg.

"We wait," suddenly with Rozsi; and Margit, with a solemn face, repeated, "We wait."

Swithin's eyes swelled a little with his desire to see what they were waiting for. How queer they were, with their eyes that gazed beyond him! He looked at their figures. 'She would pay for dressing,' he thought, and he tried to imagine Rozsi in a skirt with proper flounces, a thin waist, and hair drawn back over her ears. She would pay for dressing, with that supple figure, fluffy hair, and little hands! And instantly his own hands, face, and clothes disturbed him. He got up, examined the pistols on the wall, and felt resentment at the faded, dusty room. 'Smells like a pot-house!' he thought. He sat down again close to Rozsi.

"Do you love to dance?" she asked: "to dance is to live. First you hear the music—how your feet itch! It is wonderful! You begin slow, quick—quicker; you fly—you know nothing—your feet are in the air. It is wonderful!"

A slow flush had mounted into Swithin's face.

"Ah!" continued Rozsi, her eyes fixed on him, "when I am dancing—out there I see the plains—your feet go one—two—three—quick, quick, quick, quicker—you fly."

She stretched herself, a shiver seemed to pass all down her. "Margit! dance!" and, to Swithin's consternation, the two girls—their hands on each other's shoulders—began shuffling their feet and swaying to and fro. Their heads were thrown back, their eyes half-closed; suddenly the step quickened, they swung to one side, then to the other, and began whirling round in front of him. The sudden fragrance of rose leaves enveloped him. Round they flew again. While they were still dancing, Boleskey came into the room. He caught Swithin by both hands.

"Brother, welcome! Ah! your arm is hurt! I do not forget." His yellow face and deep-set eyes expressed a dignified gratitude. "Let me introduce to you my friend Baron Kasteliz."

Swithin bowed to a man with a small forehead, who had appeared softly, and stood with his gloved hands touching his waist. Swithin conceived a sudden aversion for this cat-like man. About Boleskey there was that which made contempt impossible—the sense of comradeship begotten in the fight; the man's height; something lofty and savage in his face; and an obscure instinct that it would not pay to show distaste; but this Kasteliz, with his neat jaw, low brow, and velvety, volcanic look, excited his proper English animosity. "Your friends are mine," murmured Kasteliz. He spoke with suavity, and hissed his s's. A long, vibrating twang quavered through the room. Swithin turned and saw Rozsi sitting at the czymbal; the notes rang under the little hammers in her hands, incessant, metallic, rising and falling with that strange melody. Kasteliz had fixed his glowing eyes on her; Boleskey, nodding his head, was staring at the floor; Margit, with a pale face, stood like a statue.

'What can they see in it?' thought Swithin; 'it's not a tune.' He took up his hat. Rozsi saw him and stopped; her lips had parted with a faintly dismayed expression. His sense of personal injury diminished; he even felt a little sorry for her. She jumped up from her seat and twirled round with a pout. An inspiration seized on Swithin. "Come

and dine with me," he said to Boleskey, "to-morrow—the Goldene
Alp—bring your friend." He felt the eyes of the whole room on
him—the Hungarian's fine eyes; Margit's wide glance; the narrow,
hot gaze of Kasteliz; and lastly—Rozsi's. A glow of satisfaction
ran down his spine. When he emerged into the street he thought
gloomily, 'Now I've done it!' And not for some paces did he look
round; then, with a forced smile, turned and removed his hat to the
faces at the window.

Notwithstanding this moment of gloom, however, he was in an
exalted state all day, and at dinner kept looking at his brother and
Traquair enigmatically. 'What do they know of life?' he thought;
'they might be here a year and get no farther.' He made jokes, and
pinned the menu to the waiter's coat-tails. "I like this place," he said,
"I shall spend three weeks here." James, whose lips were on the point
of taking in a plum, looked at him uneasily.

IV

On the day of the dinner Swithin suffered a good deal. He reflected
gloomily on Boleskey's clothes. He had fixed an early hour—there
would be fewer people to see them. When the time approached he
attired himself with a certain neat splendour, and though his arm
was still sore, left off the sling. . . .

Nearly three hours afterwards he left the Goldene Alp between
his guests. It was sunset, and along the river-bank the houses stood
out, unsoftened by the dusk; the streets were full of people hurrying
home. Swithin had a hazy vision of empty bottles, of the ground
before his feet, and the accessibility of all the world. Dim recollections
of the good things he had said, of his brother and Traquair seated in
the background eating ordinary meals with inquiring, acid visages,
caused perpetual smiles to break out on his face, and he steered
himself stubbornly, to prove that he was a better man than either of
his guests. He knew, vaguely, that he was going somewhere with an
object; Rozsi's face kept dancing before him, like a promise. Once or
twice he gave Kasteliz a glassy stare. Towards Boleskey, on the other
hand, he felt quite warm, and recalled with admiration the way he
had set his glass down empty, time after time. 'I like to see him take
his liquor,' he thought; 'the fellow's a gentleman, after all.'

Boleskey strode on, savagely inattentive to everything; and Kasteliz had become more like a cat than ever. It was nearly dark when they reached a narrow street close to the cathedral. They stopped at a door held open by an old woman. The change from the fresh air to a heated corridor, the noise of the door closed behind him, the old woman's anxious glances, sobered Swithin.

"I tell her," said Boleskey, "that I reply for you as for my son."

Swithin was angry. What business had this man to reply for him!

They passed into a large room, crowded with men and women; Swithin noticed that they all looked at him. He stared at them in turn—they seemed of all classes, some in black coats or silk dresses, others in the clothes of work-people; one man, a cobbler, still wore his leather apron, as if he had rushed there straight from his work. Laying his hand on Swithin's arm, Boleskey evidently began explaining who he was; hands were extended, people beyond reach bowed to him. Swithin acknowledged the greetings with a stiff motion of his head; then seeing other people dropping into seats, he, too, sat down. Some one whispered his name—Margit and Rozsi were just behind him.

"Welcome!" said Margit; but Swithin was looking at Rozsi. Her face was so alive and quivering! 'What's the excitement all about?' he thought. 'How pretty she looks!' She blushed, drew in her hands with a quick tense movement, and gazed again beyond him in the room. 'What is it?' thought Swithin; he had a longing to lean back and kiss her lips. He tried angrily to see what she was seeing in those faces turned all one way.

Boleskey rose to speak. No one moved; not a sound could be heard but the tone of his deep voice. On and on he went, fierce and solemn, and with the rise of his voice, all those faces—fair or swarthy—seemed to be glowing with one and the same feeling. Swithin felt the white heat in those faces—it was not decent! In that whole speech he only understood the one word—"Magyar"— which came again and again. He almost dozed off at last. The twang of a czymbal woke him. 'What?' he thought, 'more of that infernal music!' Margit, leaning over him, whispered: "Listen! Racoczy! it is forbidden!" Swithin saw that Rozsi was no longer in her seat; it was she who was striking those forbidden notes. He looked round— everywhere the same unmoving faces, the same entrancement, and fierce stillness. The music sounded muffled, as if it, too, were bursting its heart in silence. Swithin felt within him a touch of panic. Was this a den of tigers? The way these people listened, the ferocity of their stillness, was frightful!

He gripped his chair and broke into a perspiration; was there no chance to get away? 'When it stops,' he thought, 'there'll be a rush!' But there was only a greater silence. It flashed across him that any hostile person coming in then would be torn to pieces. A woman sobbed. The whole thing was beyond words unpleasant. He rose, and edged his way furtively towards the doorway. There was a cry of "Police!" The whole crowd came pressing after him. Swithin would soon have been out, but a little behind he caught sight of Rozsi swept off her feet. Her frightened eyes angered him. 'She doesn't deserve it,' he thought sulkily; 'letting all this loose!' and forced his way back to her. She clung to him, and a fever went stealing through his veins; he butted forward at the crowd, holding her tight. When they were outside he let her go.

"I was afraid," she said.

"Afraid!" muttered Swithin; "I should think so." No longer touching her, he felt his grievance revive.

"But you are so strong," she murmured.

"This is no place for you," growled Swithin. "I'm going to see you home."

"Oh!" cried Rozsi; "but papa and—Margit!"

"That's their lookout!" and he hurried her away.

She slid her hand under his arm; the soft curves of her form brushed him gently, each touch only augmented his ill-humour. He burned with a perverse rage, as if all the passions in him were simmering and ready to boil over; it was as if a poison were trying to work its way out of him through the layers of his stolid flesh. He maintained a dogged silence; Rozsi, too, said nothing, but when they reached the door, she drew her hand away.

"You are angry!" she said.

"Angry," muttered Swithin; "no! How d'you make that out?" He had a torturing desire to kiss her.

"Yes, you are angry," she repeated; "I wait here for papa and Margit."

Swithin also waited, wedged against the wall. Once or twice, for his sight was sharp, he saw her steal a look at him, a beseeching look, and hardened his heart with a kind of pleasure. After five minutes Boleskey, Margit, and Kasteliz appeared. Seeing Rozsi they broke into exclamations of relief and Kasteliz, with a glance at Swithin, put his lips to her hand. Rozsi's look said, "Wouldn't you like to do that?" Swithin turned short on his heel, and walked away.

V

All night he hardly slept, suffering from fever, for the first time in his life. Once he jumped out of bed, lighted a candle, and going to the glass, scrutinised himself long and anxiously. After this he fell asleep, but had frightful dreams. His first thought when he woke was, 'My liver's out of order!' and, thrusting his head into cold water, he dressed hastily and went out. He soon left the house behind. Dew covered everything; blackbirds whistled in the bushes, the air was fresh and sweet. He had not been up so early since he was a boy. Why was he walking through a damp wood at this hour of the morning? Something intolerable and unfamiliar must have sent him out. No fellow in his senses would do such a thing! He came to a dead stop, and began unsteadily to walk back. Regaining the hotel, he went to bed again, and dreamed that in some wild country he was living in a room full of insects, where a housemaid—Rozsi—holding a broom, looked at him with mournful eyes. There seemed an unexplained need for immediate departure; he begged her to forward his things, and shake them out carefully before she put them into the trunk. He understood that the charge for sending would be twenty-two shillings, thought it a great deal, and had the horrors of indecision. "No," he muttered, "pack, and take them myself." The housemaid turned suddenly into a lean creature; and he awoke with a sore feeling in his heart.

His eye fell on his wet boots. The whole thing was scaring, and jumping up, he began to throw his clothes into his trunks. It was twelve o'clock before he went down, and found his brother and Traquair still at the table arranging an itinerary; he surprised them by saying that he too was coming; and without further explanation set to work to eat. James had heard that there were salt-mines in the neighbourhood—his proposal was to start, and halt an hour or so on the road for their inspection: he said: "Everybody'll ask you if you've seen the salt-mines: I shouldn't like to say I hadn't seen the salt-mines. What's the good, they'd say, of your going there if you haven't seen the salt-mines?" He wondered, too, if they need fee the second waiter—an idle chap!

A discussion followed; but Swithin ate on glumly, conscious that his mind was set on larger affairs. Suddenly on the far side of the street Rozsi and her sister passed, with little baskets on their arms. He started up, and at that moment Rozsi looked round—her face was the incarnation of enticement, the chin tilted, the lower lip thrust a little forward, her round neck curving back over her shoulder. Swithin muttered, "Make your own arrangements—leave me out!" and hurried from the room, leaving James beside himself with interest and alarm.

When he reached the street, however, the girls had disappeared. He hailed a carriage. "Drive!" he called to the man, with a flourish of his stick, and as soon as the wheels had begun to clatter on the stones he leaned back, looking sharply to right and left. He soon had to give up thought of finding them, but made the coachman turn round and round again. All day he drove about, far into the country, and kept urging the driver to use greater speed. He was in a strange state of hurry and elation. Finally, he dined at a little country inn; and this gave the measure of his disturbance—the dinner was atrocious.

Returning late in the evening he found a note written by Traquair. "Are you in your senses, man?" it asked; "we have no more time to waste idling about here. If you want to rejoin us, come on to Danielli's Hotel, Venice." Swithin chuckled when he read it, and feeling frightfully tired, went to bed and slept like a log.

VI

Three weeks later he was still in Salzburg, no longer at the Goldene Alp, but in rooms over a shop near the Boleskeys'. He had spent a small fortune in the purchase of flowers. Margit would croon over them, but Rozsi, with a sober "Many tanks!" as if they were her right, would look long at herself in the glass, and pin one into her hair. Swithin ceased to wonder; he ceased to wonder at anything they did. One evening he found Boleskey deep in conversation with a pale, dishevelled-looking person.

"Our friend Mr. Forsyte—Count D——," said Boleskey.

Swithin experienced a faint, unavoidable emotion; but looking at the Count's trousers, he thought: 'Doesn't look much like one!' And with an ironic bow to the silent girls, he turned, and took his hat. But when he had reached the bottom of the dark stairs he heard footsteps. Rozsi came running down, looked out at the door, and put her hands up to her breast as if disappointed: suddenly with a quick glance round she saw him. Swithin caught her arm. She slipped away, and her face seemed to bubble with defiance or laughter; she ran up three steps, looked at him across her shoulder, and fled on up the stairs. Swithin went out bewildered and annoyed.

'What was she going to say to me?' he kept thinking. During these three weeks he had asked himself all sorts of questions: whether he were being made a fool of; whether she were in love with him; what he was doing there, and sometimes at night, with all his candles burning as if he wanted light, the breeze blowing on him through the window, his cigar, half smoked, in his hand, he sat, an hour or more, staring at the wall. 'Enough of this!' he thought every morning. Twice he packed fully—once he ordered his travelling carriage, but countermanded it the following day. What definitely he hoped, intended, resolved, he could not have said. He was always thinking of Rozsi, he could not read the riddle in her face—she held him in a vice, notwithstanding that everything about her threatened the very fetishes of his existence. And Boleskey! Whenever he looked at him he thought, 'If he were only clean?' and mechanically fingered his own well-tied cravate. To talk with the fellow, too, was like being forced to look at things which had no place in the light of day. Freedom, equality, self-sacrifice!

'Why can't he settle down at some business,' he thought, 'instead of all this talk?' Boleskey's sudden diffidences, self-depreciation, fits of despair, irritated him. "Morbid beggar!" he would mutter; "thank God I haven't a thin skin." And proud too! Extraordinary! An impecunious fellow like that! One evening, moreover, Boleskey had returned home drunk. Swithin had hustled him away into his bedroom, helped him to undress, and stayed until he was asleep. 'Too much of a good thing!' he thought, 'before his own daughters, too!' It was after this that he ordered his travelling carriage. The other occasion on which he packed was one evening, when not only Boleskey, but Rozsi herself had picked chicken bones with her fingers.

Often in the mornings he would go to the Mirabell Garden to smoke his cigar; there, in stolid contemplation of the statues—rows of half-heroic men carrying off half-distressed females—he would spend an hour pleasantly, his hat tilted to keep the sun off his nose. The day after Rozsi had fled from him on the stairs, he came there as usual. It was a morning of blue sky and sunlight glowing on the old prim garden, on its yew-trees, and serio-comic statues, and walls covered, with apricots and plums. When Swithin approached his usual seat, who should be sitting there but Rozsi!

"Good-morning," he stammered; "you knew this was my seat then?"

Rozsi looked at the ground. "Yes," she answered.

Swithin felt bewildered. "Do you know," he said, "you treat me very funnily?"

To his surprise Rozsi put her little soft hand down and touched his; then, without a word, sprang up and rushed away. It took him a minute to recover. There were people present; he did not like to run, but overtook her on the bridge, and slipped her hand beneath his arm.

"You shouldn't have done that," he said; "you shouldn't have run away from me, you know."

Rozsi laughed. Swithin withdrew his arm; a desire to shake her seized him. He walked some way before he said, "Will you have the goodness to tell me what you came to that seat for?"

Rozsi flashed a look at him. "To-morrow is the *fête*," she answered.

Swithin muttered, "Is that all?"

"If you do not take us, we cannot go."

"Suppose I refuse," he said sullenly, "there are plenty of others."

Rozsi bent her head, scurrying along. "No," she murmured, "if *you* do not go—I do not wish."

Swithin drew her hand back within his arm. How round and soft it was! He tried to see her face. When she was nearly home he said good-bye, not wishing, for some dark reason, to be seen with her. He watched till she had disappeared; then slowly retraced his steps to the Mirabell Garden. When he came to where she had been sitting, he slowly lighted his cigar, and for a long time after it was smoked out remained there in the silent presence of the statues.

VII

A crowd of people wandered round the booths, and Swithin found himself obliged to give the girls his arms. 'Like a little Cockney clerk!' he thought. His indignation passed unnoticed; they talked, they laughed, each sight and sound in all the hurly-burly seemed to go straight into their hearts. He eyed them ironically—their eager voices, and little coos of sympathy seemed to him vulgar. In the thick of the crowd he slipped his arm out of Margit's, but, just as he thought that he was free, the unwelcome hand slid up again. He tried again, but again Margit reappeared, serene, and full of pleasant humour; and his failure this time appeared to him in a comic light. But when Rozsi leaned across him, the glow of her round cheek, her curving lip, the inscrutable grey gleam of her eyes, sent a thrill of longing through him. He was obliged to stand by while they parleyed with a gipsy, whose matted locks and skinny hands inspired him with a not unwarranted disgust. "Folly!" he muttered, as Rozsi held out her palm. The old woman mumbled, and shot a malignant look at him. Rozsi drew back her hand, and crossed herself. 'Folly!' Swithin thought again; and seizing the girls' arms, he hurried them away.

"What did the old hag say?" he asked.

Rozsi shook her head.

"You don't mean that you believe?"

Her eyes were full of tears. "The gipsies are wise," she murmured.

"Come, what did she tell you?"

This time Rozsi looked hurriedly round, and slipped away into the crowd. After a hunt they found her, and Swithin, who was scared, growled: "You shouldn't do such things—it's not respectable."

On higher ground, in the centre of a clear space, a military band was playing. For the privilege of entering this charmed circle Swithin paid three *kronen*, choosing naturally the best seats. He ordered wine, too, watching Rozsi out of the corner of his eye as he poured it out. The protecting tenderness of yesterday was all lost in this medley. It was every man for himself, after all! The colour had deepened again in her cheeks, she laughed, pouting her lips. Suddenly she put her glass aside. "Thank you, very much," she said, "it is enough!"

Margit, whose pretty mouth was all smiles, cried, "*Lieber Gott!* is it not good—life?" it was not a question Swithin could undertake to answer. The band began to play a waltz. "Now they will dance. *Lieber Gott!* and are the lights not wonderful?" Lamps were flickering beneath the trees like a swarm of fireflies. There was a hum as from a gigantic beehive. Passers-by lifted their faces, then vanished into the crowd; Rozsi stood gazing at them spell-bound, as if their very going and coming were a delight.

The space was soon full of whirling couples. Rozsi's head began to beat time. "O Margit!" she whispered.

Swithin's face had assumed a solemn, uneasy expression. A man, raising his hat, offered his arm to Margit. She glanced back across her shoulder to reassure Swithin. "It is a friend," she said.

Swithin looked at Rozsi—her eyes were bright, her lips tremulous. He slipped his hand along the table and touched her fingers. Then she flashed a look at him—appeal, reproach, tenderness, all were expressed in it. Was she expecting him to dance? Did she want to mix with the riff-raff there; wish *him* to make an exhibition of himself in this hurly-burly? A voice said, "Good-evening!" Before them stood Kasteliz, in a dark coat tightly buttoned at the waist.

"You are not dancing, *Rozsi Kozsanony*?" (Miss Rozsi). "Let me, then, have the pleasure." He held out his arm. Swithin stared in front of him. In the very act of going she gave him a look that said as plain as words: "Will you not?" But for answer he turned his eye away, and when he looked again she was gone. He paid the score and made his way into the crowd. But as he went she danced by close to him, all flushed and panting. She hung back as if to stop him, and he caught the glistening of tears. Then he lost sight of her again. To be deserted the first minute he was alone with her, and for that jackanapes with the small head and volcanic glances! It was too much! And suddenly it occurred to him that she was alone with Kasteliz—alone at night, and far from home. 'Well,' he thought, 'what do I care?' and shouldered his way on through the crowd. It served him right for mixing with such people here. He left the fair, but the further he went, the more he nursed his rage, the more heinous seemed her offence, the sharper grew his jealousy. 'A beggarly baron!' was his thought.

A figure came alongside—it was Boleskey. One look showed Swithin his condition. Drunk again! This was the last straw!

Unfortunately Boleskey had recognised him. He seemed violently excited. "Where—where are my daughters?" he began.

Swithin brushed past, but Boleskey caught his arm. "Listen—brother!" he said; "news of my country! After to-morrow———"

"Keep it to yourself!" growled Swithin, wrenching his arm free. He went straight to his lodgings, and, lying on the hard sofa of his unlighted sitting-room, gave himself up to bitter thoughts. But in spite of all his anger, Rozsi's supply-moving figure, with its pouting lips, and roguish appealing eyes, still haunted him.

VIII

Next morning there was not a carriage to be had, and Swithin was compelled to put off his departure till the morrow. The day was grey and misty; he wandered about with the strained, inquiring look of a lost dog in his eyes.

Late in the afternoon he went back to his lodgings. In a corner of the sitting-room stood Rozsi. The thrill of triumph, the sense of appeasement, the emotion, that seized on him, crept through to his lips in a faint smile. Rozsi made no sound, her face was hidden by her hands. And this silence of hers weighed on Swithin. She was forcing him to break it. What was behind her hands? His own face was visible! Why didn't she speak? Why was she here? Alone? That was not right surely.

Suddenly Rozsi dropped her hands; her flushed face was quivering—it seemed as though a word, a sign, even, might bring a burst of tears.

He walked over to the window. 'I must give her time!' he thought; then seized by unreasoning terror at this silence, spun round, and caught her by the arms. Rozsi held, back from him, swayed forward and buried her face on his breast. . . .

Half an hour later Swithin was pacing up and down his room. The scent of rose leaves had not yet died away. A glove lay on the floor; he picked it up, and for a long time stood weighing it in his

hand. All sorts of confused thoughts and feelings haunted him. It was
the purest and least selfish moment of his life, this moment after she
had yielded. But that pure gratitude at her fiery, simple abnegation
did not last; it was followed by a petty sense of triumph, and by
uneasiness. He was still weighing the little glove in his hand, when
he had another visitor. It was Kasteliz.

"What can I do for you?" Swithin asked ironically.

The Hungarian seemed suffering from excitement. Why had
Swithin left his charges the night before? What excuse had he to
make? What sort of conduct did he call this?

Swithin, very like a bull-dog at that moment, answered:

What business was it of his?

The business of a gentleman! What right had the Englishman to
pursue a young girl?

"Pursue?" said Swithin; "you've been spying, then?"

"Spying—I—Kasteliz—Maurus Johann—an insult!"

"Insult!" sneered Swithin; "d'you mean to tell me you weren't in
the street just now?"

Kasteliz answered with a hiss, "If you do not leave the city I will
make you, with my sword—do you understand?"

"And if you do not leave my room I will throw you out of the
window!"

For some minutes Kasteliz spoke in pure Hungarian while
Swithin waited, with a forced smile and a fixed look in his eye. He
did not understand Hungarian.

"If you are still in the city to-morrow evening," said Kasteliz at last
in English, "I will spit you in the street."

Swithin turned to the window and watched his visitor's retiring
back with a queer mixture of amusement, stubbornness, and anxiety.
'Well,' he thought, 'I suppose he'll run me through!' The thought
was unpleasant; and it kept recurring, but it only served to harden
his determination. His head was busy with plans for seeing Rozsi; his
blood on fire with the kisses she had given him.

IX

Swithin was long in deciding to go forth next day. He had made up
his mind not to go to Rozsi till five o'clock. 'Mustn't make myself

too cheap,' he thought. It was a little past that hour when he at last
sallied out, and with a beating heart walked towards Boleskey's. He
looked up at the window, more than half expecting to see Rozsi
there; but she was not, and he noticed with faint surprise that the
window was not open; the plants, too, outside, looked singularly
arid. He knocked. No one came. He beat a fierce tattoo. At last the
door was opened by a man with a reddish beard, and one of those
sardonic faces only to be seen on shoemakers of Teutonic origin.

"What do you want, making all this noise?" he asked in German.

Swithin pointed up the stairs. The man grinned, and shook his
head.

"I want to go up," said Swithin.

The cobbler shrugged his shoulders, and Swithin rushed upstairs.
The rooms were empty. The furniture remained, but all signs of life
were gone. One of his own bouquets, faded, stood in a glass; the
ashes of a fire were barely cold; little scraps of paper strewed the
hearth; already the room smelt musty. He went into the bedrooms,
and with a feeling of stupefaction stood staring at the girls' beds, side
by side against the wall. A bit of ribbon caught his eye; he picked it
up and put it in his pocket—it was a piece of evidence that she had
once existed. By the mirror some pins were dropped about a little
powder had been spilled. He looked at his own disquiet face and
thought, 'I've been cheated!'

The shoemaker's voice aroused him. "*Tausend Teufel! Eilen Sie, nur!
Zeit is Geld! Kann nich' länger warten!*" Slowly he descended.

"Where have they gone?" asked Swithin painfully. "A pound for
every English word you speak. A pound!" and he made an O with
his fingers.

The corners of the shoemaker's lips curled. "*Geld! Mff! Eilen Sie,
nur!*"

But in Swithin a sullen anger had begun to burn. "If you don't tell
me," he said, "it'll be the worse for you."

"*Sind ein komischer Kerl!*" remarked the shoemaker. "*Hier ist meine
Frau!*"

A battered-looking woman came hurrying down the passage,
calling out in German, "Don't let him go!"

With a snarling sound the shoemaker turned his back, and
shambled off.

The woman furtively thrust a letter into Swithin's hand, and furtively waited.

The letter was from Rozsi.

"Forgive me"—it ran—"that I leave you and do not say good-bye. To-day our father had the call from our dear Father-town so long awaited. In two hours we are ready. I pray to the Virgin to keep you ever safe, and that you do not quite forget me.—Your unforgetting good friend,

ROZSI."

When Swithin read it his first sensation was that of a man sinking in a bog; then his obstinacy stiffened. 'I won't be done,' he thought. Taking out a sovereign he tried to make the woman comprehend that she could earn it, by telling him where they had gone. He got her finally to write the words out in his pocket-book, gave her the sovereign, and hurried to the Goldene Alp, where there was a waiter who spoke English.

The translation given him was this:

"At three o'clock they start in a carriage on the road to Linz—they have bad horses—the Herr also rides a white horse."

Swithin at once hailed a carriage and started at full gallop on the road to Linz. Outside the Mirabell Garden he caught sight of Kasteliz and grinned at him. 'I've sold *him* anyway,' he thought; 'for all their talk, they're no good, these foreigners!'

His spirits rose, but soon fell again. What chance had he of catching them? They had three hours' start! Still, the roads were heavy from the rain of the last two nights—they had luggage and bad horses; his own were good, his driver bribed—he might overtake them by ten o'clock! But did he want to? What a fool he had been not to bring his luggage; he would then have had a respectable position. What a brute he would look without a change of shirt, or anything to shave with! He saw himself with horror, all bristly, and in soiled linen. People would think him mad. 'I've given myself away,' flashed across him, 'what the devil can I say to them?' and he stared sullenly at the driver's back. He read Rozsi's letter again; it had a scent of her. And in the growing darkness, jolted by the swinging of the carriage, he suffered tortures from his prudence, tortures from his passion.

It grew colder and dark. He turned the collar of his coat up to his ears. He had visions of Piccadilly. This wild-goose chase appeared suddenly a dangerous, unfathomable business. Lights, fellowship, security! 'Never again!' he brooded; 'why won't they let me alone?' But it was not clear whether by 'they' he meant the conventions, the Boleskeys, his passions, or those haunting memories of Rozsi. If he had only had a bag with him! What was he going to say? What was he going to get by this? He received no answer to these questions. The darkness itself was less obscure than his sensations. From time to time he took out his watch. At each village the driver made inquiries. It was past ten when he stopped the carriage with a jerk. The stars were bright as steel, and by the side of the road a reedy lake showed in the moonlight. Swithin shivered. A man on a horse had halted in the centre of the road. "Drive on!" called Swithin, with a stolid face. It turned out to be Boleskey, who, on a gaunt white horse, looked like some winged creature. He stood where he could bar the progress of the carriage, holding out a pistol.

'Theatrical beggar!' thought Swithin, with a nervous smile. He made no sign of recognition. Slowly Boleskey brought his lean horse up to the carriage. When he saw who was within he showed astonishment and joy.

"You?" he cried, slapping his hand on his attenuated thigh, and leaning over till his beard touched Swithin. "You have come? You followed us?"

"It seems so," Swithin grunted out.

"You throw in your lot with us. Is it possible? You—you are a knight-errant then!"

"Good God!" said Swithin. Boleskey, flogging his dejected steed, cantered forward in the moonlight. He came back, bringing an old cloak, which he insisted on wrapping round Swithin's shoulders. He handed him, too, a capacious flask.

"How cold you look!" he said. "Wonderful! Wonderful! you English!" His grateful eyes never left Swithin for a moment. They had come up to the heels of the other carriage now, but Swithin, hunched in the cloak, did not try to see what was in front of him. To the bottom of his soul he resented the Hungarian's gratitude. He remarked at last, with wasted irony:

"You're in a hurry, it seems!"

"If we had wings," Boleskey answered, "we would use them."

"Wings!" muttered Swithin thickly; "legs are good enough for me."

X

Arrived at the inn where they were to pass the night, Swithin waited, hoping to get into the house without a "scene," but when at last he alighted the girls were in the doorway, and Margit greeted him with an admiring murmur, in which, however, he seemed to detect irony. Rozsi, pale and tremulous, with a half-scared look, gave him her hand, and, quickly withdrawing it, shrank behind her sister. When they had gone up to their room Swithin sought Boleskey. His spirits had risen remarkably. "Tell the landlord to get us supper," he said; "we'll crack a bottle to our luck." He hurried on the landlord's preparations. The window of the room faced a wood, so near that he could almost touch the trees. The scent from the pines blew in on him. He turned away from that scented darkness, and began to draw the corks of wine-bottles. The sound seemed to conjure up Boleskey. He came in, splashed all over, smelling slightly of stables; soon after, Margit appeared, fresh and serene, but Rozsi did not come.

"Where is your sister?" Swithin said. Rozsi, it seemed, was tired. "It will do her good to eat," said Swithin. And Boleskey, murmuring, "She must drink to our country," went out to summon her, Margit followed him, while Swithin cut up a chicken. They came back without her. She had "a megrim of the spirit."

Swithin's face fell. "Look here!" he said, "*I'll* go and try. Don't wait for me."

"Yes," answered Boleskey, sinking mournfully into a chair; "try, brother, try—by all means, try."

Swithin walked down the corridor with an odd, sweet, sinking sensation in his chest; and tapped on Rozsi's door. In a minute, she peeped forth, with her hair loose, and wondering eyes.

"Rozsi," he stammered, "what makes you afraid of me, *now*?"

She stared at him, but did not answer.

"Why won't you come?"

Still she did not speak, but suddenly stretched out to him her bare arm. Swithin pressed his face to it. With a shiver, she whispered above him, "I will come," and gently shut the door.

Swithin stealthily retraced his steps, and paused a minute outside the sitting-room to regain his self-control.

The sight of Boleskey with a bottle in his hand steadied him.

"She is coming," he said. And very soon she did come, her thick hair roughly twisted in a plait.

Swithin sat between the girls; but did not talk, for he was really hungry. Boleskey too was silent, plunged in gloom; Rozsi was dumb; Margit alone chattered.

"You will come to our Father-town? We shall have things to show you. Rozsi, what things we will show him!" Rozsi, with a little appealing movement of her hands, repeated, "What things we will show you!" She seemed suddenly to find her voice, and with glowing cheeks, mouth full, and eyes bright as squirrels, they chattered reminiscences of the "dear Father-town," of "dear friends," of the "dear home."

'A poor place!' Swithin could not help thinking. This enthusiasm seemed to him common; but he was careful to assume a look of interest, feeding on the glances flashed at him from Rozsi's restless eyes.

As the wine waned Boleskey grew more and more gloomy, hut now and then a sort of gleaming flicker passed over his face. He rose to his feet at last.

"Let us not forget," he said, "that we go perhaps to ruin, to death; in the face of all this we go, because our country needs—in this there is no credit, neither to me nor to you, my daughters; but for this noble Englishman, what shall we say? Give thanks to God for a great heart. He comes—not for country, not for fame, not for money, but to help the weak and the oppressed. Let us drink, then, to him; let us drink again and again to heroic Forsyte!" In the midst of the dead silence, Swithin caught the look of suppliant mockery in Rozsi's eyes. He glanced at the Hungarian. Was he laughing at him? But Boleskey, after drinking up his wine, had sunk again into his seat; and there suddenly, to the surprise of all, he began to snore. Margit rose and, bending over him like a mother, murmured: "He is tired—it is the ride!" She raised him in her strong arms, and leaning on her shoulder Boleskey staggered from the room. Swithin and Rozsi were left alone. He slid his hand towards her hand that lay so close, on the rough tablecloth. It seemed to await his touch.

Something gave way in him, and words came welling up; for the moment he forgot himself, forgot everything but that he was near her. Her head dropped on his shoulder, he breathed the perfume of her hair. "Good-night!" she whispered, and the whisper was like a kiss; yet before he could stop her she was gone. Her footsteps died away in the passage, but Swithin sat gazing intently at a single bright drop of spilt wine quivering on the table's edge. In that moment she, in her helplessness and emotion, was all in all to him—his life nothing; all the real things—his conventions, convictions, training, and himself—all seemed remote, behind a mist of passion and strange chivalry. Carefully with a bit of bread he soaked up the bright drop; and suddenly, he thought:

'This is tremendous!' For a long time he stood there in the window, close to the dark pine-trees.

XI

In the early morning he awoke, full of the discomfort of this strange place and the medley of his dreams. Lying, with his nose peeping over the quilt, he was visited by a horrible suspicion. When he could bear it no longer, he started up in bed. What if it were all a plot to get him to marry her? The thought was treacherous, and inspired in him a faint disgust. Still, *she* might be ignorant of it! But was she so innocent? What innocent girl would have come to his room like that? What innocent girl? Her father, who pretended to be caring only for his country? It was not probable that any man was such a fool; it was all part of the game—a scheming rascal! Kasteliz, too—his threats! They intended him to marry her? And the horrid idea was strengthened by his reverence for marriage. It was the proper, the respectable condition; he was genuinely afraid of this other sort of *liaison*—it was somehow too primitive! And yet the thought of that marriage made his blood run cold. Considering that she had already yielded, it would be all the more monstrous! With the cold, fatal clearness of the morning light he now for the first time saw his position in its full bearings. And, like a fish pulled out of water, he gasped at what was disclosed. Sullen resentment against this attempt to force him settled deep into his soul.

He seated himself on the bed, holding his head in his hands, solemnly thinking out what such marriage meant. In the first place

it meant ridicule, in the next place ridicule, in the last place ridicule.
She would eat chicken bones with her fingers—those fingers his
lips still burned to kiss. She would dance wildly with other men.
She would talk of her "dear Father-town," and all the time her eyes
would look beyond him, somewhere or other into some d———d
place he knew nothing of. He sprang up and paced the room, and
for a moment thought he would go mad.

They meant him to marry her! Even she—she meant him to marry
her! Her tantalising inscrutability; her sudden little tendernesses;
her quick laughter; her swift, burning kisses; even the movements
of her hands; her tears—all were evidence against her. Not one of
these things that Nature made her do counted on her side, but how
they fanned his longing, his desire, and distress. He went to the glass
and tried to part his hair with his fingers, but being rather fine,
it fell into lank streaks. There was no comfort to be got from it.
He drew his muddy boots on. Suddenly he thought: 'If I could see
her alone, I could arrive at some arrangement!' Then, with a sense
of stupefaction, he made the discovery that no arrangement could
possibly be made that would not be dangerous, even desperate. He
seized his hat, and, like a rabbit that has been fired at, bolted from the
room. He plodded along amongst the damp woods with his head
down, and resentment and dismay in his heart. But, as the sun rose,
and the air grew sweet with pine scent, he slowly regained a sort of
equability. After all, she had already yielded; it was not as if——! And
the tramp of his own footsteps lulled him into feeling that it would
all come right. 'Look at the thing practically,' he thought. The faster
he walked the firmer became his conviction that he could still see
it through. He took out his watch—it was past seven—he began
to hasten back. In the yard of the inn his driver was harnessing the
horses; Swithin went up to him.

"Who told you to put them in?" he asked.

The driver answered, "*Der Herr*."

Swithin turned away. 'In ten minutes,' he thought, 'I shall be in
that carriage again, with this going on in my head! Driving away
from England, from all I'm used to—driving to—what?' Could he
face it? Could he face all that he had been through that morning;
face it day after day, night after night? Looking up, he saw Rozsi at
her open window gazing down at him; never had she looked sweeter,

more roguish. An inexplicable terror seized on him; he ran across the yard and jumped into his carriage. "To Salzburg!" he cried; "drive on!" And rattling out of the yard without a look behind, he flung a sovereign at the hostler. Flying back along the road faster even than he had come, with pale face, and eyes blank and, staring like a pug-dog's, Swithin spoke no single word; nor, till he had reached the door of his lodgings, did he suffer the driver to draw rein.

XII

Towards evening, five days later, Swithin, yellow and travel-worn, was ferried in a gondola to Danielli's Hotel. His brother, who was on the steps, looked at him with an apprehensive curiosity.

"Why, it's you!" he mumbled. "So you've got here safe?"

"Safe?" growled Swithin.

James replied, "I thought you wouldn't leave your friends!" Then, with a jerk of suspicion, "You haven't brought your friends?"

"What friends?" growled Swithin.

James changed the subject. "You don't look the thing," he said.

"Really!" muttered Swithin; "what's that to you?"

He appeared at dinner that night, but fell asleep over his coffee. Neither Traquair nor James asked him any further question, nor did they allude to Salzburg; and during the four days which concluded the stay in Venice Swithin went about with his head up, but his eyes half-closed like a dazed man. Only after they had taken ship at Genoa did he show signs of any healthy interest in life, when, finding that a man on board was perpetually strumming, he locked the piano up and pitched the key into the sea.

That winter in London he behaved much as usual, but fits of moroseness would seize on him, during which he was not pleasant to approach.

One evening when he was walking with a friend in Piccadilly, a girl coming from a side-street accosted him in German. Swithin, after staring at her in silence for some seconds, handed her a five-pound note, to the great amazement of his friend; nor could he himself have explained the meaning of this freak of generosity.

Of Rozsi he never heard again. . . .

This, then, was the substance of what he remembered as he lay ill in bed. Stretching out his hand he pressed the bell. His valet appeared, crossing the room like a cat; a Swede, who had been with Swithin many years; a little man with a dried face and fierce moustache, morbidly sharp nerves, and a queer devotion to his master.

Swithin made a feeble gesture. "Adolf," he said, "I'm very bad."

"Yes, sir!"

"Why do you stand there like a cow?" asked Swithin; "can't you see I'm very bad?"

"Yes, sir!" The valet's face twitched as though it masked the dance of obscure emotions.

"I shall feel better after dinner. What time is it?"

"Five o'clock."

"I thought it was more. The afternoons are very long."

"Yes, sir!"

Swithin sighed, as though he had expected the consolation of denial.

"Very likely I shall have a nap. Bring up hot water at half-past six and shave me before dinner."

The valet moved towards the door. Swithin raised himself.

"What did Mr. James say to you!"

"He said you ought to have another doctor; two doctors, he said, better than one. He said, also, he would look in again on his way 'home.'"

Swithin grunted, "Umph! What else did he say?"

"He said you didn't take care of yourself."

Swithin glared.

"Has anybody else been to see me?"

The valet turned away his eyes. "Mrs. Thomas Forsyte came last Monday fortnight."

"How long have I been ill?"

"Five weeks on Saturday."

"Do you think I'm very bad?"

Adolf's face was covered suddenly with crow's-feet. "You have no business to ask me question like that! I am not paid, sir, to answer question like that."

Swithin said faintly: "You're a peppery fool! Open a bottle of champagne!"

Adolf took a bottle of champagne from a cupboard and held nippers to it. He fixed his eyes on Swithin. "The doctor said——"

"Open the bottle!"

"It is not—"

"Open the bottle—or I give you warning."

Adolf removed the cork. He wiped a glass elaborately, filled it, and bore it scrupulously to the bedside. Suddenly twirling his moustaches, he wrung his hands, and burst out:

"It is poison."

Swithin grinned faintly. "You foreign fool!" he said. "Get out!"

The valet vanished.

'He forgot himself!' thought Swithin. Slowly he raised the glass, slowly put it back, and sank gasping on his pillows. Almost at once he fell asleep.

He dreamed that he was at his club, sitting after dinner in the crowded smoking-room, with its bright walls and trefoils of light. It was there that he sat every evening, patient, solemn, lonely, and sometimes fell asleep, his square, pale old face nodding to one side. He dreamed that he was gazing at the picture over the fireplace, of an old statesman with a high collar, supremely finished face, and sceptical eyebrows—the picture, smooth, and reticent as sealing-wax, of one who seemed for ever exhaling the narrow wisdom of final judgments. All round him, his fellow-members were chattering. Only he himself, the old sick member, was silent. If fellows only knew what it was like to sit by yourself and feel ill all the time! What they were saying he had heard a hundred times. They were talking of investments, of cigars, horses, actresses, machinery. What was that? A foreign patent for cleaning boilers? There was no such thing; boilers couldn't be cleaned, any fool knew that! If an Englishman couldn't clean a boiler, no foreigner could clean one. He appealed to the old statesman's eyes. But for once those eyes seemed hesitating, blurred, wanting in finality. They vanished. In their place were Rozsi's little deep-set eyes, with their wide and far-off look; and as he gazed they seemed to grow bright as steel, and to speak to him. Slowly the whole face grew to be there, floating on the dark background of the picture; it was pink, aloof, unfathomable, enticing, with its fluffy hair and quick lips, just as he had last seen it. "Are you looking for something?" she seemed to say: "I could show you."

"I have everything safe enough," answered Swithin, and in his sleep he groaned.

He felt the touch of fingers on his forehead. 'I'm dreaming,' he thought in his dream.

She had vanished; and far away, from behind the picture, came a sound of footsteps.

Aloud, in his sleep, Swithin muttered: "I've missed it."

Again he heard the rustling of those light footsteps, and close in his ear a sound, like a sob. He awoke; the sob was his own. Great drops of perspiration stood on his forehead. 'What is it?' he thought; 'what have I lost?' Slowly his mind travelled over his investments; he could not think of any single one that was unsafe. What was it, then, that he had lost? Struggling on his pillows, he clutched the wine-glass. His lips touched the wine. 'This isn't the "Heidseck"!' he thought angrily, and before the reality of that displeasure all the dim vision passed away. But as he bent to drink, something snapped, and, with a sigh, Swithin Forsyte died above the bubbles. . . .

When James Forsyte came in again on his way home, the valet, trembling, took his hat and stick.

"How's your master?"

"My master is dead, sir!"

"Dead! He can't be! I left him safe an hour ago!"

On the bed Swithin's body was doubled like a sack; his hand still grasped the glass.

James Forsyte paused. "Swithin!" he said, and with his hand to his ear he waited for an answer; but none came, and slowly in the glass a last bubble rose and burst.

[*December, 1900*]

A STOIC

I

I §

Aequam memento rebus in arduis
Servare mentem.—HORACE.

In the City of Liverpool, on a January day of 1905, the Board-room of "The Island Navigation Company" rested, as it were, after the labours of the afternoon. The long table was still littered with the ink, pens, blotting-paper, and abandoned documents of six persons—a deserted battlefield of the brain. And, lonely, in his chairman's seat at the top end old Sylvanus Heythorp sat, with closed eyes, still and heavy as an image. One puffy, feeble hand, whose fingers quivered, rested on the arm of his chair; the thick white hair on his massive head glistened in the light from a green-shaded lamp. He was not asleep, for every now and then his sanguine cheeks filled, and a sound half sigh, half grunt, escaped his thick lips between a white moustache and the tiny tuft of white hairs above his cleft chin. Sunk in the chair, that square thick trunk of a body in short black-braided coat seemed divested of all neck.

Young Gilbert Farney, secretary of "The Island Navigation Company," entering his hushed Board-room, stepped briskly to the table, gathered some papers, and stood looking at his chairman. Not more than thirty-five, with the bright hues of the optimist in his hair, beard, cheeks, and eyes, he had a nose and lips which curled ironically. For, in his view, he *was* the Company; and its Board did but exist to chequer his importance. Five days in the week for seven hours a day he wrote, and thought, and wove the threads of its business, and this lot came down once a week for two or three hours, and taught their grandmother to suck eggs. But watching that red-cheeked, white-haired, somnolent figure, his smile was not so contemptuous as might have been expected. For after all, the chairman was a wonderful old boy. A man of go and insight could not but respect him. Eighty! Half paralysed, over head and ears in debt, having gone the pace all his life—or so they said!—till at last that mine in Ecuador had done for him—before the secretary's day, of course, but he had heard of it. The old chap had bought it up on spec'—"*de l'audace, toujours de l'audace*," as he was so fond of saying—paid for it half in cash and half in promises, and then— the thing had turned out empty, and left him with £20,000 worth of the old shares unredeemed. The old boy had weathered it out without a bankruptcy so far. Indomitable old buffer; and never fussy like the rest of them! Young Farney, though a secretary, was capable of attachment; and his eyes expressed a pitying affection. The Board meeting had been long and "snaggy"—a final settling of that Pillin business. Rum go the chairman forcing it on them like this! And with quiet satisfaction the secretary thought: 'And he never would have got it through if I hadn't made up my mind that it really is good business!' For to expand the Company was to expand himself. Still, to buy four ships with the freight market so depressed was a bit startling, and there would be opposition at the general meeting. Never mind! He and the chairman could put it through—put it through. And suddenly he saw the old man looking at him.

Only from those eyes could one appreciate the strength of life yet flowing underground in that well-nigh helpless carcase—deep-coloured little blue wells, tiny, jovial, round windows.

A sigh travelled up through layers of flesh, and he said almost inaudibly:

"Have they come, Mr. Farney?"

"Yes, sir. I've put them in the transfer office; said you'd be with them in a minute; but I wasn't going to wake you."

"Haven't been asleep. Help me up."

Grasping the edge of the table with his trembling hands, the old man pulled, and, with Farney heaving him behind, attained his feet. He stood about five feet ten, and weighed fully fourteen stone; not corpulent, but very thick all through; his round and massive head alone would have outweighed a baby. With eyes shut, he seemed to be trying to get the better of his own weight, then he moved with the slowness of a barnacle towards the door. The secretary, watching him, thought: 'Marvellous old chap! How he gets about by himself is a miracle! And he can't retire, they say—lives on his fees!'

But the chairman was through the green baize door. At his tortoise gait he traversed the inner office, where the youthful clerks suspended their figuring—to grin behind his back—and entered the transfer office, where eight gentlemen were sitting. Seven rose, and one did not. Old Heythorp raised a saluting hand to the level of his chest and moving to an armchair, lowered himself into it.

"Well, gentlemen?"

One of the eight gentlemen got up again.

"Mr. Heythorp, we've appointed Mr. Brownbee to voice our views. Mr. Brownbee!" And down he sat.

Mr. Brownbee rose—a stoutish man some seventy years of age, with little grey side whiskers, and one of those utterly steady faces only to be seen in England, faces which convey the sense of business from father to son for generations; faces which make wars, and passion, and free thought seem equally incredible; faces which inspire confidence, and awaken in one a desire to get up and leave the room. Mr. Brownbee rose, and said in a suave voice:

"Mr. Heythorp, we here represent about £14,000. When we had the pleasure of meeting you last July, you will recollect that you held out a prospect of some more satisfactory arrangement by Christmas. We are now in January, and I am bound to say we none of us get younger."

From the depths of old Heythorp a preliminary rumble came travelling, reached the surface, and materialised:

"Don't know about you—feel a boy, myself."

The eight gentlemen looked at him. Was he going to try and put them off again? Mr. Brownbee said with unruffled calm:

"I'm sure we're very glad to hear it. But to come to the point. We have felt, Mr. Heythorp, and I'm sure you won't think it unreasonable, that—er—bankruptcy would be the most satisfactory solution. We have waited a long time, and we want to know definitely where we stand; for, to be quite frank, we don't see any prospect of improvement; indeed, we fear the opposite."

"You think I'm going to join the majority."

This plumping out of what was at the back of their minds produced in Mr. Brownbee and his colleagues a sort of chemical disturbance. They coughed, moved their feet, and turned away their eyes, till the one who had not risen, a solicitor named Ventnor, said bluffly:

"Well, put it that way if you like."

Old Heythorp's little deep eyes twinkled.

"My grandfather lived to be a hundred; my father ninety-six—both of them rips. I'm only eighty, gentlemen; blameless life compared with theirs."

"Indeed," Mr. Brownbee said, "we hope you have many years of this life before you."

"More of this than of another." And a silence fell, till old Heythorp added: "You're getting a thousand a year out of my fees. Mistake to kill the goose that lays the golden eggs. I'll make it twelve hundred. If you force me to resign my directorships by bankruptcy, you won't get a rap, you know."

Mr. Brownbee cleared his throat:

"We think, Mr. Heythorp, you should make it at least fifteen hundred. In that case we might perhaps consider——"

Old Heythorp shook his head.

"We can hardly accept your assertion that we should get nothing in the event of bankruptcy. We fancy you greatly underrate the possibilities. Fifteen hundred a year is the least you can do for us."

"See you d——d first."

Another silence followed, then Ventnor, the solicitor, said irascibly:

"We know where we are, then."

Mr. Brownbee added almost nervously:

"Are we to understand that twelve hundred a year is your—your last word?"

Old Heythorp nodded. "Come again this day month, and I'll see what I can do for you;" and he shut his eyes.

Round Mr. Brownbee six of the gentlemen gathered, speaking in low voices; Mr. Ventnor nursed a leg and glowered at old Heythorp, who sat with his eyes closed. Mr. Brownbee went over and conferred with Mr. Ventnor, then clearing his throat, he said:

"Well, sir, we have considered your proposal; we agree to accept it for the moment. We will come again, as you suggest, in a month's time. We hope that you will by then have seen your way to something more substantial, with a view to avoiding what we should all regret, but which I fear will otherwise become inevitable."

Old Heythorp nodded. The eight gentlemen took their hats, and went out one by one, Mr. Brownbee courteously bringing up the rear.

The old man, who could not get up without assistance, stayed musing in his chair. He had diddled 'em for the moment into giving him another month, and when that month was up—he would diddle 'em again! A month ought to make the Pillin business safe, with all that hung on it. That poor funkey chap Joe Pillin! A gurgling chuckle escaped his red lips. What a shadow the fellow had looked, trotting in that evening just a month ago, behind his valet's announcement: "Mr. Pillin, sir."

What a parchmenty, precise, threadpaper of a chap, with his bird's claw of a hand, and his muffled-up throat, and his quavery:

"How do you do, Sylvanus? I'm afraid you're not——"

"First rate. Sit down. Have some port."

"Port! I never drink it. Poison to me! Poison!"

"Do you good!"

"Oh! I know, that's what you always say. You've a monstrous constitution, Sylvanus. If I drank port and smoked cigars and sat up till one o'clock, I should be in my grave to-morrow. I'm not the man I was. The fact is I've come to see if you can help me. I'm getting old; I'm growing nervous——"

"You always were as chickeny as an old hen, Joe."

"Well, my nature's not like yours. To come to the point, I want to sell my ships and retire. I need rest. Freights are very depressed. I've got my family to think of."

"Crack on, and go broke: buck you up like anything!"

"I'm quite serious, Sylvanus."

"Never knew you anything else, Joe."

A quavering cough, and out it had come:

"Now—in a word—won't your 'Island Navigation Company' buy my ships?"

A pause, a twinkle, a puff of smoke. "Make it worth my while!" He had said it in jest; and then, in a flash, the idea had come to him. Rosamund and her youngsters! What a chance to put something between them and destitution when he had joined the majority! And so he said: "We don't want your silly ships."

That claw of a hand waved in deprecation. "They're very good ships—doing quite well. It's only my wretched health. If I were a strong man I shouldn't dream—"

"What d'you want for 'em?" Good Lord! how he jumped if you asked him a plain question. The chap was as nervous as a guinea-fowl!

"Here are the figures—for the last four years. I think you'll agree that I couldn't ask less than seventy thousand."

Through the smoke of his cigar old Heythorp had digested those figures slowly, Joe Pillin feeling his teeth and sucking lozenges the while; then he said:

"Sixty thousand! And out of that you pay me ten per cent, if I get it through for you. Take it or leave it."

"My dear Sylvanus, that's almost—cynical."

"Too good a price—you'll never get it without me."

"But a—but a commission! You could never disclose it!"

"Arrange that all right. Think it over. Freights'll go lower yet. Have some port."

"No, no! Thank you. No! So you think freights will go lower?"

"Sure of it."

"Well, I'll be going. I'm sure I don't know. It's—it's—I must think."

"Think your hardest."

"Yes, yes. Good-bye. I can't imagine how you still go on smoking those things and drinking port."

"See you in your grave yet, Joe." What a feeble smile the poor fellow had! Laugh—he couldn't! And, alone again, he had browsed, developing the idea which had come to him.

Though, to dwell in the heart of shipping, Sylvanus Heythorp had lived at Liverpool twenty years, he was from the Eastern Counties, of a family so old that it professed to despise the Conquest. Each of its generations occupied nearly twice as long as those of less tenacious men. Traditionally of Danish origin, its men folk had as a rule bright reddish-brown hair, red cheeks, large round heads, excellent teeth and poor morals. They had done their best for the population of any county in which they had settled; their offshoots swarmed. Born in

the early twenties of the nineteenth century, Sylvanus Heythorp, after
an education broken by escapades both at school and college, had
fetched up in that simple London of the late forties, where claret,
opera, and eight per cent for your money ruled a cheery roost.
Made partner in his shipping firm well before he was thirty, he had
sailed with a wet sheet and a flowing tide; dancers, claret, Clicquot,
and piquet; a cab with a tiger; some travel—all that delicious early-
Victorian consciousness of nothing save a golden time. It was all so
full and mellow that he was forty before he had his only love affair of
any depth—with the daughter of one of his own clerks, a *liaison* so
awkward as to necessitate a sedulous concealment. The death of that
girl, after three years, leaving him a natural son, had been the chief,
perhaps the only real, sorrow of his life. Five years later he married.
What for? God only knew! as he was in the habit of remarking.
His wife had been a hard, worldly, well-connected woman, who
presented him with two unnatural children, a girl and a boy, and grew
harder, more worldly, less handsome, in the process. The migration to
Liverpool, which took place when he was sixty and she forty-two,
broke what she still had of heart, but she lingered on twelve years,
finding solace in bridge, and being haughty towards Liverpool. Old
Heythorp saw her to her rest without regret. He had felt no love
for her whatever, and practically none for her two children—they
were in his view colourless, pragmatical, very unexpected characters.
His son Ernest—in the Admiralty—he thought a poor, careful stick.
His daughter Adela, an excellent manager, delighting in spiritual
conversation and the society of tame men, rarely failed to show him
that she considered him a hopeless heathen. They saw as little as need
be of each other. She was provided for under that settlement he had
made on her mother fifteen years ago, well before the not altogether
unexpected crisis in his affairs. Very different was the feeling he had
bestowed on that son of his "under the rose." The boy, who had always
gone by his mother's name of Lame, had on her death been sent to
some relations of hers in Ireland, and there brought up. He had been
called to the Dublin bar, and married, young, a girl half Cornish and
half Irish; presently, having cost old Heythorp in all a pretty penny, he
had died impecunious, leaving his fair Rosamund at thirty with a girl
of eight and a boy of five. She had not spent six months of widowhood
before coming over from Dublin to claim the old man's guardianship.

A remarkably pretty woman, like a full-blown rose, with greenish hazel eyes, she had turned up one morning at the offices of "The Island Navigation Company," accompanied by her two children—for he had never divulged to them his private address. And since then they had always been more or less on his hands, occupying a small house in a suburb of Liverpool. He visited them there, but never asked them to the house in Sefton Park, which was in fact his daughter's; so that his proper family and friends were unaware of their existence.

Rosamund Larne was one of those precarious ladies who make uncertain incomes by writing full-bodied storyettes. In the most dismal circumstances she enjoyed a buoyancy bordering on the indecent, which always amused old Heythorp's cynicism. But of his grandchildren Phyllis and Jock (wild as colts) he had become fond. And this chance of getting six thousand pounds settled on them at a stroke had seemed to him nothing but heaven-sent. As things were, if he "went off"—and, of course, he might at any moment—there wouldn't be a penny for them; for he would "cut up" a good fifteen thousand to the bad. He was now giving them some three hundred a year out of his fees; and dead directors unfortunately earned no fees! Six thousand pounds at four and a half per cent settled so that their mother couldn't "blue it," would give them a certain two hundred and fifty pounds a year—better than beggary. And the more he thought the better he liked it, if only that shaky chap, Joe Pillin, didn't shy off when he'd bitten his nails short over it!

Four evenings later, the "shaky chap" had again appeared at his house in Sefton Park.

"I've thought it over, Sylvanus. I don't like it."

"No; but you'll do it."

"It's a sacrifice. Fifty-four thousand for four ships—it means a considerable reduction in my income."

"It means security, my boy."

"Well, there is that; but you know, I really can't be party to a secret commission. If it came out, think of my name and goodness knows what."

"It won't come out."

"Yes, yes, so you say, but—"

"All you've got to do's to execute a settlement on some third parties that I'll name. I'm not going to take a penny of it myself. Get

your own lawyer to draw it up and make him trustee. You can sign it
when the purchase has gone through. I'll trust you, Joe. What stock
have you got that gives four and a half per cent?"

"Midland——"

"That'll do. You needn't sell."

"Yes, but who *are* these people?"

"Woman and her children I want to do a good turn to." What
a face the fellow had made! "Afraid of being connected with a
woman, Joe?"

"Yes, you may laugh—I *am* afraid of being connected with
someone else's woman. I don't like it—I don't like it at all. I've not
led your, life, Sylvanus."

"Lucky for you; you'd have been dead long ago. Tell your lawyer
it's an old flame of yours—you old dog!"

"Yes, there it is at once, you see. I might be subject to blackmail."

"Tell him to keep it dark, and just pay over the income,
quarterly."

"I don't like it, Sylvanus—I don't like it."

"Then leave it, and be hanged to you. Have a cigar?"

"You know I never smoke. Is there no other way?"

"Yes. Sell stock in London, bank the proceeds there, and bring
me six thousand pounds in notes. I'll hold 'em till after the general
meeting. If the thing doesn't go through, I'll hand 'em back to you."

"No; I like that even less."

"Rather I trusted *you*, eh!"

"No, not at all, Sylvanus, not at all. But it's all playing round the
law."

"There's no law to prevent you doing what you like with your
money. What I do's nothing to you. And mind you, I'm taking
nothing from it—not a mag. You assist the widowed and the
fatherless—just your line, Joe!"

"What a fellow you are, Sylvanus; you don't seem capable of
taking anything seriously."

"Care killed the cat!"

Left alone after this second interview he had thought: 'The
beggar'll jump.'

And the beggar *had*. That settlement was drawn and only awaited
signature. The Board to-day had decided on the purchase; and all

that remained was to get it ratified at the general meeting. Let him but get that over, and this provision for his grandchildren made, and he would snap his fingers at Brownbee and his crew—the canting humbugs! "Hope you have many years of this life before you!" As if they cared for anything but his money—*their* money rather! And becoming conscious of the length of his reverie, he grasped the arms of his chair, heaved at his own bulk, in an effort to rise, growing redder and redder in face and neck. It was one of the hundred things his doctor had told him not to do for fear of apoplexy, the humbug! Why didn't Farney or one of those young fellows come and help him up? To call out was undignified. But was he to sit there all night? Three times he failed, and after each failure sat motionless again, crimson and exhausted; the fourth time he succeeded, and slowly made for the office. Passing through, he stopped and said in his extinct voice:

"You young gentlemen had forgotten me."

"Mr. Farney said you didn't wish to be disturbed, sir."

"Very good of him. Give me my hat and coat."

"Yes, sir."

"Thank you. What time is it?"

"Six o'clock, sir."

"Tell Mr. Farney to come and see me to-morrow at noon, about my speech for the general meeting."

"Yes, sir."

"Good-night to you."

"Good-night, sir."

At his tortoise gait he passed between the office stools to the door, opened it feebly, and slowly vanished.

Shutting the door behind him, a clerk said:

"Poor old chairman! He's on his last!"

Another answered;

"Gosh! He's a tough old hulk. He'll go down fightin'."

2 §

Issuing from the offices of "The Island Navigation Company," Sylvanus Heythorp moved towards the corner whence he always took tram to Sefton Park. The crowded street had all that prosperous air of catching or missing something which characterises the town where London and New York and Dublin meet. Old Heythorp had to cross to the far side, and he sallied forth without regard to traffic. That snail-like passage had in it a touch of the sublime; the old man seemed saying:

"Knock me down and be d——d to you—I'm not going to hurry." His life was saved perhaps ten times a day by the British character at large, compounded of phlegm and a liking to take something under its protection. The train conductors on that line were especially used to him, never failing to catch him under the arms and heave him like a sack of coals, while with trembling hands he pulled hard at the rail and strap.

"All right, sir?"

"Thank you."

He moved into the body of the tram, where somebody would always get up from kindness and the fear that he might sit down on them; and there he stayed motionless, his little eyes tight closed. With his red face, tuft of white hairs above his square cleft block of shaven chin, and his big high-crowned bowler hat, which yet seemed too petty for his head with its thick hair—he looked like some kind of an idol dug up and decked out in gear a size too small.

One of those voices of young men from public schools and exchanges where things are bought and sold, said:

"How de do, Mr. Heythorp?"

Old Heythorp opened his eyes. That sleek cub, Joe Pillin's son! What a young pup—with his round eyes, and his round cheeks, and his little moustache, his fur coat, his spats, his diamond pin!

"How's your father?" he said.

"Thanks, rather below par, worryin' about his ships. Suppose you haven't any news for him, sir?"

Old Heythorp nodded. The young man was one of his pet abominations, embodying all the complacent, little-headed mediocrity of this new generation; natty fellows all turned out of the same mould, sippers and tasters, chaps without drive or capacity, without even vices; and he did not intend to gratify the cub's curiosity.

"Come to my house," he said; "I'll give you a note for him."

"Tha—anks; I'd like to cheer the old man up."

The old man! Cheeky brat! And closing his eyes he relapsed into immobility. The tram wound and ground its upward way, and he mused. When he was that cub's age—twenty-eight or whatever it might be—he had done most things; been up Vesuvius, driven four-in-hand, lost his last penny on the Derby and won it back on the Oaks, known all the dancers and operatic stars of the day, fought a duel with a Yankee at Dieppe and winged him for saying through his confounded nose that Old England was played out; been a controlling voice already in his shipping firm; drunk five other of the best men in London under the table; broken his neck steeplechasing; shot a burglar in the legs; been nearly drowned, for a bet; killed snipe in Chelsea; been to Court for his sins; stared a ghost out of countenance; and travelled with a lady of Spain. If this young pup had done the last, it would be all he had; and yet, no doubt, he would call himself a "spark."

The conductor touched his arm.

"'Ere you are, sir."

"Thank you."

He lowered himself to the ground, and moved in the bluish darkness towards the gate of his daughter's house. Bob Pillin walked beside him, thinking: 'Poor old josser, he *is* gettin' a back number!' And he said: "I should have thought you ought to drive, sir. My old guv-nor would knock up at once if he went about at night like this."

The answer rumbled out into the misty air:

"Your father's got no chest; never had."

Bob Pillin gave vent to one of those fat cackles which come so readily from a certain type of man; and old Heythorp thought: 'Laughing at his father! Parrot!'

They had reached the porch.

A woman with dark hair and a thin, straight face and figure was arranging some flowers in the hall. She turned and said:

"You really ought not to be so late, Father! It's wicked at this time of year. Who is it—oh! Mr. Pillin, how do you do? Have you had tea? Won't you come to the drawing-room; or do you want to see my father?"

"Tha—anks! I believe your father——" And he thought: 'By Jove! the old chap *is* a caution!' For old Heythorp was crossing the hall without having paid the faintest attention to his daughter. Murmuring again:

"Tha—anks awfully; he wants to give me something," he followed. Miss Heythorp was not his style at all; he had a kind of dread of that thin woman who looked as if she could never be unbuttoned. They said she was a great churchgoer and all that sort of thing.

In his sanctum old Heythorp had moved to his writing-table, and was evidently anxious to sit down.

"Shall I give you a hand, sir?"

Receiving a shake of the head, Bob Pillin stood by the fire and watched. The old "sport" liked to paddle his own canoe. Fancy having to lower yourself into a chair like that! When an old Johnny got to such a state it was really a mercy when he snuffed out, and made way for younger men. How his Companies could go on putting up with such a fossil for chairman was a marvel! The fossil rumbled and said in that almost inaudible voice:

"I suppose you're beginning to look forward to your father's shoes?"

Bob Pillin's mouth opened. The voice went on:

"Dibs and no responsibility. Tell him from me to drink port—add five years to his life."

To this unwarranted attack Bob Pillin made no answer save a laugh; he perceived that a manservant had entered the room.

"A Mrs. Larne, sir. Will you see her?"

At this announcement the old man seemed to try and start; then he nodded, and held out the note he had written. Bob Pillin received it together with the impression of a murmur which sounded like: "Scratch a poll, Poll!" and passing the fine figure of a woman in a fur coat, who seemed to warm the air as she went by, he was in the hall again before he perceived that he had left his hat.

A young and pretty girl was standing on the bearskin before the fire, looking at him with round-eyed innocence. He thought: 'This is better; I mustn't disturb them for my hat'; and approaching the fire, he said:

"Jolly cold, isn't it?"

The girl smiled: "Yes—jolly."

He noticed that she had a large bunch of violet at her breast, a lot of fair hair, a short straight nose, and round blue-grey eyes very frank and open. "Er—" he said, "I've left my hat in there."

"What larks!" And at her little clear laugh something moved within Bob Pillin.

"You know this house well?"

She shook her head. "But it's rather scrummy, isn't it?"

Bob Pillin, who had never yet thought so, answered:

"Quite O.K."

'The girl threw up her head to laugh again. "O.K.? What's that?"

Bob Pillin saw her white round throat, and thought: 'She is a ripper!' And he said with a certain desperation:

"My name's Pillin. Yours is Larne, isn't it? Are you a relation here?"

"He's our Guardy. Isn't he a chook?"

That rumbling whisper like "Scratch a poll, Poll!" recurring to Bob Pillin, he said with reservation:

"You know him better than I do."

"Oh! Aren't you his grandson, or something?" Bob Pillin did not cross himself.

"Lord! No! My dad's an old friend of his; that's all."

"Is your dad like him?"

"Not much."

"What a pity! It would have been lovely if they'd been Tweedles."

Bob Pillin thought: 'This bit is something new. I wonder what her Christian name is.' And he said:

"What did your godfather and godmothers in your baptism——?"

The girl laughed; she seemed to laugh at everything.

"Phyllis."

Could he say: "Is my only joy"? Better keep it! But—for what? He wouldn't see her again if he didn't look out! And he said:

"I live at the last house in the park—the red one. D'you know it? Where do you?"

"Oh! a long way—23, Millicent Villas. It's a poky little house. I hate it. We have awful larks, though."

"Who are we?"

"Mother, and myself, and Jock—he's an awful boy. You can't conceive what an awful boy he is. He's got nearly red hair; I think he'll be just like Guardy when he gets old. He's *awful*!"

Bob Pillin murmured:

"I should like to see him."

"Would you? I'll ask mother if you can. You won't want to again;
he goes off all the time like a squib." She threw back her head,
and again Bob Pillin felt a little giddy. He collected himself, and
drawled:

"Are you going in to see your Guardy?"

"No. Mother's got something special to say. We've never been here
before, you see. Isn't he fun, though?"

"Fun!"

"I think he's the greatest lark: but he's awfully nice to me. Jock
calls him the last of the Stoic'uns."

A voice called from old Heythorp's den:

"Phyllis!" It had a particular ring, that voice, as if coming from
beautifully formed red lips, of which the lower one must curve the
least bit over; it had, too, a caressing vitality, and a kind of warm falsity.

The girl threw a laughing look back over her shoulder, and
vanished through the door into the room.

Bob Pillin remained with his back to the fire and his puppy
round eyes fixed on the air that her figure had last occupied. He
was experiencing a sensation never felt before. Those travels with
a lady of Spain, charitably conceded him by old Heythorp, had
so far satisfied the emotional side of this young man; they had
stopped short at Brighton and Scarborough, and been preserved
from even the slightest intrusion of love. A calculated and hygienic
career had caused no anxiety either to himself or his father; and
this sudden swoop of something more than admiration gave him an
uncomfortable choky feeling just above his high round collar, and
in the temples a sort of buzzing—those first symptoms of chivalry.
A man of the world does not, however, succumb without a struggle;
and if his hat had not been out of reach, who knows whether he
would not have left the house hurriedly, saying to himself: "No, no,
my boy; Millicent Villas is hardly your form, when your intentions
are honourable"? For somehow that round and laughing face, bob
of glistening hair, those wide-opened grey eyes, refused to awaken
the beginnings of other intentions—such is the effect of youth and
innocence on even the steadiest young men. With a kind of moral
stammer, he was thinking:

'Can I—dare I offer to see them to their tram? Couldn't I even
nip out and get the car round and send them home in it? No, I

might miss them—better stick it out here! What a jolly laugh! What a ripping face—strawberries and cream, hay, and all that! Millicent Villas!' And he wrote it on his cuff.

The door was opening; he heard that warm vibrating voice:

"Come along, Phyllis!"—the girl's laugh so high and fresh:

"Right-o! Coming!" And with, perhaps, the first real tremor he had ever known, he crossed to the front door. All the more chivalrous to escort them to the tram without a hat! And suddenly he heard: "I've got your hat, young man!" And her mother's voice, warm, and simulating shock: "Phyllis, you awful gairl! Did you ever see such an awful gairl, Mr.——"

"Pillin, Mother."

And then—he did not quite know how—insulated from the January air by laughter and the scent of fur and violets, he was between them walking to their tram. It was like an experience out of the "Arabian Nights," or something of that sort, an intoxication which made one say one was going their way, though one would have to come all the way back in the same beastly tram. Nothing so warming had ever happened to him as sitting between them on that drive, so that he forgot the note in his pocket, and his desire to relieve the anxiety of the "old man," his father. At the tram's terminus they all got out. There issued a purr of invitation to come and see them some time; a clear: "Jock'll love to see you!" A low laugh: "You awful gairl!" And a flash of cunning zigzagged across his brain. Taking off his hat, he said:

"Thanks awfully; rather!" and put his foot back on the step of the tram. Thus did he delicately expose the depths of his chivalry!

"Oh! you *said* you were going our way! What one-ers you do tell! Oh!" The words were as music; the sight of those eyes growing rounder, the most perfect he had ever seen; and Mrs. Larne's low laugh, so warm yet so preoccupied, and the tips of the girl's fingers waving back above her head. He heaved a sigh and knew no more till he was seated at his club before a bottle of champagne. Home! Not he! He wished to drink and dream. "The old man" would get his news all right to-morrow!

3 §

The words: "A Mrs. Larne to see you, sir," had been of a nature
to astonish weaker nerves. What had brought her here? She knew
she mustn't come! Old Heythorp had watched her entrance with
cynical amusement. The way she whiffed herself at that young pup in
passing, the way her eyes slid round! He had a very just appreciation
of his son's widow; and a smile settled deep between his chin tuft
and his moustache. She lifted his hand, kissed it, pressed it to her
splendid bust, and said:

"So here I am at last, you see. Aren't you surprised?"

Old Heythorp shook his head.

"I really had to come and see you, Guardy; we haven't had a sight
of you for such an age. And in this awful weather! How are you, dear
old Guardy?"

"Never better." And, watching her green-grey eyes, he added
"Haven't a penny for you!"

Her face did not fall; she gave her feather-laugh.

"How dreadful of you to think I came for that! But I *am* in an
awful fix, Guardy."

"Never knew you not to be."

"Just let me tell you, dear; it'll be some relief. I'm having the most
terrible time."

She sank into a low chair; disengaging an overpowering scent of
violets, while melancholy struggled to subdue her face and body.

"The most awful fix. I expect to be sold up any moment. We
may be on the streets to-morrow. I daren't tell the children; they're
so happy, poor darlings. I shall be obliged to take Jock away from
school. And Phyllis will have to stop her piano and dancing; it's an
absolute crisis. And all due to those Midland Syndicate people. I've
been counting on at least two hundred for my new story, and the
wretches have refused it."

With a tiny handkerchief she removed one tear from the corner of
one eye. "It *is* hard, Guardy; I worked my brain silly over that story."

From old Heythorp came a mutter which sounded suspiciously
like "Rats!"

Heaving a sigh, which conveyed nothing but the generosity of her
breathing apparatus, Mrs. Larne went on:

"You couldn't, I suppose, let me have just one hundred?"

"Not a bob."

She sighed again, her eyes slid round the room; then in her warm voice she murmured:

"Guardy, you *were* my dear Philip's father, weren't you? I've never said anything; but *of course* you were. He was so like you, and so is Jock."

Nothing moved in old Heythorp's face. No pagan image consulted with flowers and song and sacrifice could have returned less answer. Her dear Philip! She had led him the devil of a life, or he was a Dutchman! And what the deuce made her suddenly trot out the skeleton like this? But Mrs. Larne's eyes were still wandering.

"What a lovely house! You know, I think you ought to help me, Guardy. Just imagine if your grandchildren were thrown out into the street!"

The old man grinned. He was not going to deny his relationship—it was her look-out, not his. But neither was he going to let her rush him.

"And they will be; you *couldn't* look on and see it. Do come to my rescue this once. You really might do something for them."

With a rumbling sigh he answered:

"Wait. Can't give you a penny now. Poor as a church mouse."

"Oh! Guardy!"

"Fact."

Mrs. Larne heaved one of her most buoyant sighs. She certainly did not believe him.

"Well!" she said; "you'll be sorry when we come round one night and sing for pennies under your window. Wouldn't you like to see Phyllis? I left her in the hall. She's growing such a sweet gairl. Guardy—just fifty!"

"Not a rap."

Mrs. Larne threw up her hands. "Well! You'll repent it. I'm at my last gasp." She sighed profoundly, and the perfume of violets escaped in a cloud. Then, getting up, she went to the door and called: "Phyllis!"

When the girl entered old Heythorp felt the nearest approach to a flutter of the heart for many years. She had put her hair up! She was like a spring day in January; such a relief from that scented humbug, her mother. Pleasant, the touch of her lips on his forehead, the sound of her clear voice, the sight of her slim movements, the feeling that she did him credit—clean-run stock, she and that young scamp Jock—better than the holy woman, his daughter Adela, would produce if anyone were ever fool enough to marry her, or that pragmatical fellow, his son Ernest.

And when they were gone he reflected with added zest on the six thousand pounds he was getting for them out of Joe Pillin and his ships. He would have to pitch it strong in his speech at the general meeting. With freights so low, there was bound to be opposition. No dash nowadays; nothing but flabby caution! They were a scrim-shanking lot on the Board—he had had to put them round one by one—the deuce of a tug getting this thing through! And yet, the business was sound enough. Those ships would earn money, properly handled—good money!

His valet, coming in to prepare him for dinner, found him asleep. He had for the old man as much admiration as may be felt for one who cannot put his own trousers on. He would say to the housemaid Molly: "He's a game old blighter—must have been a rare one in his day. Cocks his hat at you, even now, I see!" To which the girl, Irish pretty, would reply: "Well, an' sure I don't mind, if it gives um a pleasure. 'Tis better annyway than the sad eye I get from herself."

At dinner, old Heythorp always sat at one end of the rose-wood table and his daughter at the other. It was the eminent moment of the day. With napkin tucked high into his waistcoat, he gave himself to the meal with passion. His palate was undimmed, his digestion unimpaired. He could still eat as much as two men, and drink more than one. And while he savoured each mouthful he never spoke if he could help it. The holy woman had nothing to say that he cared to hear, and he nothing to say that she cared to listen to. She had a horror, too, of what she called "the pleasures of the table"—those lusts of the flesh! She was always longing to dock his grub, he knew. Would see her further first! What other pleasures were there at his age? Let her wait till *she* was eighty. But she never would be; too thin and holy!

This evening, however, with the advent of the partridge she *did* speak.

"Who were your visitors, Father?"

Trust her for nosing anything out! Fixing his little blue eyes on her, he mumbled with a very full mouth: "Ladies."

"So I saw; what ladies?"

He had a longing to say: 'Part of one of my families under the rose.' As a fact it was the best part of the only one, but the temptation to multiply exceedingly was almost overpowering. He checked himself, however, and went on eating partridge, his secret irritation crimsoning his cheeks; and he watched her eyes, those cold precise and round grey eyes, noting it, and knew she was thinking: 'He eats too much.'

She said: "Sorry I'm not considered fit to be told. You ought not to be drinking hock."

Old Heythorp took up the long green glass, drained it, and repressing fumes and emotion went on with his partridge. His daughter pursed her lips, took a sip of water, and said:

"I know their name is Larne, but it conveyed nothing to me; perhaps it's just as well."

The old man, mastering a spasm, said with a grin:

"My daughter-in-law and my granddaughter."

"What! Ernest married—Oh! nonsense!"

He chuckled, and shook his head.

"Then do you mean to say, Father, that you were married before you married my mother?"

"No."

The expression on her face was as good as a play!

She said with a sort of disgust: "Not married! I see. I suppose those people are hanging round your neck, then; no wonder you're always in difficulties. Are there any more of them?"

Again the old man suppressed that spasm, and the veins in his neck and forehead swelled alarmingly. If he had spoken he would infallibly have choked. He ceased eating, and putting his hands on the table tried to raise himself. He could not, and subsiding in his chair sat glaring at the stiff, quiet figure of his daughter.

"Don't be silly, Father, and make a scene before Meller. Finish your dinner."

He did not answer. He was not going to sit there to be dragooned and insulted! His helplessnes had never so weighed on him before.

It was like a revelation. A log—that had to put up with anything! A log! And, waiting for his valet to return, he cunningly took up his fork.

In that saintly voice of hers she said:

"I suppose you don't realise that it's a shock to me. I don't know what Ernest will think——"

"Earnest be d——d."

"I do wish, Father, you wouldn't swear."

Old Heythorp's rage found vent in a sort of rumble. How the devil had he gone on all these years in the same house with that woman, dining with her day after day! But the servant had come back now, and putting down his fork he said:

"Help me up!"

The man paused, thunderstruck, with the *soufflé* balanced.

To leave dinner unfinished—it was a portent!

"Help me up!"

"Mr. Heythorp's not very well, Meller; take his other arm."

The old man shook off her hand.

"I'm very well. Help me up. Dine in my own room in future."

Raised to his feet, he walked slowly out; but in his sanctum he did not sit down, obsessed by this first overwhelming realisation of his helplessness. He stood swaying a little, holding on to the table, till the servant, having finished serving dinner, brought in his port.

"Are you, waiting to sit down, sir?"

He shook his head. Hang it, he could do that for himself, anyway. He must think of something to fortify his position against that woman. And he said:

"Send me Molly!"

"Yes, sir." The man put down the port and went.

Old Heythorp filled his glass, drank, and filled again. He took a cigar from the box and lighted it. The girl came in, a grey-eyed, dark-haired damsel, and stood with her hands folded, her head a little to one side, her lips a little parted. The old man said:

"You're a human being."

"I would, hope so, sirr."

"I'm going to ask you something as a human being—not a servant—see?"

"No, sirr; but I will be glad to do annything you like."

"Then put your nose in here every now and then, to see if I want anything. Meller goes out sometimes. Don't say anything; just put your nose in."

"Oh! an' I will; 'tis a pleasure 'twill be to do ut."

He nodded, and when she had gone lowered himself into his chair with a sense of appeasement. Pretty girl! Comfort to see a pretty face—not a pale, peeky thing like Adela's. His anger burned up anew. So she counted on his helplessness, had begun to count on that, had she? She should see that there was life in the old dog yet! And his sacrifice of the uneaten *soufflé*, the still less eaten mushrooms, the peppermint sweet with which he usually concluded dinner, seemed to consecrate that purpose. They all thought he was a hulk, without a shot left in the locker! He had seen a couple of them at the Board that afternoon shrugging at each other, as though saying: 'Look at him!' And young Farney pitying him. Pity, forsooth! And that coarse-grained solicitor chap at the creditors' meeting curling his lips as much to say: 'One foot in the grave!' He had seen the clerks dowsing the glim of their grins; and that young pup Bob Pillin screwing up his supercilious mug over his dog-collar. He knew that scented humbug Rosamund was getting scared that he'd drop off before she'd squeezed him dry. And his valet was always looking him up and down queerly. As to that holy woman—! Not quite so fast! Not quite so fast! And filling his glass for the fourth time, he slowly sucked down the dark red fluid, with the "old boots" flavour which his soul loved, and, drawing deep at his cigar, closed his eyes.

II

I §

The room in the hotel where the general meetings of "The Island Navigation Company" were held was nearly full when the secretary came through the door which as yet divided the shareholders from their directors. Having surveyed their empty chairs, their ink and papers, and nodded to a shareholder or two, he stood, watch in hand, contemplating the congregation. A thicker attendance than he had ever seen! Due, no doubt, to the lower dividend, and this Pillin business. And his tongue curled. For if he had a natural contempt for his Board, with the exception of the chairman, he had a still more natural

contempt for his shareholders. Amusing spectacle when you come
to think of it, a general meeting! Unique! Eighty or a hundred men,
and five women, assembled through sheer devotion to their money.
Was any other function in the world so single-hearted. Church was
nothing to it—so many motives were mingled there with devotion
to one's soul. A well-educated young man—reader of Anatole France,
and other writers—he enjoyed ironic speculation. What earthly good
did they think they got by coming here? Half-past two! He put his
watch back into his pocket, and passed into the Board-room.

There, the fumes of lunch and of a short preliminary meeting
made cosy the February atmosphere. By the fire four directors were
conversing rather restlessly; the fifth was combing his beard; the
chairman sat with eyes closed and red lips moving rhythmically in
the sucking of a lozenge, the slips of his speech ready in his hand.
The secretary said in his cheerful voice:

"Time, sir."

Old Heythorp swallowed, lifted his arms, rose with help, and
walked through to his place at the centre of the table. The five
directors followed. And, standing at the chairman's right, the
secretary read the minutes, forming the words precisely with his
curling tongue. Then, assisting the chairman to his feet, he watched
those rows of faces, and thought: 'Mistake to let them see he can't
get up without help. He ought to have let me read his speech—I
wrote it.'

The chairman began to speak:

"It is my duty and my pleasure, ladies and gentlemen, for the
nineteenth consecutive year to present to you the directors' report
and the accounts for the past twelve months. You will all have
had special notice of a measure of policy on which your Board
has decided, and to which you will be asked to-day to give your
adherence—to that I shall come at the end of my remarks. . . .'"

"Excuse me, sir; we can't hear a word down here."

'Ah!' thought the secretary, 'I was expecting that.'

The chairman went on, undisturbed. But several shareholders now
rose, and the same speaker said testily: "We might as well go home. If
the chairman's got no voice, can't somebody read for him?"

The chairman took a sip of water, and resumed. Almost all in the
last six rows were now on their feet, and amid a hubbub of murmurs

the chairman held out to the secretary the slips of his speech, and fell heavily back into his chair.

The secretary re-read from the beginning; and as each sentence fell from his tongue, he thought: 'How good that is!' 'That's very clear!' 'A neat touch!' 'This is getting them.' It seemed to him a pity they could not know it was all his composition. When at last he came to the Pillin sale he paused for a second.

"I come now to the measure of policy to which I made allusion at the beginning of my speech. Your Board has decided to expand your enterprise by purchasing the entire fleet of Pillin & Co., Ltd. By this transaction we become the owners of the four steamships *Smyra*, *Damascus*, *Tyre* and *Sidon*, vessels in prime condition with a total freight-carrying capacity of fifteen thousand tons, at the low inclusive price of sixty thousand pounds. Gentlemen, '*Vestigia nulla retrorsum!*'"—it was the chairman's phrase, his bit of the speech, and the secretary did it more than justice. "Times are bad, but your Board is emphatically of the opinion that they are touching bottom; and this, in their view, is the psychological moment for a forward stroke. They confidently recommend your adoption of their policy and the ratification of this purchase, which they believe will, in the not far distant future, substantially increase the profits of the Company." The secretary sat down with reluctance. The speech should have continued with a number of appealing sentences which he had carefully prepared, but the chairman had cut them out with the simple comment: "They ought to be glad of the chance." It was, in his view, an error.

The director who had combed his beard now rose—a man of presence, who might be trusted to say nothing long and suavely. While he was speaking the secretary was busy noting whence opposition was likely to come. The majority were sitting owl-like—a good sign; but some dozen were studying their copies of the report, and three at least were making notes—Westgate, for instance, who wanted to get on the Board, and was sure to make himself unpleasant—the time-honoured method of vinegar; and Batterson, who also desired to come on, and might be trusted to support the Board—the time-honoured method of oil; while, if one knew anything of human nature, the fellow who had complained that he might as well go home would have something uncomfortable to say.

The director finished his remarks, combed his beard with his fingers, and sat down.

A momentary pause ensued. Then Messieurs Westgate and Batterson rose together. Seeing the chairman nod towards the latter, the secretary thought: 'Mistake! He should have humoured Westgate by giving him precedence.' But that was the worst of the old man, he had no notion of the *suaviter in modo!* Mr. Batterson—thus unchained—would like, if he might be so allowed, to congratulate the Board on having piloted their ship so smoothly through the troublous waters of the past year. With their worthy chairman still at the helm, he had no doubt that in spite of the still low—he would not say falling—barometer, and the—er—unseasonable climacteric, they might rely on weathering the—er—he would not say storm. He would confess that the present dividend of four per cent. was not one which satisfied every aspiration (Hear, hear!), but speaking for himself, and he hoped for others—and here Mr. Batterson looked round—he recognised that in all the circumstances it was as much as they had the right—er—to expect. But following the bold but to *his* mind prudent development which the Board proposed to make, he thought that they might reasonably, if not sanguinely, anticipate a more golden future. ("No, no!") A shareholder said, "No, no!" That might seem to indicate a certain lack of confidence in the special proposal before the meeting. ("Yes!") From that lack of confidence he would like at once to dissociate himself. Their chairman, a man of foresight and acumen, and valour proved on many a field and—er—sea, would not have committed himself to this policy without good reason. In his opinion they were in safe hands, and he was glad to register his support of the measure proposed. The chairman had well said in his speech: "*Vestigia in retrorsum!*" Shareholders would agree with him that there could be no better motto for Englishmen. Ahem!

Mr. Batterson sat down. And Mr. Westgate rose: He wanted—he said—to know more, much more, about this proposition, which to his mind was of a very dubious wisdom . . . 'Ah!' thought the secretary, 'I told the old boy he must tell them more.' . . . To whom, for instance, had the proposal first been made? To him!—the chairman said. Good! But why were Pillins selling, if freights were to go up, as they were told?

"Matter of opinion."

"Quite so; and in my opinion they are going lower, and Pillins were right to sell. It follows that we are wrong to buy." ("Hear, hear!" "No, no!") "Pillins are shrewd people. What does the chairman say? Nerves! Does he mean to tell us that this sale was the result of nerves?"

The chairman nodded.

"That appears to me a somewhat fantastic theory; but I will leave that and confine myself to asking the grounds on which the chairman bases his confidence; in fact, what it is which is actuating the Board in pressing on us at such a time what I have no hesitation in stigmatising as a rash proposal. In a word, I want light as well as leading in this matter."

Mr. Westgate sat down.

What would the chairman do now? The situation was distinctly awkward—seeing his helplessness and the luke-warmness of the Board behind him. And the secretary felt more strongly than ever the absurdity of his being an underling, he who in a few well-chosen words could so easily have twisted the meeting round his thumb. Suddenly he heard the long, rumbling sigh which preluded the chairman's speeches.

"Has any other gentleman anything to say before I move the adoption of the report?"

Phew! That would put their backs up. Yes, sure enough it had brought that fellow, who had said he might as well go home, to his feet! Now for something nasty!

"Mr. Westgate requires answering. I don't like this business. I don't impute anything to anybody; but it looks to me as if there were something behind it which the shareholders ought to be told. Not only that; but, to speak frankly, I'm not satisfied to be ridden over roughshod in this fashion by one who, whatever he may have been in the past, is obviously not now in the prime of his faculties."

With a gasp the secretary thought: 'I knew that was a plain-spoken man!'

He heard again the rumbling beside him. The chairman had gone crimson, his mouth was pursed, his little eyes were very blue.

"Help me up," he said.

The secretary helped him, and waited, rather breathless.

The chairman took a sip of water, and his voice, unexpectedly loud, broke an ominous hush:

"Never been so insulted in my life. My best services have been at your disposal for nineteen years; you know what measure of success this Company has attained. I am the oldest man here, and my experience of shipping is, I hope, a little greater than that of the two gentlemen who spoke last. I have done my best for you, ladies and gentlemen, and we shall see whether you are going to endorse an indictment of my judgment and of my honour, if I am to take the last speaker seriously. This purchase is for your good. 'There is a tide in the affairs of men'—and I for one am not content, never have been, to stagnate. If that is what you want, however, by all means give your support to these gentlemen and have done with it. I tell you freights will go up before the end of the year; the purchase is a sound one, more than a sound one—I, at any rate, stand or fall by it. Refuse to ratify it, if you like; if you do, I shall resign."

He sank back into his seat. The secretary, stealing a glance, thought with a sort of enthusiasm: 'Bravo! Who'd have thought he could rally his voice like that? A good touch, too, about his honour! I believe he's knocked them. It's still dicky, though, if that fellow at the back gets up again; the old chap can't work that stop a second time.' Ah! here was 'old Apple-pie' on his hind legs. That was all right!

"I do not hesitate to say that I am an old friend of the chairman; we are, many of us, old friends of the chairman, and it has been painful to me, and I doubt not to others, to hear an attack made on him. If he is old in body, he is young in mental vigour and courage. I wish we were all as young. We ought to stand by him; I say, we ought to stand by him." ("Hear, hear! Hear, hear!") And the secretary thought:

'That's done it!' And he felt a sudden odd emotion, watching the chairman bobbing his body, like a wooden toy, at old Appleby; and old Appleby bobbing back. Then, seeing a shareholder close to the door get up, thought: 'Who's that? I know his face—Ah! yes; Ventnor, the solicitor—he's one of the chairman's creditors that are coming again this afternoon. What now?'

"I can't agree that we ought to let sentiment interfere with our judgment in this matter. The question is simply: How are our pockets going to be affected? I came here with some misgivings, but the attitude of the chairman has been such as to remove them; and I shall support the proposition." The secretary thought: 'That's all right—only, he said it rather queerly—rather queerly.'

Then, after a long silence, the chairman, without rising, said:

"I move the adoption of the report and accounts."

"I second that."

"Those in favour signify the same in the usual way. Contrary? Carried." The secretary noted the dissentients, six in number, and that Mr. Westgate did not vote.

A quarter of an hour later he stood in the body of the emptying room supplying names to one of the gentlemen of the Press.

The passionless fellow said: "Haythorp, with an 'a'; oh! an 'e'; he seems an old man. Thank you. I may have the slips? Would you like to see a proof? With an 'a' you said—oh! an 'e'. Good afternoon!" And the secretary thought:

'Those fellows, what *does* go on inside them? Fancy not knowing the old chairman by now!' . . .

II §

Back in the proper office of "The Island Navigation Company" old Heythorp sat smoking a cigar and smiling like a purring cat. He was dreaming a little of his triumph, sifting with his old brain, still subtle, the wheat from the chaff of the demurrers: Westgate—nothing in that—professional discontent till they silenced him with a place on the Board—but not while *he* held the reins! That chap at the back— an ill-conditioned fellow! "Something behind!" Suspicious brute! There was something—but—hang it! they might think themselves lucky to get four ships at that price, and all due to him! It was on the last speaker that his mind dwelt with a doubt. That fellow Ventnor, to whom he owed money—there had been something just a little queer about his tone—as much as to say, "I smell a rat." Well! one would see that at the creditors' meeting in half an hour.

"Mr. Pillin, sir."

"Show him in!"

In a fur coat which seemed to extinguish his thin form, Joe Pillin entered. It was snowing, and the cold had nipped and yellowed his meagre face between its slight grey whiskering. He said thinly:

"How are you, Sylvanus? Aren't you perished in this cold?"

"Warm as toast. Sit down. Take off your coat."

"Oh! I should be lost without it. You must have a fire inside you. So—so it's gone through?"

Old Heythorp nodded; and Joe Pillin, wandering like a spirit, scrutinised the shut door. He came back to the table, and said in a low voice:

"It's a great sacrifice."

Old Heythorp smiled.

"Have you signed the deed poll?"

Producing a parchment from his pocket Joe Pillin unfolded it with caution to disclose his signature, and said:

"I don't like it—it's irrevocable."

A chuckle escaped old Heythorp.

"As death."

Joe Pillin's voice passed up into the treble clef.

"I can't bear irrevocable things. I consider you stampeded me, playing on my nerves."

Examining the signatures old Heythorp murmured:

"Tell your lawyer to lock it up. He must think you a sad dog, Joe."

"Ah! Suppose on my death it comes to the knowledge of my wife!"

"She won't be able to make it hotter for you than you'll be already."

Joe Pillin replaced the deed within his coat, emitting a queer thin noise. He simply could not bear joking on such subjects.

"Well," he said, "you've got your way; you always do. Who is this Mrs. Larne? You oughtn't to keep me in the dark. It seems my boy met her at your house. You told me she didn't come there."

Old Heythorp said with relish:

"Her husband was my son by a woman I was fond of before I married; her children are my grandchildren. You've provided for them. Best thing you ever did."

"I don't know—I don't know. I'm sorry you told me. It makes it all the more doubtful. As soon as the transfer's complete, I shall get away abroad. This cold's killing me. I wish you'd give me your recipe for keeping warm."

"Get a new inside."

Joe Pillin regarded his old friend with a sort of yearning.

"And yet," he said, "I suppose, with your full-blooded habit, your life hangs by a thread, doesn't it?"

"A stout one, my boy!"

"Well, good-bye, Sylvanus. You're a Job's comforter; I must be getting home." He put on his hat, and, lost in his fur coat, passed out into the corridor. On the stairs he met a man who said:

"How do you do, Mr. Pillin? I know your son. Been seeing the chairman? I see your sale's gone through all right. I hope that'll do us some good, but I suppose you think the other way?"

Peering at him from under his hat, Joe Pillin said:

"Mr. Ventnor, I think? Thank you! It's very cold, isn't it?" And, with that cautious remark, he passed on down.

Alone again, old Heythorp thought: 'By George! What a wavering, quavering, thread-paper of a fellow! What misery life must be to a chap like that! He walks in fear—he wallows in it. Poor devil!' And a curious feeling swelled his heart, of elation, of lightness such as he had not known for years. Those two young things were safe now from penury—safe! After dealing with those infernal creditors of his he would go round and have a look at the children. With a hundred and twenty a year the boy could go into the Army—best place for a young scamp like that. The girl would go off like hot cakes, of course, but she needn't take the first calf that came along. As for their mother, she must look after herself; nothing under two thousand a year would keep *her* out of debt. But trust her for wheedling and bluffing her way out of any scrape! Watching his cigar-smoke curl and disperse he was conscious of the strain he had been under these last six weeks, aware suddenly of how greatly he had baulked at thought of to-day's general meeting. Yes! It might have turned out nasty. He knew well enough the forces on the Board, and off, who would be only too glad to shelve him. If he were shelved here his other two Companies would be sure to follow suit, and bang would go every penny of his income—he would be a pauper dependent on that holy woman. Well! Safe now for another year if he could stave off these sharks once more. It might be a harder job this time, but he was in luck—in luck, and it must hold. And taking a luxurious pull at his cigar, he rang the handbell.

"Bring 'em in here, Mr. Farney. And let me have a cup of China tea as strong as you can make it."

"Yes, sir. Will you see the proof of the press report, or will you leave it to me?"

"To you."

"Yes, sir. It was a good meeting, wasn't it?"

Old Heythorp nodded.

"Wonderful how your voice came back just at the right moment. I was afraid things were going to be difficult. The insult did it, I think. It was a monstrous thing to say. I could have punched his head."

Again old Heythorp nodded; and, looking into the secretary's fine blue eyes, he repeated: "Bring 'em in."

The lonely minute before the entrance of his creditors passed in the thought: 'So that's how it struck him! Short shrift I should get if it came out.'

The gentlemen, who numbered ten this time, bowed to their debtor, evidently wondering why the deuce they troubled to be polite to an old man who kept them out of their money. Then, the secretary reappearing with a cup of China tea, they watched while their debtor drank it. The feat was tremulous. Would he get through without spilling it all down his front, or choking? To those unaccustomed to his private life it was slightly miraculous. He put the cup down empty, tremblingly removed some yellow drops from the little white tuft below his lip, relit his cigar, and said:

"No use beating about the bush, gentlemen; I can offer you fourteen hundred a year so long as I live and hold my directorships, and not a penny more. If you can't accept that, you must make me bankrupt and get about sixpence in the pound. My qualifying shares will fetch a couple of thousand at market price. I own nothing else. The house I live in, and everything in it, barring my clothes, my wine, and my cigars, belong to my daughter under a settlement fifteen years old. My solicitors and bankers will give you every information. That's the position in a nutshell."

In spite of business habits the surprise of the ten gentlemen was only partially concealed. A man who owed them so much would naturally say he owned nothing, but would he refer them to his solicitors and bankers unless he were telling the truth? Then Mr. Ventnor said:

"Will you submit your pass books?"

"No, but I'll authorise my bankers to give you a full statement of my receipts for the last five years—longer, if you like."

The strategic stroke of placing the ten gentlemen round the Board table had made it impossible for them to consult freely without being overheard, but the low-voiced transference of thought travelling round was summed up at last by Mr. Brownbee.

"We think, Mr. Heythorp, that your fees and dividends should enable you to set aside for us a larger sum. Sixteen hundred, in fact, is what we think you should give us yearly. Representing, as we do, sixteen thousand pounds, the prospect is not cheering, but we hope you have some good years before you yet. We understand your income to be two thousand pounds."

Old Heythorp shook his head. "Nineteen hundred and thirty pounds in a good year. Must eat and drink; must have a man to look after me—not as active as I was. Can't do on less than five hundred pounds. Fourteen hundred's all I can give you, gentlemen; it's an advance of two hundred pounds. That's my last word."

The silence was broken by Mr. Ventnor.

"And it's my last word that I'm not satisfied. If these other gentlemen accept your proposition I shall be forced to consider what I can do on my own account."

The old man stared at him, and answered:

"Oh! you will, sir; we shall see."

The others had risen and were gathered in a knot at the end of the table; old Heythorp and Mr. Ventnor alone remained seated. The old man's lower lip projected till the white hairs below stood out like bristles. 'You ugly dog,' he was thinking, 'you think you've got something up your sleeve. Well, do your worst!' The "ugly dog" rose abruptly and joined the others. And old Heythorp closed his eyes, sitting perfectly still, with his cigar, which had gone out, sticking up between his teeth. Mr. Brownbee turning to voice the decision come to, cleared his throat.

"Mr. Heythorp," he said, "if your bankers and solicitors bear out your statements, we shall accept your offer *faute de mieux*, in consideration of your—" but meeting the old man's eyes, which said so very plainly: "Blow your consideration!" he ended with a stammer: "Perhaps you will kindly furnish us with the authorisation you spoke of?"

Old Heythorp nodded, and Mr. Brownbee, with a little bow, clasped his hat to his breast and moved towards the door. The nine gentlemen followed. Mr. Ventnor, bringing up the rear, turned and looked back. But the old man's eyes were already closed again.

The moment his creditors were gone, old Heythorp sounded the hand-bell.

"Help me up, Mr. Farney. That Ventnor—what's his holding?"

"Quite small. Only ten shares, I think."

"Ah! What time is it?"

"Quarter to four, sir."

"Get me a taxi."

After visiting his bank and his solicitors he struggled once more into his cab and caused it to be driven towards Millicent Villas. A kind of sleepy triumph permeated his whole being, bumped and shaken by the cab's rapid progress. So! He was free of those sharks now so long as he could hold on to his Companies; and he would still have a hundred a year or more to spare for Rosamund and her youngsters. He could live on four hundred, or even three-fifty, without losing his independence, for there would be no standing life in that holy woman's house unless he could pay his own scot! A good day's work! The best for many a long month!

The cab stopped before the villa.

3 §

There are rooms which refuse to give away their owners, and rooms which seem to say: 'They really are like this.' Of such was Rosamund Larne's—a sort of permanent confession, seeming to remark to anyone who entered: 'Her taste? Well, you can see— cheerful and exuberant; her habits—yes, she sits here all the morning in a dressing-gown, smoking cigarettes and dropping ink; kindly observe my carpet. Notice the piano—it has a look of coming and going, according to the exchequer. This very deep-cushioned sofa is permanent, however; the water colours on the walls are safe, too—they're by herself. Mark the scent of mimosa—she likes flowers, and likes them strong. No clock, of course. Examine the bureau—she is obviously always ringing for "the drumstick," and saying: "Where's this, Ellen, and where's that? You naughty gairl, you've been tidying." Cast an eye on that pile of manuscript—she has evidently a genius for composition; it flows off her pen—like Shakespeare, she never blots a line. See how she's had the electric light put in, instead of that horrid gas; but try and turn either of them on—you can't; last quarter isn't paid, of course; and she uses an oil lamp, you can tell that by the ceiling. The dog over there, who will not answer to the name of "Carmen," a Pekinese spaniel like a little Djin, all prominent eyes rolling their blacks, and no nose between—yes, Carmen looks as if she didn't know what was coming next; she's right—it's a pet-and-slap-again life! Consider, too, the fittings of the tea-tray, rather soiled, though not quite tin, but I say unto you that no millionaire's in all its glory ever had a liqueur bottle on it.'

When old Heythorp entered this room, which extended from back to front of the little house, preceded by the announcement "Mr. Æsop, it was resonant with a very clatter-bodandigo of noises, from Phyllis playing the Machiche; from the boy Jock on the hearthrug, emitting at short intervals the most piercing notes from an ocarina; from Mrs. Larne on the sofa, talking with her trailing volubility to Bob Pillin; from Bob Pillin muttering: "Ye—es! Qui—ite! Ye—es!" and gazing at Phyllis over his collar. And, on the window-sill, as far as she could get from all this noise, the little dog Carmen was rolling her eyes. At sight of their visitor Jock blew one rending screech, and bolting behind the sofa, placed his chin on its top, so that nothing but his round pink unmoving face was visible, and the dog Carmen tried to climb the blind cord.

Encircled from behind by the arms of Phyllis and preceded by the gracious perfumed bulk of Mrs. Larne, old Heythorp was escorted to the sofa. It was low, and when he had plumped down on to it, the boy Jock emitted a hollow groan. Bob Pillin was the first to break the silence.

"How are you, sir? I hope it's gone through."

Old Heythorp nodded. His eyes were fixed on the liqueur, and Mrs. Larne murmured:

"Guardy, you *must* try our new liqueur. Jock, you awful boy, get up and bring Guardy a glass."

The boy Jock approached the tea-table, took up a glass, put it to his eye and filled it rapidly.

"You horrible boy, you could see that glass has been used."

In a high round voice rather like an angel's, Jock answered:

"All right, Mother; I'll get rid of it," and rapidly swallowing the yellow liqueur, took up another glass.

Mrs. Larne laughed.

"What am I to do with him?"

A loud shriek prevented a response. Phyllis, who had taken her brother by the ear to lead him to the door, let him go to clasp her injured self. Bob Pillin went hastening towards her; and following the young man with her chin, Mrs. Larne said, smiling:

"Aren't those children awful? He's such a nice fellow. We like him so much, Guardy."

The old man grinned. So she was making up to that young pup! Rosamund Larne, watching him, murmured:

"Oh! Guardy, you're as bad as Jock. He takes after you terribly. Look at the shape of his head. Jock, come here!" The innocent boy approached with his girlish complexion, his flowery blue eyes, his perfect mouth, he stood before his mother like a large cherub. And suddenly he blew his ocarina in a dreadful manner. Mrs. Larne launched a box at his ears, and receiving the wind of it he fell prone.

"That's the way he behaves. Be off with you, you awful boy. I want to talk to Guardy."

The boy withdrew on his stomach, and sat against the wall cross-legged, fixing his innocent round eyes on old Heythorp. Mrs. Larne sighed.

"Things are worse and worse, Guardy. I'm at my wits' end to tide over this quarter. You wouldn't advance me a hundred on my new story? I'm sure to get two for it in the end."

The old man shook his head.

"I've done something for you and the children," he said. "You'll get notice of it in a day or two; ask no questions."

"Oh! Guardy! Oh! you dear!" And her gaze rested on Bob Pillin, leaning over the piano, where Phyllis again sat.

Old Heythorp snorted. "What are you cultivating that young gaby for? She mustn't be grabbed up by any fool who comes along."

Mrs. Larne murmured at once:

"Of course, the dear gairl is *much* too young. Phyllis, come and talk to Guardy!"

When the girl was installed beside him on the sofa, and he had felt
that little thrill of warmth the proximity of youth can bring, he said:

"Been a good girl?"

She shook her head.

"Can't when Jock's not at school. Mother can't pay for him this
term."

Hearing his name, the boy Jock blew his ocarina till Mrs. Larne
drove him from the room, and Phyllis went on:

"He's more awful than anything you can think of. Was my dad
at all like him, Guardy? Mother's always so mysterious about him. I
suppose you knew him well."

Old Heythorp, incapable of confusion, answered stolidly:

"Not very."

"Who was *his* father? I don't believe even mother knows."

"Man about town in my day."

"Oh! your day must have been jolly. Did you wear peg-top
trousers, and dundrearies?"

Old Heythorp nodded.

"What larks! And I suppose you had lots of adventures with
opera dancers and gambling. The young men are all so good now."
Her eyes rested on Bob Pillin. "That young man's a perfect stick of
goodness."

Old Heythorp grunted.

"You wouldn't know how good he was," Phyllis went on musingly,
"unless you'd sat next him in a tunnel. The other day he had his waist
squeezed and he simply sat still and did nothing. And then when the
tunnel ended, it was Jock after all, not me. His face was—Oh! ah! ha!
ha! Ah! ha!" She threw back her head, displaying all her white, round
throat. Then edging near, she whispered:

"He likes to pretend, of course, that he's fearfully lively. He's
promised to take mother and me to the theatre and supper afterwards.
Won't it be scrummy! Only, I haven't anything to go in."

Old Heythorp said: "What do you want? Irish poplin?"

Her mouth opened wide: "Oh! Guardy! Soft white satin!"

"How many yards'll go round you?"

"I should think about twelve. We could make it ourselves. You are
a chook!"

A scent of hair, like hay, enveloped him, her lips bobbed against

his nose, and there came a feeling in his heart as when he rolled
the first sip of a special wine against his palate. This little house was
a rumpty-too affair, her mother was a humbug, the boy a cheeky
young rascal, but there was a warmth here he never felt in that big
house which had been his wife's and was now his holy daughter's.
And once more he rejoiced at his day's work, and the success of his
breach of trust, which put some little ground beneath these young
feet, in a hard and unscrupulous world. Phyllis whispered in his
ear:

"Guardy, do look; he *will* stare at me like that. Isn't it awful—like
a boiled rabbit?"

Bob Pillin, attentive to Mrs. Larne, was gazing with all his might
over her shoulder at the girl. The young man was moonstruck, that
was clear! There was something almost touching in the stare of those
puppy dog's eyes. And he thought:

'Young beggar—wish I were his age!' The utter injustice of having
an old and helpless body, when your desire for enjoyment was as
great as ever! They said a man was as old as he felt! Fools! A man was
as old as his legs and arms, and not a day younger. He heard the girl
beside him utter a discomfortable sound, and saw her face cloud as if
tears were not far off; she jumped up, and going to the window, lifted
the little dog and buried her face in its brown and white fur. Old
Heythorp thought: 'She sees that her humbugging mother is using
her as a decoy.' But she had come back, and the little dog, rolling its
eyes horribly at the strange figure on the sofa, in a desperate effort to
escape succeeded in reaching her shoulder, where it stayed perched
like a cat, held by one paw and trying to back away into space. Old
Heythorp said abruptly:

"Are you very fond of your mother?"

"Of course I am, Guardy. I adore her."

"H'm! Listen to me. When you come of age or marry, you'll have
a hundred and twenty a year of your own that you can't get rid
of. Don't ever be persuaded into doing what you don't want. And
remember: Your mother's a sieve, no good giving her money; keep
what you'll get for yourself—it's only a pittance, and you'll want it
all—every penny."

Phyllis's eyes had opened very wide; so that he wondered if she
had taken in his words.

"Oh! Isn't money horrible, Guardy?"

"The want of it."

"No, it's beastly altogether. If only we were like birds. Or if one could put out a plate overnight, and have just enough in the morning to use during the day."

Old Heythorp sighed.

"There's only one thing in life that matters—independence. Lose that, and you lose everything. That's the value of money. Help me up."

Phyllis stretched out her hands, and the little dog, running down her back, resumed its perch on the windowsill, close to the blind cord.

Once on his feet, old Heythorp said:

"Give me a kiss. You'll have your satin to-morrow."

Then looking at Bob Pillin, he remarked:

"Going my way? I'll give you a lift."

The young man, giving Phyllis one appealing look, answered dully: "Tha—anks!" and they went out together to the taxi. In that draughtless vehicle they sat, full of who knows what contempt of age for youth, and youth for age; the old man resenting this young pup's aspiration to his granddaughter; the young man annoyed that this old image had dragged him away before he wished to go. Old Heythorp said at last:

"Well?"

Thus expected to say something, Bob Pillin muttered:

"Glad your meetin' went off well, sir. You scored a triumph I should think."

"Why?"

"Oh! I don't know. I thought you had a good bit of opposition to contend with."

Old Heythorp looked at him.

"Your grandmother!" he said; then, with his habitual instinct of attack, added: "You make the most of your opportunities, I see."

At this rude assault Bob Pillin's red-cheeked face assumed a certain dignity. "I don't know what you mean, sir. Mrs. Larne is very kind to me."

"No doubt. But don't try to pick the flowers."

Thoroughly upset, Bob Pillin preserved a dogged silence. This fortnight, since he had first met Phyllis in old Heythorp's hall, had been the most singular of his existence up to now. He would never have believed that a fellow could be so quickly and completely bowled, could succumb without a kick, without even wanting to kick. To one with his philosophy of having a good time and never committing himself too far, it was in the nature of "a fair knock-out," and yet so pleasurable, except for the wear and tear about one's chances. If only he knew how far the old boy really counted in the matter! To say: "My intentions are strictly honourable" would be old-fashioned; besides—the old fellow might have no right to hear it. They called him Guardy, but without knowing more he did not want to admit the old curmudgeon's right to interfere.

"Are you a relation of theirs, sir?"

Old Heythorp nodded.

Bob Pillin went on with desperation:

"I should like to know what your objection to me is."

The old man turned his head so far as he was able; a grim smile bristled the hairs about his lips, and twinkled in his eyes. What did he object to? Why—everything! Object to! That sleek head, those puppy-dog eyes, fattish red cheeks, high collars, pearl pin, spats, and drawl—pah! the imbecility, the smugness of his mug; no go, no devil in any of his sort, in any of these fish-veined, coddled-up young bloods, nothing but playing for safety! And he wheezed out:

"Milk and water masquerading as port wine."

Bob Pillin frowned.

It was almost too much for the composure even of a man of the world. That this paralytic old fellow should express contempt for his virility was really the last thing in jests. Luckily he could not take it seriously. But suddenly he thought:

'What if he really has the power to stop my going there, and means to turn them against me!' And his heart quailed.

"Awfully sorry, sir," he said, "if you don't think I'm wild enough. Anything I can do for you in that line—"

The old man grunted; and realising that he had been quite witty, Bob Pillin went on:

"I know I'm not in debt, no entanglements, got a decent income, pretty good expectations and all that; but I can soon put that all right if I'm not fit without."

It was perhaps his first attempt at irony, and he could not help thinking how good it was.

But old Heythorp preserved a deadly silence. He looked like a stuffed man, a regular Aunt Sally sitting there, with the fixed red in his cheeks, his stivered hair, square block of a body, and no neck that you could see—only wanting the pipe in his mouth! Could there really be danger from such an old idol? The idol spoke:

"I'll give you a word of advice. Don't hang round there, or you'll burn your fingers. Remember me to your father. Good-night!"

The taxi had stopped before the house in Sefton Park. An insensate impulse to remain seated and argue the point fought in Bob Pillin with an impulse to leap out, shake his fist in at the window, and walk off. He merely said, however:

"Thanks for the lift. Good-night!" And, getting out deliberately, he walked off.

Old Heythorp, waiting for the driver to help him up, thought: 'Fatter, but no more guts than his father!'

In his sanctum he sank at once into his chair. It was wonderfully still there every day at this hour; just the click of the coals, just the faintest ruffle from the wind in the trees of the park. And it was cosily warm, only the fire lightening the darkness. A drowsy beatitude pervaded the old man. A good day's work! A triumph—that young pup had said. Yes! Something of a triumph! He had held on, and won. And dinner to look forward to, yet. A nap—a nap! And soon, rhythmic, soft, sonorous, his breathing rose, with now and then that pathetic twitching of the old who dream.

III

I §

When Bob Pillin emerged from the little front garden of 23, Millicent Villas ten days later, his sentiments were ravelled, and he could not get hold of an end to pull straight the stuff of his mind.

He had found Mrs. Larne and Phyllis in the sitting-room, and Phyllis had been crying; he was sure she had been crying; and that memory still infected the sentiments evoked by later happenings. Old Heythorp had said: "You'll burn your fingers." The process had begun. Having sent her daughter away on a pretext really a bit too thin, Mrs. Larne had installed him beside her scented bulk on the sofa, and poured into his ear such a tale of monetary woe and entanglement, such a mass of present difficulties and rosy prospects, that his brain still whirled, and only one thing emerged clearly—that she wanted fifty pounds, which she would repay him on quarter-day; for their Guardy had made a settlement by which, until the dear children came of age, she would have sixty pounds every quarter. It was only a question of a few weeks; he might ask Messrs. Scriven and Coles; they would tell him the security was quite safe. He certainly might ask Messrs. Scriven and Coles—they happened to be his father's solicitors; but it hardly seemed to touch the point. Bob Pillin had a certain shrewd caution, and the point was whether he was going to begin to lend money to a woman who, he could see, might borrow up to seventy times seven on the strength of his infatuation for her daughter. That was rather too strong! Yet, if he didn't—she might take a sudden dislike to him, and where would he be then? Besides, would not a loan make his position stronger? And then—such is the effect of love even on the younger generation—that thought seemed to him unworthy. If he lent at all, it should be from chivalry—ulterior motives might go hang! And the memory of the tear-marks on Phyllis's pretty pale-pink cheeks; and her petulantly mournful: "Oh! young man, isn't money beastly!" scraped his heart, and ravished his judgment. All the same, fifty pounds was fifty pounds, and goodness knew how much more; and what did he know of Mrs. Larne, after all, except that she was a relative of old Heythorp's and wrote stories—told them too, if he was not mistaken? Perhaps it would be better to see Scrivens'. But again that absurd nobility assaulted him. Phyllis! Phyllis! Besides, were not settlements always drawn so that they refused to form security for anything? Thus, hampered and troubled, he hailed a cab. He was dining with the Ventnors on the Cheshire side, and would be late if he didn't get home sharp to dress.

Driving, white-tied and waistcoated, in his father's car, he thought with a certain contumely of the younger Ventnor girl, whom he had been wont to consider pretty before he knew Phyllis. And seated next her at dinner, he quite enjoyed his new sense of superiority to her charms, and the ease with which he could chaff and be agreeable. And all the time he suffered from the suppressed longing which scarcely ever left him now, to think and talk of Phyllis. Ventnor's fizz was good and plentiful, his old Madeira absolutely first chop, and the only other man present a teetotal curate, who withdrew with the ladies to talk his parish shop. Favoured by these circumstances, and the perception that Ventnor was an agreeable fellow, Bob Pillin yielded to his secret itch to get near the subject of his affections.

"Do you happen," he said airily, "to know a Mrs. Larne— relative of old Heythorp's—rather a handsome woman—she writes stories."

Mr. Ventnor shook his head. A closer scrutiny than Bob Pillin's would have seen that he also moved his ears.

"Of old Heythorp's? Didn't know he had any, except his daughter, and that son of his in the Admiralty."

Bob Pillin felt the glow of his secret hobby spreading within him.

"She is, though—lives rather out of town; got a son and daughter. I thought you might know her stories—clever woman."

Mr. Ventnor smiled.

"Ah!" he said enigmatically, "these lady novelists! Does she make any money by them?"

Bob Pillin knew that to make money by writing meant success, but that not to make money by writing was artistic, and implied that you had private means, which perhaps was even more distinguished. And he said:

"Oh! she has private means, I know."

Mr. Ventnor reached for the Madeira.

"So she's a relative of old Heythorp's," he said. "He's a very old friend of your father's. He ought to go bankrupt, you know."

To Bob Pillin, glowing with passion and Madeira, the idea of bankruptcy seemed discreditable in connection with a relative of Phyllis. Besides, the old boy was far from that! Had he not just made this settlement on Mrs. Larne? And he said:

"I think you're mistaken. That's of the past."

Mr. Ventnor smiled.

"Will you bet?" he said.

Bob Pillin also smiled. "I should be bettin' on a certainty."

Mr. Ventnor passed his hand over his whiskered face. "Don't you believe it; he hasn't a mag to his name. Fill your glass."

Bob Pillin said, with a certain resentment:

"Well, I happen to know he's just made a settlement of five or six thousand pounds. Don't know if you call that being bankrupt."

"What! On this Mrs. Larne?"

Confused, uncertain whether he had said something derogatory or indiscreet, or something which added distinction to Phyllis, Bob Pillin hesitated, then gave a nod.

Mr. Ventnor rose and extended his short legs before the fire.

"No, my boy," he said. "No!"

Unaccustomed to flat contradiction, Bob Pillin reddened.

"I'll bet you a tenner. Ask Scrivens'."

Mr. Ventnor ejaculated:

"Scrivens'—but they're not——" then, staring rather hard he added: "I won't bet. You may be right. Scrivens' are your father's solicitors too, aren't they? Always been sorry he didn't come to me. Shall we join the ladies?" And to the drawing-room he preceded a young man more uncertain in his mind than on his feet.

Charles Ventnor was not one to let you see that more was going on within than met the eye. But there was a good deal going on that evening, and after his conversation with young Bob he had occasion more than once to turn away and rub his hands together. When, after that second creditors' meeting, he had walked down the stairway which led to the offices of "The Island Navigation Company," he had been deep in thought. Short, squarely built, rather stout, with moustache and large mutton-chop whiskers of a red-brown, and a faint floridity in face and dress, he impressed at first sight only by a certain truly British vulgarity. One felt that here was a hail-fellow-well-met man who liked lunch and dinner, went to Scarborough for his summer holidays, sat on his wife, took his daughters out in a boat and was never sick. One felt that he went to church every Sunday morning, looked upwards as he moved through life, disliked the unsuccessful, and expanded with his second glass of wine. But then a clear look into his well-clothed face and red-brown eyes would give the feeling: 'There's something fulvous here; he might be a bit too foxy.' A third look brought the thought: 'He's certainly a bully.' He was not a large creditor of old Heythorp. With interest on the original, he calculated his claim at three hundred pounds— unredeemed shares in that old Ecuador mine. But he had waited for his money eight years, and could never imagine how it came about that he had been induced to wait so long. There had been, of course, for one who liked "big pots," a certain glamour about the personality of old Heythorp, still a bit of a swell in shipping circles, and a bit of an aristocrat in Liverpool. But during the last year Charles Ventnor had realised that the old chap's star had definitely set—when that happens, of course, there is no more glamour, and the time has come to get your money. Weakness in oneself and others is despicable! Besides, he had food for thought, and descending the stairs he chewed it. He smelt a rat—creatures for which both by nature and profession he had a nose. Through Bob Pillin, on whom he sometimes dwelt in connection with his younger daughter, he knew that old Pillin and old Heythorp had been friends for thirty years and more. That, to an astute mind, suggested something behind this sale. The thought had already occurred to him when he read his copy of the report. A commission would be a breach of trust, of course, but there were ways of doing things; the old chap was devilish hard pressed, and human nature was human nature! His lawyerish mind habitually put two and two together. The old fellow had deliberately appointed to meet his creditors again just after the general meeting which would decide the purchase—had said he might do something for them then. Had that no significance?

In these circumstances Charles Ventnor had come to the meeting with eyes wide open and mouth tight closed. And he had watched. It was certainly remarkable that such an old and feeble man with no neck at all, who looked indeed as if he might go off with apoplexy any moment, should actually say that he "stood or fell" by this purchase, knowing that if he fell he would be a beggar. Why should the old chap be so keen on getting it through? It would do him personally no good, unless—Exactly! He had left the meeting, therefore, secretly confident that old Heythorp had got something out of this transaction which would enable him to make a substantial proposal to his creditors. So that when the old man had declared that he was going to make none, something had turned sour in his heart, and he had said to himself: "All right, you old rascal! You don't know C.V." The cavalier manner of that beggarly old rip, the defiant look of his deep little eyes, had put a polish on the rancour of one who prided himself on letting no man get the better of him. All that evening, seated on one side of the fire, while Mrs. Ventnor sat on the other, and the younger daughter played Gounod's Serenade on the violin—he cogitated. And now and again he smiled, but not too much. He did not see his way as yet, but had little doubt that before long he would. It would not be hard to knock that chipped old idol off his perch. There was already a healthy feeling among the shareholders that he was past work and should be scrapped. The old chap should find that Charles V. was not to be defied; that when he got his teeth into a thing, he did not let it go. By hook or crook he would have the old man off his Boards, or his debt out of him as the price of leaving him alone. His life or his money—and the old fellow should determine which. With the memory of that defiance fresh within him, he almost hoped it might come to be the first, and turning to Mrs. Ventnor, he said abruptly:

"Have a little dinner Friday week, and ask young Pillin and the curate." He specified the curate, a teetotaller, because he had two daughters, and males and females must be paired, but he intended to pack him off after dinner to the drawing-room to discuss parish matters while he and Bob Pillin sat over their wine. What he expected to get out of the young man he did not as yet know.

On the day of the dinner, before departing for the office, he had gone to his cellar. Would three bottles of Perrier Jouet do the trick, or must he add one of the old Madeira? He decided to be on the safe side. A bottle or so of champagne went very little way with him personally, and young Pillin might be another.

The Madeira having done its work by turning the conversation into such an admirable channel, he had cut it short for fear young Pillin might drink the lot or get wind of the rat. And when his guests were gone, and his family had retired, he stood staring into the fire, putting together the pieces of the puzzle. Five or six thousand pounds—six would be ten per cent, on sixty! Exactly! Scrivens'—young Pillin had said! But Crow & Donkin, not Scriven & Coles, were old Heythorp's solicitors. What could that mean, save that the old man wanted to cover the tracks of a secret commission, and had handled the matter through solicitors who did not know the state of his affairs! But why Pillin's solicitors? With this sale just going through, it must look deuced fishy to them too. Was it all a mare's nest, after all? In such circumstances he himself would have taken the matter to a London firm who knew nothing of anybody.

Puzzled, therefore, and rather disheartened, feeling too that touch of
liver which was wont to follow his old Madeira, he went up to bed
and woke his wife to ask her why the dickens they couldn't always
have soup like that!

Next day he continued to brood over his puzzle, and no fresh light
came; but having a matter on which his firm and Scrivens' were in
touch, he decided to go over in person, and see if he could surprise
something out of them. Feeling, from experience, that any really
delicate matter would only be entrusted to the most responsible
member of the firm, he had asked to see Scriven himself, and just as
he had taken his hat to go, he said casually:

"By the way, you do some business for old Mr. Heythorp, don't
you?"

Scriven, raising his eyebrows a little, muttered: "Er—no," in
exactly the tone Mr. Ventnor himself used when he wished to imply
that though he didn't as a fact do business, he probably soon would.
He knew therefore that the answer was a true one. And nonplussed,
he hazarded:

"Oh! I thought you did, in regard to a Mrs. Larne."

This time he had certainly drawn blood of sorts, for down came
Scriven's eyebrows, and he said:

"Mrs. Larne—we know a Mrs. Larne, but not in that connection.
Why?"

"Oh! Young Pillin told me."

"Young Pillin? Why, it's his——!" A little pause, and then: "Old
Mr. Heythorp's solicitors are Crow & Donkin, I believe."

Mr. Ventnor held out his hand. "Yes, yes," he said; "good-bye. Glad
to have got that matter settled up," and out he went, and down
the street, important, smiling. By George! He had got it! "It's his
father"—Scriven had been going to say. What a plant! Exactly! Oh!
neat! Old Pillin had made the settlement direct; and the solicitors
were in the dark; that disposed of his difficulty about *them*. No
money had passed between old Pillin and old Heythorp—not a
penny. Oh! neat! But not neat enough for Charles Ventnor, who
had that nose for rats. Then his smile died, and with a little chill
he perceived that it was all based on supposition—not quite good
enough to go on! What then? Somehow he must see this Mrs. Larne,
or better—old Pillin himself. The point to ascertain was whether

she had any connection of her own with Pillin. Clearly young Pillin
didn't know of it; for, according to him, old Heythorp had made
the settlement. By Jove! That old rascal was deep—all the more
satisfaction in proving that he was not as deep as C.V. To unmask
the old cheat was already beginning to seem in the nature of a public
service. But on what pretext could he visit Pillin? A subscription to
the Windeatt almshouses! That would make him talk in self-defence
and he would take care to press the request to the actual point of
getting a subscription. He caused himself to be driven to the Pillin
residence in Sefton Park. Ushered into a room on the ground floor,
heated in American fashion, Mr. Ventnor unbuttoned his coat. A
man of sanguine constitution, he found this hot-house atmosphere
a little trying. And having sympathetically obtained Joe Pillin's
reluctant refusal—Quite so! One could not indefinitely extend one's
subscriptions even for the best of causes!—he said gently:

"By the way, you know Mrs. Larne, don't you?"

The effect of that simple shot surpassed his highest hopes. Joe
Pillin's face, never highly coloured, turned a sort of grey; he opened
his thin lips, shut them quickly, as birds do, and something seemed
to pass with difficulty down his scraggy throat. The hollows, which
nerve exhaustion delves in the cheeks of men whose cheek-bones
are not high, increased alarmingly. For a moment he looked deathly;
then, moistening his lips, he said:

"Larne—Larne? No, I don't seem——"

Mr. Ventnor, who had taken care to be drawing on his gloves,
murmured:

"Oh! I thought—your son knows her; a relation of old Heythorp's,"
and he looked up.

Joe Pillin had his handkerchief to his mouth; he coughed feebly,
then with more and more vigour:

"I'm in very poor health," he said, at last. "I'm getting abroad
at once. This cold's killing me. What name did you say?" And he
remained with his handkerchief against his teeth.

Mr. Ventnor repeated:

"Larne. Writes stories."

Joe Pillin muttered into his handkerchief:

"Ah! H'm! No—I—no! My son knows all sorts of people. I shall
have to try Mentone. Are you going? Good-bye! Good-bye! I'm

sorry; ah! ha! My cough—ah! ha h'h'm! Very distressing. Ye-hes! My cough—ah! ha h'h'm! Most distressing. Ye-hes!"

Out in the drive Mr. Ventnor took a deep breath of the frosty air. Not much doubt now! The two names had worked like charms. This weakly old fellow would make a pretty witness, would simply crumple under cross-examination. What a contrast to that hoary old sinner Heythorp, whose brazenness nothing could affect. The rat was as large as life! And the only point was how to make the best use of it. Then—for his experience was wide—the possibility dawned on him, that after all, this Mrs. Larne might only have been old Pillin's mistress—or be his natural daughter, or have, some other blackmailing hold on him. Any such connection would account for his agitation, for his denying her, for his son's ignorance. Only it wouldn't account for young Pillin's saying that old Heythorp had made the settlement. He could only have got that from the woman herself. Still, to make absolutely sure, he had better try and see her. But how? It would never do to ask Bob Pillin for an introduction, after this interview with his father. He would have to go on his own and chance it. Wrote stories did she? Perhaps a newspaper would know her address; or the Directory would give it—not a common name! And, hot on the scent, he drove to a post office. Yes, there it was, right enough! "Larne, Mrs. R.—23, Millicent Villas." And thinking to himself: 'No time like the present,' he turned in that direction. The job was delicate. He must be careful not to do anything which might compromise his power of making public use of his knowledge. Yes—ticklish! What he did now must have a proper legal bottom. Still, anyway you looked at it, he had a *right* to investigate a fraud on himself as a shareholder of "The Island Navigation Company," and a fraud on himself as a creditor of old Heythorp. Quite! But suppose this Mrs. Larne was really entangled with old Pillin, and the settlement a mere reward of virtue, easy or otherwise. Well! in that case there'd be no secret commission to make public, and he needn't go further. So that, in either event, he would be all right. Only—how to introduce himself? He might pretend he was a newspaper man wanting a story. No, that wouldn't do! He must not represent that he was what he was not, in case he had afterwards to justify his actions publicly, always a difficult thing, if you were not careful! At that moment there came into his mind a question Bob Pillin had asked the other night. "By the way, you can't borrow on a settlement can you? Isn't there generally some clause against it?" Had this woman been trying to borrow from him on that settlement? But at this moment he reached the house, and got out of his cab still undecided as to how he was going to work the oracle. Impudence, constitutional and professional, sustained him in saying to the little maid:

"Mrs. Larne at home? Say Mr. Charles Ventnor, will you?" His quick brown eyes took in the apparel of the passage which served for hall—the deep blue paper on the walls, lilac-patterned curtains over the doors, the well-known, print of a nude young woman looking over her shoulder, and he thought: 'H'm! Distinctly tasty!' They noted, too, a small brown-and-white dog cowering in terror at the very end of the passage, and he murmured affably: "Fluffy! Come here, Fluffy!" till Carmen's teeth chattered in her head.

"Will you come in, sir?"

Mr. Ventnor ran his hand over his whiskers, and, entering a room, was impressed at once by its air of domesticity. On a sofa a handsome woman and a pretty young girl were surrounded by sewing apparatus and some white material. The girl looked up, but the elder lady rose.

Mr. Ventnor said easily:

"You know my young friend, Mr. Robert Pillin, I think."

The lady, whose bulk and bloom struck him to the point of admiration, murmured in a full sweet drawl:

"Oh! Ye—es. Are you from Messrs. Scrivens'?"

With the swift reflection: 'As I thought!' Mr. Ventnor answered:

"Er—not exactly. I *am* a solicitor though; came just to ask about a certain settlement that Mr. Pillin tells me you're entitled under."

"Phyllis dear!"

Seeing the girl about to rise from underneath the white stuff, Mr. Ventnor said quickly:

"Pray don't disturb yourself—just a formality!" It had struck him at once that the lady would have to speak the truth in the presence of this third party, and he went on:

"Quite recent, I think. This'll be your first interest—on six thousand pounds? Is that right?" And at the limpid assent of that rich, sweet voice, he thought: 'Fine woman; what eyes!'

"Thank you; that's quite enough. I can go to Scrivens' for any detail. Nice young fellow, Bob Pillin, isn't he?" He saw the girl's chin tilt, and Mrs. Larne's full mouth curling in a smile.

"Delightful young man; we're very fond of him."

And he proceeded:

"I'm quite an old friend of his; have you known him long?"

"Oh! no. How long, Phyllis, since we met him at Guardy's? About a month. But he's so unaffected—quite at home with us. A nice fellow."

Mr. Ventnor murmured:

"Very different from his father, isn't he?"

"Is he! We don't know his father; he's a shipowner, I think."

Mr. Ventnor rubbed his hands: "Ye—es," he said, "just giving up— a warm man. Young Pillin's a lucky fellow—only son. So you met him at old Mr. Heythorp's. I know him too—relation of yours, I believe."

"Our dear Guardy—such a wonderful man."

Mr. Ventnor echoed: "Wonderful—regular old Roman."

"Oh! but he's so *kind*!" Mrs. Larne lifted the white stuff:

"Look what he's given this naughty gairl!"

Mr. Ventnor murmured: "Charming! Charming! Bob Pillin said, I think, that Mr. Heythorp was your settlor."

One of those little clouds which visit the brows of women who have owed money in their time passed swiftly athwart Mrs. Larne's eyes. For a moment they seemed saying: 'Don't you want to know too much?' Then they slid from under it.

"Won't you sit down?" she said. "You must forgive our being at work."

Mr. Ventnor, who had need of sorting his impressions, shook his head.

"Thank you; I must be getting on. Then Messrs. Scriven can—a mere formality! Good-bye! Good-bye Miss Larne. I'm sure the dress will be most becoming."

And with memories of a too clear look from the girl's eyes, of a warm firm pressure from the woman's hand, Mr. Ventnor backed towards the door and passed away just in time to avoid hearing in two voices:

"What a nice lawyer!"

"What a horrid man!"

Back in his cab, he continued to rub his hands. No, she *didn't* know old Pillin! That was certain; not from her words, but from her face. She wanted to know him, or about him, anyway. She was trying to hook young Bob for that sprig of a girl—it was clear as mud. H'm! it would astonish his young friend to hear that he had called. Well, let it! And a curious mixture of emotions beset Mr. Ventnor. He saw the whole thing now so plainly, and really could not refrain from a certain admiration. The law had been properly diddled! There was nothing to prevent a man from settling money on a woman he had never seen; and so old Pillin's settlement could probably not be upset. But old Heythorp could. It was neat, though, oh! neat! And that was a fine woman—remarkably! He had a sort of feeling that if only the settlement had been in danger, it might have been worth while to have made a bargain—a woman like that could have made it worth while! And he believed her quite capable of entertaining the proposition! Her eye! Pity—quite a pity! Mrs. Ventnor was not a wife who satisfied every aspiration. But alas! the settlement was safe. This baulking of the sentiment of love, whipped up, if anything, the longing for justice in Mr. Ventnor. That old chap should feel his teeth now. As a piece of investigation it was not so bad—not so bad at all! He had had a bit of luck, of course—no, not luck—just that knack of doing the right thing at the right moment which marks a real genius for affairs.

But getting into his train to return to Mrs. Ventnor, he thought: 'A woman like that would have been——!' And he sighed.

2 §

With a neatly written cheque for fifty pounds in his pocket Bob Pillin turned in at 23, Millicent Villas on the afternoon after Mr. Ventnor's visit. Chivalry had won the day. And he rang the bell with an elation which astonished him, for he knew he was doing a soft thing.

"Mrs. Larne is out, sir; Miss Phyllis is at home."

His heart leaped.

"Oh—h! I'm sorry. I wonder if she'd see me?"

The little maid answered:

"I think she's been washin' 'er 'air, sir, but it may be dry be now. I'll see."

Bob Pillin stood stock still beneath the young woman on the wall. He could scarcely breathe. If her hair were not dry— how awful! Suddenly he heard floating down a clear but smothered: "Oh! Gefoozleme!" and other words which he could not catch. The little maid came running down.

"Miss Phyllis says, sir, she'll be with you in a jiffy. And I was to tell you that Master Jock is loose, sir."

Bob Pillin answered "Tha—anks," and passed into the drawing-room. He went to the bureau, took an envelope, enclosed the cheque, and addressing it: "Mrs. Larne," replaced it in his pocket. Then he crossed over to the mirror. Never till this last month had he really doubted his own face; but now he wanted for it things he had never wanted. It had too much flesh and colour. It did not reflect his passion. This was a handicap. With a narrow white piping round his waistcoat opening, and a button-hole of tuberoses, he had tried to repair its deficiencies. But do what he would, he was never easy about himself nowadays, never up to that pitch which could make him confident in her presence. And until this month to lack confidence had never been his wont. A clear, high, mocking voice said:

"Oh—h! Conceited young man!"

And spinning round he saw Phyllis in the doorway. Her light brown hair was fluffed out on her shoulders, so that he felt a kind of fainting-sweet sensation, and murmured inarticulately:

"Oh! I say—how jolly!"

"Lawks! It's awful! Have you come to see mother?"

Balanced between fear and daring, conscious of a scent of hay and verbena and camomile, Bob Pillin stammered:

"Ye—es. I—I'm glad she's not in, though."

Her laugh seemed to him terribly unfeeling.

"Oh! oh! Don't be foolish. Sit down. Isn't washing one's head awful?"

Bob Pillin answered feebly:

"Of course, I haven't much experience."

Her mouth opened.

"Oh! You *are*—aren't you?"

And he thought desperately: 'Dare I—oughtn't I—couldn't I somehow take her hand or put my arm round her, or something?' Instead, he sat very rigid at his end of the sofa, while she sat lax and

lissom at the other, and one of those crises of paralysis which beset
would-be lovers fixed him to the soul.

Sometimes during this last month memories of a past existence,
when chaff and even kisses came readily to the lips, and girls were
fair game, would make him think: 'Is she really such an innocent?
Doesn't she really want me to kiss her?' Alas! such intrusions lasted
but a moment before a blast of awe and chivalry withered them, and
a strange and tragic delicacy—like nothing he had ever known—
resumed its sway. And suddenly he heard her say:

"Why do you know such awful men?"

"What? I don't know any *awful* men."

"Oh yes, you do; one came here yesterday; he had whiskers, and
he was awful."

"Whiskers?" His soul revolted in disclaimer. "I believe I only
know one man with whiskers—a lawyer."

"Yes—that was him; a perfectly horrid man. Mother didn't mind
him, but *I* thought he was a beast."

"Ventnor! Came here? How d'you mean?"

"He did; about some business of yours, too." Her face had clouded
over. Bob Pillin had of late been harassed by the still-born beginning
of a poem:

> I rode upon my way and saw
> A maid who watched me from the door.

It never grew longer, and was prompted by the feeling that her
face was like an April day. The cloud which came on it now was like
an April cloud, as if a bright shower of rain must follow. Brushing
aside the two distressful lines, he said:

"Look here, Miss Larne—Phyllis—look here!"

"All right, I'm looking!"

"What does it mean—how did he come? What did he say?"
She shook her head, and her hair quivered; the scent of camomile,
verbena, hay, was wafted; then looking at her lap, she muttered:

"I wish you wouldn't—I wish mother wouldn't—I hate it. Oh!
Money! Beastly—beastly!" and a tearful sigh shivered itself into Bob
Pillin's reddening ears.

"I say—don't! And do tell me, because——"

"Oh! you *know*."

"I don't—I don't know anything at all. I never—"

Phyllis looked up at him. "Don't tell fibs; you know mother's borrowing money from you, and it's hateful!"

A desire to lie roundly, a sense of the cheque in his pocket, a feeling of injustice, the emotion of pity, and a confused and black astonishment about Ventnor, caused Bob Pillin to stammer:

"Well, I'm d——d!" and to miss the look which Phyllis gave him through her lashes—a look saying:

"Ah! that's better!"

"I *am* d——d! Look here! D'you mean to say that Ventnor came here about my lending money? I never said a word to him——"

"There you see—you *are* lending!"

He clutched his hair.

"We've got to have this out," he added.

"Not by the roots! Oh! you do look funny. I've never seen you with your hair untidy. Oh! oh!"

Bob Pillin rose and paced the room. In the midst of his emotion he could not help seeing himself sidelong in the mirror; and on pretext of holding his head in both his hands, tried earnestly to restore his hair. Then coming to a halt he said:

"Suppose I *am* lending money to your mother, what does it matter? It's only till quarter-day. Anybody might want money."

Phyllis did not raise her face.

"Why are you lending it?"

"Because—because—why shouldn't I?" and diving suddenly, he seized her hands.

She wrenched them free; and with the emotion of despair, Bob Pillin took out the envelope.

"If you like," he said, "I'll tear this up. I don't want to lend it, if you don't want me to; but I thought—I thought—" It was for her alone he had been going to lend this money!

Phyllis murmured through her hair:

"Yes! You thought that *I*—that's what's so hateful!"

Apprehension pierced his mind.

"Oh? I never—I swear I never——"

"Yes, you did; you thought I wanted you to lend it." She jumped up, and brushed past him into the window. So she thought she was being used as a decoy! That was awful—especially since it was true. He knew well enough that Mrs. Larne was working his admiration for her daughter for all that it was worth. And he said with simple fervour:

"What rot!" It produced no effect, and at his wits' end, he almost shouted: "Look, Phyllis! If you don't want me to—here goes!" Phyllis turned. Tearing the envelope across he threw the bits into the fire. "There it is," he said.

Her eyes grew round; she said in an awed voice: "Oh!" In a sort of agony of honesty he said:

"It was only a cheque. Now you've got your way."

Staring at the fire she answered slowly:

"I expect you'd better go before mother comes."

Bob Pillin's mouth fell ajar; he secretly agreed, but the idea of sacrificing a moment alone with her was intolerable, and he said hardily:

"No, I shall stick it!"

Phyllis sneezed.

"My hair isn't a bit dry," and she sat down on the fender with her back to the fire.

A certain spirituality had come into Bob Pillin's face. If only he could get that wheeze off: "Phyllis is my only joy!" or even: "Phyllis—do you—won't you—mayn't I?" But nothing came—nothing.

And suddenly she said:

"Oh! don't breathe so loud; it's awful!"

"Breathe? I wasn't!"

"You were; just like Carmen when she's dreaming."

He had walked three steps towards the door, before he thought: 'What does it matter? I can stand anything from her'; and walked the three steps back again.

She said softly:

"Poor young man!"

He answered gloomily:

"I suppose you realise that this may be the last time you'll see me?"

"Why? I thought you were going to take us to the theatre."

"I don't know whether your mother will—after——" Phyllis gave a little clear laugh.

"You don't know mother. Nothing makes any difference to her."

And Bob Pillin muttered:

"I see." He did not, but it was of no consequence. Then the thought of Ventnor again ousted all others. What on earth—how on earth! He searched his mind for what he could possibly have said the other night. Surely he had not asked him to do anything; certainly not given him their address. There was something very odd about it that had jolly well got to be cleared up! And he said:

"Are you sure the name of that johnny who came here yesterday was Ventnor?"

Phyllis nodded.

"And he was short, and had whiskers?"

"Yes; red, and red eyes."

He murmured reluctantly: "It must be him. Jolly good cheek; I simply can't understand. I shall go and see him. How on earth did he know your address?"

"I expect you gave it him."

"I did not. I won't have you thinking me a squirt."

Phyllis jumped up. "Oh! Lawks! Here's mother!" Mrs. Larne was coming up the garden. Bob Pillin made for the door. "Good-bye," he said; "I'm going." But Mrs. Larne was already in the hall. Enveloping him in fur and her rich personality, she drew him with her into the drawing-room, where the back window was open and Phyllis gone.

"I hope," she said, "those naughty children have been making you comfortable. That nice lawyer of yours came yesterday. He seemed quite satisfied."

Very red above his collar, Bob Pillin stammered:

"I never told him to; he isn't my lawyer. I don't know what it means."

Mrs. Larne smiled. "My dear boy, it's all right. You needn't be so squeamish. I want it to be quite on a business footing."

Restraining a fearful inclination to blurt out: "It's not going to be on any footing!" Bob Pillin mumbled: "I must go; I'm late."

"And when will you be able——?"

"Oh! I'll—I'll send—I'll write. Good-bye!" And suddenly he found that Mrs. Larne had him by the lapel of his coat. The scent of violets and fur was overpowering, and the thought flashed through him: 'I believe she only wanted to take money off old Joseph in the Bible. I can't leave my coat in her hands! What shall I do?'

Mrs. Larne was murmuring:

"It would be *so* sweet of you if you could manage it to-day"; an her hand slid over his chest. "Oh! You *have* brought your cheque-book—what a nice boy!"

Bob Pilin took it out in desperation, and, sitting down at the bureau, wrote a cheque similar to that which he had torn and burned. A warm kiss lighted on his eyebrow, his head was pressed for a moment to a furry bosom; a hand took the cheque; a voice said: "How delightful!" and a sigh immersed him in a bath of perfume. Backing to the door, he gasped:

"Don't mention it; and—and *don't tell Phyllis, please*. Good-bye!"

Once through the garden gate, he thought: 'By gum! I've done it now. That Phyllis should know about it at all! That beast Ventnor!'

His face grew almost grim. He would go and see what that meant anyway!

3 §

Mr. Ventnor had not left his office when his young friend's card was brought to him. Tempted for a moment to deny his own presence, he thought: 'No! What's the good? Bound to see him sometime!' If he had not exactly courage, he had that particular blend of self-confidence and insensibility which must needs distinguish those who follow the law; nor did he ever forget that he was in the right.

"Show him in!" he said.

He would be quite bland, but young Pillin might whistle for an explanation; he was still tormented, too, by the memory of rich curves and moving lips, and the possibilities of better acquaintanceship.

While shaking the young man's hand his quick and fulvous eye detected at once the discomposure behind that mask of cheek and collar, and relapsing into one of those swivel chairs which give one an advantage over men more statically seated, he said:

"You look pretty bobbish. Anything I can do for you?"

Bob Pillin, in the fixed chair of the consulter, nursed his bowler on his knee.

"Well, yes, there is. I've just been to see Mrs. Larne."

Mr. Ventnor did not flinch.

"Ah! Nice woman; pretty daughter, too!" And into those words he put a certain meaning. He never waited to be bullied. Bob Pillin felt the pressure of his blood increasing.

"Look here, Ventnor," he said, "I want an explanation."

"What of?"

"Why, of your going there, and using my name, and God knows what."

Mr. Ventnor gave his chair two little twiddles before he said:

"Well, you won't get it."

Bob Pillin remained for a moment taken aback; then he muttered resolutely:

"It's not the conduct of a gentleman."

Every man has his illusions, and no man likes them disturbed. The gingery tint underlying Mr. Ventnor's colouring overlaid it; even the whites of his eyes grew red.

"Oh!" he said; "indeed. You mind your own business, will you?"

"It is my business—very much so. You made use of my name, and I don't choose——"

"The devil you don't! Now, I tell you what——" Mr. Ventnor leaned forward—"you'd better hold your tongue, and not exasperate me. I'm a good-tempered man, but I won't stand your impudence."

Clenching his bowler hat, and only kept in his seat by that sense of something behind, Bob Pillin ejaculated:

"Impudence! That's good—after what you did! Look here, why did you? It's so extraordinary!"

Mr. Ventnor answered:

"Oh! is it? You wait a bit, my friend!"

Still more moved by the mystery of this affair, Bob Pillin could only mutter:

"I never gave you their address; we were only talking about old Heythorp."

And at the smile which spread between Mr. Ventnor's whiskers, he jumped up, crying:

"It's not the thing, and you're not going to put me off. I insist on an explanation."

Mr. Ventnor leaned back, crossing his stout legs, joining the tips of his thick fingers. In this attitude he was always self-possessed.

"You do—do you?"

"Yes. You must have had some reason."

Mr. Ventnor gazed up at him.

"I'll give you a piece of advice, young cock, and charge you nothing for it, too: Ask no questions, and you'll be told no lies. And here's another: Go away before you forget yourself again."

The natural stolidity of Bob Pillin's face was only just proof against this speech. He said thickly:

"If you go there again and use my name, I'll—Well, it's lucky for you you're not my age. Anyway I'll relieve you of my acquaintanceship in future. Good-evening!" and he went to the door. Mr. Ventnor had risen.

"Very well," he said loudly. "Good riddance! You wait and see which boot the leg is on!"

But Bob Pillin was gone, leaving the lawyer with a very red face, a very angry heart, and a vague sense of disorder in his speech. Not only Bob Pillin, but his tender aspirations had all left him; he no longer dallied with the memory of Mrs. Larne, but like a man and a Briton thought only of how to get his own back and punish evildoers. The atrocious words of his young friend, "It's not the conduct of a gentleman," festered in the heart of one who was made gentle not merely by nature but by Act of Parliament, and he registered a solemn vow to wipe the insult out, if not with blood, with verjuice. It was his duty, and they should d——d well see him do it!

IV

I §

Sylvanus Heythorp seldom went to bed before one or rose before eleven. The latter habit alone kept his valet from handing in the resignation which the former habit prompted almost every night.

Propped on his pillows in a crimson dressing-gown, and freshly shaved, he looked more Roman than he ever did, except in his bath. Having disposed of coffee, he was wont to read his letters, and *The Morning Post*, for he had always been a Tory, and could not stomach paying a halfpenny for his news. Not that there were many letters—when a man has reached the age of eighty, who should write to him, except to ask for money?

It was Valentine's Day. Through his bedroom window he could
see the trees of the park, where the birds were in song, though he
could not hear them. He had never been interested in Nature—full-
blooded men with short necks seldom are.

This morning indeed there were two letters, and he opened that
which smelt of something. Inside was a thing like a Christmas card,
save that the naked babe had in his hands a bow and arrow, and
words coming out of his mouth: "To be your Valentine." There was
also a little pink note with one blue forget-me-not printed at the
top. It ran:

"DEAREST GUARDY,—I'm sorry this is such a mangy little valentine;
I couldn't go out to get it because I've got a beastly cold, so I asked
Jock, and the pig bought this. The satin is simply scrumptious. If
you don't come and see me in it some time soon, I shall come and
show it to you. I wish I had a moustache, because my top lip feels
just like a matchbox, but it's rather ripping having breakfast in bed.
Mr. Pillin's taking us to the theatre the day after to-morrow evening.
Isn't it nummy! I'm going to have rum and honey for my cold.

> "Good-bye,
> "Your PHYLLIS."

So this that quivered in his thick fingers, too insensitive to feel
it, was a valentine for *him!* Forty years ago that young thing's
grandmother had given him his last. It made him out a very old
chap! Forty years ago! Had that been himself living then? And
himself, who, as a youth, came on the town in 'forty-five? Not a
thought, not a feeling the same! They said you changed your body
every seven years. The mind with it, too, perhaps. Well, he had come
to the last of his bodies, now! And that holy woman had been urging
him to take it to Bath, with her face as long as a tea-tray, and some
gammon from that doctor of his. Too full a habit—dock his port—
no alcohol—might go off in a coma any night! Knock off—not he!
Rather die any day than turn teetotaller! When a man had nothing
left in life except his dinner, his bottle, his cigar, and the dreams they
gave him—these doctors forsooth must want to cut them off! No,
no! *Carpe diem!* while you lived, get something out of it. And now
that he had made all the provision he could for those youngsters,

his life was no good to anyone but himself; and the sooner he went off the better, if he ceased to enjoy what there was left, or lost the power, to say:

"I'll do this and that, and you be jiggered!" Keep a stiff lip until you crashed, and then go clean! He sounded the bell beside him twice—for Molly, not his man. And when the girl came in, and stood, pretty in her print frock, her fluffy over-fine dark hair escaping from under her cap, he gazed at her in silence.

" Yes, sirr?"

"Want to look at you, that's all."

"Oh! an' I'm not tidy, sirr."

"Never mind. Had your valentine?"

"No, sirr; who would send me one, then?"

"Haven't you a young man?"

"Well, I might. But he's over in my country."

"What d'you think of this?"

He held out the little boy.

The girl took the card and scrutinised it reverently; she said in a detached voice:

"Indeed, an' ut's pretty, too."

"Would you like it?"

"Oh; if 'tis not taking ut from you."

Old Heythorp shook his head, and pointed to the dressing-table.

"Over there—you'll find a sovereign. Little present for a good girl."

She uttered a deep sigh. " Oh, sirr, 'tis too much; 'tis kingly."

"Take it."

She took it, and came back, her hands clasping the sovereign and the valentine, in an attitude as of prayer.

The old man's gaze rested on her with satisfaction.

"I like pretty faces—can't bear sour ones. Tell Meller to get my bath ready."

When she had gone he took up the other letter—some lawyer's writing—and opening it with the usual difficulty read:

                                                    "February 13th, 1905.

"Sir,—Certain facts having come to my knowledge, I deem it my duty to call a special meeting of the shareholders of 'The Island

Navigation Coy.,' to consider circumstances in connection with the purchase of Mr. Joseph Pillin's fleet. And I give you notice that at this meeting your conduct will be called in question.

   "I am sir"

     "Yours faithfully,

          "CHARLES VENTNOR.

  Having read this missive, old Heythorp remained some minutes without stirring. Ventnor! That solicitor chap who had made himself unpleasant at the creditors' meetings!

  There are men whom a really bad bit of news at once stampedes out of all power of coherent thought and action, and men who at first simply do not take it in. Old Heythorp took it in fast enough; coming from a lawyer it was about as nasty as it could be. But, at once, with stoic wariness his old brain began casting round. What did this fellow really know? And what exactly could he do? One thing was certain; even if he knew everything, he couldn't upset that settlement. The youngsters were all right. The old man grasped the fact that only his own position was at stake. But this was enough in all conscience; a name which had been before the public fifty odd years—income, independence, more perhaps. It would take little, seeing his age and feebleness, to make his Companies throw him over. But what had the fellow got hold of? How decide whether or not to take notice; to let him do his worst, or to try and get into touch with him? And what was the fellow's motive? He held ten shares! That would never make a man take all this trouble, and over a purchase which was really first-rate business for the Company. Yes! His conscience was quite clean. He had not betrayed his Company—on the contrary, had done it a good turn, got them four sound ships at a low price—against much opposition. That he might have done the Company a better turn, and got the ships at fifty-four thousand, did not trouble him—the six thousand was a deuced sight better employed; and he had not pocketed a penny piece himself! But the fellow's motive? Spite? Looked like it. Spite, because he had been disappointed of his money, and defied into the bargain! H'm! If that were so, he might still be got to blow cold again. His eyes lighted on the pink note with the blue forget-me-not. It marked as it were the high-water mark of what was left to him of life; and this other letter in his hand—by Jove!—low-

water mark! And with a deep and rumbling sigh he thought: 'No, I'm
not going to be beaten by this fellow.'

"Your bath is ready, sir."

Crumpling the two letters into the pocket of his dressing-gown,
he said:

"Help me up; and telephone to Mr. Farney to be good enough
to come round." . . .

An hour later, when the secretary entered, his chairman was
sitting by the fire perusing the articles of association. And, waiting
for him to look up, watching the articles shaking in that thick, feeble
hand, the secretary had one of those moments of philosophy not too
frequent with his kind. Some said the only happy time of life was
when you had no passions, nothing to hope and live for. But did you
really ever reach such a stage? The old chairman, for instance, still
had his passion for getting his own way, still had his prestige, and set
a lot of store by it! And he said:

"Good-morning, sir; I hope you're all right in this east wind. The
purchase is completed."

"Best thing the Company ever did. Have you heard from a
shareholder called Ventnor. You know the man I mean."

"No, sir. I haven't."

"Well! You may get a letter that'll make you open your eyes. An
impudent scoundrel! Just write at my dictation."

                                              "*February* 14th, 1905.
"CHARLES VENTNOR, Esq.

"SIR,—I have your letter of yesterday's date, the contents of which
I am at a loss to understand. My solicitors will be instructed to take
the necessary measures."

'Phew! What's all this about?' the secretary thought.

                    "Yours truly . . . I'll sign."

And the shaky letters closed the page:

                              "SYLVANUS HEYTHORP."

"Post that as you go."

"Anything else I can do for you, sir?"

"Nothing, except to let me know if you hear from this fellow."

When the secretary had gone the old man thought: 'So! The

ruffian hasn't called the meeting yet. That'll bring him round here fast enough if it's his money he wants—blackmailing scoundrel!'

"Mr. Pillin, sir; and will you wait lunch, or will you have it in the dining-room?"

"In the dining-room."

At the sight of that death's-head of a fellow, old Heythorp felt a sort of pity. He looked bad enough already—and this news would make him look worse. Joe Pillin glanced round at the two closed doors.

"How are you, Sylvanus? I'm very poorly." He came closer, and lowered his voice: "Why did you get me to make that settlement? I must have been mad. I've had a man called Ventnor—I didn't like his manner. He asked me if I knew a Mrs. Larne."

"Ha! What did you say?"

"What could I say? I *don't* know her. But why did he ask?"

"Smells a rat."

Joe Pillin grasped the edge of the table with both hands. "Oh!" he murmured. "Oh, don't say that!"

Old Heythorp held out to him the crumpled letter. When he had read it Joe Pillin sat down abruptly before the fire.

"Pull yourself together, Joe; they can't touch you, and they can't upset either the purchase or the settlement. They can upset me, that's all."

Joe Pillin answered, with trembling lips:

"How you can sit there, and look the same as ever! Are you sure they can't touch me?"

Old Heythorp nodded grimly.

"They talk of an Act, but they haven't passed it yet. They might prove a breach of trust against me. But I'll diddle them. Keep your pecker up, and get off abroad."

"Yes, yes. I must. I'm very bad. I was going to-morrow. But I don't know, I'm sure, with this hanging over me. My son knowing her makes it worse. He knows this man Ventnor, too. And I daren't say anything to Bob. What are you thinking of Sylvanus? You look very funny."

Old Heythorp seemed to rouse himself from a sort of coma. "I want my lunch," he said. "Will you stop and have some?"

Joe Pillin stammered out:

"Lunch! I don't know when I shall eat again. What are you going to do, Sylvanus?"

"Bluff the beggar out of it."

"But suppose you can't?"

"Buy him off. He's one of my creditors."

Joe Pillin stared at him afresh. "You always had such nerve," he said yearningly. "Do you ever wake up between two and four? I do—and everything's black."

"Put a good stiff nightcap on, my boy, before going to bed."

"Yes; I sometimes wish I was less temperate. But I couldn't stand it. I'm told your doctor forbids you alcohol."

"He does. That's why I drink it."

Joe Pillin, brooding over the fire, said: "This meeting—d'you think they mean to have it? D'you think this man really knows? If my name gets into the newspapers——" but encountering his old friend's deep little eyes, he stopped. "So you advise me to get off to-morrow, then?"

Old Heythorp nodded.

"Your lunch is served, sir."

Joe Pillin started violently, and rose.

"Well, good-bye, Sylvanus—good-bye! I don't suppose I shall be back till the summer, if I ever come back!" He sank his voice: "I shall rely on you. You won't let them, will you?"

Old Heythorp lifted his hand, and Joe Pillin put into that swollen shaking paw his pale and spindly fingers. "I wish I had your pluck," he said sadly. "Good-bye, Sylvanus," and turning, he passed out.

Old Heythorp thought: 'Poor shaky chap. All to pieces at the first shot!' And, going to his lunch, ate more heavily than usual.

2 §

Mr. Ventnor, on reaching his office and opening his letters, found, as he had anticipated, one from "that old rascal." Its contents excited in him the need to know his own mind. Fortunately this was not complicated by a sense of dignity—he only had to consider the position with an eye on not being made to look a fool. The point was simply whether he set more store by his money than by his desire for—er—justice. If not, he had merely to convene the special meeting, and lay before it the plain fact that Mr. Joseph Pillin, selling his ships for sixty thousand pounds, had just made a settlement of six thousand pounds on a lady whom he did not know, a daughter, ward, or what-not—of the purchasing Company's chairman, who had said, moreover, at the general meeting, that he stood or fell by the transaction; he had merely to do this, and demand that an explanation be required from the old man of such a startling coincidence. Convinced that no explanation would hold water, he felt sure that his action would be at once followed by the collapse, if nothing more, of that old image, and the infliction of a nasty slur on old Pillin and his hopeful son. On the other hand, three hundred pounds was money; and if old Heythorp were to say to him: "What do you want to make this fuss for?—here's what I owe you!" could a man of business and the world let his sense of justice—however he might itch to have it satisfied—stand in the way of what was after all also his sense of justice?—for this money had been owing to him for the deuce of a long time. In this dilemma, the words: "My solicitors will be instructed" were of notable service in helping him to form a decision, for he had a certain dislike of other solicitors, and an intimate knowledge of the law of libel and slander; if by any remote chance there should be a slip between the cup and the lip, Charles Ventnor might be in the soup—a position which he deprecated both by nature and profession. High thinking, therefore, decided him at last to answer thus:

"*February* 15th, 1905.

"SIR,—I have received your note. I think it may be fair, before taking further steps in this matter, to ask you for a personal explanation of the circumstances to which I alluded. I therefore propose with your permission to call on you at your private residence at five o'clock to-morrow afternoon.

Yours faithfully,
"CHARLES VENTNOR.

Having sent this missive, and arranged in his mind, the damning, if circumstantial, evidence he had accumulated, he awaited the hour with confidence, for his nature was not lacking in the cock-surety of a Briton. All the same, he dressed himself particularly well that morning, putting on a blue and white striped waistcoat which, with a cream-coloured tie, set off his fulvous whiskers and full blue eyes; and he lunched, if anything, more fully than his wont, eating a

stronger cheese and taking a glass of special Club ale. He took care
to be late, too, to show the old fellow that his coming at all was in
the nature of an act of grace. A strong scent of hyacinths greeted
him in the hall; and Mr. Ventnor, who was an amateur of flowers,
stopped to put his nose into a fine bloom and think uncontrollably
of Mrs. Larne. Pity! The things one had to give up in life—fine
women—one thing and another. Pity! The thought inspired in him
a timely anger; and he followed the servant, intending to stand no
nonsense from this paralytic old rascal.

The room he entered was lighted by a bright fire, and a single
electric lamp with an orange shade on a table covered by a black
satin cloth. There were heavily gleaming oil paintings on the walls, a
heavy old brass chandelier without candles, heavy dark red curtains,
and an indefinable scent of burnt acorns, coffee, cigars, and old man.
He became conscious of a candescent spot on the far side of the
hearth, where the light fell on old Heythorp's thick white hair.

"Mr. Ventnor, sir."

The candescent spot moved. A voice said: "Sit down?"

Mr. Ventnor sat in an armchair on the opposite side of the fire; and,
finding a kind of somnolence creeping over him, pinched himself.
He wanted all his wits about him.

The old man was speaking in that extinct voice of his, and Mr.
Ventnor said rather pettishly:

"Beg pardon, I don't get you."

Old Heythorp's voice swelled with sudden force:

"Your letters are Greek to me."

"Oh! indeed! I think we can soon make them into plain
English!"

"Sooner the better."

Mr. Ventnor passed through a moment of indecision. Should he lay
his cards on the table? It was not his habit, and the proceeding was
sometimes attended with risk. The knowledge, however, that he could
always take them up again, seeing there was no third person here to
testify that he had laid them down, decided him, and he said:

"Well, Mr. Heythorp, the long and short of the matter is this: Our
friend Mr. Pillin paid you a commission of ten per cent. on the sale
of his ships. Oh! yes. He settled the money not on you, but on your
relative Mrs. Larne and her children. This, as you know, is a breach

of trust on your part."

The old man's voice: "Where did you get hold of that cock-and-bull story?" brought him to his feet before the fire.

"It won't do, Mr. Heythorp. My witnesses are Mr. Pillin, Mrs. Larne, and Mr. Scriven."

"What have you come here for, then—blackmail?"

Mr. Ventnor straightened his waistcoat; a rush of conscious virtue had dyed his face.

"Oh! you take that tone," he said, "do you? You think you can ride roughshod over everything? Well, you're very much mistaken. I advise you to keep a civil tongue and consider your position, or I'll make a beggar of you. I'm not sure this isn't a case for a prosecution!"

"Gammon!"

The choler in Charles Ventnor kept him silent for a moment; then he burst out:

"Neither gammon nor spinach. You owe me three hundred pounds, you've owed it me for years, and you have the impudence to take this attitude with me, have you? Now, I never bluster; I say what I mean. You just listen to me. Either you pay me what you owe me at once, or I call this meeting and make what I know public. You'll very soon find out where you are. And a good thing, too, for a more unscrupulous—unscrupulous——" he paused for breath.

Occupied with his own emotion, he had not observed the change in old Heythorp's face. The imperial on that lower lip was bristling, the crimson of those cheeks had spread to the roots of his white hair. He grasped the arms of his chair, trying to rise; his swollen hands trembled; a little saliva escaped one corner of his lips. And the words came out as if shaken by his teeth:

"So—so—you—you bully me!"

Conscious that the interview had suddenly passed from the phase of negotiation, Mr. Ventnor looked hard at his opponent. He saw nothing but a decrepit, passionate, crimson-faced old man at bay, and all the instincts of one with everything on his side boiled up in him. The miserable old turkey-cock—the apoplectic image! And he said:

"And you'll do no good for yourself by getting into a passion. At your age, and in your condition, I recommend a little prudence.

Now just take my terms quietly, or you know what'll happen. I'm not to be intimidated by any of your airs." And seeing that the old man's rage was such that he simply could not speak, he took the opportunity of going on: "I don't care two straws which you do—I'm out to show you who's master. If you think in your dotage you can domineer any longer—well, you'll find two can play at that game. Come, now, which are you going to do?"

The old man had sunk back in his chair, and only his little deep-blue eyes seemed living. Then he moved one hand, and Mr. Ventnor saw that he was fumbling to reach the button of an electric bell at the end of a cord. 'I'll show him,' he thought, and stepping forward, he put it out of reach.

Thus frustrated, the old man remained motionless, staring up. The word "blackmail" resumed its buzzing in Mr. Ventnor's ears. The impudence—the consummate impudence of it from this fraudulent old ruffian with one foot in bankruptcy and one foot in the grave, if not in the dock.

"Yes," he said, "it's never too late to learn; and for once you've come up against someone a leetle bit too much for you. Haven't you now? You'd better cry '*Peccavi*.'"

Then, in the deathly silence of the room, the moral force of his position, and the collapse as it seemed of his opponent, awakening a faint compunction, he took a turn over the Turkey carpet to readjust his mind.

"You're an old man, and I don't want to be too hard on you. I'm only showing you that you can't play fast and loose as if you were God Almighty any longer. You've had your own way too many years. And now you can't have it, see!" Then, as the old man again moved forward in his chair, he added: "Now, don't get into a passion again; calm yourself, because I warn you—this is your last chance. I'm a man of my word; and what I say, I do."

By a violent and unsuspected effort the old man jerked himself up and reached the bell. Mr. Ventnor heard it ring, and said sharply:

"Mind you, it's nothing to me which you do. I came for your own good. Please yourself. Well?"

He was answered by the click of the door and the old man's husky voice:

"Show this hound out! And then come back!"

Mr. Ventnor had presence of mind enough not to shake his fist. Muttering: "Very well, Mr. Heythorp! Ah! *Very* well!" he moved with dignity to the door. The careful shepherding of the servant renewed the fire of his anger. Hound! he had been called a hound!

3 §

After seeing Mr. Ventnor off the premises the man Meller returned to his master, whose face looked very odd—"all patchy-like," as he put it in the servants' hall, as though the blood driven to his head had mottled for good the snowy whiteness of the forehead. He received the unexpected order:

"Get me a hot bath ready, and put some pine stuff in it."

When the old man was seated there, the valet asked:

"How long shall I give you, sir?"

"Twenty minutes."

"Very good, sir."

Lying in that steaming brown fragrant liquid, old Heythorp heaved a stertorous sigh. By losing his temper with that ill-conditioned cur he had cooked his goose. It was done to a turn; and he was a ruined man. If only—oh! if only he could have seized the fellow by the neck and pitched him out of the room! To have lived to be so spoken to; to have been unable to lift hand or foot, hardly even his voice—he would sooner have been dead! Yes—sooner have been dead! A dumb and measureless commotion was still at work in the recesses of that thick old body, silver-brown in the dark water, whose steam he drew deep into his wheezing lungs, as though for spiritual relief. To be beaten by a cur like that! To have a common cad of a petti-fogging lawyer drag him down and kick him about; tumble a name which had stood high, in the dust! The fellow had the power to make him a byword and a beggar! It was incredible! But it was a fact. And to-morrow he would begin to do it—perhaps had begun already. His tree had come down with a crash! Eighty years—eighty good years! He regretted none of them—regretted nothing; least of all this breach of trust which had provided for his grandchildren—one of the best things he had ever done. The fellow was a cowardly hound, too! The way he had snatched the bell-pull out of his reach—despicable cur! And a chap like that was to put "paid" to the account of Sylvanus Heythorp, to "scratch" him out of life—so near the end of everything, the very end. His hand raised above the surface fell back on his stomach through the dark water, and a bubble or two rose. Not so fast—not so fast! He had but to slip down a foot, let the water close over his head, and "Goodbye" to Master Ventnor's triumph! Dead men could not be kicked off the Boards of Companies. Dead men could not be beggared, deprived of their independence. He smiled and stirred a little in the bath till the water reached the white hairs on his lower lip. It smelt nice! And he took a long sniff. He had had a good life, a good life! And with the thought that he had it in his power at any moment to put Master Ventnor's nose out of joint—to beat the beggar after all, a sense of assuagement and well-being crept over him. His blood ran more evenly again. He closed his eyes. They talked about an after-life— people like that holy woman. Gammon! You went to sleep—a long sleep; no dreams. A nap after dinner! Dinner! His tongue sought his palate! Yes! he could eat a good dinner! That dog hadn't put him off his stroke! The best dinner he had ever eaten was the one he gave to Jack Herring, Chichester, Thornworthy, Nick Treffry and Jolyon Forsyte at Pole's. Good Lord! In 'sixty—yes—'sixty-five? Just before he fell in love with Alice Larne—ten years before he came to Liverpool. That was a dinner! Cost twenty-four pounds for the six of them—and Forsyte an absurdly moderate fellow. Only Nick Treffry and himself had been three-bottle men! Dead! Every jack man of them. And suddenly he thought: 'My name's a good one—I was never down before—never beaten!'

A voice above the steam said:

"The twenty minutes is up, sir."

"All right; I'll get out. Evening clothes."

And Meller, taking out dress suit and shirt, thought: 'Now, what does the old bloomer want dressin' up again for; why can't he go to bed and have his dinner there? When a man's like a baby, the cradle's the place for him.' . . .

An hour later, at the scene of his encounter with Mr. Ventnor, where the table was already laid for dinner, old Heythorp stood and gazed. The curtains had been drawn back, the window thrown open to air the room, and he could see out there the shapes of the dark trees and a sky grape-coloured, in the mild, moist night. It smelt good. A sensuous feeling stirred in him, warm from his bath, clothed from head to foot in fresh garments. Deuce of a time since he had dined in full fig! He would have liked a woman dining opposite—but not the holy woman; no, by George!—would have liked to see light falling on a woman's shoulders once again, and a pair of bright eyes! He crossed, snail-like, towards the fire. There that bullying fellow had stood with his back to it—confound his impudence!—as if the place belonged to him. And suddenly he had a vision of his three secretaries' faces—especially young Farney's—as they would look when the pack got him by the throat and pulled him down. His co-directors, too! Old Heythorp! How are the mighty fallen! And that hound jubilant!

His valet passed across the room to shut the window and draw the curtains. This chap too! The day he could no longer pay his wages, and had lost the power to say "Shan't want your services any more"—when he could no longer even pay his doctor for doing his best to kill him off! Power, interest, independence, all—gone! To be dressed and undressed, given pap, like a baby in arms, served as they chose to serve him, and wished out of the way—broken, dishonoured! By money alone an old man had his being! Meat, drink, movement, breath! When all his money was gone the holy woman would let him know it fast enough. They would all let him know it; or if they didn't, it would be out of pity! He had never been pitied yet—thank God! And he said:

"Get me up a bottle of Perrier Jouet. What's the menu?"

"Germane soup, sir; filly de sole; sweetbread; cutlet soubees, rum souffly."

"Tell her to give me a *hors d'oeuvre*, and put on a savoury."

"Yes, sir."

When the man had gone, he thought: 'I should have liked an oyster—too late now!' and going over to his bureau he fumblingly pulled out the top drawer. There was little in it—just a few papers, business papers on his Companies, and a schedule of his debts; not even a copy of his will—he had not made one, nothing to leave! Letters he had never kept. Half a dozen bills, a few receipts, and the little pink note with the blue forget-me-not. That was the lot. An old tree gives up bearing leaves, and its roots dry up, before it comes down in a wind; an old man's world slowly falls away from him till he stands alone in the night. Looking at the pink note, he thought:

'Suppose I'd married Alice—a man never had a better mistress!' He fumbled the drawer to; but still he strayed feebly about the room, with a curious shrinking from sitting down, legacy from the quarter of an hour he had been compelled to sit while that hound worried at his throat. He was opposite one of the pictures now. It gleamed, dark and oily, limning a Scots Grey who had mounted a wounded Russian on his horse, and was bringing him back prisoner from the Balaclava charge. A very old friend—bought in 'fifty-nine. It had hung in his chambers in the Albany—hung with him ever since. With whom would it hang when he was gone? For that holy woman would scrap it, to a certainty, and stick up some Crucifixion or other, some new-fangled high art thing! She could even do that now if she liked—for she owned it, owned every mortal stick in the room, to the very glass he would drink his champagne from; all made over under the settlement fifteen years ago, before his last big gamble went wrong. "*De l'audace, toujours de l'audace!*" The gamble which had brought him down till his throat at last was at the mercy of a bullying hound. The pitcher and the well! At the mercy—! The sound of a popping cork dragged him from reverie. He moved to his seat, back to the window, and sat down to his dinner. By George! They had got him an oyster! And he said:

"I've forgotten my teeth!"

While the man was gone for them, he swallowed the oysters, methodically touching them one by one with cayenne, Chili vinegar, and lemon. Ummm! Not quite what they used to be at Pimm's in the best days, but not bad—not bad! Then seeing the little blue bowl lying before him, he looked up and said:

"My compliments to cook on the oysters. Give me the champagne." And he lifted his trembling teeth. Thank God, he could still put 'em in for himself! The creaming goldenish fluid from the napkined bottle slowly reached the brim of his glass, which had a hollow stem; raising it to his lips, very red between the white hairs above and below, he drank with a gurgling noise, and put the glass down—empty. Nectar! And just cold enough!

"I frapped it the least bit, sir."

"Quite right. What's that smell of flowers?"

"It's from those 'yacinths on the sideboard, sir. They come from Mrs. Larne, this afternoon."

"Put 'em on the table. Where's my daughter?"

"She's had dinner, sir; goin' to a ball, I think."

"A ball!"

"Charity ball, I fancy, sir."

"Ummm! Give me a touch of the old sherry with the soup."

"Yes, sir. I shall have to open a bottle."

"Very well, then, do!"

On his way to the cellar the man confided to Molly, who was carrying the soup:

"The Gov'nor's going it to-night! What he'll be like tomorrow I dunno."

The girl answered softly:

"Poor old man, let um have his pleasure." And, in the hall, with the soup tureen against her bosom, she hummed above the steam, and thought of the ribbons on her new chemises, bought out of the sovereign he had given her.

And old Heythorp, digesting his oysters, snuffed the scent of the hyacinths, and thought of the St. Germain, his favourite soup. It wouldn't be first-rate, at this time of year—should be made with little young home-grown peas. Paris was the place for it. Ah! The French were the fellows for eating, and—looking things in the face! Not hypocrites—not ashamed of their reason or their senses!

The soup came in. He sipped it, bending forward as far as he could, his napkin tucked in over his shirt-front like a bib. He got the bouquet of that sherry to a T—his sense of smell was very keen to-night; rare old stuff it was—more than a year since he had tasted it—but no one drank sherry nowadays, hadn't the constitution for it! The fish came up, and went down; and with the sweetbread he took his second glass of champagne. Always the best, that second glass—the stomach well warmed, and the palate not yet dulled. Umm! So that fellow thought he had him beaten, did he? And he said suddenly:

"The fur coat in the wardrobe, I've no use for it. You can take it away to-night."

With tempered gratitude the valet answered:

"Thank you, sir; much obliged, I'm sure." So the old buffer had found out there was moth in it!

"Have I worried you much?"

"No, sir; not at all, sir—that is, no more than reason."

"Afraid I have. Very sorry—can't help it. You'll find that, when you get like me."

"Yes, sir; I've always admired your pluck, sir."

"Um! Very good of you to say so."

"Always think of you keepin' the flag flyin', sir."

Old Heythorp bent his body from the waist.

"Much obliged to you."

"Not at all, sir. Cook's done a little spinach in cream with the soubees."

"Ah! Tell her from me it's a capital dinner, so far."

"Thank you, sir."

Alone again, old Heythorp sat unmoving, his brain just narcotically touched. "The flag flyin'—the flag flyin'!" He raised his glass and sucked. He had an appetite now, and finished the three cutlets, and all the sauce and spinach. Pity! he could have managed a snipe— fresh shot! A desire to delay, to lengthen dinner, was strong upon him; there were but the *soufflé* and the savoury to come. He would have enjoyed, too, someone to talk to. He had always been fond of good company—been good company himself, or so they said—not that he had had a chance of late. Even at the Boards they avoided talking to him, he had noticed for a long time. Well! that wouldn't trouble him again—he had sat through his last Board, no doubt. They shouldn't kick him off, though; he wouldn't give them that pleasure—had seen the beggars hankering after his chairman's shoes too long. The *soufflé* was before him now, and lifting his glass, he said:

"Fill up."

"These are the special glasses, sir; only four to the bottle."

"Fill up."

The servant filled, screwing up his mouth.

Old Heythorp drank, and put the glass down empty with a sigh. He had been faithful to his principles, finished the bottle before touching the sweet—a bottle—of a good brand! And now for the *soufflé*! Delicious, flipped down with the old sherry! So that holy woman was going to a ball, was she? How deuced funny! Who would dance with a dry stick like that, all eaten up with a piety which was just sexual disappointment? Ah! yes, lots of women like that—had often noticed 'em—pitied 'em too, until you had to do with them and they made you as unhappy as themselves, and were tyrants into the bargain. And he asked:

"What's the savoury?"

"Cheese remmykin, sir."

His favourite.

"I'll have my port with it—the 'sixty-eight.'"

The man stood gazing with evident stupefaction. He had not expected this. The old man's face was very flushed, but that might be the bath. He said feebly:

"Are you sure you ought, sir?"

"No, but I'm going to."

"Would you mind if I spoke to Miss Heythorp, sir?"

"If you do, you can leave my service."

"Well, sir, I don't accept the responsibility."

"Who asked you to?"

"No, sir."

"Well, get it, then; and don't be an ass."

"Yes, sir."

If the old man were not humoured he would have a fit, perhaps!

And the old man sat quietly staring at the hyacinths. He felt happy, his whole being lined and warmed and drowsed—and there was more to come! What had the holy folk to give you compared with the comfort of a good dinner? Could they make you dream, and see life rosy for a little? No, they could only give you promissory notes which would never be cashed. A man had nothing but his pluck—they only tried to undermine it, and make him squeal for help. He could see his precious doctor throwing up his hands: "Port after a bottle of champagne—you'll die of it!" And a very good death too—none better. A sound broke the silence of the closed-up room. Music? His daughter playing the piano overhead. Singing too! What a trickle of a voice! Jenny Lind! The Swedish nightingale—he had never missed the nights when she was singing—Jenny Lind!

"It's very hot, sir. Shall I take it out of the case?"

Ah. The ramequin!

"Touch of butter, and the cayenne!"

"Yes, sir."

He ate it slowly, savouring each mouthful; had never tasted a better. With cheese—port! He drank one glass, and said:

"Help me to my chair."

And settled there before the fire with decanter and glass and hand-bell on the little low table by his side, he murmured:

"Bring coffee, and my cigar, in twenty minutes."

To-night he would do justice to his wine, not smoking till he had finished. As old Horace said:

> Aequam memento rebus in arduis
> Servare mentem.

And, raising his glass, he sipped slowly, spilling a drop or two, shutting his eyes.

The faint silvery squealing of the holy woman in the room above, the scent of hyacinths, the drowse of the fire, on which a cedar log had just been laid, the feeling of the port soaking down into the crannies of his being, made up a momentary Paradise. Then the music stopped; and no sound rose but the tiny groans of the log trying to resist the fire. Dreamily he thought: 'Life wears you out wears you out. Logs on a fire!' And he filled his glass again. That fellow had been careless; there were dregs at the bottom of the decanter and he had got down to them! Then, as the last drop from his tilted glass trickled into the white hairs on his chin, he heard the coffee tray put down, and taking his cigar he put it to his ear, rolling it in his thick fingers. In prime condition! And drawing a first whiff, he said:

"Open that bottle of the old brandy in the sideboard."

"Brandy, sir? I really daren't, sir."

"Are you my servant or not?"

"Yes, sir, but——"

A minute of silence, then the man went hastily to the sideboard, took out the bottle, and drew the cork. The tide of crimson in the old man's face had frightened him.

"Leave it there."

The unfortunate valet placed the bottle on the little table. 'I'll have to tell her,' he thought; 'but if I take away the port decanter and the glass, it won't look so bad.' And, carrying them, he left the room.

Slowly the old man drank his coffee, and the liqueur of brandy. The whole gamut! And watching his cigar-smoke wreathing blue in the orange glow, he smiled. The last night to call his soul his own, the last night of his independence. Send in his resignations to-morrow—not wait to be kicked off! Not give that fellow a chance!

A voice which seemed to come from far off, said:

"Father! You're drinking brandy! How *can* you—you know it's simple poison to you!" A figure in white, scarcely actual, loomed up close. He took the bottle to fill up his liqueur glass, in defiance; but a hand in a long white glove, with another dangling from its wrist, pulled it away, shook it at him, and replaced it in the sideboard. And, just as when Mr. Ventnor stood there accusing him, a swelling and churning in his throat prevented him from speech; his lips moved, but only a little froth came forth.

His daughter had approached again. She stood quite close, in white satin, thin-faced, sallow, with eyebrows raised, and her dark hair frizzed—yes! frizzed—the holy woman! With all his might he tried to say: 'So you bully me, do you—you bully me *to-night*!' but only the word "so" and a sort of whispering came forth. He heard her speaking. "It's no good your getting angry, Father. After champagne—it's wicked!" Then her form receded in a sort of rustling white mist; she was gone; and he heard the spluttering and growling of her taxi, bearing her to the ball. So! She tyrannised and bullied, even before she had him at her mercy, did she? She should see! Anger had brightened his eyes; the room came clear again. And slowly raising himself he sounded the bell twice, for the girl, not for that fellow Meller, who was in the plot. As soon as her pretty black and white-aproned figure stood before him, he said:

"Help me up!"

Twice her soft pulling was not enough, and he sank back. The third time he struggled to his feet.

"Thank you; that'll do." Then, waiting till she was gone, he crossed the room, fumbled open the sideboard door, and took out the bottle. Reaching over the polished oak, he grasped a sherry glass; and holding the bottle with both hands, tipped the liquor into it, put it to his lips and sucked. Drop by drop it passed over his palate— mild, very old, old as himself, coloured like sunlight, fragrant. To the last drop he drank it, then hugging the bottle to his shirt-front, he moved snail-like to his chair, and fell back into its depths.

For some minutes he remained there motionless, the bottle clasped to his chest, thinking: 'This is not the attitude of a gentleman. I must put it down on the table—on the table;' but a thick cloud was between him and everything. It was with his hands he would have to put the bottle on the table! But he could not find his hands, could not feel them. His mind see-sawed in strophe and antistrophe: "You can't move!"— "I will move!" "You're beaten"—"I'm not beat." "Give up"—"I won't." That struggle to find his hands seemed to last for ever—he must find them! After that—go down—all standing—after that! Everything round him was red. Then the red cloud cleared just a little, and he could hear the clock—"tick—tick—tick"; a faint sensation spread from his shoulders down to his wrists, down his palms; and yes—he could feel the bottle! He redoubled his struggle to get forward in his chair; to get forward and put the bottle down. It was not dignified like this! One arm he could move now; but he could not grip the bottle nearly tight enough to put it down. Working his whole body forward, inch by inch, he shifted himself up in the chair till he could lean sideways, and the bottle, slipping down his chest, dropped slanting to the edge of the low stool-table. Then with all his might he screwed his trunk and arms an inch further, and the bottle stood. He had done it— done it! His lips twitched into a smile; his body sagged back to its old position. He had done it! And he closed his eyes. . . .

At half-past eleven the girl Molly, opening the door, looked at him and said softly: "Sirr! there's some ladies, and a gentleman!" But he did not answer. And, still holding the door, she whispered out into the hall:

"He's asleep, miss."

A voice whispered back:

"Oh! Just let me go in, I won't wake him unless he does. But I do want to show him my dress."

The girl moved aside; and on tiptoe Phyllis passed in. She walked to where, between the lamp-glow and the fire-glow, she was lighted up. White satin—her first low-cut dress—the flush of her first supper party—a gardenia at her breast, another in her fingers! Oh! what a pity he was asleep! How red he looked! How funnily old men breathed! And mysteriously, as a child might, she whispered:

"Guardy!"

No answer! And pouting, she stood twiddling the gardenia. Then suddenly she thought: 'I'll put it in his buttonhole! When he wakes up and sees it, how he'll jump!'

And stealing close, she bent, and slipped it in. Two faces looked at her from round the door; she heard Bob Pillin's smothered chuckle; her mother's rich and feathery laugh. Oh! How red his forehead was! She touched it with her lips; skipped back, twirled round, danced silently a second, blew a kiss, and like quicksilver was gone.

And the whispering, the chuckling, and one little outpealing laugh rose in the hall.

But the old man slept. Nor until Meller came at his usual hour of half-past twelve, was it known that he would never wake.

[*1916*]

A PORTRAIT

It is at the age of eighty that I picture him, without the vestige of a stoop, rather above middle height, of very well-proportioned figure, whose flatness of back and easy movements were the admiration of all who saw them. His iron-grey eyes had lost none of their colour, they were set in deep, so that their upper lids were invisible, and had a peculiar questioning directness, apt to change suddenly into twinkles. His head was of fine shape—one did not suspect that it required a specially made hat, being a size larger than almost any other head; it was framed in very silky silvery hair, brushed in an arch across his forehead, and falling in becoming curves over the tips of his ears; and he wore always a full white beard and moustaches, which concealed a jaw and chin of great determination cleft by a dimple. His nose had been broken in his early boyhood; it was the nose of a thinker, broad and of noticeable shape. The colour of his cheeks was a fine dry brown; his brow very capacious, both wide and high, and endowed with a singular serenity. But it was the balance and poise of his head which commanded so much attention. In a theatre, church, concert-hall, there was never any head so fine as his, for the silvery hair and beard lent to its massiveness a curious grace and delicacy.

The owner of that head could not but be endowed with force, sagacity, humour, and the sense of justice. It expressed, indeed, his essential quality—equanimity; for there were two men in him—he of the chin and jaw, a man of action and tenacity, and he of the nose and brow, the man of speculation and impersonality; yet these two were so curiously balanced and blended that there was no harsh ungraceful conflict. And what made this equanimity so memorable was the fact that both his power of action and his power of speculation were of high quality. He was not a commonplace person content with a little of both. He wanted and had wanted throughout life, if one may judge by records, a good deal of both, ever demanding with one half of him strong and continuous action, and with the other half high and clean thought and behaviour. The desire for the best both in material and spiritual things remained with him through life. He felt things deeply; and but for his strange balance, and a yearning for inward peace which never seems to have deserted him, his ship might well have gone down in tragedy.

To those who had watched that journey, his voyage through life seemed favourable, always on the top of the weather. He had worked hard, and he had played hard, but never too hard. And though one might often see him irritated, I think no one ever saw him bored. He perceived a joke quicker than most of us; he was never eccentric, yet fundamentally independent of other people's opinions, and perhaps a little unconscious that there were better men than he. Not that he was conceited, for of this quality, so closely allied to stupidity and humbug, he had about as much as the babe unborn. He was, indeed, a natural foe to anæmia in any of its forms, just as he was instinctively hostile to gross bull-beef men and women. The words, "a bullying chap," were used by him as crushing dispraise. I can recall him now in his chair after dinner, listening to one who, puffing his cigarette, is letting himself go on a stream of robustious, rather swaggering complacencies; with what a comprehending straight look he regards the speaker, not scornful, not sarcastic, but simply, as it were, saying: "No, my young buck, for all your fine full-blooded talk, and all your red face, you are what I see you to be, and you will do what I tell you to do!" Such men had no chance with him when it came to the tug of war; he laid his will on them as if they had been children.

He was that rather rare thing, a pure-blooded Englishman; having no strain of Scotch, Welsh, Irish, or foreign blood in his pedigree for four hundred years at least. He sprang from a long line of farmers intermarrying with their kind in the most southern corner of Devonshire, and it is probable that Norse and British blood were combined in him in a high state of equality. Even in the actual situation of his place of origin, the principle of balance had been maintained, for the old farm house from which his grandfather had emerged had been perched close to the cliff. Thus, to the making of him had gone land and sea, the Norseman and the Celt.

Articled to the Law at the age of sixteen by his father, a Plymouth merchant, whose small ancient ships traded to the Mediterranean in fruits, leather, and wines, he had come to London, and at the earliest possible date (as was the habit with men in those times) had been entered on the rolls as a solicitor. Often has he told me of the dinner he gave in honour of that event. "I was a thread-paper, then," he would say (indeed, he never became fat),—"We began with a barrel of oysters." About that and other festivities of his youth there was all the rich and rollicking flavour of the days of Pickwick. He was practically dependent on his own exertions from the time he began to practise his profession, and it was characteristic of him that he never seems to have been hard pressed for money. The inherent sanity and moderation of his instincts preserved him, one imagines, from the financial ups and downs of most young men, for there was no niggardliness in him, and a certain breadth of conception characterised his money affairs throughout life. It was rather by the laws of gravity, therefore, whereby money judiciously employed attracts money, and the fact that he lived in that moneymaker's Golden Age, the nineteenth century, that he had long been (at the age of eighty) a wealthy man. Money was to him the symbol of a well-spent, well-ordered life, provocative of warmth in his heart because he loved his children, and was careful of them to a fault. He did not marry till he was forty-five, but his feeling for the future of his family manifested itself with the birth of his first child. Selecting a fair and high locality, not too far away from London, he set himself at once to make a country place, where the little things should have fresh air, new milk, and all the fruits of the earth, home-grown round them. Quite wonderful was the forethought he lavished on that house and little estate stretching down the side of a hill, with its walled gardens, pasture, corn-land and coppice. All was solid, and of the best, from the low four-square red brick house with its concrete terrace and French windows, to the cow-houses down by the coppice. From the oak trees, hundreds of years old, on the lawns, to the peach trees just planted along the south sunny walls. But here, too, there was no display for the sake of it, and no extravagance. Everything was at hand, from home baked bread, to mushrooms wild and tame; from the stables with their squat clock-tower, to pigsties; from roses that won all the local prizes, to bluebells; but nothing redundant or pretentious.

The place was an endless pleasure to him, who to the last preserved his power of taking interest, not only in great, but in little things. Each small triumph over difficulty—the securing of hot water in such a quarter, the better lighting of another, the rescue of the nectarines from wasps, the quality of his Alderney cows, the encouragement of rooks—afforded him as much simple and sincere satisfaction as every little victory he achieved in his profession, or in the life of the Companies which he directed. But with all his shrewd practical sense, and almost naïve pleasure in material advantage, he combined a very real spiritual life of his own. Nor was there anything ascetic in that inner life. It was mellow as the music of Mozart, his most beloved composer; Art and Nature, both had their part in it. He was, for instance, very fond of opera, but only when it could be called "grand"; and it grieved him that opera was no longer what it had been, yet was it secretly a grave satisfaction that he had known those classical glories denied to the present generation. He loved indeed almost all classical music, but (besides Mozart) especially Beethoven, Gluck, and Meyerbeer, whom he insisted (no less than Herbert Spencer) on considering a great composer. Wagner he tried very hard to appreciate and, after visiting Bayreuth, even persuaded himself that he had succeeded, though he never ceased to point out the great difference that existed between this person and Mozart. He loved the Old Masters of painting, having for favourites amongst the Italians: Rafael, Correggio, Titian, Tintoretto; and amongst Englishmen Reynolds and Romney. On the other hand, he regarded Hogarth and Rubens as coarse, but Vandyke he very much admired, because of his beautiful painting of hands, the hallmark, he would maintain, of an artist's quality. I cannot remember his feeling about Rembrandt, but Turner he certainly distrusted as extravagant. Botticelli and the earlier masters he had not as yet quite learned to relish; and Impressionism, including Whistler, never really made conquest of his taste, though he always resolutely kept his mind open to what was modern—feeling himself young at heart.

Once on a spring day, getting over a stile, I remember him saying:

"Eighty! I can't believe it. Seems very queer. I don't feel it. Eighty!" And, pointing to a blackbird that was singing, he added: "That takes the years off you!" His love of Nature was very intimate, simple, and unconscious. I can see him standing by the pond of a summer evening watching the great flocks of starlings that visited those fields; or, with his head a little to one side, listening rapturously to a skylark. He would contemplate, too, with a sort of serene passion, sunset effects, and every kind of view.

But his greatest joy in life had been his long summer holidays, in Italy or among the Alps, and his memory was a perfect storehouse of peaks, passes, and arrivals at Italian inns. He had been a great walker, and, as an old man, was still very active. I can remember him on horseback at the age of sixty, though he had never been a sportsman—not being in the way of hunting, having insufficient patience for fishing, and preferring to spend such time as he might have had for shooting, in communing with his beloved mountains. His love for all kinds of beauty, indeed, was strangely potent; and perhaps the more natural and deep for its innocence of all tradition and formal culture. He got it, I think, from his mother, of whom he always spoke with reverence as "the most beautiful woman in the Three Towns." Yes, his love of beauty was a sensuous, warm glow pervading the whole of him, secretly separating him from the majority of his associates. A pretty face, a beautiful figure, a mellow tune, the sight of dancing, a blackbird's song, the moon behind a poplar tree, starry nights, sweet scents, and the language of Shakespeare—all these moved him deeply, the more perhaps because he had never learned to express his feelings. His attempts at literature indeed were strangely naïve and stilted; his verse, in the comic vein, rather good; but all, as it were, like his period, ashamed to express any intimate feeling except in classical language. Yet his literary tastes were catholic; Milton was his favourite poet, Byron he also admired; Browning he did not care for; his favourite novelist was George Eliot, and, curiously enough—in later life—Turgenev. I well remember when the translated volumes of that author were coming out, how he would ask for another of those yellow books. He did not know why he liked them, with all those "crack-jaw" Russian names; but assuredly it was because they were written by one who worshipped beauty.

The works of Dickens and Thackeray he read with appreciation, on the whole, finding the first perhaps a little too grotesque, and the second a little too satiric. Scott, Trollope, Marryat, Blackmore, Hardy, and Mark Twain also pleased him; but Meredith he thought too "misty."

A great theatre-goer all his life, he was very lukewarm towards modern actors, comparing them adversely with those constellations of the past, Edmund and Charles Kean, Charlie Mathews, Farren, Power, "little Robson," and Helen Faucit. He was, however, a great lover of Kate Vaughan's dancing; an illustration of the equanimity of one who had formed his taste on Taglioni.

Irving he would only accept in *Louis XI*, *The Bells*, and, I think, *Charles I*, and for his mannerisms he had a great aversion. There was something of the old grand manner about his theatre habits. He attended with the very best and thinnest lavender kid gloves on his hands, which he would hold up rather high and, clap together at the end of an act which pleased him; even, on memorable occasions adding the word "Bravo." He never went out before the end of a play, however vehemently he might call it "poor stuff," which, to be quite honest, he did about nine times out of ten. And he was ever ready to try again, having a sort of touching confidence in an art which had betrayed him so often. His opera hats were notable, usually of such age as to have lost shape, and surely the largest in London. Indeed, his dress was less varied than that of any man I have ever seen; but always neat and well-cut, for he went habitually to the best shops, and without eccentricity of any kind. He carried a repeating gold watch and thin round gold chain which passed, smooth and sinuous as a little snake, through a small black seal with a bird on it; and he never abandoned very well made side-spring boots with cork soles, greatly resenting the way other boots dirtied his hands, which were thin and brown with long polished nails, and blue veins outstanding. For reading only, he wore tortoise-shelled eyeglasses, which he would perch low down on the bridge of his nose, so that he could look over them, for his eyes were very long-sighted. He was extremely fastidious in his linen, and all personal matters, yet impatient of being mollycoddled, or in any way over-valeted. Even on the finest days, he carried an umbrella, the ferrule of which, from his habit of stumping it on the pavement, had a worn and harassed look, and was rarely more than half present.

Having been a Conservative Liberal in politics till well past sixty, it was not until Disraeli's time that he became a Liberal Conservative. This was curious, for he always spoke doubtfully of "Dizzy," and even breathed the word "humbug" in connection with him.

Probably he was offended by what he termed "the extravagance" in
Dizzy's rival. For the Duke of Devonshire and Lord Salisbury he had
respect without enthusiasm; and conceived for John Bright a great
admiration as soon as he was dead. But on the whole the politician
who had most attracted him had been Palmerston, because—if
memory serves—he had in such admirable degree the faculty of
"astonishing their weak nerves." For, though never a Jingo, and in
later days both cautious and sane in his Imperialism, he had all a
Briton's essential deep-rooted distrust of the foreigner. He felt that
they were not quite safe, not quite sound, and must from time to
time be made to feel this. Born two years after the battle of Waterloo,
he had inherited a certain high pride of island birth. And yet in one
case, where he was for years in close contact with a foreigner he
conceived for him so grave a respect, that it was quite amusing to
watch the discomfiture of his traditional distrust. It was often a matter
of wonder amongst those who knew him that a man of his ability
and judgment had never even sought to make his mark in public
affairs. Of the several reasons for this, the chief was, undoubtedly, the
extraordinary balance of his temperament. To attain pre-eminence
in any definite department of life would have warped and stunted
too many of his instincts, removed too many of his interests; and so
he never specialised in any thing. He was quite unambitious, always
taking the lead in whatever field he happened to be, by virtue of
his great capacity and will-power, but never pushing himself, and
apparently without any life-aim, but that of leading a sane, moderate,
and harmonious existence.

And it is for this that he remains written on the national page, as
the type of a lost and golden time, when life to each man seemed
worth living for its own sake, without thought of its meaning as
a whole, or much speculation as to its end. There was something
classical, measured, and mellow in his march down the years, as if he
had been god-mothered by Harmony. And yet, though he said his
prayers and went to church, he could not fairly have been called a
religious man; for at the time when he formed his religious habits,
"religion" had as yet received no shocks, and reigned triumphant
over an unconscious nation whose spirit was sleeping; and when
"religion," disturbed to its foundations, began to die, and people all
round him were just becoming religious enough to renounce the

beliefs they no longer held, he was too old to change, and continued to employ the mechanism of a creed which had never really been vital to him. He was in essence pagan: All was right with his world! His love was absorbed by Nature, and his wonder by the Great Starry Scheme he felt all around. This was God to him; for it was ever in the presence of the stars that he was most moved to a sense of divine order. Looking up at those tremulous cold companions he seemed more reverent, and awed, than ever he was in the face of creeds or his fellow man. Whether stirred by the sheer beauty of Night, or by its dark immensity swarming with those glittering worlds, he would stand silent, and then, perhaps, say wistfully: "What little bits of things we are! Poor little wretches!" Yes, it was then that he really worshipped, adoring the great wonders of Eternity. No one ever heard him talk with conviction of a future life. He was far too self-reliant to accept what he was told, save by his own inner voice; and that did not speak to him with certainty. In fact, as he grew old, to be uncertain of all such high things was part of his real religion; it seemed to him, I think, impertinent to pretend to intimate knowledge of what was so much bigger than himself. But neither his conventional creed, nor that awed uncertainty which was his real religion were ever out of hand; they jogged smoothly on in double harness, driven and guided by a supremer power—his reverence for Life. He abhorred fanaticism. In this he truly mirrored the spirit of that great peacefully expanding river, the Victorian Era, which began when he came of age. And yet, in speaking before him of deep or abstract things, it was not safe to reckon without his criticism, which would sometimes make powerfully shrewd deductions out of the sheer logical insight of a nature neither fundamentally concerned with other worlds, nor brought up to the ways of discussion. He was pre-eminently the son of a time between two ages—a past age of old, unquestioning faith in authority; a future age of new faith, already born but not yet grown. Still sheltering in the shade of the old tree which was severed at the roots and toppling, he never, I think, clearly saw—though he may have had glimpses—that men, like children whose mother has departed from their home, were slowly being forced to trust in, and be good to, themselves and to one another, and so to form out of their necessity, desperately, unconsciously, their new great belief in Humanity. Yes, he was the son of *a time between two ages*—the product of an era without real faith—an individualist to the core.

His attitude towards the poor, for instance, was essentially that of man to man. Save that he could not tolerate impostors (one of his favourite words), and saw through them with almost startling rapidity, he was compassionate to any who had fallen on evil fortune, and especially to those who had been in any way connected with him. But in these almonary transactions he was always particularly secretive, as if rather doubting their sagacity, and the wisdom of allowing them to become known—himself making up and despatching the parcels of old clothes, and rather surreptitiously producing such coins and writing such cheques as were necessary. But "the poor," in bulk, were always to him the concern of the Poor Law pure and simple, and in no sense of the individual citizen. It was the same with malefactors, he might pity as well as condemn them, but the idea that the society to which he and they belonged was in any way responsible for them, would never have occurred to him. His sense of justice, like that of his period, was fundamentally based on the notion that every man had started with equal, or at all events, with quite sufficient opportunities, and must be judged as if he had. But, indeed, it was not the custom in his day to concern oneself with problems outside one's own class. Within that class, and in all matters domestic, no man was ever born with a nicer sense of justice. It was never overridden by his affections; very seldom, and that with a certain charming *naïveté*, by his interests. This sense of justice, however, in no way prevented him from being loved; for, in spite of a temper apt to take fire, flare up, and quickly die down again, he was one of the most lovable of men. There was not an ounce of dourness or asperity in his composition. His laughter was of a most infectious kind, singularly spontaneous and delightful, resembling the laughter of a child. The change which a joke wrought in the aspect of his large, dignified, and rather noble face, was disconcerting. It became wrinkled, or, as it were, crumpled; and such a twinkling overcame his eyes as was frequently only to be extinguished by moisture. "That's rich!" was his favourite expression to describe what had tickled him; for he had preserved the use of Devonshire expressions, bringing them forth from an intimate pet drawer of memory, and lingering over them with real gusto. He still loved, too, such Devonshire dishes of his boyhood as "junket" and "toad in the hole"; and one of his favourite memories was that of the meals snatched at the old coaching inn at Exeter, while they changed the horses of the Plymouth to London coach. Twenty-four hours at ten miles an hour, without ever a break! Glorious drive! Glorious the joints of beef, the cherry brandy! Glorious the old stage coachman, a "monstrous fat chap" who at that time ruled the road!

In the City, where his office was situated, he was wont, though at all times a very moderate eater, to frequent substantial, old-fashioned hostelries such as Roche's, Pim's, or Birch's in preference to newer and more pretentious places of refreshment. He had a remarkable palate too, and though he drank very little, was, in his prime, considered as fine a judge of wine as any in London. Of tea he was particularly fond, and always consumed the very best Indian, made with extreme care, maintaining that the Chinese variety was only fit for persons of no taste.

He had little liking for his profession, believing it to be beneath him, and that Heaven had intended him for an advocate; in which he was probably right, for his masterful acumen could not have failed to assure him a foremost position at the Bar. And in him, I think, it is certain that a great Judge was lost to the State. Despite this contempt for what he called the "pettifogging" character of his occupation, he always inspired profound respect in his clients; and among the shareholders of his Companies, of which he directed several, his integrity and judgment stood so high that he was enabled to pursue successfully a line of policy often too comprehensive and far-seeing for the temper of the times. The reposeful dignity, and courage, of his head and figure when facing an awkward General Meeting could hardly have been exceeded. He sat, as it were, remote from its gusty temper, quietly determining its course.

Truly memorable were his conflicts with the only other man of his calibre on those Boards, and I cannot remember that he was ever beaten. He was at once the quicker tempered and more cautious. And if he had not the other's stoicism and iron nerve, he saw further into the matter in hand, was more unremitting in his effort, equally tenacious of purpose, and more magnetic. In fact, he had a way with him.

But, after all said, it was in his dealings with children that the best and sweetest side of his personality was manifested. With them he became completely tender, inexhaustibly interested in their interests, absurdly patient, and as careful as a mother. No child ever resisted him, or even dreamed of doing so. From the first moment they loved his white hair and beard, his "feathers" as one little thing called them. They liked the touch of his thin hand, which was never wet or cold; and, holding to it, were always ready to walk with him—wandering with complete unanimity, not knowing quite where or for what reason. How often have I not watched him starting out on that high adventure with his grandson, his face turned gravely down towards a smaller face turned not quite so gravely up; and heard their voices tremendously concerned with all the things they might be going to do together! How often have I not seen them coming back tired as cats, but still concerned about what was next going to happen! And children were always willing to play cricket with him because he bowled to them very slowly, pitching up what he called "three-quarter" balls, and himself always getting "out" almost before he went in. For, though he became in his later years a great connoisseur of cricket, spending many days at Lord's or the Oval, choosing out play of the very highest class, and quite impatient of the Eton and Harrow Match, he still performed in a somewhat rococo fashion, as of a man taught in the late twenties of the last century, and having occasion to revive that knowledge about 1895. He bent his back knee, and played with a perfectly crooked bat, to the end that when he did hit the ball, which was not too often, it invariably climbed the air. There was, too, about his batting, a certain vein of recklessness or bravado, somewhat out of keeping with his general character, so that, as has been said, he was never in too long. And when he got out he would pitch the bat down as if he were annoyed, which would hugely please his grandson, showing of course that he had been trying his very best, as indeed he generally had. But his bowling was extremely impressive, being effected with very bent knees, and a general air of first putting the ball to the eye, as if he were playing bowls; in this way he would go on and on giving the boy "an innings," and getting much too hot. In fielding he never could remember on the spur of the moment whether it was his knees or his feet that he ought to close; and this, in combination with a habit of bending rather cautiously, because he was liable to lumbago, detracted somewhat from his brilliance; but when the ball was once in his hands, it was

most exciting—impossible to tell whether he would throw it at the
running batsman, the wicket, or the bowler, according as the game
appeared to him at the moment to be double wicket, single wicket,
or rounders. He had lived in days when games were not the be-all
and end-all of existence, and had never acquired a proper seriousness
in such matters. Those who passed from cricket with him to cricket
in the cold wide world found a change for which at first they were
unable to account. But even more fascinating to children than his
way of playing cricket was his perfect identification with whatever
might be the matter in hand. The examination of a shell, the listening
to the voice of the sea imprisoned in it, the making of a cocked
hat out of *The Times* newspaper, the doing up of little buttons, the
feeding of pigeons with crumbs, the holding fast of a tiny leg while
walking beside a pony, all these things absorbed him completely, so
that no visible trace was left of the man whose judgment on affairs
was admirable and profound. Nor, whatever the provocation, could
he ever bring himself to point the moral of anything to a child,
having that utter toleration of their foibles which only comes from a
natural and perfectly unconscious love of being with them. His face,
habitually tranquil, wore in their presence a mellow look of almost
devil-may-care serenity.

   Their sayings, too, he treasured, as though they were pearls. First
poems, such as

> I sorr a worm,
> It was half-ly dead;
> I took a great spud,
> And speared through his head

were to him of singular fair promise. Their diagnoses of character,
moreover, especially after visiting a circus, filled him with pure
rapture, and he would frequently repeat this one:

   "Father, is Uncle a clever man?"

   "H'm! well—yes, certainly."

   "I never seen no specimens. He can't balance a pole on his nose,
for instance."

   To the declining benison of their prayers, from their "darling father
and mother," to "all poor people who are in distress," he loved to

listen, not so much for the sentiments expressed, as because, in their little night-gowns, they looked so sweet, and were so roundabout in their way of getting to work.

Yes, children were of all living things his chosen friends, and they knew it.

But in his long life he made singularly few fast friendships with grown-up people, and, as far as I know, no enemies. For there was in him, despite his geniality, a very strong vein of fastidiousness, and such essential deep love of domination, that he found, perhaps, few men of his own age and standing to whom he did not feel natively superior. His most real and lifelong friendship was for a certain very big man with a profound hatred of humbug and a streak of "the desperate character" in him. They held each other in the highest esteem, or, as they would probably have put it, swore by one another; the one grumbling at, but reverencing, the other's high and resolute equanimity; the other deploring and admiring the one's deep and generous recklessness. The expressions: "Just like John, the careful fellow!" "Just like Sil, reckless beggar!" were always on their lips; for like all their generation they were sparing of encomium; and great, indeed, must have been their emotion before they would show their feelings. Dear as they were to each other's hearts, they never talked together of spiritual things, they never spoke in generalities, but gravely smoking their cigars, discussed their acquaintances, investments, wine, their nephews and grandchildren, and the affairs of the State—condemning the advertising fashion in which everything was now done. Once in a while they would tell a story—but they knew each other's stories too well; once in a while quote a line of Byron, Shakespeare, or Milton; or whistle to each other, inharmoniously, a bar or two from some song that Grisi, Mario, or Jenny Lind had sung. Once in a while memories of the heyday of their youth, those far-off golden hours, stealing over them, they would sit silent, with their grave steady eyes following the little rings of bluish smoke. . . . Yes, for all their lack of demonstration, they loved each other well.

I seem still to see the subject of this portrait standing at his friend's funeral one bleak November day, the pale autumn sun light falling on the silver of his uncovered head a little bowed, and on his grave face, for once so sad. I hear the tones of his voice, still full and steady; and from the soul in his eyes, looking as it were, through and through those forms of death to some deep conclusion of his own. I know how big and sane and sweet he was.

His breed is dying now, it has nearly gone. But as I remember him with that great quiet forehead, with his tenderness, and his glance which travelled to the heart of what it rested on, I despair of seeing his like again. For, with him there seems to me to have passed away a principle, a golden rule of life, nay, more, a spirit—the soul of Balance. It has stolen away, as in the early morning the stars steal out of the sky. *He* knew its tranquil secret, and where he is, there must it still be hovering.

[*1910*]

THE GREY ANGEL

HER predilection for things French came from childish recollections of schooldays in Paris and a hasty removal thence by her father during the revolution of '48; of later travels as a little maiden, by diligence, to Pau and the then undiscovered Pyrenees, to Montpellier, and a Nice as yet unspoiled. Unto her seventy-eighth year, her French accent had remained unruffled, her soul in love with French gloves and dresses; and her face had the pale, unwrinkled, slightly aquiline perfection of the French marquise type—it may, perhaps, be doubted whether any French marquise ever looked the part so perfectly.

How it came about that she had settled down in a southern French town, in the summer of 1914, only her roving spirit knew. She had been a widow ten years, which she had passed in the quest of perfection; all her life she had been haunted by that instinct, half-smothered in ministering to her husband, children, and establishments in London and the country. Now, in loneliness, the intrinsic independence of her soul was able to assert itself, and from hotel to hotel she had wandered in England, Wales, Switzerland, France, till she had found what seemingly arrested her. Was it the age of that oldest of Western cities, that little mother of Western civilisation, which captured her fancy? Or did a curious perversity turn her from more obvious abodes; or, again, was she kept there by the charm of a certain church which she would enter every day to steep herself in mellow darkness, the scent of incense, the drone of incantations, and quiet communion with a God higher indeed than she had been brought up to, high-church though she had always been? She had a pretty little apartment, where for very little—the bulk of her small wealth was habitually at the service of others—she could manage with one maid and no "fuss." She had some "nice" French friends there, too. But more probably it was simply the war which kept her, waiting, like so many other people, till it seemed worth while to move and re-establish herself. The immensity and wickedness of this strange event held her suspended, body and spirit, high up on the hill which had seen the ancient peoples, the Romans, Gauls, Saracens, and still looked out towards the flat Camargue. Here in her three rooms, with a little kitchen, the maid Augustine, a parrot, and the Paris *Daily Mail*, she dwelt marooned by a world event which stunned her. Not that she worried, exactly. The defeat of her country and France never entered her head. She only grieved quietly over the dreadful things that were being done, and every now and then would glow with admiration at the beautiful way the King and Queen were behaving. It was no good to "fuss," and one must make the best of things, as the "dear little Queen" was doing—for each Queen in turn, and she had seen three reign in her time, was always that to her. Her ancestors had been uprooted from their lands, their house burned, her pedigree diverted, in the Stuart wars; and a reverence for royalty was fastened in her blood.

Quite early in the business she had begun to knit, moving her slim fingers not too fast, gazing at the grey wool through glasses, rimless and invisible, perched on the bridge of her firm well-shaped nose, and now and then speaking to her parrot. The bird could say, "Scratch a poll, Poll," and "Hullo!"—those keys to the English language. The maid Augustine, having completed some small duty, would come and stand, her head on one side, gazing down with inquiring compassion in her young, clear-brown eyes. It seemed to her, straight and sturdy as a young tree, both wonderful and sad that *Madame* should be seventy-seven, and so frail—*Madame* who had no lines in her face and such beautiful grey hair; who had so strong a will-power, too, and knitted such soft comforters "*pour nos braves chers poilus.*" And suddenly she would say: "*Madame n'est pas fatiguée?*" And *Madame* would answer: "No. Speak English, Augustine—Polly will pick up your French!" And, reaching up a pale hand, she would set straight a stray fluff of the girl's dark-brown hair or improve the set of her fichu.

Those two got on extremely well, for though Madame was—oh! but very particular, she was always "*très gentille et toujours grande dame.*" And that love of form deep in the French soul promoted the girl's admiration for one whom she could see would in no circumstances lose her dignity. Besides, *Madame* was full of dainty household devices, and could not bear waste; and these, though exacting, were qualities which appealed to Augustine. With her French passion for "the family," she used to wonder how in days like these *Madame* could endure to be far away from her son and daughter and the grandchildren, whose photographs hung on the walls; and the long letters her mistress was always writing in a beautiful, fine hand, beginning, "My darling Sybil," "My darling Reggie," and ending always, "Your devoted mother," seemed to a warm and simple heart but meagre substitutes for flesh-and-blood realities. But, as *Madame* would inform her, they were so busy doing things for the dear soldiers, and working for the war; they could not come to her—that would never do. And to go to them would give so much trouble, when the railways were so wanted for the troops; and she had their lovely letters, which she kept—as Augustine observed—in a lavender-scented sachet, and frequently took out to read. Another point of sympathy between those two was their passion for military music and seeing soldiers pass. Augustine's brother and father were at the front, and *Madame's* dead brother had been a soldier in the Crimean War—"long before you were born, Augustine, when the French and English fought the Russians: I was in France then, too, a little girl, and we lived at Nice; the flowers were so lovely, you can't think! And my poor brother was so cold in the siege of Sebastopol." Somehow, that time and that war were more real to her than this.

In December, when the hospitals were already full, her French friends took her to the one which they attended. She went in, her face very calm, with that curious inward composure which never deserted it, carrying in front of her a black silk bag, wherein she had concealed an astonishing collection of treasures for the poor men. A bottle of acidulated drops, packets of cigarettes, two of her own mufflers, a pocket set of draughts, some English riddles translated by herself into French (very curious), some ancient copies of an illustrated paper, boxes of chocolate, a ball of string to make "cats' cradles" (such an amusing game), her own packs of patience cards, some photograph frames, postcards of Aries, and, most singular, a kettle-holder. At the head of each bed she would sit down and rummage in the bag, speaking in her slow but quite good French, to explain the use of the acidulated drops, or to give a lesson in cats' cradles. And the *poilus* would listen with their polite, ironic patience, and be left smiling, curiously fascinated, as if they had been visited by a creature from another world.

She would move on to other beds, quite unconscious of the effect she had produced on them and of their remarks: "*L'ange aux cheveux gris*" became her name within those walls. And the habit of filling that black silk bag and going there to distribute its contents soon grew to be with her a ruling passion which neither weather nor her own aches and pains, not inconsiderable, must interfere with. The things she brought became more marvellous every week. But, however much she carried coals to Newcastle, or tobacco pouches to those who did not smoke, or homeopathic globules to such as crunched up the whole bottleful for the sake of the sugar as soon as her back was turned, no one ever smiled now with anything but real pleasure at the sight of her calm and truly sweet smile and the scent of soap on her pale hands. "*Cher fils, je croyais que ceci vous donnerait un peu de plaisir. Voyez-vous comme c'est commode n'est ce pas?*" Each newcomer to the wards was warned by his comrades that the angel with the grey hair was to be taken without a smile, exactly as if she were his grandmother.

In the walk to the hospital Augustine would accompany her, carrying the bag and a large peasant's umbrella to cover them both, for the winter was hard and snowy, and carriages cost money, which must now be kept entirely for the almost daily replenishment of the bag and other calls of war. The girl, to her chagrin, was always left in a safe place, for it would never do to take her in and put fancies into her head, or excite the dear soldiers with anything so taking. The visit over, they would set forth home, walking very slowly in the high narrow streets, Augustine pouting a little and shooting swift glances at anything in uniform, and *Madame* making firm her lips against a fatigue which sometimes almost overcame her before she could get home and up the stairs. And the parrot would greet them indiscreetly with new phrases—"Keep smiling!" and "Kiss Augustine!" which he sometimes varied with "Kiss a poll, Poll!" or "Scratch Augustine!" to *Madame's* regret. Tea would revive her, and then she would knit, for as time went on and the war seemed to get farther from that end which, in common with so many, she had expected before now, it seemed dreadful not to

be always doing something to help the poor dear soldiers; and for
dinner, to Augustine's horror, she now had nothing but soup, or an
egg beaten up with milk and brandy. It saved time and expense—
she was sure people ate too much; and afterward she would read
the *Daily Mail*, often putting it down to sigh, and press her lips
together, and think, "One must look on the bright side of things,"
and wonder a little where it was. And Augustine, finishing her
work in the tiny kitchen, would sigh too, and think of red trousers
and peaked caps, not yet out of date in that southern region, and
of her own heart saying "Kiss Augustine!" and she would peer out
between the shutters at the stars sparkling over the Camargue, or
look down where the ground fell away beyond an old wall, and
nobody walked in the winter night; and muse on her nineteenth
birthday coming, and sigh with the thought that she would be old
before anyone had loved her; and of how *Madame* was looking
"*très fatiguée.*"

Indeed, *Madame* was *très fatiguée* in these days. The world's vitality
and her own were at January ebb. But to think of oneself was
impossible; it would be all right presently, and one must not fuss, or
mention in one's letters to the dear children that one felt poorly. As for
a doctor—that would be sinful waste, and besides, what use were they
except to tell you what you knew? And she was terribly vexed when
Augustine found her in a faint one morning, and she found Augustine
in tears, with her hair all over her face. She rated the girl soundly for
making such a fuss over "a little thing like that," and with extremely
trembling fingers pushed the brown hair back and told her to wash
her face, while the parrot said reflectively, "Scratch a poll—Hullo!"
The girl, who had seen her own grandmother die not long before,
and remembered how "*fatiguée*" she had been during her last days,
was frightened. Coming back after washing her face, she found her
mistress writing on a number of little envelopes the same words: "*En
bonne Amitié.*"

"Take this hundred-franc note, Augustine, and get it changed into
single francs—the ironmonger will do it if you say it's for me. I am
going to take a rest. I shan't buy anything for the bag for a whole
week. I shall take francs instead."

"Oh, Madame! You must not go out: *vous êtes trop fatiguée.*"

"Nonsense! How do you suppose our dear little Queen in England would get on with all she has to do, if she were to give in like that? We must none of us give up in these days. Help me to put on my things; I am going to church."

"Oh, *Madame*! Must you go to church? It is not your kind of church. You do not pray there, do you?"

"Of course I pray there. I am very fond of the dear old church. God is in every church, Augustine; you ought to know that at your age."

"But *Madame* has her own religion?"

"Don't be silly. What does that matter? Help me into my cloth coat—not the fur, it's too heavy—and then go and get that money changed."

"But *Madame* should see a doctor. If *Madame* faints again I shall die with fright. *Madame* has no colour—but no colour at all; it must be that there is something wrong."

Madame rose, and taking the girl's ear between thumb and finger pinched it gently.

"You are a very silly girl. What would our soldiers do if all the nurses were like you?"

Reaching the church she sat down gladly, turning her face up toward her favourite picture, a Virgin standing with her Baby in her arms. It was only faintly coloured now; but there were those who said that an Arlésienne must have sat for it. Why it pleased her so she never quite knew, unless by its cool, unrestored devotion, and the faint smiling in the eyes. Religion with her was strange yet very real. She was not clever, and never even began to try and understand what she believed. If she tried to be good she would go to God—wherever God might be; and rarely did she forget to try to be good. Sitting there she thought, or rather prayed: "Let me forget that I have a body, and remember the poor soldiers."

She shivered. It struck cold that morning in the church—the wind bitter from the north-east; some women in black were kneeling, and four candles burned in the gloom of a side aisle—thin, steady little spires of gold. There was no sound at all. A smile came on her lips. She was remembering all those young faces in the wards, the faces, too, of her own children far away, the faces of all she loved; and all the poor souls on land and sea, fighting and working and dying. Her lips moved in prayer:

"O God, who makes the birds sing and the stars shine and gives us little children, strengthen my heart so that I may forget my own aches and think of those of other people."

On reaching home again she took gelsemium, her favourite remedy against that shivering which would keep coming; then, covering herself with her fur coat, she lay down. Augustine, returning with the hundred single francs, placed them noiselessly beside the little pile of envelopes, and, after looking at the motionless face of her mistress, withdrew. Two tears came out of those closed eyes and clung on the pale cheeks below. The seeming sleeper was thinking of her children, away over there in England, her children and their children. Almost unbearably she was longing for a sight of them, recalling each face, voice, different way they had of saying "Mother darling," or "Granny, look what I've got!" and thinking that if only the war would end she would pack at once and go to them—that is, if they would not come to her for a nice long holiday in this beautiful place. She thought of spring and how lovely it would be to see the trees come out again, and almond blossom against a blue sky. The war seemed so long, and winter too. But she must not complain; others had much greater sorrows—the poor widowed women kneeling in the church; the poor boys freezing in the trenches. God in His great mercy would not allow it to last much longer! It would not be like Him! Her eyes rested gloatingly on the piles of francs and envelopes. How could she reduce still further her personal expenditure? It was so dreadful to spend on oneself—an old woman like her. Doctor, indeed! If Augustine fussed any more she would send her away and do for herself! And the parrot, leaving his cage, which he could always do, perched just behind her and said: "Hullo! Kiss me, too!"

That afternoon in the hospital everyone noticed what a beautiful colour she had. "*L'ange au cheveux gris*" had never been more popular.

She had not meant to give all the francs that day, but she saw how pleased they were, and so the whole ninety-seven had their franc each. The three over would buy Augustine a little brooch to make up to the silly child for her fright in the morning. The buying of this brooch took a long time at the jeweller's, and she had only just fixed on an amethyst before feeling deadly ill with a dreadful pain through her lungs. She went out with her tiny package quickly, not wanting any fuss, and began to mount toward home. She had only three hundred yards to go, and with each step said to herself: "Nonsense! What would the Queen think of you? Remember the poor soldiers with only one leg! You have got both your legs! And the poor men who walk from the battlefield with bullets through the lungs. What is your pain to theirs?" But the pain, like none she had ever felt—having sharp knife edges—kept passing through and through her; her legs had no strength at all, seeming to move simply because her will said: "If you don't, I'll leave you behind. So there!" She felt as if perspiration were flowing down, yet her face was dry as a dead leaf when she put up her hand to it. Her brain stammered, came to a sudden standstill. Her eyes searched painfully each grey-shuttered window for her own house, though she knew quite well that she had not reached it yet. From sheer pain she stood still, a wry smile on her lips, thinking how Polly would say:

"Keep smiling!" Then she moved on, holding out her hand, as if to pull on some imaginary rope. So, foot by foot, she crept to her door. A peculiar floating sensation had come over her. The pain ceased, and—as if she had passed through no doors, mounted no stairs—she was up in her room, lying on her sofa, conscious that she was not in control of her thoughts, and that Augustine must be thinking her ridiculous. Making a great effort, she said:

"I forbid you to send for a doctor, Augustine. I shall be all right in a day or two. And you must put on this little brooch—I bought it for you. The war will be over to-morrow, and then we will all go and have tea together in a wood. Granny will come to you, my darlings."

And when the terrified girl had rushed out she thought:

"There now! I shall get up and do for myself." The doctor found her half-dressed, trying to feed a perch in the empty cage with a spoon, while the parrot sat on the mantelpiece, with his head on one side.

When she had been properly undressed and made to lie down on the sofa, for she would not go to bed and they dared not oppose her, the doctor made his diagnosis. It was that of double pneumonia, which declares for life or death in forty-eight hours. At her age a desperate case. Her children must be wired to at once. She had sunk back, seemingly unconscious; and Augustine slipped out the lavender sachet where the letters were kept and gave it to the doctor. When he had left the room to extract addresses and send those telegrams, the girl sat down by the foot of the couch, staring at that motionless form, with tears running down her broad cheeks. For many minutes neither of them stirred, and the only sound was the restless stropping of the parrot's beak against a wire of his cage. Then the lips moved, and the girl bent forward. A whispering came forth:

"Mind, Augustine—no one is to tell my children—I can't have them disturbed—over a little thing—like this—and in my purse you'll find another—hundred-franc note. I shall want some more francs for the day after to-morrow. Be a good girl and don't fuss. Give me my gelsemium and my prayer-book. And go to bed just as usual—we must all—keep smiling—like the dear soldiers—" The whispering ceased; then began again in delirious incoherence. The girl sat trembling, covering her ears from those uncanny sounds. She could not follow—with her little English—the swerving, intricate flights of that old spirit amazed by fever—the memories released, the longings disclosed, the half-uttered prayers, the little half-conscious efforts to regain form and dignity. She could only pray to the Virgin. When relieved by the daughter of *Madame's* French friend, who spoke good English, she murmured: "*Oh! Mademoiselle, Madame est très, très fatiguée—la pauvre tête—faut-il enlever les cheveux? Elle fait ça toujours pour elle même.*" To the girl it seemed sacrilege to take off that crown of fine grey hair. Yet, when the old face was covered only by the thin white hair of nature, dignity still surmounted the wandering talk and the moaning from the parched lips, which smiled and pouted, as if remembering the maxims of the parrot. So the night passed. Once her spirit seemed to recover its coherence, and she was heard to whisper: "God has given me this so that I may know what the poor soldiers suffer. Oh! they've forgotten to cover Polly's cage." But high fever soon passes from the very old; and early morning brought a deathlike exhaustion, with utter silence, save for the licking of the flames at the olive-wood logs, and the sound as they slipped or settled down, calcined. The firelight crept fantastically about the walls covered with tapestry of French-grey silk, crept round the screen-head of the couch, and exhibited the pallor of that mask-like face, which covered such tenuous threads of life. Augustine, who had come on guard when the fever died away, sat in the armchair before those flames, trying to watch, but dropping off into the healthy sleep of youth. And out in the clear, hard shivering Southern cold, the old clocks chimed the hours into the winter dark, where the old town brooded above plain and river under the morning stars. The girl dreamed—dreamed of a sweetheart under the acacias by her home, of his pinning their white flowers into her hair; and woke with a little laugh. Light was already coming through the shutter chinks, the fire was but red embers and white ash. She gathered it stealthily together, put on fresh logs, and stole over to the couch. How white! how still! Dead? She jerked her hands up to her full breast, and a cry mounted to her throat. The eyes opened. The lips parted, as if to smile; the voice whispered: "Don't be silly!" The girl's cry changed into a little sob, and bending down she put her lips to the hand outside the quilt. It moved faintly, the lips whispered: "The emerald ring is for you, Augustine. Is it morning? Uncover Polly's cage and open his door."

A telegram had come. Her son and daughter would arrive next morning early. They waited for a moment of consciousness to tell her; but the day went by, and it did not come. She was sinking fast; her only movements were a tiny compression now and then of the lips, a half-opening of the eyes, and once a smile when the parrot spoke. The rally came at eight o'clock. *Mademoiselle* was sitting by the couch when the voice came fairly strong: "Give my love to my dear soldiers, and take them their francs out of my purse, please. Augustine, take care of Polly. I want to see if the emerald ring fits you. Take it off, please. There, you see, it does. That's very nice. Your sweetheart will like that when you have one. What do you say, *Mademoiselle*? My son and daughter are coming? All that way?" The lips smiled, tears forced their way into her eyes. "My darlings! How good of them! Oh! what a cold journey they'll have! Get my room ready, Augustine, with a good fire! What are you crying for? Remember what Polly says:

'Keep smiling!'"

She did not seem anxious as to whether she would live to see her children. Her smile moved *Mademoiselle* to whisper: "*Elle a la sourire divine.*"

"*Ah! Mademoiselle, elle pense toujours aux autres.*" And the girl's tears dropped on the emerald ring.

The long night fell—would she wake again? Both watched, ready at the faintest movement to administer oxygen and brandy. She was still breathing when at six o'clock they heard the express come in and presently the carriage stop before the house. *Mademoiselle* stole down to let them in.

Still in their travelling coats, her son and daughter knelt down beside the couch, watching in the dim candle-light for a sign and cherishing her cold hands. Daylight came; they put the shutters back and blew out the candles. Augustine, huddled in the far corner, cried gently to herself. *Mademoiselle* had withdrawn. The two still knelt, tears running down their cheeks. The least twitching of just-opened lips showed that she breathed. A tiny sigh escaped; her eyelids fluttered. The son, leaning forward, said:

"Sweetheart, we're here."

The eyes opened then; something more than a simple human spirit seemed to look through—the lips parted. They bent to catch the sound.

"My darlings—don't cry; smile!" The eyes closed. A smile, so touching that it rent the heart, flickered and went out. Breath had ceased to pass the lips.

In the silence the French girl's sobbing rose; the parrot stirred in his still-covered cage. And the son and daughter knelt, pressing their faces against the couch.

[*1917*]

QUALITY

I KNEW him from the days of my extreme youth, because he made my father's boots; inhabiting with his elder brother two little shops let into one, in a small by-street—now no more, but then most fashionably placed in the West End.

That tenement had a certain quiet distinction; there was no sign upon its face that he made for any of the Royal Family—merely his own German name of Gessler Brothers; and in the window a few pairs of boots. I remember that it always troubled me to account for those unvarying boots in the window, for he made only what was ordered, reaching nothing down, and it seemed so inconceivable that what he made could ever have failed to fit. Had he bought them to put there? That, too, seemed inconceivable. He would never have tolerated in his house leather on which he had not worked himself. Besides, they were too beautiful—the pair of pumps, so inexpressibly slim, the patent leathers with cloth tops, making water come into one's mouth, the tall brown riding-boots with marvellous sooty glow, as if, though new, they had been worn a hundred years. Those pairs could only have been made by one who saw before him the Soul of Boot—so truly were they prototypes incarnating the very spirit of all footgear. These thoughts, of course, came to me later, though even when I was promoted to him, at the age of perhaps fourteen, some inkling haunted me of the dignity of himself and brother. For to make boots—such boots as he made—seemed to me then, and still seems to me, mysterious and wonderful.

I remember well my shy remark, one day, while stretching out to him my youthful foot:

"Isn't it awfully hard to do, Mr. Gessler?"

And his answer, given with a sudden smile from out of the sardonic redness of his beard: "Id is an Ardt!"

Himself, he was a little as if made from leather, with his yellow crinkly face, and crinkly reddish hair and beard, and neat folds slanting down his cheeks to the corners of his mouth, and his guttural and one-toned voice; for leather is a sardonic substance, and stiff and slow of purpose. And that was the character of his face, save that his eyes, which were grey-blue had in them the simple gravity of one secretly possessed by the Ideal. His elder brother was so very like him—though watery, paler in every way, with a great industry—that sometimes in early days I was not quite sure of him until the interview was over. Then I knew that it was he, if the words, "I will ask my brudder," had not been spoken; and that, if they had, it was his elder brother.

When one grew old and wild and ran up bills, one somehow never ran them up with Gessler Brothers. It would not have seemed becoming to go in there and stretch out one's foot to that blue iron-spectacled glance, owing him for more than—say—two pairs, just the comfortable reassurance that one was still his client.

For it was not possible to go to him very often—his boots lasted terribly having something beyond the temporary—some, as it were, essence of boot stitched into them.

One went in, not as into most shops, in the mood of: "Please serve me, and let me go!" but restfully, as one enters a church; and, sitting on the single wooden chair, waited—for there was never anybody there. Soon, over the top edge of that sort of well—rather dark, and smelling soothingly of leather—which formed the shop, there would be seen his face, or that of his elder brother, peering down. A guttural sound, and the tip-tap of bast slippers beating the narrow wooden stairs, and he would stand before one without coat, a little bent, in leather apron, with sleeves turned back, blinking—as if awakened from some dream of boots, or like an owl surprised in daylight and annoyed at this interruption.

And I would say: "How do you do Mr. Gessler? Could you make me a pair of Russia leather boots?"

Without a word he would leave me, retiring whence he came, or into the other portion of the shop, and I would continue to rest in the wooden chair, inhaling the incense of his trade. Soon he would come back, holding in his thin, veined, hand a piece of gold-brown leather. With eyes fixed on it, he would remark: "What a beardiful biece!" When I, too, had admired it, he would speak again. "When do you wand dem?" And I would answer: "Oh! As soon as you conveniently can." And he would say: "To-morrow fordnighd?" Or if he were his elder brother: "I will ask my brudder!"

Then I would murmur: "Thank you! Good-morning Mr. Gessler." "Goot-morning!" he would reply, still looking at the leather in his hand. And as I moved to the door, I would hear the tip-tap of his bast slippers restoring him, up the stairs, to his dream of boots. But if it were some new kind of footgear that he had not yet made me, then indeed he would observe ceremony—divesting me of my boot and holding it long in his hand, looking at it with eyes at once critical and loving, as if recalling the glow with which he had created it, and rebuking the way in which one had disorganised this masterpiece. Then, placing my foot on a piece of paper, he would two or three times tickle the outer edges with a pencil and pass his nervous fingers over my toes, feeling himself into the heart of my requirements.

I cannot forget that day on which I had occasion to say to him: "Mr. Gessler, that last pair of town walking-boots creaked, you know."

He looked at me for a time without replying, as if expecting me to withdraw or qualify the statement, then said:

"Id shouldn'd 'ave greaked."

"It did, I'm afraid."

"You goddem wed before dey found demselves?"

"I don't think so."

At that he lowered his eyes, as if hunting for memory of those boots, and I felt sorry I had mentioned this grave thing.

"Zend dem back!" he said; "I will look at dem."

A feeling of compassion for my creaking boots surged up in me, so well could I imagine the sorrowful long curiosity of regard which he would bend on them.

"Zome boods," he said slowly, "are bad from birdt. If I can do noding wid dem, I dake dem off your bill."

Once (once only) I went absent-mindedly into his shop in a pair of boots bought in an emergency at some large firm's. He took my order without showing me any leather, and I could feel his eyes penetrating the inferior integument of my foot. At last he said:

152

"Dose are nod my boods."

The tone was not one of anger, nor of sorrow, not even of contempt, but there was in it something quiet that froze the blood. He put his hand down and pressed a finger on the place where the left boot, endeavouring to be fashionable, was not quite comfortable.

"Id 'urds you dere," he said. "Dose big virms 'ave no self respect. Drash!" And then, as if something had given way within him, he spoke long and bitterly. It was the only time I ever heard him discuss the conditions and hardships of his trade.

"Dey get id all," he said, "dey get id by adverdisement, nod by work. Dey dake it away from us, who lofe our boods. Id gomes to this—bresently I haf no work. Every year id gets less—you will see." And looking at his lined face I saw things I had never noticed before, bitter things and bitter struggle—and what a lot of grey hairs there seemed suddenly in his red beard!

As best I could, I explained the circumstances of the purchase of those ill-omened boots. But his face and voice made a so deep impression that during the next few minutes I ordered many pairs. Nemesis fell! They lasted more terribly than ever. And I was not able conscientiously to go to him for nearly two years.

When at last I went I was surprised to find that outside one of the two little windows of his shop another name was painted, also that of a bootmaker—making, of course, for the Royal Family. The old familiar boots, no longer in dignified isolation, were huddled in the single window. Inside, the now contracted well of the one little shop was more scented and darker than ever. And it was longer than usual, too, before a face peered down, and the tip-tap of the bast slippers began. At last he stood before me, and, gazing through those rusty iron spectacles, said:

"Mr.——, isn'd it?"

"Ah! Mr. Gessler," I stammered, "but your boots are really *too* good, you know! See, these are quite decent still!" And I stretched out to him my foot. He looked at it.

"Yes," he said, "beople do nod wand good boods, id seems."

To get away from his reproachful eyes and voice I hastily remarked: "What have you done to your shop?"

He answered quietly: "Id was too exbensif. Do you wand some boods?"

I ordered three pairs, though I had only wanted two, and quickly left. I had, I know not quite what feeling of being part, in his mind, of a conspiracy against him; or not perhaps so much against him as against his idea of boot. One does not, I suppose, care to feel like that; for it was again many months before my next visit to his shop, paid, I remember, with the feeling: "Oh! well, I can't leave the old boy—so here goes! Perhaps it'll be his elder brother!"

For his elder brother, I knew, had not character enough to reproach me, even dumbly.

And, to my relief, in the shop there did appear to be his elder brother, handling a piece of leather.

"Well, Mr. Gessler," I said, "how are you?"

He came close, and peered at me.

"I am breddy well," he said slowly; "but my elder brudder is dead."

And I saw that is was indeed himself—but how aged and wan! And never before had I heard him mention his brother. Much shocked, I murmured: "Oh! I am sorry!"

"Yes," he answered, "he was a good man, he made a good bood; but he is dead." And he touched the top of his head, where the hair had suddenly gone as thin as it had been on that of his poor brother, to indicate, I suppose, the cause of death. "He could nod ged over losing de oder shop. Do you wand any boods?" And he held up the leather in his hand:

"Id's a beaudiful biece."

I ordered several pairs. It was very long before they came—but they were better than ever. One simply could not wear them out. And soon after that I went abroad.

It was over a year before I was again in London. And the first shop I went to was my old friend's. I had left a man of sixty, I came back to one of seventy-five, pinched and worn and tremulous, who genuinely, this time, did not at first know me.

"Oh! Mr. Gessler," I said, sick at heart; "how splendid your boots are! See, I've been wearing this pair nearly all the time I've been abroad; and they're not halfworn out, are they?"

He looked long at my boots—a pair of Russia leather, and his face seemed to regain steadiness. Putting his hand on my instep, he said:

"Do dey vid you here? I 'ad drouble wid dat bair, I remember."

I assured him that they had fitted beautifully.

"Do you wand any boods?" he said. "I can make dem quickly; id is a slack dime."

I answered: "Please, please! I want boots all round—every kind!"

"I will make a vresh model. Your food must be bigger." And with utter slowness, he traced round my foot; and felt my toes, only once looking up to say:

"Did I dell you my brudder was dead?"

To watch him was painful, so feeble had he grown; I was glad to get away.

I had given those boots up, when one evening they came. Opening the parcel, I set the four pairs out in a row. Then one by one I tried them on. There was no doubt about it. In shape and fit, in finish and quality of leather, they were the best he had ever made me. And in the mouth of one of the town walking-boots I found his bill. The amount was the same as usual, but it gave me quite a shock. He had never before sent it in till quarter day. I flew downstairs and wrote a cheque, and posted it at once with my own hand.

A week later, passing the little street, I thought I would go in and tell him how splendidly the new boots fitted. But when I came to where his shop had been, his name was gone. Still there, in the window, were the slim pumps, the patent leathers with cloth tops, the sooty riding-boots.

I went in, very much disturbed. In the two little shops—again made into one—was a young man with an English face.

"Mr. Gessler in?" I said.

He gave me a strange, ingratiating look.

"No, sir," he said, "no. But we can attend to anything with pleasure. We've taken the shop over. You've seen our name, no doubt, next door. We make for some very good people."

"Yes, yes," I said; "but Mr. Gessler?"

"Oh!" he answered; "dead."

"Dead! But I only received these boots from him last Wednesday week."

"Ah!" he said; "a shockin' go. Poor old man starved 'imself."

"Good God!"

"Slow starvation, the doctor called it! You see he went to work in such a way! Would keep the shop on; wouldn't have a soul touch his boots except himself. When he got an order, it took him such a time. People won't wait. He lost everybody. And there he'd sit, goin' on and on—I will say that for him—not a man in London made a better boot! But look at the competition! He never advertised! Would 'ave the best leather, too, and do it all 'imself. Well, there it is. What could you expect with his ideas?"

"But starvation—!"

"That may be a bit flowery, as the sayin' is—but I know myself he was sittin' over his boots day and night, to the very last. You see I used to watch him. Never gave 'imself time to eat; never had a penny in the house. All went in rent and leather. How he lived so long I don't know. He regular let his fire go out. He was a character. But he made good boots."

"Yes," I said, "he made good boots."

[*1911*]

THE MAN WHO KEPT
HIS FORM

I these days every landmark is like Alice's flamingo-croquet-mallet—
when you refer to it, the creature curls up into an interrogation
mark and looks into your face; and every cornerstone resembles her
hedgehog-croquet-ball, which, just before you can use it, gets up
and walks away. The old flavours of life are out of fashion, the old
scents considered stale; "gentleman" is a word to sneer at, and "form"
a sign of idiocy.

And yet there are families in the British Isles in which gentility
has persisted for hundreds of years, and though you may think me
old-fashioned and romantic, I am convinced that such gentlefolk
often have a certain quality, a kind of inner pluck bred into them,
which is not to be despised at all.

This is why I tell you my recollections of Miles Ruding.

My first sight of him—if a new boy may look at a monitor—was
on my rather wretched second day at a Public School. The three other
pups who occupied an attic with me had gone out, and I was ruefully
considering whether I had a right to any wall-space on which to hang
two small oleographs depicting very scarlet horsemen on very bay
horses, jumping very brown hedges, which my mother had bought
me, thinking they might be suitable to the manly taste for which
Public Schools are celebrated. I had taken them out of my playbox,
together with the photographs of my parents and eldest sister, and
spread them all on the window-seat. I was gazing at the little show
lugubriously when the door was opened by a boy in "tails."

"Hallo!" he said. "You new?"

"Yes," I answered in a mouselike voice.

"I'm Ruding. Head of the house. You get an allowance of two

bob weekly when it's not stopped. You'll see the fagging lists on
the board. You don't get any fagging the first fortnight. What's your
name?"

"Bartlet."

"Oh! Ah!" he examined a piece of paper in his hand. "You're one
of mine. How are you getting on?"

"Pretty well."

"That's all right." He seemed about to withdraw, so I asked him
hastily: "Please, am I allowed to hang these pictures?

"Rather—any pictures you like. Let's look at them!" He came
forward. When his eyes fell on the array, he said abruptly: "Oh! Sorry!"
and, taking up the oleos, he turned his back on the photographs. A
new boy is something of a psychologist out of sheer fright, and
when he said "Sorry!" because his eyes had fallen on the effigies
of my people, I felt somehow that he couldn't be a beast. "You got
these at Tompkins'," he said. "I had the same my first term. Not bad.
I should put 'em up here."

While he was holding them to the wall I took a "squint" at
him. He seemed to me of a fabulous height—about five feet ten, I
suppose; thin, and bolt upright. He had a stickup collar—"barmaids"
had not yet come in—but not a very high one, and his neck was
rather long. His hair was peculiar, dark and crisp, with a reddish
tinge; and his dark-grey eyes were small and deep in, his cheekbones
rather high, his cheeks thin and touched with freckles. His nose,
chin, and cheekbones all seemed a little large for his face as yet. If I
may put it so, there was a sort of unfinished finish about him. But he
looked straight, and had a nice smile.

"Well, young Bartlet," he said, handing me back the pictures,
"buck up, and you'll be all right."

I put away my photographs, and hung the oleos. Ruding! The
name was familiar. Among the marriages in my family pedigree, such
as "—daughter of Fitzherbert," "daughter of Tastborough," occurred
the entry: "daughter of Ruding"— some time before the Civil War.
Daughter of Ruding! This demigod might be a far-off kinsman. But
I felt I should never dare to tell him of the coincidence.

Miles Ruding was not brilliant, but pretty good at everything. He
was not well dressed—you did not think of dress in connection with
him either one way or the other. He was not exactly popular—being

reserved, far from showy, and not rich—but he had no "side," and never either patronised or abused his juniors. He was not indulgent to himself or others, but he was very just; and, unlike many monitors, seemed to take no pleasure in "whopping." He never fell off in "trials" at the end of a term, and was always playing as hard at the finish of a match as at the start. One would have said he had an exacting conscience, but he was certainly the last person to mention such a thing. He never showed his feelings, yet he never seemed trying to hide them, as I used always to be. He was greatly respected without seeming to care; an independent, self-dependent bird, who would have cut a greater dash if he hadn't been so, as it were, uncreative. In all those two years I only had one at all intimate talk with him, which, after all, was perhaps above the average number, considering the difference in our ages. In my fifth term and Ruding's last but one, there had been some disciplinary rumpus in the house, which had hurt the dignity of the captain of the football "torpid" eleven—a big Irish boy who played back and was the mainstay of the side. It happened on the eve of our first house match, and the sensation may be imagined when this important person refused to play; physically and spiritually sore, he declared for the part of Achilles and withdrew to his tent. The house rocked with pro and con. My sympathies, in common with nearly all below the second fifth, lay with Donelly against the sixth form. His defection had left me captain of the side, so that the question whether we could play at all depended on me. If I declared a sympathetic strike, the rest would follow. That evening, after long hours of *"fronde"* with other rebellious spirits, I was alone and still in two minds, when Ruding came into my room. He leaned against the door, and said:

"Well, Bartlet, *you're* not going to rat?"

"I—I don't think Donelly ought to have been—been whopped," I stammered.

"That's as may be," he said, "but the house comes first. You know that."

Torn between the loyalties, I was silent.

"Look here, young Bartlet," he said suddenly, "it'll be a disgrace to us all, and it hangs on you."

"All right," I said sulkily, "I'll play."

"Good chap!"

"But I don't think Donelly ought to have been whopped," I

repeated inanely; "he's—he's too big."

Ruding approached till he looked right down on me in my old "froust," as we called armchairs. "One of these days," he said slowly, "you'll be head of the house yourself. You'll have to keep up the prestige of the sixth form. If you let great louts like Donelly cheek little weak six-formers with impunity" (I remember how impressed I was by the word), "you'll let the whole show down. My old governor runs a district in Bengal, about as big as Wales, entirely on prestige. He's often talked to me about it. I hate whopping anybody, but I'd much rather whop a lout like Donelly than I would a little new chap. He's a swine, anyway, for turning the house down because his back is sore."

"It isn't that," I said, "it—it wasn't just."

"If it was unjust," said Ruding, with what seems to me now extraordinary patience, "then the whole system's wrong, and that's a pretty big question, young Bartlet. Anyway, it's not for me to decide. I've got to administer what is. Shake hands, and do your damnedest to-morrow, won't you?"

I put out my hand with a show of reluctance, though secretly won over.

We got an awful hiding, but I can still hear Ruding's voice yelling: "Well played, Bartlet! Well pla-a-ayed!"

I have only one other school recollection of Miles Ruding which lets any real light in on him. On the day he left for good I happened to travel up to Town in the same carriage. He sat looking through the window back at the old Hill, and I distinctly saw a tear run down his cheek. He must have been conscious that I had remarked the phenomenon, for he said suddenly:

"Damn! I've got a grit in my eye," and began to pull the eyelid down in a manner which did not deceive me in the least.

I then lost sight of him completely for several years. His people were not well off, and he did not go up to the 'Varsity. He once said to me: "My family's beastly old, and beastly poor."

It was during one of my Odysseys in connection with sport that I saw him again. He was growing fruit on a ranch in Vancouver Island. Nothing used to strike a young Englishman travelling in the Colonies more than the difference between what he saw and what all printed matter led him to expect. When I ran across Ruding in the Club at

Victoria and he invited me to stay with him, I expected rows of fine trees with large pears and apples hanging on them, a colonial house with broad verandah, and Ruding in ducks, among rifles and fishing rods, and spirited horses. What I found was a bare new wooden house, not yet painted, in a clearing of the heavy forest. His fruit trees had only just been planted, and he would be lucky if he got a crop within three years. He wore, not white ducks, but blue jeans, and worked about twelve hours a day, felling timber and clearing fresh ground. He had one horse to ride and drive, and got off for a day's shooting or fishing about once a month. He had three Chinese boys working under him, and lived nearly as sparingly as they. He had been out of England eight years, and this was his second venture—the first in Southern California had failed after three years of drought. He would be all right for water here, he said; which seemed enough in a country whose rainfall is superior to that of England.

"How the devil do you stand the loneliness?" I said.

"Oh! one gets used to it. Besides, this isn't lonely—good Lord, no! You should see some places!"

Living this sort of life, he yet seemed exactly what he used to be—in fact, he had kept his form. He didn't precisely dress for dinner, but he washed. He had English papers sent out to him, and read Victorian poetry, and history natural and unnatural, in the evenings over his pipe. He shaved every day, had his cold tub every morning, and treated his Chinese boys just as he used to treat us new boys at school; so far as I could tell, they seemed to have for him much the feelings we used to have—a respect not amounting to fear, and a liking not quite rising to affection.

"I couldn't live here without a woman," I said one evening.

He sighed. 'I don't want to mess myself up with anything short of a wife; and I couldn't ask a girl to marry me till the place is fit for her. This fruit-growing's always a gamble at first."

"You're an idealist," I said.

He seemed to shrink, and it occurred to me suddenly that if there were anything he hated, it would be a generalisation like that. But I was in a teasing mood.

"You're keeping up the prestige of the English gentleman." His teeth gritted on his pipe-stem. "I'm dashed if I'm keeping up anything except my end; that's quite enough."

"And exactly the same thing," I murmured.

He turned away. I felt he was much annoyed with me for trying to introduce him to self-consciousness. And he was right! It's destructive; and his life held too many destructive elements—silence, solitude, distance from home, and this daily mixing with members of an Eastern race. I used to watch the faces of his Chinese boys—remote as cats, wonderfully carved, and old, and self-sufficient. I appreciate now how much of what was carved and old and self-sufficient Ruding needed in himself to live year in, year out, alone among them, without losing his form. All that week of my visit I looked with diabolical curiosity for some sign of deterioration—of the coarsening or softening which one felt ought naturally to come of such a life. Honestly, I could not find a trace, save that he wouldn't touch whisky, as if he were afraid of it, and shied away at any mention of women.

"Aren't you ever coming home?" I asked when I was taking leave.

"When I've made good here," he said, "I shall come back and marry."

"And then out again?"

"I expect so. I've got no money, you know."

Four years later I happened to see the following in *The Times*: "Ruding—Fuljambe: At St. Thomas's, Market Harborough, Miles Ruding of Bear Ranch, Vancouver Island, to Blanche, daughter of Charles Fuljambe, J.P., Market Harborough." So it seemed he *had* made good! But I wondered what "daughter of Fuljambe" would make of it out there. Well, I came across Ruding and his wife that very summer at Eastbourne, where they were spending the butt end of their long honeymoon. She was pleasant, pretty, vivacious—too vivacious I felt when I thought of Bear Ranch; and Ruding himself, under the stimulus of his new venture, was as nearly creative as I ever saw him. We dined and bathed, played tennis and went riding on the Downs together. Daughter of Fuljambe was quite "a sport" —though, indeed, in 1899 that word had hardly come into use. I confess to wondering why, exactly, she had married my friend, till she gave me the history of it one evening. It seems their families were old neighbours, and when Ruding came back after having been away in the New World for twelve years, he was something of a curiosity, if not of a hero. He had been used to take her out hunting when she was a small child, so that she had an old-time reverence for him. He seemed, in his absence of small-talk and "side," superior to the rattle-pated young men about her—here daughter of Fuljambe gave me a side-long glance—and one day he had done a thing which toppled her into his arms. She was to go to a fancy dress ball one evening as a Chinese lady. But in the morning a cat upset a bottle of ink over her dress and reduced it to ruin. What was to be done? All the elaborate mask of make-up and head-dressing, which she had rehearsed to such perfection, sacrificed for want of a dress to wear it with! Ruding left that scene of desolation possessed by his one great creative impulse. It seemed that he had in London a Chinese lady's dress which he had brought home with him from San Francisco. No trains from Market Harborough could possibly get him up to Town and back in time, so he had promptly commandeered the only neighbouring motor car, driven it up at a rate which must have approached forty miles an hour—a really fabulous speed for those days—got the dress, sent daughter of Fuljambe a wire, motored back at the same furious pace, and appeared before her door with the dress at eight forty-five. Daughter of Fuljambe received him in her dressing-gown, with her hair combed up and her face beautifully painted. Ruding said quietly: "Here you are; it's the genuine thing," and disappeared before she had time to thank him. The dress was superior to the one the cat had spoiled. That night she accepted him. "Miles didn't properly propose to me," she said; "I saw he couldn't bear to, because of what he'd done, so I just had to tell him not to keep his form so awfully. And here we are! He *is* a dear, isn't he?"

In his dealings with her he certainly was, for she was a self-centred little person.

They went off to Vancouver Island in September. The following January I heard that he had joined a Yeomanry contingent and gone out to fight the Boers. He left his wife in England with her people on his way. I met her once or twice before he was invalided home with enteric. She told me that she had opposed his going, till she found out it was making him quite miserable. "And yet, you know," she said, "he's frightfully devoted."

When he recovered they went back to Vancouver Island, where he found his ranch so let down that he had to begin nearly all over again. I can imagine what he went through with his dainty and exacting helpmate. She came home in 1904 to get over it, and again I met her out hunting.

"Miles is too good for me," she said the second day as we were jogging home; "he's got such fearful pluck. If only he'd kick his conscience out of the window sometimes. Oh! Mr. Bartlet, I don't want to go back there—I really don't; it's simply deadly. But he says if he gives this up he'll be thirty-eight without a thing to show for it, and just have to cadge round for a job, and he won't do that; but I don't believe I can stand it much longer."

I wrote to Ruding. His answer was dry and inexpressive, but I could read between the lines: Heaven forbid that he should drag his wife out to him again, but he would have to stick it there another two years; then, perhaps he could sell and buy a farm in England. To clear out now would be ruination. He missed his wife awfully, but—one must hoe one's row, and he would rather she stayed with her people than force herself to rough it out there with him.

Then, of course, came that which a man like Ruding, with his loyalty and his sense of form, is the last to imagine possible. Daughter of Fuljambe met a young man in the Buffs or Greens or Blues, and after, I am sure, a struggle—she was not a bad little sort—went off with him. That happened early in 1906, just as he was beginning to see the end of his struggle with Bear Ranch. I felt very sorry for him, yet inclined to say:

"My dear man, where was your imagination; couldn't you see this was bound to happen with 'daughter of Fuljambe' once she got away from you?" And yet, poor devil, what could he have done?

He came home six thousand miles to give her a divorce. A ghoulish curiosity took me into Court. I never had more whole-hearted admiration for Ruding than I had that day, watching him in that pretentiously crooked Court among us tight-lipped, curly-minded lawyers, giving his unemotional evidence. Straight, thin, lined and brown, with grey already in his peculiar-coloured hair, his voice low, his eyes unwavering, in all his lonely figure a sad, quiet protest—it was not I only who was moved by the little speech he made to the Judge:

"My Lord, I should like to say that I have no bitter feelings; I think it was my fault for asking a woman to share a rough, lonely life, so far away." It gave me a queer pleasure to see the little bow the Judge made him, as if saying: "Sir, as one gentleman to another." I had meant to get hold of him after the case, but when it came to the point I felt it was the last thing he would want of anyone. He went straight back the six thousand miles and sold his ranch. Cunningham, who used to be in our house, and had a Government post in Esquimault, told me that Ruding made himself quite unpopular over that sale. Some enterprising gentleman, interested in real estate, had reported the discovery of coal seams, which greatly enhanced the value of Bear Ranch and several neighbouring properties. Ruding was offered a big sum. He took it, and had already left the neighbourhood when the report about coal was duly disproved. Ruding at once offered to cancel the price, and take the agricultural value of the property. His offer was naturally accepted, and the disgust of other owners who had sold on the original report may be imagined. More wedded to the rights of property, they upheld the principle "Caveat emptor," and justified themselves by calling Ruding names. With his diminished proceeds he bought another ranch on the mainland.

How he spent the next eight years I only vaguely know. I don't think he came home at all. Cunningham spoke of him as "Still the same steady-going old chap, awfully respected; but no one knows him very well. He looks much as he did, except that he's gone grey."

Then, like a bolt from hell, came the Great War. I can imagine Ruding almost glad. His imagination would not give him the big horror of the thing; he would see it as the inevitable struggle, the long-expected chance to show what he and his country were made of. And I must confess that on the evidence he seems to have been made of even better stuff than his country. He began by dyeing his hair. By dint of this and by slurring the eight of his age so that it sounded like forty odd, he was accepted, and, owing to his Transvaal experience, given a commission in Kitchener's army. But he did not get out to France till early in 1916. He was considered by his Colonel the best officer in the regiment for training recruits, and his hair, of course, had soon gone grey again. They said he chafed terribly at being kept at home. In the spring of 1916 he was mentioned in despatches, and that summer was badly gassed on the Somme. I went to see him in hospital. He had grown a little grey moustache, but otherwise seemed quite unchanged. I grasped at once that he was one of those whose nerve—no matter what happened to him— would see it through. One had the feeling that this would be so as a matter of course, that he himself had not envisaged any other possibility. He was so completely lost in the winning of the war that his own sensations seemed to pass him by. He had become as much of a soldier as the best of those professionally unimaginative stoical creatures, and quite naturally, as if it were in his blood. He dwelt quietly, without visible emotion, in that universal atmosphere of death. All was in the day's work, so long as the country emerged victorious; nor did there seem the least doubt in his mind but that it would so emerge. A part of me went with him all the way, but a part of me stared at him in curiosity, surprise, admiration, and a sort of contempt, as at a creature too single-hearted and uncomplicated. One side of me was bred like him—armorial bearings, daughter of Ruding, and all the rest of it—the other had new blood with all its doubts and ferments.

I saw him several times in that hospital at Teignmouth, where he recovered slowly.

One day I asked him point blank whether one's nerve was not bound to go in time. He looked a little surprised and said rather coldly: "Not if your heart's in the right place."

That was it to a T. His heart was so deeply rooted in exactly the right place that nothing external could get at it. Whatever downed Ruding would have to blow him up bodily—there was no detaching his heart from the rest of him. And that's what I mean by an inbred quality, the inner pluck that you can bet on. I don't say it's not to be found in private soldiers and "new" people, but not in quite the same—shall we say? —matter-of-course way. When those others have it, they're proud of it or conscious of it, or simply primitively virile and thick-skinned; they don't—like such as Ruding—regard not having it as "impossible," a sort of disgrace. If scientists could examine the nerves of men like him, would they discern a faint difference in their colour or texture—the result of generations of nourishment above the average and of a traditional philosophy which for hundreds of years has held fear to be the cardinal offence? I wonder.

He went out again in 1917, and was out for the rest of the war. He did nothing very startling or brilliant; but, as at school, he was always on the ball, finishing as hard as when he started. At the Armistice he was a Lieutenant-Colonel, and a Major when he was gazetted out, at the age of fifty-three, with the various weaknesses which gas and a prolonged strain leave in a man of that age, but no pensionable disability. He went back to Vancouver. Anyone at all familiar with fruit-growing knows it for a pursuit demanding the most even and constant attention. When Ruding joined up he had perforce left his ranch in the first hands which came along; and at that time, with almost every rancher in like case, those hands were very poor substitutes for the hands of an owner. He went back to a property practically valueless. He was not in sufficient health to sit down for another long struggle to pull it round, as after the Boer War, so he sold it for a song and came home again, full of confidence that, with his record, he would get a job. He found that his case was that of thousands. They didn't want him back in the Army. They were awfully sorry, but they didn't know what they could do for him. The Governmental education and employment schemes, too, seemed all for younger men. He sat down on the song and the savings from his pay to wait for some ship or other out of his fleet of applications to come home. It did not come; his savings went. How did I know all this? I will tell you.

One night last January I had occasion to take a cab from a restaurant in Soho to my Club in Pall Mall. It was wet, and I got in hastily. I was sitting there comatose from my good dinner when I had a queer feeling that I knew the back of the driver. It had— what shall I call it?—a refined look. The man's hair was grey; and I began trying to recollect the profile I had glimpsed when bolting in. Suddenly with a sort of horror the thought flashed through me: Miles Ruding!

It was!

When I got out and we looked each other in the face, he smiled and my lips quivered. "Old chap," I said, "draw your cab up on that stand and get in with me."

When we were sitting together in his cab we lighted cigarettes, and didn't speak for quite a minute, till I burst out:

"Look here! What does this mean?"

"Bread and butter."

"Good God! And this is what the country——"

"Bartlet," he said, through curiously set lips, with a little fixed smile about the corners, "cut out all that about the country. I prefer this to any more cadging for a job; that's all."

Silent from shame, I broke out at last: "It's the limit! What about the Government schemes?"

"No go! they're all for younger men."

"My dear chap!" was all I could find to say.

"This isn't a bad life in good weather," he went on with that queer smile; "I haven't much of a chest now."

"Do you mean to say you contemplate going on with this?"

"Till something turns up; but I'm no good at asking for things, Bartlet; I simply can't do it."

"What about your people?"

"Dead or broke."

"Come and stay with me till your ship comes home."

He squeezed my arm and shook his head. That's what's so queer about gentility! If only I could have established a blood tie! Ruding would have taken help or support from his kinsfolk—would have inherited without a qualm from a second cousin that he'd never seen; but from the rest of the world it would be charity. Sitting in that cab of his, he told me, without bitterness, the tale which is that of hundreds since the war. Ruding one could not pity to his face, it would have been impossible. And, when he had finished, I could only mutter:

"Well, I think it's damnable, considering what the country owes you."

He did not answer. You can say what you like about his limitations, but Miles Ruding was bred to keep his form.

I nearly shook his hand off when I left him, and I could see that he disliked that excessive display of feeling. From my Club doorway I looked round. He had resumed his driver's seat, and, through the rain, I saw him with the cigarette between his lips, and the lamplight shining on his lean profile. Very still he sat—symbol of that lost cause, gentility.

[*1920*]

THE JAPANESE QUINCE

As Mr. Nilson, well known in the City, opened the window of his dressing-room on Campden Hill, he experienced a peculiar sweetish sensation in the back of his throat, and a feeling of emptiness just under his fifth rib. Hooking the window back, he noticed that a little tree in the Square Gardens had come out in blossom, and that the thermometer stood at sixty. 'Perfect morning,' he thought; 'spring at last!'

Resuming some meditations on the price of Tintos, he took up an ivory-backed hand-glass and scrutinised his face. His firm, well-coloured cheeks, with their neat brown moustaches, and his round, well-opened, clear grey eyes, wore a reassuring appearance of good health. Putting on his black frock coat, he went downstairs.

In the dining-room his morning paper was laid out on the sideboard. Mr. Nilson had scarcely taken it in his hand when he again became aware of that queer feeling. Somewhat concerned, he went to the French window and descended the scrolled iron steps into the fresh air. A cuckoo clock struck eight.

'Half an hour to breakfast,' he thought; 'I'll take a turn in the Gardens.'

He had them to himself, and proceeded to pace the circular path with his morning paper clasped behind him. He had scarcely made two revolutions, however, when it was borne in on him that, instead of going away in the fresh air, the feeling had increased. He drew several deep breaths, having heard deep breathing recommended by his wife's doctor; but they augmented rather than diminished the sensation—as if some sweetish liquor in course within him, together with a faint aching just above his heart. Running over what he had eaten the night before, he could recollect no unusual dish, and it occurred to him that it might possibly be some smell affecting him.

But he could detect nothing except a faint sweet lemony scent, rather agreeable than otherwise, which evidently emanated from the bushes budding in the sunshine. He was on the point of resuming his promenade, when a blackbird close by burst into song, and, looking up, Mr. Nilson saw at a distance of perhaps five yards a little tree, in the heart of whose branches the bird was perched. He stood staring curiously at this tree, recognising it for that which he had noticed from his window. It was covered with young blossoms, pink and white, and little bright green leaves both round and spiky; and on all this blossom and these leaves the sunlight glistened. Mr. Nilson smiled; the little tree was so alive and pretty! And instead of passing on, he stayed there smiling at the tree.

'Morning like this!' he thought; 'and here I am the only person in the Square who has the—to come out and———!' But he had no sooner conceived this thought than he saw quite near him a man with his hands behind him, who was also staring up and smiling at the little tree. Rather taken aback, Mr. Nilson ceased to smile, and looked furtively at the stranger. It was his next-door neighbour, Mr. Tandram, well known in the City, who had occupied the adjoining house for some five years. Mr. Nilson perceived at once the awkwardness of his position, for, being married, they had not yet had occasion to speak to one another. Doubtful as to his proper conduct, he decided at last to murmur: "Fine morning!" and was passing on, when Mr. Tandram answered: "Beautiful, for the time of year!"

Detecting a slight nervousness in his neighbour's voice, Mr. Nilson was emboldened to regard him openly. He was of about Mr. Nilson's own height, with firm, well-coloured cheeks, neat brown moustaches, and round, well-opened, clear grey eyes; and he was wearing a black frock coat. Mr. Nilson noticed that he had his morning paper clasped behind him as he looked up at the little tree. And, visited somehow by the feeling that he had been caught out, he said abruptly:

"Er—can you give me the name of that tree?"

Mr. Tandram answered:

"I was about to ask you that," and stepped towards it. Mr. Nilson also approached the tree.

"Sure to have its name on, I should think," he said.

Mr. Tandram was the first to see the little label, close to where the blackbird had been sitting. He read it out.

"Japanese quince!"

"Ah!" said Mr. Nilson, "thought so. Early flowerers."

"Very," assented Mr. Tandram, and added: "Quite a feelin' in the air to-day."

Mr. Nilson nodded.

"It was a blackbird singin'," he said.

"Blackbirds," answered Mr. Tandram, "I prefer them to thrushes myself; more body in the note." And he looked at Mr. Nilson in an almost friendly way.

"Quite," murmured Mr. Nilson. "These exotics, they don't bear fruit. Pretty blossom!" and he again glanced up at the blossom, thinking: 'Nice fellow, this, I rather like him.'

Mr. Tandram also gazed at the blossom. And the little tree, as if appreciating their attention, quivered and glowed. From a distance the blackbird gave a loud, clear call. Mr. Nilson dropped his eyes. It struck him suddenly that Mr. Tandram looked a little foolish; and, as if he had seen himself, he said:

"I must be going in. Good morning!"

A shade passed over Mr. Tandram's face, as if he, too, had suddenly noticed something about Mr. Nilson.

"Good morning," he replied, and clasping their journals to their backs they separated.

Mr. Nilson retraced his steps towards his garden window, walking slowly so as to avoid arriving at the same time as his neighbour. Having seen Mr. Tandram mount his scrolled iron steps, he ascended his own in turn. On the top step he paused.

With the slanting spring sunlight darting and quivering into it, the Japanese quince seemed more living than a tree. The blackbird had returned to it, and was chanting out his heart.

Mr. Nilson sighed; again he felt that queer sensation, that choky feeling in his throat.

The sound of a cough or sigh attracted his attention. There, in the shadow of his French window, stood Mr. Tandram, also looking forth across the Gardens at the little quince tree.

Unaccountably upset, Mr. Nilson turned abruptly into the house, and opened his morning paper.

[*1910*]

THE BROKEN BOOT

The actor, Gilbert Caister, who had been "out" for six months, emerged from his East-coast seaside lodging about noon in the day, after the opening of "Shooting the Rapids," on tour, in which he was playing Dr. Dominick in the last act. A salary of four pounds a week would not, he was conscious, remake his fortunes, but a certain jauntiness had returned to the gait and manner of one employed again at last.

Fixing his monocle, he stopped before a fishmonger's and, with a faint smile on his face, regarded a lobster. Ages since he had eaten a lobster! One could long for a lobster without paying, but the pleasure was not solid enough to detain him. He moved upstreet and stopped again, before a tailor's window.

Together with the actual tweeds, in which he could so easily fancy himself refitted, he could see a reflection of himself, in the faded brown suit wangled out of the production of "Marmaduke Mandeville" the year before the war. The sunlight in this damned town was very strong, very hard on seams and buttonholes, on knees and elbows! Yet he received the ghost of aesthetic pleasure from the reflected elegance of a man long fed only twice a day, of an eyeglass well rimmed out from a soft brown eye, of a velour hat salved from the production of "Educating Simon" in 1912; and in front of the window he removed that hat, for under it was his new phenomenon, not yet quite evaluated, his *mèche blanche*. Was it an asset, or the beginning of the end? It reclined backwards on the right side, conspicuous in his dark hair, above that shadowy face always interesting to Gilbert Caister. They said it came from atrophy of the—something nerve, an effect of the war, or of under-nourished tissue. Rather distinguished, perhaps, but——!

He walked on, and became conscious that he had passed a face he knew. Turning, he saw it also turned on a short and dapper figure—a face rosy, bright, round, with an air of cherubic knowledge, as of a getter-up of amateur theatricals.

Bryce-Green, by George!

"Caister? It is! Haven't seen you since you left the old camp. Remember what sport we had over 'Gotta-Grampus'? By Jove! I am glad to see you. Doing anything with yourself? Come and have lunch with me."

Bryce-Green, the wealthy patron, the moving spirit of entertainment in that south-coast convalescent camp. And, drawling slightly, Caister answered:

"I shall be delighted." But within him something did not drawl: 'By God, you're going to have a feed, my boy!'

And—elegantly threadbare, roundabout and dapper—the two walked side by side.

"Know this place? Let's go in here! Phyllis, cocktails for my friend Mr. Caister and myself, and caviare on biscuits. Mr. Caister is playing here; you must go and see him."

The girl who served the cocktails and the caviare looked up at Caister with interested blue eyes. Precious!—he had been "out" for six months!

"Nothing of a part," he drawled; "took it to fill a gap." And below his waistcoat the gap echoed: 'Yes, and it'll take some filling.'

"Bring your cocktail along, Caister; we'll go into the little further room, there'll be nobody there. What shall we have—a lobstah?"

And Caister murmured: "I love lobstahs."

"Very fine and large here. And how are you, Caister? So awfully glad to see you—only real actor we had."

"Thanks," said Caister, "I'm all right." And he thought: 'He's a damned amateur, but a nice little man.'

"Sit here. Waiter, bring us a good big lobstah and a salad; and then—er—a small fillet of beef with potatoes fried crisp, and a bottle of my special hock. Ah! and a rum omelette—plenty of rum and sugah. Twig?"

And Caister thought: 'Thank God, I do.'

They had sat down opposite each other at one of two small tables in the little recessed room.

"Luck!" said Bryce-Green.

"Luck!" replied Caister; and the cocktail trickling down him echoed: 'Luck!'

"And what do you think of the state of the drama?"

Oh! ho! A question after his own heart. Balancing his monocle by a sweetish smile on the opposite side of his mouth, Caister drawled his answer: "Quite too bally awful!"

"H'm! Yes," said Bryce-Green; "nobody with any genius, is there?"

And Caister thought: 'Nobody with any money.'

"Have you been playing anything great? You were so awfully good in 'Gotta-Grampus'!"

"Nothing particular. I've been—er—rather slack." And with their feel around his waist his trousers seemed to echo:
'Slack!'

"Ah!" said Bryce-Green. "Here we are! Do you like claws?"

"Tha-a-nks. Anything!" To eat—until warned by the pressure of his waist against his trousers! What a feast! And what a flow of his own tongue suddenly released—on drama, music, art; mellow and critical, stimulated by the round eyes and interjections of his little provincial host.

"By Jove, Caister! You've got a *mêche blanche*. Never noticed. I'm awfully interested in *mêches blanches*. Don't think me too frightfully rude—but did it come suddenly?"

"No, gradually."

"And how do you account for it?"

'Try starvation,' trembled on Caister's lips.

"I don't," he said.

"I think it's ripping. Have some more omelette? I often wish I'd gone on the regular stage myself. Must be a topping life, if one has talent, like you."

Topping?

"Have a cigar. Waiter! Coffee, and cigars. I shall come and see you to-night. Suppose you'll be here a week?"

Topping! The laughter and applause—"Mr. Caister's rendering left nothing to be desired; its—and its—are in the true spirit of—!"

Silence recalled him from his rings of smoke. Bryce-Green was sitting, with cigar held out and mouth a little open, and bright eyes round as pebbles, fixed—fixed on some object near the floor, past the corner of the tablecloth. Had he burnt his mouth? The eyelids fluttered; he looked at Caister, licked his lips like a dog, nervously, and said:

"I say, old chap, don't think me a beast, but are you at all—er—er—rocky? I mean—if I can be of any service, don't hesitate! Old acquaintance, don't you know, and all that——"

His eyes rolled out again towards the object, and Caister followed them. Out there above the carpet he saw it—his own boot. It dangled slightly, six inches off the ground—split—right across, twice, between lace and toecap. Quite! He knew it. A boot left him from the rôle of Bertie Carstairs, in "The Dupe," just before the war. Good boots. His only pair, except the boots of Dr. Dominick, which he was nursing. And from the boot he looked back at Bryce-Green, sleek and concerned. A drop, black when it left his heart, suffused his eye behind the monocle; his smile curled bitterly; he said:

"Not at all, thanks! Why?"

"Oh! n-n-nothing. It just occurred to me." His eyes—but Caister had withdrawn the boot. Bryce-Green paid the bill and rose.

"Old chap, if you'll excuse me; engagement at half-past two. So awf'ly glad to have seen you. Good-bye!"

"Good-bye!" said Caister. "Thanks."

He was alone. And, chin on hand, he stared through his monocle into an empty coffee cup. Alone with his heart, his boot, his life to come. . . . 'And what have you been in lately, Mr. Caister?' 'Nothing very much lately. Of course I've played almost everything.' 'Quite so. Perhaps you'll leave your address; can't say anything definite, I'm afraid.' 'I—I should—er—be willing to rehearse on approval; or—if I could read the part?' 'Thank you, afraid we haven't got as far as that.' 'No? Quite! Well, I shall hear from you, perhaps.' And Caister could see his own eyes looking at the manager. God! What a look! . . . A topping life! A dog's life! Cadging—cadging—cadging for work! A life of draughty waiting, of concealed beggary, of terrible depressions, of want of food!

The waiter came skating round as if he desired to clear. Must go! Two young women had come in and were sitting at the other table between him and the door. He saw them look at him, and his sharpened senses caught the whisper:

"Sure—in the last act. Don't you see his *mêche blanche*?"

"Oh! yes—of course! Isn't it—wasn't he——!"

Caister straightened his back; his smile crept out, he fixed his monocle. They had spotted his Dr. Dominick!

"If you've quite finished, sir, may I clear?"

"Certainly. I'm going." He gathered himself and rose. The young women were gazing up. Elegant, with faint smile, he passed them close, so that they could not see, managing—his broken boot.

[*1922*]

THE CHOICE

SOME years ago in Chelsea there used to stand at the crossing of a street leading to the Embankment an old man whose living was derived from the cleanliness of boots. In the intervals of plying his broom he could generally be seen seated on an upturned wooden box, talking to an Irish terrier, who belonged to a house near by, and had taken a fancy to him. He was a Cornishman by birth, had been a plumber by trade, and was a cheerful, independent old fellow with ruddy cheeks, grey hair and beard, and little, bright, rather watery, grey eyes. But he was a great sufferer from a variety of ailments. He had gout, and some trouble in his side, and feet that were like barometers in their susceptibility to weather. Of all these matters he would speak to us in a very impersonal and uncomplaining way, diagnosing himself, as it were, for the benefit of his listeners. He was, it seems, alone in the world, not having of course at that time anything to look forward to in the way of a pension, nor, one fancies, very much to look back on except the death of his near relatives and the decline of the plumbing trade. It had declined him for years, but, even before a long illness ousted him in favour of younger men, he had felt very severely the palpable difference in things. In old days plumbing had been a quiet, steady business, in which you were apparently "on your own, and knew where you were"; but latterly "you had just had to do what the builders told you, and of course they weren't going to make allowances; if you couldn't do the job as fast as a young man—out you went, and there you were." This long illness and the death of his wife coming close together (and sweeping away the last of his savings), had determined him therefore to buy a broom and seek for other occupation. To sweep a crossing was not a profession that he himself would have chosen before all others, still it was "better than the 'house—and you were your own master." The climate in those days not being the most suitable for a business which necessitated constant exposure to all elements but that of fire, his ailments were proportionately active; but the one remarkable feature of his perpetual illness was that he was always "better" than he had been. We could not at times help thinking that this continual crescendo of good health should have gradually raised him to a pinnacle of paramount robustness; and it was with a certain disappointment; in the face of his assurances, that we watched him getting, on the contrary, slowly stiffer and feebler, and noted the sure increase of the egg-like deposits, which he would proudly have us remark, about his wrists and fingers.

He was so entirely fixed and certain that he was "going in the river" before he went "in the 'house," that one hesitated to suggest that the time was at hand when he should cease to expose himself all day and every day. He had evidently pondered long and with a certain deep philosophy on this particular subject, and fortified himself by hearsay.

"The 'house ain't for a man that respects himself," he would remark. And, since that was his conviction, such as respected themselves could not very well beg him to act against it. At the same time, it became increasingly difficult to pass him without wondering how much longer it would be before he finally sought shelter in the element of water, which was so apt to pour down on him day by day.

It is uncertain whether he discussed this matter of the river *versus* the 'house with the dog, to whom he was always talking; but that they shared a certain fellow-feeling on the subject of exposure and advancing age is more than probable; for, as he would point out: The poor old feller's teeth were going; and the stiffness across his loins was always worse when it was wet. In fact, he was afraid that the old dog was gettin' old! And the dog would sit patiently for an hour at a time looking up at him, trying to find out, perhaps, from his friend's face what a dog should do, when the enemy weighed on him till he could no longer tolerate himself, not knowing, of course, that kindly humans would see to it that he did not suffer more than a dog could bear. On his face with its grizzled muzzle and rheumy eyes, thus turned up, there was never a sign of debate; it was full of confidence that, whatever decision his friend came to, in this momentous question between the river and the 'house, would be all right, perfectly satisfactory in every way to dogs and men.

One very rainy summer our old friend in a burst of confidence disclosed the wish of his heart. It was that he might be suffered to go down once more to Fowey in Cornwall, where he had been born, but had not been for fifty years. By some means or other the money was procured for this enterprise, and he was enabled to set off by excursion train for a fortnight's holiday. He was observed the day before his start talking at great length to the dog, and feeding it out of a paper bag with carraway-seed biscuits. A letter was received from him during his absence, observing certain strange laws of calligraphy, and beginning "Honoured Sir and Lady." It was full of an almost passionate description of a regatta, of a certain "Joe Petherick" who had remembered him, of the "luvly weather" and other sources of his great happiness; and ended "Yours truley obedient." On the fifteenth day he was back at his corner seated on his box in the pouring rain, saying that he was "a different man, ten years younger, and ready to 'go' now, any day"; nor could anything dissuade him from the theory that Heaven had made a special lodgment in our persons on his behalf. But only four days later, the sun being for once in the heavens, he was so long in answering a salutation that we feared he had been visited by some kind of stroke; his old face had lost colour, it seemed stiff, and his eyes had almost disappeared.

Inquiry elicited from him the information that he was better than he had been, but that the dog was dead. They had put it away while he had been gone, and he was afraid that he should miss the "faithful old feller."

"He was very good to me," he said; "always came for a bit of bread or biscuit. And he was company to me; I never knew such a sensible creature." He seemed to think that the dog must have pined during his absence, and that this had accelerated his end by making his owners think he was more decrepit than he really was.

The death of the dog, and the cold damp autumn that year, told heavily on the old man, but it was not till mid-November that he was noted one morning absent from his post. As he did not reappear his lodging was sought out. It was in a humble street, but the house was neat and clean, and the landlady seemed a good, rough woman. She informed us that our old friend was laid up "with pleurisy and the gouty rheumatics"; that by rights, of course, he ought to be in the infirmary, but she didn't like to turn him out, though where she would get her rent from she didn't know, to say nothing of his food, because she couldn't let him starve while there he was cryin' out with the pain, and no one but herself to turn a hand to him, with his door open at the top of the house, where he could holler for her if he wanted. An awful independent old feller, too, or else she wouldn't hesitate, for that was where he ought to be, and no mistake, not having a soul in the world to close his eyes, and that's what it would come to, though she would never be surprised if he got up and went out to-morrow, he was that stubborn!

Leaving her to the avocations which we had interrupted by coming in, we went upstairs.

The door of the back room at the top was, as indeed she had led us to suppose, open; and through it the sound of our friend's voice could be heard travelling forth:

"O Lord God, that took the dog from me, and gave me this here rheumatics, help me to keep a stiff and contrite heart. I am an old man, O Lord God, and I am not one to go into that *place*. So God give me a stiff heart, and I will remember you in my prayers, for that's about all I can do now, O God. I have been a good one in my time, O Lord, and cannot remember doing harm to any man for a long while now, and I have tried to keep upsides with it; so, good Lord, remember and do not forget me, now that I am down, a-lying here all day, and the rent goin' on. For ever and ever, O Lord, Amen."

We allowed a little time to pass before we went in, unwilling that he should think we had overheard that prayer. He was lying in a small dingy bed, with a medicine bottle and glass beside him on an old tin trunk. There was no fire.

He was—it seemed—better than he had been; the doctor's stuff was doing him good.

Certain arrangements were made for his benefit, and in less than three weeks he was back again at his corner.

In the spring of the following year we went abroad and were absent several months. He was no longer at his post when at last we came back, and a policeman informed us that he had not been there for some weeks. We made a second pilgrimage to his lodgings. The house had changed hands. The new landlady was a thin, anxious-looking young woman, who spoke in a thin, anxious voice. Yes, the old man had been taken very ill—double pneumonia and heart disease, she thought. Anyway, she couldn't have the worry and responsibility of him, let alone her rent. She had had the doctor, and had him taken off. Yes, it had upset him a bit; he would never have gone if he'd had his choice; but of course she had her living to get. She had his bits of things locked up all right; he owed her a little rent. In her opinion he'd never come out again. She was very sorry for him, too; he'd given no trouble till he was took ill.

Following up her information we repaired with heavy hearts to the 'house, which he had so often declared he would never enter. Having ascertained the number of his ward we mounted the beautifully clean stairs. In the fifth of a row of beds, our old friend was lying, apparently asleep. But watching him carefully, we saw that his lips, deep sunk between his frosty moustache and beard, were continually moving.

"He's not asleep," said the nurse; "he'll lie like that all the time. He frets."

At the sound of his name he had opened his eyes, which, though paler and smaller and more rheumy, were still almost bright. He fixed them on us with a peculiar stare, as much as to say: "You've taken an advantage of me, finding me here." We could hardly bear that look, and hurriedly asked him how he was. He tried to raise himself and answered huskily that he was better than he had been. We begged him not to exert himself, and told him how it was that we had been away, and so forth. He seemed to pay no attention, but suddenly said: "I'm in here; I don't mean to stay; I'll be goin' out in a day or two." We tried to confirm that theory, but the expression of his eyes seemed to take away our power of comfort, and make us ashamed of looking at him. He beckoned us closer.

"If I'd a had the use of my legs," he whispered, "they'd never have had me. I'd a-gone in the river first. But I don't mean to stay—I'm goin' back home."

The nurse told us, however, that this was out of the question; he was still very ill.

Four days later we went again to see him. He was no longer there. He had gone home. They had buried him that morning.

[*1910*]

ULTIMA THULE

ULTIMA THULE! The words come into my head this winter night. That is why I write down the story, as I know it, of a little old friend.

I used to see him first in Kensington Gardens, where he came in the afternoons, accompanied by a very small girl. One would see them silent before a shrub or flower, or with their heads inclined to heaven before a tree, or leaning above water and the ducks, or stretched on their stomachs watching a beetle, or on their backs watching the sky. Often they would stand holding crumbs out to the birds, who would perch about them, and even drop on their arms little white marks of affection and esteem. They were admittedly a noticeable couple. The child, who was fair-haired and elfinlike, with dark eyes and a pointed chin, wore clothes that seemed somewhat hard put to it. And, if the two were not standing still, she went along pulling at his hand, eager to get there; and, since he was a very little, light old man, he seemed always in advance of his own feet. He was garbed, if I remember, in a daverdy brown overcoat and broad-brimmed soft grey hat, and his trousers, what was visible of them, were tucked into half-length black gaiters which tried to join with very old brown shoes. Indeed, his costume did not indicate any great share of prosperity. But it was his face that riveted attention. Thin, cherry-red, and wind-dried as old wood, it had a special sort of brightness, with its spikes and waves of silvery hair, and blue eyes which seemed to shine. Rather mad, I used to think. Standing by the rails of an enclosure, with his withered lips pursed and his cheeks drawn in till you would think the wind might blow through them, he would emit the most enticing trills and pipings, exactly imitating various birds.

Those who rouse our interest are generally the last people we speak to, for interest seems to set up a kind of special shyness; so it was long before I made his acquaintance. But one day by the Serpentine, I saw him coming along alone, looking sad, but still with that queer brightness about him. He sat down on my bench with his little dried hands on his thin little knees, and began talking to himself in a sort of whisper. Presently I caught the words: "God cannot be like us." And for fear that he might go on uttering such precious remarks that were obviously not intended to be heard, I had either to go away or else address him. So, on an impulse, I said:

"Why?"

He turned without surprise.

"I've lost my landlady's little girl," he said. "Dead! And only seven years old."

"That little thing I used to watch you with?"

"Did you? Did you? I'm glad you saw her."

"I used to see you looking at flowers, and trees, and those ducks."

His face brightened wistfully. "Yes; she was a great companion to an old man like me." And he relapsed into his contemplation of the water. He had a curious, precise way of speaking, that matched his pipchinesque little old face. At last he again turned to me those blue youthful eyes which seemed to shine out of a perfect little nest of crow's-feet.

"We were great friends! But I couldn't expect it. Things don't last, do they?" I was glad to notice that his voice was getting cheerful. "When I was in the orchestra at the Harmony Theatre, it never used to occur to me that some day I shouldn't play there any more. One felt like a bird. That's the beauty of music, sir. You lose yourself; like that blackbird there." He imitated the note of a blackbird so perfectly that I could have sworn the bird started.

"Birds and flowers! Wonderful things; wonderful! Why, even a buttercup!" He pointed at one of those little olden flowers with his toe. "Did you ever see such a marvellous thing?" And he turned his face up at me. "And yet, somebody told me once that they don't agree with cows. Now can that be? I'm not a countryman—though I was born at Kingston."

"The cows do well enough on them," I said, "in my part of the world. In fact, the farmers say they like to see buttercups."

"I'm glad to hear you say that. I was always sorry to think they disagreed."

When I got up to go, he rose, too.

"I take it as very kind of you," he said, "to have spoken to me."

"The pleasure was mine. I am generally to be found hereabouts in the afternoons any time you like a talk."

"Delighted," he said; "delighted. I make friends of the creatures and flowers as much as possible, but they can't always make us understand." And after we had taken off our respective hats, he reseated himself, with his hands on his knees.

Next time I came across him standing by the rails of an enclosure, and, in his arms, an old and really wretched-looking cat.

"I don't like boys," he said, without preliminary of any sort. "What do you think they were doing to this poor old cat? Dragging it along by a string to drown it; see where it's cut into the fur! I think boys despise the old and weak!" He held it out to me. At the ends of those little sticks of arms the beast looked more dead than alive; I had never seen a more miserable creature.

"I think a cat," he said, "is one of the most marvellous things in the world. Such a depth of life in it."

And, as he spoke, the cat opened its mouth as if protesting at that assertion. It *was* the sorriest-looking beast.

"What are you going to do with it?"

"Take it home; it looks to me as if it might die."

"You don't think that might be more merciful?"

"It depends; it depends. I shall see. I fancy a little kindness might do a great deal for it. It's got plenty of spirit. I can see from its eye."

"May I come along with you a bit?"

"Oh!" he said; "delighted."

We walked on side by side, exciting the derision of nearly everyone we passed—his face looked so like a mother's when she is feeding her baby!

"You'll find this'll be quite a different cat tomorrow," he said. "I shall have to get in, though, without my landlady seeing; a funny woman! I have two or three strays already."

"Can I help in any way?"

"Thank you," he said. "I shall ring the area bell, and as she comes out below I shall go in above. She'll think it's boys. They *are* like that."

"But doesn't she do your rooms, or anything?"

A smile puckered his face. "I've only one; I do it myself. Oh, it'd never do to have her about, even if I could afford it. But," he added, "if you're so kind as to come with me to the door, you might engage her by asking where Mr. Thompson lives. That's me. In the musical world my name was Moronelli; not that I have Italian blood in me, of course."

"And shall I come up?"

"Honoured; but I live very quietly."

We passed out of the gardens at Lancaster Gate, where all the house-fronts seem so successful, and out of it into a little street that was extremely like a grubby child trying to hide under its mother's skirts. Here he took a newspaper from his pocket and wrapped it round the cat.

"She's a funny woman," he repeated; "Scotch descent, you know." Suddenly he pulled an area bell and scuttled up the steps.

When he had opened the door, however, I saw before him in the hall a short, thin woman dressed in black, with a sharp and bumpy face. Her voice sounded brisk and resolute.

"What have you got there, Mr. Thompson?"

"Newspaper, Mrs. March."

"Oh, indeed! Now, you're not going to take that cat upstairs!"

The little old fellow's voice acquired a sudden shrill determination. "Stand aside, please. If you stop me, I'll give you notice. The cat is going up. It's ill, and it is going up."

It was then I said:

"Does Mr. Thompson live here?"

In that second he shot past her, and ascended.

"That's him," she said; "and I wish it wasn't, with his dirty cats. Do you want him?"

"I do."

"He lives at the top." Then, with a grudging apology:

"I can't help it; he tries me—he's very trying."

"I am sure he is."

She looked at me. The longing to talk that comes over those who answer bells all day, and the peculiar Scottish desire to justify oneself, rose together in that face which seemed all promontories dried by an east wind.

"Ah!" she said; "he is. I don't deny his heart; but he's got no sense of anything. Goodness knows what he hasn't got up there. I wonder

I keep him. An old man like that ought to know better; half-starving himself to feed them." She paused, and her eyes, which had a cold and honest glitter, searched me closely.

"If you're going up," she said, "I hope you'll give him good advice. He never lets me in. I wonder I keep him."

There were three flights of stairs, narrow, clean, and smelling of oilcloth. Selecting one of two doors at random, I knocked. His silvery head and bright, pinched face were cautiously poked out.

"Ah!" he said; "I thought it might be her!"

The room, which was fairly large, had a bare floor with little on it save a camp-bed and chest of drawers with jug and basin. A large bird-cage on the wall hung wide open. The place smelt of soap and a little of beasts and birds. Into the walls, whitewashed over a green wall-paper which stared through in places, were driven nails with their heads knocked off, on to which bits of wood had been spiked, so that they stood out as bird-perches high above the ground. Over the open window a piece of wire-netting had been fixed. A little spirit-stove and an old dressing-gown hanging on a peg completed the accoutrements of a room which one entered with a certain diffidence. He had not exaggerated. Besides the new cat, there were three other cats and four birds, all—save one, a bullfinch—invalids. The cats kept close to the walls, avoiding me, but wherever my little old friend went they followed him with their eyes. The birds were in the cage, except the bullfinch, which had perched on his shoulder.

"How on earth," I said, "do you manage to keep cats and birds in one room?"

"There is danger," he answered, "but I have not had a disaster yet. Till their legs or wings are mended, they hardly come out of the cage; and after that they keep up on my perches. But they don't stay long, you know, when they're once well. That wire is only put over the window while they're mending; it'll be off to-morrow for this lot."

"And then they'll go?"

"Yes. The sparrow first, and then the two thrushes."

"And this fellow?"

"Ask him," he said. "Would *you* go, bully?" But the bullfinch did not deign to answer.

"And were all those cats, too, in trouble?"

"Yes," he said. "They wouldn't want me if they weren't."

Thereupon he began to warm some blue-looking milk, contemplating the new cat, which he had placed in a round basket close to the little stove, while the bullfinch sat on his head. It seemed time to go.

"Delighted to see you, sir," he said, "any day." And, pointing up at the bullfinch on his head, he added: "Did you ever see anything so wonderful as that bird? The size of its heart! Really marvellous."

To the rapt sound of that word marvellous, and full of the memory of his mysterious brightness while he stood pointing upward to the bird perched on his thick, silvery hair, I went.

The landlady was still at the bottom of the stairs, and began at once. "So you found him! I don't know why I keep him. Of course, he was kind to my little girl." I saw tears gather in her eyes.

"With his cats and his birds, I wonder I keep him! But where would he go? He's no relations, and no friends—not a friend in the world, I think! He's a character. Lives on air—feeding them cats! I've no patience with them, eating him up. He never lets me in. Cats and birds! I wonder I keep him. Losing himself for those rubbishy things! It's my belief he was always like that; and that's why he never got on. He's no sense of anything."

And she gave me a shrewd look, wondering, no doubt, what the deuce I had come about.

I did not come across him again in the gardens for some time, and went at last to pay him a call. At the entrance to a mews just round the corner of his grubby little street, I found a knot of people collected round one of those bears that are sometimes led through the less conspicuous streets of our huge towns. The yellowish beast was sitting up in deference to its master's rod, uttering little grunts, and moving its uplifted snout from side to side, in the way bears have. But it seemed to be extracting more amusement than money from its audience.

"Let your bear down off its hind legs and I'll give you a penny." And suddenly I saw my little old friend under his flopping grey hat, amongst the spectators, all taller than himself. But the bear's master only grinned and prodded the animal in the chest. He evidently knew a good thing when he saw it.

"I'll give you twopence to let him down."

Again the bear-man grinned. "More!" he said, and again prodded the bear's chest. The spectators were laughing now.

"Threepence! And if you don't let him down for that, I'll hit you in the eye."

The bear-man held out his hand. "All a-right," he said, "threepence: I let him down."

I saw the coins pass and the beast dropping on his forefeet; but just then a policeman coming in sight, the man led his bear off, and I was left alone with my little old friend.

"I wish I had that poor bear," he said: 'I could teach him to be happy. But, even if I could buy him, what could I do with him up there? She's such a funny woman."

He looked quite dim, but brightened as we went along.

"A bear," he said, "is really an extraordinary animal. What wise little eyes he has! I do think he's a marvellous creation! My cats will have to go without their dinner, though. I was going to buy it with that threepence."

I begged to be allowed the privilege.

"Willingly!" he said. "Shall we go in here? They like cod's head best."

While we stood waiting to be served I saw the usual derisive smile pass over the fishmonger's face. But my little old friend by no means noticed it; he was too busy looking at the fish. "A fish is a marvellous thing, when you come to think of it," he murmured. "Look at its scales. Did you ever see such mechanism?"

We bought five cod's heads, and I left him carrying them in a bag, evidently lost in the anticipation of five cats eating them.

After that I saw him often, going with him sometimes to buy food for his cats, which seemed ever to increase in numbers. His talk was always of his strays, and the marvels of creation, and that time of his life when he played the flute at the Harmony Theatre. He had been out of a job, it seemed, for more than ten years; and, when questioned, only sighed and answered:

"Don't talk about it, please!"

His bumpy landlady never failed to favour me with a little conversation. She was one of those women who have terrific consciences, and terrible grudges against them.

"I never get out," she would say.

"Why not?"

"Couldn't leave the house."

"It won't run away!"

But she would look at me as if she thought it might, and repeat:

"Oh! I never get out."

An extremely Scottish temperament.

Considering her descent, however, she was curiously devoid of success, struggling on apparently from week to week, cleaning, and answering the bell, and never getting out, and wondering why she kept my little old friend; just as he struggled on from week to week, getting out and collecting strays, and discovering the marvels of creation, and finding her a funny woman. Their hands were joined, one must suppose, by that dead child.

One July afternoon, however, I found her very much upset. He had been taken dangerously ill three days before.

"There he is," she said; "can't touch a thing. It's my belief he's done for himself, giving his food away all these years to those cats of his. I shooed 'em out to-day, the nasty creatures; they won't get in again."

"Oh!" I said, "you shouldn't have done that. It'll only make him miserable."

She flounced her head up. "Hoh!" she said: "I wonder I've kept him all this time, with his birds and his cats dirtying my house. And there he lies, talking gibberish about them. He made me write to a Mr. Jackson, of some theatre or other—I've no patience with him. And that little bullfinch all the time perching on his pillow, the dirty little thing! I'd have turned it out, too, only it wouldn't let me catch it."

"What does the doctor say?"

"Double pneumonia—caught it getting his feet wet, after some stray, I'll be bound. I'm nursing him. There has to be someone with him all the time."

He was lying very still when I went up, with the sunlight falling across the foot of his bed, and, sure enough, the bullfinch perching on his pillow. In that high fever he looked brighter than ever. He was not exactly delirious, yet not exactly master of his thoughts.

"Mr. Jackson! He'll be here soon. Mr. Jackson! He'll do it for me. I can ask him, if I die. A funny woman. I don't want to eat; I'm not a great eater—I want my breath, that's all."

At sound of his voice the bullfinch fluttered off the pillow and flew round and round the room, as if alarmed at something new in the tones that were coming from its master.

Then he seemed to recognise me. "I think I'm going to die," he said; "I'm very weak. It's lucky there's nobody to mind. If only he'd come soon. I wish"—and he raised himself with feeble excitement— "I wish you'd take that wire off the window; I want my cats. She turned them out. I want him to promise me to take them, and bully-boy, and feed them with my money, when I'm dead."

Seeing that excitement was certainly worse for him than cats, I took the wire off. He fell back, quiet at once; and presently, first one and then another cat came stealing in, till there were four or five seated against the walls. The moment he ceased to speak the bullfinch, too, came back to his pillow. His eyes looked most supernaturally bright, staring out of his little, withered-up old face at the sunlight playing on his bed; he said just audibly: "Did you ever see anything more wonderful than that sunlight? It's really marvellous!" After that he fell into a sort of doze or stupor. And I continued to sit there in the window, relieved, but rather humiliated, that he had not asked me to take care of his cats and bullfinch.

Presently there came the sound of a motor-car in the little street below. And almost at once the landlady appeared. For such an abrupt woman, she entered very softly.

"Here he is," she whispered.

I went out and found a gentleman, perhaps sixty years of age, in a black coat, buff waistcoat, gold watch-chain, light trousers, patent-leather boots, and a wonderfully shining hat. His face was plump and red, with a glossy grey moustache; indeed, he seemed to shine everywhere, save in the eyes, which were of a dull and somewhat liverish hue.

"Mr. Jackson?"

"The same. How is the little old chap?"

Opening the door of the next room, which I knew was always empty, I beckoned Mr. Jackson in.

"He's really very ill; I'd better tell you what he wants to see you about."

He looked at me with that air of "You can't get at me—whoever you may be," which belongs to the very successful.

"Right-o!" he said. "Well?"

I described the situation. "He seems to think," I ended, "that you'll be kind enough to charge yourself with his strays, in case he should die."

Mr. Jackson prodded the unpainted washstand with his gold-. headed cane.

"Is he really going to kick it?"

"I'm afraid so; he's nothing but skin, bone, and spirit, as it is."

"H'm! Stray cats, you say, and a bird! Well, there's no accounting. He was always a cracky little chap. So that's it! When I got the letter I wondered what the deuce! We pay him his five quid a quarter regular to this day. To tell truth, he deserved it. Thirty years he was at our shop; never missed a night. First-rate flute he was. He ought never to have given it up, though I always thought it showed a bit of heart in him. If a man don't look after number one, he's as good as gone; that's what I've always found. Why, I was no more than he was when I started. Shouldn't have been worth a plum if I'd gone on his plan, that's certain." And he gave that profound chuckle which comes from the very stomach of success. "We were having a rocky time at the Harmony; had to cut down everything we could—music, well, that came about first. Little old Moronelli, as we used to call him—old Italian days before English names came in, you know— he was far the best of the flutes; so I went to him and said: 'Look here, Moronelli, which of these other boys had better go?' 'Oh!' he said—I remember his funny little old mug now—'has one of them to go, Mr. Jackson? Timminsa'—that was the elder— 'he's a wife and family; and Smetoni'—Smith, you know—'he's only a boy. Times are bad for flutes.' 'I know it's a bit hard,' I said, 'but this theatre's goin' to be run much cheaper; one of 'em's got to get.' 'Oh!' he said, 'dear me!' he said. What a funny little old chap it was! Well—what, do you think? Next day I had his resignation. Give you my word I did my best to turn him. Why, he was sixty then if he was a day—at sixty a man don't get jobs in a hurry. But not a bit of it! All he'd say was: 'I shall get a place all right!' But that's it, you know—he never did. Too long in one shop. I heard by accident he was on the rocks; that's how I make him that allowance. But that's the sort of hopeless little old chap he is—no idea of himself. Cats! Why not? I'll take his old cats on; don't you let him worry about that. I'll see to his bird, too. If I can't give 'em a better time than ever they have here, it'll be funny!" And, looking round the little empty room, he again uttered that profound chuckle: "Why, he was with us at the Harmony thirty years—that's time, you know; I made my fortune in it."

"I'm sure," I said, "it'll be a great relief to him."

"Oh! Ah! That's all right. You come down to my place"—he handed me a card: 'Mr. Cyril Porteous Jackson, Ultima Thule, Wimbledon'— "and see how I fix 'em up. But if he's really going to kick it, I'd like to have a look at the little old chap, just for old times' sake."

We went, as quietly as Mr. Jackson's bright boots would permit, into his room, where the landlady was sitting gazing angrily at the cats. She went out without noise, flouncing her head as much as to say: "Well, now you can see what I have to go through, sitting up here. I never get out."

Our little old friend was still in that curious stupor. He seemed unconscious, but his blue eyes were not closed, staring brightly out before them at things we did not see. With his silvery hair and his flushed frailty, he had an unearthly look. After standing perhaps three minutes at the foot of the bed, Mr. Jackson whispered:

"Well, he does look queer. Poor little old chap! You tell him from me I'll look after his cats and bird; he needn't worry. And now, I think I won't keep the car. Makes me feel a bit throaty, you know. Don't move; he might come to."

And, leaning all the weight of his substantial form on those bright and creaking toes, he made his way to the door, flashed at me a diamond ring, whispered hoarsely: "So long! That'll be all right!" and vanished. And soon I heard the whirring of his car and just saw the top of his shiny hat travelling down the little street.

Some time I sat on there, wanting to deliver that message. An uncanny vigil in the failing light, with those five cats—yes, five at least—lying or sitting against the walls, staring like sphinxes at their motionless protector. I could not make out whether it was he in his stupor with his bright eyes that fascinated them, or the bullfinch perched on his pillow, who they knew perhaps might soon be in their power. I was glad when the landlady came up and I could leave the message with her.

When she opened the door to me next day at six o'clock I knew that he was gone. There was about her that sorrowful, unmistakable importance, that peculiar mournful excitement, which hovers over houses where death has entered.

"Yes," she said, "he went this morning. Never came round after you left. Would you like to see him?"

We went up.

He lay, covered with a sheet, in the darkened room. The landlady pulled the window-curtains apart. His face, as white now almost as his silvery head, had in the sunlight a radiance like that of a small, bright angel gone to sleep. No growth of hair, such as comes on most dead faces, showed on those frail cheeks that were now smooth and lineless as porcelain. And on the sheet above his chest the bullfinch sat, looking into his face.

The landlady let the curtains fall, and we went out.

"I've got the cats in here"—she pointed to the room where Mr. Jackson and I had talked—"all ready for that gentleman when he sends. But that little bird, I don't know what to do; he won't let me catch him, and there he sits. It makes me feel all funny."

It had made me feel all funny, too.

"He hasn't left the money for his funeral. Dreadful, the way he never thought about himself. I'm glad I kept him, though." And, not to my astonishment, she suddenly began to cry.

A wire was sent to Mr. Jackson, and on the day of the funeral I went down to "Ultima Thule," Wimbledon, to see if he had carried out his promise.

He had. In the grounds, past the vinery, an outhouse had been cleaned and sanded, with cushions placed at intervals against the wall, and a little trough of milk. Nothing could have been more suitable or luxurious.

"How's that?" he said. "I've done it thoroughly." But I noticed that he looked a little glum.

"The only thing," he said, "is the cats. First night they seemed all right; and the second, there were three of 'em left. But to-day the gardener tells me there's not the ghost of one anywhere. It's not for want of feeding. They've had tripe, and liver, and milk—as much as ever they liked. And cod's heads, you know—they're very fond of them. I must say it's a bit of a disappointment to me."

As he spoke, a sandy cat which I perfectly remembered, for it had only half of its left ear, appeared in the doorway, and stood, crouching, with its green eyes turned on us; then, hearing Mr. Jackson murmur, "Puss, puss!" it ran for its life, slinking almost into the ground, and vanished among some shrubs.

Mr. Jackson sighed. "Perversity of the brutes!" he said. He led me back to the house through a conservatory full of choice orchids. A gilt bird-cage was hanging there, one of the largest I had ever seen, replete with every luxury the heart of bird could want.

"Is that for the bullfinch?" I asked him.

"Oh!" he said; "didn't you know? The little beggar wouldn't let himself be caught, and the second morning, when they went up, there he lay on the old chap's body, dead. I thought it was very touchin'. But I kept the cage hung up for you to see that I should have given him a good time here. Oh, yes, 'Ultima Thule' would have done him well!"

And from a bright leather case Mr. Jackson offered me a cigar.

The question I had long been wishing to ask him slipped out of me then:

"Do you mind telling me why you called your house 'Ultima Thule?'"

"Why?" he said. "Found it on the gate. Think it's rather *distingué*, don't you?" and he uttered his profound chuckle.

"First-rate. The whole place is the last word in comfort."

"Very good of you to say so," he said. "I've laid out a goodish bit on it. A man must have a warm corner to end his days in. 'Ultima Thule,' as you say—it isn't bad. There's success about it, somehow."

And with that word in my ears, and in my eyes a vision of the little old fellow in his "Ultima Thule," with the bullfinch lying dead on a heart that had never known success, I travelled back to town.

[*1914*]

COURAGE

AT that time (said Ferrand) I was in poverty. Not the kind of poverty that goes without dinner, but the sort that goes without breakfast, lunch, and dinner, and exists as it can on bread and tobacco. I lived in one of those fourpenny lodging-houses, Westminster way. Three, five, seven beds in a room; if you pay regularly, you keep your own bed; if not, they put someone else there who will certainly leave you a memento of himself. It's not the foreigners' quarter; they are nearly all English, and drunkards. Three-quarters of them don't eat—can't; they have no capacity for solid food. They drink and drink. They're not worth wasting your money on—cab-runners, newspaper-boys, sellers of laces, and what you call sandwich-men; three-fourths of them brutalised beyond the power of recovery. What can you expect? They just live to scrape enough together to keep their souls in their bodies; they have no time or strength to think of anything but that. They come back at night and fall asleep—and how dead that sleep is! No, they never eat—just a bit of bread; the rest is drink!

There used to come to that house a little Frenchman, with a yellow, crow's-footed face; not old either, about thirty. But his life had been hard—no one comes to these houses if life is soft, especially no Frenchman; a Frenchman hates to leave his country. He came to shave us—charged a penny; most of us forgot to pay him, so that in all he shaved about three for a penny. He went to others of these houses—this gave him his income—he kept the little shop next door, too, but he never sold anything. How he worked! He also went to one of your Public Institutions; this was not so profitable, for there he was paid a penny for ten shaves. He used to say to me, moving his tired fingers like little yellow sticks: " Pff! I slave! To gain a penny, friend, I'm spending fourpence. What would you have? One must nourish oneself to have the strength to shave ten people for a penny." He was like an ant, running round and round in his little hole, without any chance but just to live; and always in hopes of saving enough to take him back to France, and set him up there. We had a liking for each other. He was the only one, in fact—except a sandwich-man who had been an actor, and was very intelligent, when he wasn't drunk—the only one in all that warren who had ideas. He was fond of pleasure and loved his music-hall—must have gone at least twice a year, and was always talking of it. He had little knowledge of its joys, it's true—hadn't the money for that, but his intentions were good. He used to keep me till the last, and shave me slowly.

"This rests me," he would say. It was amusement for me, too, for I had got into the habit of going for days without opening my lips. It's only a man here and there one can talk with; the rest only laugh; you seem to them a fool, a freak—something that should be put into a cage or tied by the leg.

"Yes," the little man would say, "when I came here first I thought I should soon go back, but now I'm not so sure. I'm losing my illusions. Money has wings, but it's not to *me* it flies. Believe me, friend, I am shaving my soul into these specimens. And how unhappy they are, poor creatures; how they must suffer! Drink! you say. Yes, that saves them—they get a little happiness from that. Unfortunately, I haven't the constitution for it—here." And he would show me where he had no constitution. "You, too, comrade, you don't seem to be in luck; but then, you're young. Ah, well, *faut être philosophe*—but imagine what kind of a game it is in this climate, especially if you come from the South!"

When I went away, which was as soon as I had nothing left to pawn, he gave me money—there's no question of lending in those houses: if a man parts with money he gives it; and lucky if he's not robbed into the bargain. There are fellows there who watch for a new pair of shoes, or a good overcoat, profit by their wakefulness as soon as the other is asleep, and promptly disappear. There's no morality in the face of destitution—it needs a man of iron, and these are men of straw. But one thing I will say of the low English—they are not bloodthirsty, like the low French and Italians.

Well, I got a job as fireman on a steamer, made a tour tramping, and six months later I was back again. The first morning I saw the Frenchman. It was shaving-day; he was more like an ant than ever, working away with all his legs and arms; a little yellower, and perhaps more wrinkled.

"Ah!" he called out to me in French, "there you are—back again.
I knew you'd come. Wait till I've finished with this specimen—I've
a lot to talk about."

We went into the kitchen, a big stone-floored room, with tables
for eating—and sat down by the fire. It was January, but, summer or
winter, there's always a fire burning in that kitchen.

"So," he said, "you have come back? No luck? Eh! Patience! A few
more days won't kill you at your age. What fogs, though! You see, I'm
still here, but my comrade, Pigon, is dead. You remember him—the
big man with black hair who had the shop down the street. Amiable
fellow, good friend to me; and married. Fine woman his wife—a
little ripe, seeing she has had children, but of good family. He died
suddenly of heart disease. Wait a bit; I'll tell you about that ...

"It was not long after you went away, one fine day in October, when
I had just finished with these specimens here, and was taking my coffee
in the shop, and thinking of that poor Pigon—dead then just three
days—when *pom!* comes a knock, and there is Madame Pigon! Very
calm—a woman of good family, well brought up, well made—fine
woman. But the cheeks pale, and the eyes so red, poor soul.

"'Well, Madame,' I asked her, 'what can I do for you?'

"It seems this poor Pigon died bankrupt; there was not a cent in
the shop. He was two days in his grave, and the bailiffs in already.

"'Ah, Monsieur!' she says to me, 'what am I to do?'

"'Wait a bit, Madame!' I get my hat and go back to the shop with
her.

"What a scene! Two bailiffs, who would have been the better
for a shave, sitting in a shop before the basins; and everywhere, *ma
foi*, everywhere, children. Tk! Tk! A little girl of ten, very like her
mother; two little boys with little trousers, and one with nothing but
a chemise; and others—two, quite small, all rolling on the floor; and
what a horrible noise!—all crying, all but the little girl, fit, to break
themselves in two. The bailiffs seemed perplexed. It was enough to
make one weep! Seven! some quite small! That poor Pigon, I had no
idea he was so good a rabbit!

"The bailiffs behaved very well.

"'Well,' said the biggest, 'you can have four-and-twenty hours to
find this money; my mate can camp out here in the shop—we don't
want to be hard on you!

"I helped Madame to soothe the children.

"'If I had the money,' I said, 'it should be at your service, Madame—in each well-born heart there should exist humanity; but I have no money. Try and think whether you have no friends to help you.'

"'Monsieur,' she answered, 'I have none. Have I had time to make friends—I, with seven children?'

"'But in France, Madame?'

"'None, Monsieur. I have quarrelled with my family; and reflect—it is now seven years since we came to England, and then only because no one would help us.' That seemed to me bad, but what could I do? I could only say:

"'Hope always, Madame—trust in me!'

"I went away. All day long I thought how calm she was—magnificent! And I kept saying to myself: 'Come, tap your head! tap your head! Something must be done!' But nothing came.

"The next morning it was my day to go to that sacred Institution, and I started off still thinking what on earth could be done for the poor woman; it was as if the little ones had got hold of my legs and were dragging at me. I arrived late, and, to make up time, I shaved them as I have never shaved them; a hot morning—I perspired! Ten for a penny! Ten for a penny! I thought of that, and of the poor woman. At last I finished and sat down. I thought to myself: 'It's too strong! Why do you do it? It's stupid! You are wasting yourself!' And then, my idea came to me! I asked for the manager.

"'Monsieur,' I said, 'it is impossible for me to come here again.'

"'What do you mean?' says he.

"'I have had enough of your—"ten for a penny"—I am going to get married; I can't afford to come here any longer. I lose too much flesh for the money.'

"'What?' he says, 'you're a lucky man if you can afford to throw away your money like this!'

"'Throw away my money! Pardon, Monsieur, but look at me'—I was still very hot—'for every penny I make I lose threepence, not counting the boot leather to and fro. While I was still a bachelor, Monsieur, it was my own affair—I could afford these extravagances; but now—it must finish—I have the honour, Monsieur!'

"I left him, and walked away. I went to the Pigons' shop. The bailiff was still there—Pfui! He must have been smoking all the time.

"'I can't give them much longer,' he said to me.

"'It is of no importance,' I replied; and I knocked, and went into the back room.

"The children were playing in the corner, that little girl, a heart of gold, watching them like a mother; and Madame at the table with a pair of old black gloves on her hands. My friend, I have never seen such a face—calm, but so pale, so frightfully discouraged, so overwhelmed. One would say she was waiting for her death. It was bad, it was bad—with the winter coming on!

"'Good morning, Madame,' I said. 'What news? Have you been able to arrange anything?'

"'No, Monsieur. And you?'

"'No!' And I looked at her again—a fine woman; ah! a fine woman.

"'But,' I said, 'an idea has come to me this morning. Now, what would you say if I asked you to marry me? It might possibly be better than nothing.'

"She regarded me with her black eyes, and answered:

"'But willingly, Monsieur!' and then, comrade, but not till then, she cried."

The little Frenchman stopped, and stared at me hard.

"H'm!" I said at last, "you have courage!"

He looked at me again; his eyes were troubled, as if I had paid him a bad compliment.

"You think so?" he said at last, and I saw that the thought was gnawing at him, as if I had turned the light on some desperate, dark feeling in his heart.

"Yes!" he said, taking his time, while his good yellow face wrinkled and wrinkled, and each wrinkle seemed to darken:

"I was afraid of it even when I did it. Seven children!" Once more he looked at me: "And since!—sometimes—sometimes—I could——" He broke off, then burst out again:

"Life is hard! What would you have? I knew her husband. Could I leave her to the streets?"

[1904]

THE BRIGHT SIDE

A LITTLE Englishwoman, married to a German, had dwelt with him eighteen years in humble happiness and the district of Putney, where her husband worked in the finer kinds of leather.

He was a harmless, busy little man with the gift for turning his hand to anything, which is bred into the peasants of the Black Forest, who on their upland farms make all the necessaries of daily life—their coarse linen from home-grown flax, their leather gear from the hides of their beasts, their clothes from the wool thereof, their furniture from the pine logs of the forest, their bread from home-grown flour milled in simple fashion and baked in the home-made ovens, their cheese from the milk of their own goats. Why he had come to England he probably did not remember—it was so long ago; but he would still know why he had married Dora, the daughter of the Putney carpenter, she being, as it were, salt of the earth: one of those Cockney women, deeply sensitive beneath a well-nigh impermeable mask of humour and philosophy, who quite unselfconsciously are always doing things for others. In their little grey Putney house they had dwelt those eighteen years, without perhaps ever having had time to move, though they had often had the intention of doing so for the sake of the children, of whom they had three, a boy and two girls. Mrs. Gerhardt—as I will call her, for her husband had a very German name, and there is more in a name than Shakespeare dreamed of—Mrs. Gerhardt was a little woman with large hazel eyes and dark crinkly hair, in which there were already a few threads of grey when the war broke out. Her boy David, the eldest, was fourteen at that date, and her girls, Minnie and Violet, were eight and five, rather pretty children, especially the little one. Gerhardt, perhaps because he was so handy, had never risen. His firm regarded him as indispensable and paid him fair wages, but he had

no "push," having the craftsman's temperament, and employing his
spare time in little neat jobs for his house and his neighbours, which
brought him no return. They made their way, therefore, without
that provision for the future which necessitates the employment
of one's time for one's own ends. But they were happy, and had
no enemies; and each year saw some mild improvements in their
studiously clean house and tiny back garden. Mrs. Gerhardt, who was
cook, seamstress, washerwoman, besides being wife and mother, was
almost notorious in that street of semi-detached houses for being at
the disposal of anyone in sickness or trouble. She was not strong in
body, for things had gone wrong when she bore her first, but her
spirit had that peculiar power of seeing things as they were, and yet
refusing to be dismayed, which so embarrasses Fate. She saw her
husband's defects clearly, and his good qualities no less distinctly—
they never quarrelled. She gauged her children's characters, too, with
an admirable precision, which left, however, loopholes of wonder as
to what they would become.

The outbreak of the war found them on the point of going to
Margate for Bank Holiday, an almost unparalleled event; so that the
importance of the world catastrophe was brought home to them
with a vividness which would otherwise have been absent from folk
so simple, domestic, and far-removed from that atmosphere in which
the egg of war is hatched. Over the origin and merits of the struggle,
beyond saying to each other several times that it was a dreadful thing,
Mr. and Mrs. Gerhardt held but one little conversation, lying in their
iron bed with an immortal brown eiderdown, patterned with red
wriggles, over them. They agreed that it was a cruel, wicked thing
to invade "that little Belgium," and there left a matter which seemed
to them a mysterious and insane perversion of all they had hitherto
been accustomed to think of as life. Reading their papers—a daily
and a weekly, in which they had as much implicit faith as a million
other readers—they were soon duly horrified by the reports therein
of "Hun" atrocities; so horrified that they would express their
condemnation of the Kaiser and his militarism as freely as if they
had been British subjects. It was, therefore, with an uneasy surprise
that they began to find these papers talking of "the Huns at large in
our midst," of "spies," and the national danger of "nourishing such
vipers." They were deeply conscious of not being "vipers," and such

sayings began to awaken in both their breasts a humble sense of injustice, as it were. This was more acute in the breast of little Mrs Gerhardt, because, of course, the shafts were directed not at her, but at her husband. She knew her husband so well, knew him incapable of anything but homely kindly busyness, and that he should be lumped into the category of "Huns" and "spies" and tarred with the brush of mass hatred amazed and stirred her indignation, or would have, if her Cockney temperament had allowed her to take it very seriously. As for Gerhardt, he became extremely silent, so that it was ever more and more difficult to tell what he was feeling. The patriotism of the newspapers took a considerable time to affect the charity of the citizens of Putney, and so long as no neighbour showed signs of thinking that little Gerhardt was a monster and a spy, it was fairly easy for Mrs. Gerhardt to sleep at night, with the feeling that the remarks in the papers were not really intended for Gerhardt and herself. But she noticed that her man had given up reading them and would push them away, if, in the tiny sitting-room with the heavily-flowered walls, they happened to rest beside him. He had perhaps a closer sense of impending Fate than she. The boy, David, went to his first work, and the girls to their school, and so things dragged on through that first long war winter and spring. Mrs. Gerhardt, in the intervals of doing everything, knitted socks for "our poor cold boys in the trenches," but Gerhardt no longer sought out little jobs to do in the houses of his neighbours. Mrs. Gerhardt thought that he "fancied" they would not like it. It was early in that spring that she took a deaf aunt to live with them, the wife of her mother's brother, no blood-relation, but the poor woman had nowhere else to go; so David was put to sleep on the horsehair sofa in the sitting-room because she "couldn't refuse the poor thing." And then, of an April afternoon, while she was washing the household sheets, her neighbour, Mrs. Clirehugh, a little spare woman, all eyes, cheekbones, hair and decision, came in breathless and burst out:

"Oh! Mrs. Gerhardt, 'ave you 'eard? They've sunk the *Loositania*! Has I said to Will: Isn't it horful?"

Mrs. Gerhardt, her round arms dripping soapsuds, answered:

"What a dreadful thing! The poor drowning people! Dear! Oh, dear!"

"Oh! those Huns! I'd shoot the lot, I would!"

"They *are* wicked!" Mrs. Gerhardt echoed: "that was a dreadful thing to do!"

But it was not till Gerhardt came in at five o'clock, white as a sheet, that she perceived how this catastrophe affected them.

"I have been called a German," were the first words he uttered; "Dollee, I have been called a German."

"Well, so you are, my dear," said Mrs. Gerhardt.

"You do not see," he answered, with a heat and agitation which surprised her. "I tell you this *Lusitania* will finish our business. They will have me. They will take me away from you all. Already the papers have: 'Intern all the Huns.'" He sat down at the kitchen table and buried his face in hands still grimy from his leather work. Mrs. Gerhardt stood beside him, her eyes unnaturally big.

"But, Max," she said, "what has it to do with you? You couldn't help it, Max!"

Gerhardt looked up; his white face, broad in the brow and tapering to a thin chin, seemed distraught.

"What do they care for that? Is my name Max Gerhardt? What do they care if I hate the war? I am a German. That's enough. You will see."

"Oh!" murmured Mrs. Gerhardt, "they won't be so unjust."

Gerhardt reached up and caught her chin in his hand, and for a moment those two pairs of eyes gazed, straining, into each other. Then he said:

"I don't want to be taken, Dollee. What shall I do away from you and the children? I don't want to be taken, Dollee."

Mrs. Gerhardt, with a feeling of terror and a cheerful smile, answered:

"You mustn't go fancyin' things, Max. I'll make you a nice cup of tea. Cheer up, old man! Look on the bright side!"

But Gerhardt lapsed into the silence which of late she had begun to dread.

That night some shop windows were broken, some German names effaced. The Gerhardts had no shop, no name painted up, and they escaped. In Press and Parliament the cry against "the Huns in our midst" rose with a fresh fury; but, for the Gerhardts, the face of Fate was withdrawn. Gerhardt went to his work as usual, and their laborious and quiet existence remained undisturbed; nor could Mrs.

Gerhardt tell whether her "man's" ever-deepening silence was due to his "fancying things" or to the demeanour of his neighbours and fellow-workmen. One would have said that he, like the derelict aunt, was deaf, so difficult to converse with had he become. His length of sojourn in England and his value to his employers, for he had real skill, had saved him for the time being; but, behind the screen, Fate twitched her grinning chaps.

Not till the howl which followed some air raids in 1916 did they take off Gerhardt, with a variety of other elderly men, whose crime it was to have been born in Germany. They did it suddenly, and perhaps it was as well, for a prolonged sight of his silent misery must have upset his family till they would have been unable to look on that bright side of things which Mrs. Gerhardt had, as it were, always up her sleeve. When, in charge of a big and sympathetic constable, he was gone, taking all she could hurriedly get together for him, she hastened to the police station. They were friendly to her there—she must cheer up, 'e'd be all right, she needn't worry. Ah! she could go down to the 'Ome Office, if she liked, and see what could be done. But they 'eld out no 'ope! Mrs. Gerhardt waited till the morrow, having the little Violet in bed with her, and crying quietly into her pillow; then, putting on her Sunday best, she went down to a building in Whitehall, larger than any she had ever entered. Two hours she waited, sitting unobtrusive, with big, anxious eyes, and a line between her brows. At intervals of half an hour she would get up and ask the messenger cheerfully: "I 'ope they haven't forgotten me, sir. Perhaps you'd see to it." And because she was cheerful the messenger took her under his protection, and answered:

"All right, Missis. They're very busy, but *I'll* wangle you in some'ow."

When at length she was "wangled" into the presence of a grave gentleman in eye-glasses, realisation of the utter importance of this moment overcame her so that she could not speak.

"Oh! dear," she thought, while her heart fluttered like a bird— "he'll never understand; I'll never be able to make him." She saw her husband buried under the dead leaves of despair; she saw her children getting too little food; the deaf aunt, now bedridden, neglected in the new pressure of work which must fall on the only bread-winner left. And choking a little, she said:

"I'm sure I'm very sorry to take up your time, sir; but my 'usband's been taken to the Palace; and we've been married over twenty years, and he's been in England twenty-five; and he's a very good man and a good workman; and I thought perhaps they didn't understand that; and we've got three children and a relation that's bedridden. And of course, we understand that the Germans have been very wicked; Gerhardt always said that himself. And it isn't as if he was a spy; so I thought if you could do something for us, sir, I being English myself."

The gentleman, looking past her at the wall, answered wearily:

"Gerhardt—I'll look into it. We have to do very hard things, Mrs. Gerhardt."

Little Mrs. Gerhardt, with big eyes almost starting out of her head, for she was no fool, and perceived that this was the end, said eagerly:

"Of course I know that there's a big outcry, and the papers are askin' for it; but the people in our street don't mind 'im, sir. He's always done little things for them; so I thought perhaps you might make an exception in his case."

She noticed that the gentleman's lips tightened at the word outcry, and that he was looking at her now.

"His case was before the Committee, no doubt; but I'll inquire. Good-morning."

Mrs. Gerhardt, accustomed to not being troublesome, rose; a tear rolled down her cheek and was arrested by her smile.

"Thank you sir, I'm sure. Good-morning, sir."

And she went out. Meeting the messenger in the corridor, and hearing his: "Well, Missis?" she answered: "I don't know. I must look on the bright side. Good-bye, and thank you for your trouble." And she turned away feeling as if she had been beaten all over.

The bright side on which she looked did not include the return to her of little Gerhardt, who was duly detained for the safety of the country. Obedient to economy, and with a dim sense that her favourite papers were in some way responsible for this, she ceased to take them in, and took in sewing instead. It had become necessary to do so, for the allowance she received from the Government was about a quarter of Gerhardt's weekly earnings. In spite of its inadequacy it was something, and she felt she must be grateful.

But, curiously enough, she could not forget that she was English, and it seemed strange to her that, in addition to the grief caused by separation from her husband, from whom she had never been parted, not even for a night, she should now be compelled to work twice as hard and eat half as much because that husband had paid her country the compliment of preferring it to his own. But, after all, many other people had much worse trouble to grieve over, so she looked on the bright side of all this, especially on those days once a week when alone, or accompanied by the little Violet, she visited that Palace where she had read in her favourite journals to her great comfort that her husband was treated like a prince. Since he had no money, he was in what they called "the battalion," and their meetings were held in the bazaar, where things that "the princes" made were exposed for sale. Here Mr. and Mrs. Gerhardt would stand in front of some doll, some blotting-book, calendar, or walking-stick, which had been fashioned by one of "the princes." There they would hold each other's hands and try to imagine themselves unsurrounded by other men and wives, while the little Violet would stray and return to embrace her father's leg spasmodically. Standing there, Mrs. Gerhardt would look on the bright side, and explain to Gerhardt how well everything was going, and he mustn't fret about them, and how kind the police were, and how auntie asked after him, and Minnie would get a prize; and how he oughtn't to mope but eat his food, and look on the bright side. And Gerhardt would smile the smile which went into her heart just like a sword, and say:

"All right, Dollee. I'm getting on fine." Then, when the whistle blew and he had kissed little Violet, they would be quite silent, looking at each other. And she would say in a voice so matter-of-fact that it could have deceived no one:

"Well, I must go now. Good-bye, old man."

And he would say:

"Good-bye, Dollee. Kiss me."

They would kiss, and holding little Violet's hand very hard, she would hurry away in the crowd, taking care not to look back for fear she might suddenly lose sight of the bright side. But as the months went on, became a year, eighteen months, two years, and still she went weekly to see her "prince" in his Palace, that visit became for her the hardest experience of all her hard week's doings. For she was a realist, as well as a heroine, and she could see the lines of despair not only in her man's heart, but in his face. For a long time he had not said:

"I'm getting on fine, Dollee." His face had a beaten look, his figure had wasted, he complained of his head.

"It's so noisy," he would say constantly; "oh! it's so noisy, never a quiet moment—never alone—never—never—never. And not enough to eat; it's all reduced now, Dollee."

She learned to smuggle food into his hands, but it was very little, for they had not enough at home either, with the price of living ever going up and her depleted income ever stationary. They had—her "man" told her—made a fuss in the papers about their being fed like turkey-cocks, while the "Huns" were sinking the ships. Gerhardt, always a spare little man, had lost eighteen pounds. She, naturally well-covered, was getting thin herself, but that she did not notice, too busy all day long, and too occupied in thinking of her "man." To watch him week by week, more hopeless as the months dragged on, was an acute torture, to disguise which was torture even more acute. She had long seen that there *was* no bright side, but if she admitted that, she knew she would go down; so she did not. And she carefully kept from Gerhardt such matters as David's overgrowing his strength because she could not feed him properly; the completely bedridden nature of auntie; and, worse than these, the growing coldness and unkindness of her neighbours. Perhaps they did not mean to be unkind, perhaps they did, for it was not in their nature to withstand the pressure of mass sentiment, the continual personal discomfort of having to stand in queues, the fear of air raids, the cumulative indignation caused by stories of atrocities, true and untrue. In spite of her record of kindliness towards them, she became tarred with the brush at last, for her nerves had given way once or twice, and she had said it was a shame to keep her "man" like that gettin' iller and iller, who had never done a thing. Even her reasonableness—and she was very reasonable—succumbed to the strain of that weekly sight of him, till she could no longer allow for the difficulties which Mrs. Clirehugh assured her the Government had to deal with. Then one day she used the words "fair play," and at once it became current that she had "German sympathies." From that time on she was somewhat doomed. Those who had received kindnesses from her were foremost in showing her coldness, being wounded in their self-esteem. To have received little benefits, such as being nursed when they were sick, from one who had "German sympathies" was too much for the pride which is in every human being, however humble an inhabitant of Putney. Mrs. Gerhardt's Cockney spirit could support this for herself, but she could not bear it for her children. David came home with a black eye and would not say why he had got it. Minnie missed her prize at school, though she had clearly won it. That was just after the last German offensive began; but Mrs. Gerhardt refused to see that this was any reason. Little Violet twice put the heart-rending question to her: "Aren't I English, mummy?"

She was answered: "Yes, my dear, of course."

But the child obviously remained unconvinced in her troubled mind.

And then they took David for the British Army. It was that which so upset the apple-cart in Mrs. Gerhardt that she broke out to her last friend, Mrs. Clirehugh:

"I do think it's hard, Eliza. They take his father and keep him there for a dangerous Hun, year after year like that; and then they take his boy for the army to fight against him. And how I'm to get on without him I don't know."

Little Mrs. Clirehugh, who was Scotch, with a Gloucestershire accent, replied:

"Well, we've got to beat them. They're such a wicked lot. I daresay it's 'ard on you, but we've got to beat them."

"But we never did nothing," cried Mrs. Gerhardt; "it isn't us that's wicked. We never wanted the war; it's nothing but ruin to him. They did ought to let me have my man or my boy, one or the other."

"You should 'ave some feeling for the Government, Dora; they 'ave to do 'ard things."

Mrs. Gerhardt, with a quivering face, had looked at her friend.

"I have," she said at last in a tone which implanted in Mrs. Clirehugh's heart the feeling that Dora was "bitter."

She could not forget it; and she would flaunt her head at any mention of her former friend. It was a blow to Mrs. Gerhardt, who had now no friends, except the deaf and bedridden aunt, to whom all things were the same, war or no war, Germans or no Germans, so long as she was fed.

About then it was that the tide turned, and the Germans began to know defeat. Even Mrs. Gerhardt, who read the papers no longer, learned it daily, and her heart relaxed; that bright side began to reappear a little. She felt they could not feel so hardly toward her "man" now as when they were all in fear; and perhaps the war would be over before her boy went out. But Gerhardt puzzled her. He did not brighten up. The iron seemed to have entered his soul too deeply. And one day, in the bazaar, passing an open doorway, Mrs. Gerhardt had a glimpse of why. There, stretching before her astonished eyes, was a great, as it were, encampment of brown blankets, slung and looped up anyhow, dividing from each other countless sordid beds, which were almost touching, and a whiff of huddled humanity came out to her keen nostrils, and a hum of sound to her ears. So that was where her "man" had dwelt these thirty months, in that dirty, crowded, noisy place with dirty-looking men, such as those she could see lying on the beds, or crouching by the side of them over their work. He had kept neat somehow, at least on the days when she came to him—but *that* was where he lived! Alone again (for she no longer brought the little Violet to see her German father), she grieved all the way home. Whatever happened to him now, even if she got him back, she knew he would never quite get over it.

And then came the morning when she came out of her door like the other inhabitants of Putney, at sound of the maroons, thinking it was an air raid; and, catching the smile on the toothless mouth of one of her old neighbours, hearing the cheers of the boys in the school round the corner, knew that it was Peace. Her heart overflowed then, and, withdrawing hastily, she sat down in a shiny chair in her empty parlour. Her face crumpled suddenly, the tears came welling forth, and she cried, alone in the little cold room. She cried from relief and utter thankfulness. It was over—over at last! The long waiting—the long misery—the yearning for her "man" —the grieving for all those poor boys in the mud and the dreadful shell-holes and the fighting, the growing terror of anxiety for her own boy—over, all over! Now they would let Max out, now David would come back from the army; and people would not be unkind and spiteful to her and the children any more!

For all she was a Cockney, hers was a simple soul, associating peace with goodwill. Drying her tears, she stood up, and in the little cheap mirror above the empty grate looked at her face. It was lined, and she was grey; for more than two years her "man" had not seen her without her hat. Whatever would he say? And she rubbed and rubbed her cheeks, trying to smooth them out. Then her conscience smote her, and she ran upstairs to the back bed-room, where the deaf aunt lay. Taking up the amateur ear-trumpet which Gerhardt himself had made for "auntie," before he was taken away, she bawled into it:

"Peace, Auntie; it's Peace! Think of that. It's Peace!"

"What's that?" answered the deaf woman.

"It's Peace, Auntie, Peace!"

The dear lady roused herself a little, and some meaning came into the lack-lustre black eyes of her long, leathery face. "You don't say," she said in her wooden voice. "I'm so hungry, Dolly; isn't it time for my dinner?"

"I was just goin' to get it, dearie," replied Mrs. Gerhardt, and hurried back downstairs with her brain teeming, to make the deaf woman's bowl of bread, pepper, salt and onions.

All that day and the next and the next she saw the bright side of things with almost dazzling clearness, waiting to visit her "prince" in his Palace. She found him in a strange and pitiful state of nerves. The news had produced too intense and varied emotions among those crowded thousands of men buried away from normal life so long. She spent all her hour and a half trying desperately to make him see the bright side, but he was too full of fears and doubts, and she went away smiling, but utterly exhausted. Slowly in the weeks which followed she learned that nothing was changed. In the fond hope that Gerhardt might be home now any day, she was taking care that his slippers and some clothes of David's were ready for him, and the hip bath handy for him to have a lovely hot wash. She had even bought a bottle of beer and some of his favourite pickle, saving the price out of her own food, and was taking in the paper again, letting bygones be bygones. But he did not come. And soon the paper informed her that the English prisoners were returning—many in wretched state, poor things, so that her heart bled for them, and made her fiercely angry with the cruel men who had treated them so; but it informed her too that, if the paper had its way, no "Huns" would be tolerated in this country for the future.

"Send them all back!" were the words it used. She did not realise at first that this applied to Gerhardt; but when she did she dropped the journal as if it had been a living coal of fire. Not let him come back to his home, and family, not let him stay, after all they'd done to him, and he never did anything to them! Not let him stay, but send him out to that dreadful country, which he had almost forgotten in these thirty years; and he with an English wife and children! In this new terror of utter dislocation the bright side so slipped from her that she was obliged to go out into the back garden in the dark, where a sou'westerly wind was driving the rain. There, lifting her eyes to the evening sky, she uttered her little moan. It couldn't be true; and yet, what they said in her paper had always turned out true, like the taking of Gerhardt away, and the reduction of his food. And the face of the gentleman in the building at Whitehall came before her out of the long past, with his lips tightening, and his words:

"We have to do very hard things, Mrs. Gerhardt." Why had they to do them? Her "man" had never done no harm to no one! A flood, bitter as sea water, surged in her, and seemed to choke her very being. Those gentlemen in the papers—why should they go on like that? Had they no hearts, no eyes to see the misery they brought to humble folk? 'I wish them nothing worse than what they've brought to him and me,' she thought wildly, 'nothing worse!'

The rain beat on her face, wetted her grey hair, cooled her eyeballs. 'I mustn't be spiteful,' she thought; and, bending down in the dark, she touched the glass of the tiny conservatory up against the warm kitchen wall, heated by the cunning hot-water pipe that her "man" had put there in his old handy days. Under it were one monthly rose, which still had blossoms, and some straggly small chrysanthemums. She had been keeping them for the feast when he came home; but if he wasn't to come, what should she do? She raised herself. Above the wet roofs, sky-rack was passing wild and dark, but in a cleared space one or two stars shone the brighter for the blackness below. 'I must look on the bright side,' she thought, 'or I can't bear myself.' And she went in to cook the porridge for the evening meal.

The winter passed for her in the most dreadful anxiety. "Repatriate the Huns!" That cry continued to spurt up in her paper like a terrible face seen in some recurrent nightmare; and each week that she went to visit Gerhardt brought solid confirmation to her terror. He was taking it hard, so that sometimes she was afraid that "something" was happening in him. This was the utmost she went towards defining what doctors might have diagnosed as incipient softening of the brain. He seemed to dread the prospect of being sent to his native country.

"I couldn't stick it, Dollee," he would say. "What should I do—whatever should I do? I haven't a friend. I haven't a spot to go to. I should be lost. I'm afraid, Dollee. How could you come out there, you and the children? I couldn't make a living for you. I couldn't make one for myself now."

And she would say: "Cheer up, old man. Look on the bright side. Think of the others." For, though those others were not precisely the bright side, the mental picture of their sufferings, all those poor "princes" and their families, some how helped her to bear her own. But he shook his head:

"No, I should never see you again."

"I'd follow you," she answered. "Never fear, Max, we'd work in the fields—me and the children. We'd get on somehow. Bear up, my dearie. It'll soon be over now. I'll stick to you, Max, never you fear. But they won't send you, they never will."

And then, like a lump of ice pressed on her breast, came the thought: 'But if they do! Auntie! My boy! My girls! However shall I manage if they do?'

Then long lists began to appear, and in great batches men were shovelled wholesale back to the country whose speech some of them had well-nigh forgotten. Gerhardt's name had not appeared yet. The lists were hung up the day after Mrs. Gerhardt's weekly visit, but she urged him if his name did appear to appeal against repatriation. It was with the greatest difficulty that she roused in him the energy to promise. "Look on the bright side, Max," she implored him. "You've got a son in the British Army; they'll never send you. They wouldn't be so cruel. Never say die, old man."

His name appeared, but was taken out, and the matter hung again in awful suspense, while the evil face of the recurrent nightmare confronted Mrs. Gerhardt out of her favourite journal. She read that journal again, because so far as in her gentle spirit lay, she hated it. It was slowly killing her "man," and all her chance of future happiness; she hated it, and read it every morning. To the monthly rose and straggly brown-red chrysanthemums in the tiny hothouse there had succeeded spring flowers—a few hardy January snowdrops, and one by one blue scillas, and pale daffodils called "angels' tears."

Peace tarried, but the flowers came up long before their time in their tiny hothouse against the kitchen flue. Then one wonderful day there came to Mrs. Gerhardt a strange letter, announcing that Gerhardt was coming home. He would not be sent to Germany— he was coming home! To-day, that very day—any moment he might be with her. When she received it, who had long received no letters save the weekly letters of her boy still in the army, she was spreading margarine on auntie's bread for breakfast, and, moved beyond all control, she spread it thick, wickedly, wastefully thick, then dropped the knife, sobbed, laughed, clasped her hands on her breast, and without rhyme or reason began singing, "Hark! the herald angels sing." The girls had gone to school already, auntie in the room above could not hear her, no one heard her, nor saw her drop suddenly into the wooden chair, and, with her bare arms stretched out one on either side of the plate of bread and margarine, cry her heart out against the clean white table. Coming home, coming home, coming home! The bright side! The white stars!

It was a quarter of an hour before she could trust herself to answer the knocking on the floor, which meant that auntie was missing her breakfast. Hastily she made the tea and went up. The woman's dim long face gleamed greedily when she saw how thick the margarine was spread; but little Mrs. Gerhardt said no word of the reason for that feast. She just watched her only friend eating it, while moisture still trickled out from her eyes on to her flushed cheeks, and the words still hummed in her brain:

> Peace on earth and mercy mild,
> Jesus Christ a little child.

Then, still speaking no word, she ran out and put clean sheets on her and her "man's" bed. She was on wires, she could not keep still, and all the morning she polished. About noon she went out into her garden, and from under the glass plucked every flower that grew there—snowdrops, scillas, "angels' tears," quite two dozen blossoms. She brought them into the parlour and opened its window wide. The sun was shining, and fell on the flowers strewn on the table, ready to be made into the nosegay of triumphant happiness. While she stood fingering them, delicately breaking half an inch off their stalks so that they should last the longer in water, she became conscious of someone on the pavement outside the window, and looking up saw Mrs. Clirehugh. The past, the sense of having been deserted by her friends, left her, and she called out:

"Come in, Eliza; look at my flowers!"

Mrs. Clirehugh came in; she was in black, her cheekbones higher, her hair looser, her eyes bigger. Mrs. Gerhardt saw tears starting from those eyes, wetting those high cheekbones, and cried out:

"Why, what's the matter, dear?"

Mrs. Clirehugh choked. "My baby!"

Mrs. Gerhardt dropped an "angel's tear" and went up to her.

"Whatever's happened?" she cried.

"Dead!" replied Mrs. Clirehugh. "Dead o' the influenza. 'E's to be buried to-day. I can't—I can't——" Wild choking stopped her utterance. Mrs. Gerhardt put an arm round her and drew her head on to her shoulder.

"I can't"—sobbed Mrs. Clirehugh "find any flowers. It's seein' yours made me cry."

"There, there!" cried Mrs. Gerhardt. "Have them. I'm sure you're welcome, dearie. Have them—I'm so sorry!"

"I don't know," choked Mrs. Clirehugh; "I 'aven't deserved them." Mrs. Gerhardt gathered up the flowers.

"Take them," she said. "I couldn't think of it. Your poor little baby. Take them! There, there, he's spared a lot of trouble. You must look on the bright side, dearie."

Mrs. Clirehugh tossed up her head.

"You're an angel, that's what *you* are!" And grasping the flowers, she hurried out, a black figure passing the window in the sunlight.

Mrs. Gerhardt stood above the emptied table, thinking:

"Poor dear—I'm glad she had the flowers. It was a mercy I didn't call out that Max was coming!" And from the floor she picked up the "angel's tear" she had dropped, and set it in a glass of water, where the sunlight fell. She was still gazing at it, pale, slender, lonely in that coarse tumbler, when she heard a knock on the parlour door and went to open it. There stood her "man," with a large brown-paper parcel in his hand. He stood quite still, his head down, the face very grey. She cried out: "Max!" but the thought flashed through her: "He knocked on the door! It's *his* door—he knocked on the door!"

"Dollee?" he said, with a sort of question in his voice.

She threw her arms round him, drew him into the room, and, shutting the door, looked hard into his face. Yes, it was his face, but in the eyes something wandered—lit up, went out, lit up.

"Dollee," he said again, and clutched her hand.

She strained him to her with a sob.

"I'm not well, Dollee," he murmured.

"No, of course not, my dearie man; but you'll soon be all right now—home again with me. Cheer up, cheer up!"

"I'm not well," he said again.

She caught the parcel out of his hand, and, taking the "angel's tear" from the tumbler, fixed it in his coat.

"Here's a spring flower for you, Max; out of your own little hothouse. You're home again; home again, my dearie. Auntie's upstairs, and the girls' be coming soon. And we'll have dinner."

"I'm not well, Dollee," he said.

Terrified by that reiteration, she drew him down on the little horsehair sofa, and sat on his knee. "You're home, Max; kiss me. There's my man!" and she rocked him to and fro against her, yearning yet fearing to look into his face and see that "something" wander there—light up, go out, light up. "Look, dearie," she said, "I've got some beer for you. You'd like a glass of beer?"

He made a motion of his lips, a sound that was like the ghost of a smack. It terrified her, so little life was there in it.

He clutched her close, and repeated feebly:

"Yes, all right in a day or two. They let me come—I'm not well, Dollee." He touched his head.

Straining him to her, rocking him, she murmured over and over again, like a cat purring to its kitten:

"It's all right, my dearie—soon be well—soon be well! We must look on the bright side—My man!"

[*1919*]

THE BLACK GODMOTHER

SITTING out on the lawn at tea with our friend and his retriever, we had been discussing those massacres of the helpless which had of late occurred, and wondering that they should have been committed by the soldiery of so civilised a State, when, in a momentary pause of our astonishment, our friend, who had been listening in silence, crumpling the drooping soft ear of his dog, looked up and said, "The cause of atrocities is generally the violence of Fear. Panic's at the back of most crimes and follies."

Knowing that his philosophical statements were always the result of concrete instance, and that he would not tell us what that instance was if we asked him—such being his nature—we were careful not to agree.

He gave us a look out of those eyes of his, so like the eyes of a mild eagle, and said abruptly: "What do you say to this, then? . . . I was out in the dog-days last year with this fellow of mine, looking for Osmunda, and stayed some days in a village—never mind the name. Coming back one evening from my tramp, I saw some boys stoning a mealy-coloured dog. I went up and told the young devils to stop it. They only looked at me in the injured way boys do, and one of them called out, 'It's mad, guv'nor!' I told them to clear off, and they took to their heels. The dog followed me. It was a young, leggy, mild-looking mongrel, cross—I should say—between a brown retriever and an Irish terrier. There was froth about its lips, and its eyes were watery; it looked indeed as if it might be in distemper. I was afraid of infection for this fellow of mine, and whenever it came too close shooed it away, till at last it slunk off altogether. Well, about nine o'clock, when I was settling down to write by the open window of my sitting-room—still daylight, and very quiet and warm—there began that most maddening sound, the barking of an unhappy dog.

I could do nothing with that continual 'Yap—yap!' going on, and it was too hot to shut the window; so I went out to see if I could stop it. The men were all at the pub, and the women just finished with their gossip; there was no sound at all but the continual barking of this dog, somewhere away out in the fields. I travelled by ear across three meadows, till I came on a hay-stack by a pool of water. There was the dog sure enough—the same mealy-coloured mongrel, tied to a stake, yapping, and making frantic little runs on a bit of rusty chain; whirling round and round the stake, then standing quite still, and shivering. I went up and spoke to it, but it backed into the hay-stack, and there it stayed shrinking away from me, with its tongue hanging out. It had been heavily struck by something on the head; the cheek was cut, one eye half-closed, and an ear badly swollen. I tried to get hold of it, but the poor thing was beside itself with fear. It snapped and flew round so that I had to give it up and sit down with this fellow here beside me to try and quiet it—a strange dog, you know, will generally form his estimate of you from the way it sees you treat another dog. I had to sit there quite half an hour before it would let me go up to it, pull the stake out, and lead it away. The poor beast, though it was so feeble from the blows it had received, was still half-frantic, and I didn't dare to touch it; and all the time I took good care that this fellow here didn't come too near. Then came the question what was to he done. There was no vet, of course, and I'd no place to put it except my sitting-room, which didn't belong to me. But, looking at its battered head, and its half-mad eyes, I thought: 'No trusting you with these bumpkins; you'll have to come in here for the night!' Well, I got it in, and heaped two or three of those hairy little red rugs landladies are so fond of, up in a corner, and got it on to them, and put down my bread and milk. But it wouldn't eat—its sense of proportion was all gone, fairly destroyed by terror. It lay there moaning, and every now and then it raised its head with a 'yap' of sheer fright, dreadful to hear, and bit the air, as if its enemies were on it again; and this fellow of mine lay in the opposite corner, with his head on his paw, watching it. I sat up for a long time with that poor beast, sick enough, and wondering how it had come to be stoned and kicked and battered into this state; and next day I made it my business to find out." Our friend paused, scanned us a little angrily, and then went on: "It had made its first appearance,

it seems, following a bicyclist. There are men, you know—save
the mark—who, when their beasts get ill or too expensive, jump
on their bicycles and take them for a quick run, taking care never
to look behind them. When they get back home they say: 'Hullo!
Where's Fido?' Fido is nowhere, and there's an end! Well, this poor
puppy gave up just as it got to our village; and, roaming about in
search of water, attached itself to a farm labourer. The man—with
excellent intentions, as he told me himself—tried to take hold of it,
but too abruptly, so that it was startled, and snapped at him. Whereon
he kicked it for a dangerous cur, and it went drifting back towards
the village, and fell in with the boys coming home from school. It
thought, no doubt, that they were going to kick it too, and nipped
one of them who took it by the collar. Thereupon they hullabalooed
and stoned it down the road to where I found them. Then I put in
my little bit of torture, and drove it away, through fear of infection
to my own dog. After that it seems to have fallen in with a man who
told me: 'Well, you see, he came sneakin' round my house, with the
children playin', and snapped at them when they went to stroke him,
so that they came running in to their mother, an' she called to me
in a fine takin' about a mad dog. I ran out with a shovel and gave
'im one, and drove him out. I'm sorry if he wasn't mad; he looked
it right enough. You can't be too careful with strange dogs.' Its next
acquaintance was an old stone-breaker, a very decent sort. 'Well!
you see,' the old man explained to me, 'the dog came smellin' round
my stones, an' it wouldn' come near, an' it wouldn' go away; it was
all froth and blood about the jaw, and its eyes glared green at me. I
thought to meself, bein' the dog-days—I don't like the look o' you,
you look funny! So I took a stone, an' got it here, just on the ear;
an' it fell over. And I thought to meself: Well, you've got to finish it,
or it'll go bitin' somebody, for sure! But when I come to it with my
hammer, the dog it got up—an' you know how it is when there's
somethin' you've 'alf killed, and you feel sorry, and yet you feel you
must finish it, an' you hit at it blind, you hit at it agen an' agen. The
poor thing, it wriggled and snapped, an' I was terrified it'd bite me,
an' some 'ow it got away.'" Again our friend paused, and this time we
dared not look at him.

"The next hospitality it was shown," he went on presently, "was
by a farmer, who, seeing it all bloody, drove it off, thinking it had

been digging up a lamb that he'd just buried. The poor homeless beast came sneaking back, so he told his men to get rid of it. Well, they got hold of it somehow—there was a hole in its neck that looked as if they'd used a pitchfork—and, mortally afraid of its biting them, but not liking, as they told me, to drown it, for fear the owner might come on them, they got a stake and a chain, and fastened it up, and left it in the water by the hay-stack where I found it. I had some conversation with that farmer. 'That's right,' he said, 'but who was to know? I couldn't have my sheep worried. The brute had blood on his muzzle. These curs do a lot of harm when they've once been blooded. You can't run risks.'" Our friend cut viciously at a dandelion with his stick. "Run risks!" he broke out suddenly. "That was it—from beginning to end of that poor beast's sufferings, fear! From that fellow on the bicycle, afraid of the worry and expense, as soon as it showed signs of distemper, to myself and the man with the pitchfork—not one of us, I daresay, would have gone out of our way to do it a harm. But we felt fear, and so—by the law of self-preservation, or whatever you like—it all began, till there the poor thing was, with a battered head and a hole in its neck, ravenous with hunger, and too distraught even to lap my bread and milk. Yes, there's something uncanny about a suffering animal—we sat watching it, and again we were afraid, looking at its eyes and the way it bit the air. Fear! It's the black godmother of all damnable things!"

Our friend bent down, crumpling and crumpling at his dog's ears. We, too, gazed at the ground, thinking of that poor lost puppy, and the horrible inevitability of all that happens, seeing men are what they are; thinking of all the foul doings in the world, whose black godmother is Fear.

"And what became of the poor dog?" one of us asked at last.

"When," said our friend slowly, "I'd had my fill of watching, I covered it with a rug, took this fellow away with me, and went to bed. There was nothing else to do. At dawn I was awakened by three dreadful cries—not like a dog's at all. I hurried down. There was the poor beast—wriggled out from under the rug—stretched on its side, dead. This fellow of mine had followed me in, and he went and sat down by the body. When I spoke to him he just looked round, and wagged his tail along the ground, but would not come away; and there he sit till it was buried, very interested but not sorry at all."

Our friend was silent, looking angrily at something in the distance.

And we, too, were silent, seeing in spirit that vigil of early morning: The thin, lifeless, sandy-coloured body, stretched on those red mats; and this black creature now lying at our feet—propped on its haunches like the dog in "The Death of Procris," patient, curious, ungrieved, staring down at it with his bright, interested eyes.

[*1912*]

PHILANTHROPY

MIST enwrapped Restington-on-Sea; not very thick, but exceedingly clammy. It decked the autumn trees in weirdness, cobwebbed the tamarisks, and compelled Henry Ivor to shut his window, excluding the faint hiss and rustle from the beach. He seldom wrote after tea without the accompaniment of fresh air, and was drowsing over his pen when his housekeeper entered.

"A couple to see you, sir; they came once before, when you was away."

Ivor blinked. "Well, show them in."

When the door was again opened a scent of whisky came in first, then a man, a woman, and a dog.

Ivor laid down his pen and rose; he had never seen any of them before, and immediately doubted whether he wanted to see any of them again. Never able, however, to be disagreeable at a moment's notice, he waited defensively. The man, who might have been thirty-five pale, warped, and thin, seemed to extract his face from the grip of nerves.

"Hearing you were down here, sir, and being in the printing trade, if you understand my meaning——"

Ivor nodded; he did not want to nod, but it seemed unavoidable and he looked at the woman. Her face was buttoned, the most expressionless he had ever seen.

"Well?" he said.

The man's lips, thin and down at one corner, writhed again.

"You being a well-known writer," he said, and the scent of whisky deepened.

Ivor thought: 'It wants courage to beg; it's damp too. Perhaps he's only primed himself.'

"Well" he said again.

"If you understand me," said the man, "I'm in a very delicate position. I expect you know Mr. Gloy—Charles Gloy—editor of Cribbage——"

"No," said Ivor. "But will you sit down?" And he placed two chairs.

The man and the woman sat down on their edges, the dog, too, sat on its edge! Ivor regarded it—a Schipperke—thinking:

"Did they bring their dog to undermine me?" As to that, it was the only kind of dog he did not like, but it looked damp and woeful.

"My brother works for Mr. Gloy," said the man; "so, being at Beachhampton—out of a job, if you understand my meaning—I brought my wife—you being a well-known philanthropist——"

Ivor nervously took out a cigarette, and nervously put it back.

"I don't know what I can do for you," he murmured.

"I'm one to speak the truth," resumed the man, "if you follow me——" And Ivor did—he followed on and on behind a wandering tale of printing, the war, ill-health. At last he said in despair:

"I really can't recommend people I know nothing about. What exactly do you want me to do?"

The woman's face seemed suddenly to lose a button, as if she were going to cry, but just then the dog whimpered; she took it up on her lap. Ivor thought:

'How much have I got on me?'

"The fact is, Mr. Ivor," said the man, "I'm broke to the world, if you understand my meaning. If once I could get back to London."

"What do you say, madam?"

The woman's mouth quivered and mumbled; Ivor stopped her with his hand.

"Well," he said, "I can give you enough to get up to London with, and a little over. But that's all, I'm afraid. And, forgive me, I'm very busy." He stood up. The man rose also.

"I don't want to say anything about my wife; you'll forgive my mentioning it, but there's not a lady in England that's her equal at makin' babies' slippers."

"Indeed!" said Ivor. "Well, here you are!" And he held out some pound notes. The man took the notes; one of his trouser-legs was pitiably patched.

"I'm sure I'm more than grateful——" he said; and looking at Ivor as if he expected to be contradicted, added: "I can't say better than that, can I?"

"No," said Ivor, and opened the door.

"I'll be ready to repay you as soon as ever I can—if you understand my meaning.'

"Yes," said Ivor. "Good-day! Good-day, Mrs.—! Goodbye, little dog!"

One by one the three passed him and went out into the mist. Ivor saw them trailing down the road, shut the outer door, returned to his chair, sighed profoundly, and took up his pen.

When he had written three pages, and it was getting too dusk to see, his housekeeper came in.

"There's a boy from the Black Cow, sir, come to say they want you down there."

"Want me?"

"Yes, sir. That couple—the boy says they don't know what to do with them. They gave your name as being a friend."

"Good Lord!"

"Yes, sir; and the landlord says they don't seem to know where they come from like."

"Heavens!" said Ivor. He got up, however, put on his overcoat, and went out.

In the lighted doorway of the Black Cow stood the landlord.

"Sorry to have troubled you, sir, but really I can't tell how to deal with these friends of yours."

Ivor frowned. "I only saw them for the first time this afternoon. I just gave them money to go up to London with. Are they drunk?"

"Drunk!" said the landlord. "Well, if I'd known the man was half gone when he came in—of course I'd never— As to the woman, she sits and smiles. I can't get them to budge, and it's early closin'——"

"Well," muttered Ivor, "let's look at them!" And he followed the landlord in.

On the window-seat in the bar parlour those two were sitting, with mugs beside them, and the dog asleep on the feet of the woman, whose lips were unbuttoned in a foolish smile. Ivor looked at the man; his face was blank and beatific. Specimens of a damp and doleful world, they now seemed almost blissful.

"Mist' Ivor," he said. "Thought so—I'm not tight——"

"Yes," said Ivor, "but I thought you wanted to go up to London.

The station's not half a mile."

"Cert'nly—go up to London."

"Come along, then; I'll show you the way."

"Ve'y good, we can walk, if you understand my meaning." And the man stood up, the dog and the woman also. All three passed unsteadily out.

The man walked first, then the woman, then the dog, wavering into the dusky mist. Ivor followed, praying that they might meet no traffic. The man's voice broke the silence in front.

"Hen'y Ivor!" Ivor closed up nervously.

"Hen'y Ivor! I see 'm sayin' to 'mself: 'What'll they move on for!' I see him, if y' understand my meaning. Wha'sh he good for—Hen'y Ivor—only writer o' books. Is he any better than me—no! Not's good, if you f-follow me. I see 'm thinkin': 'How can I get rid of 'm?'" He stood still suddenly, almost on Ivor's toes. "Where's dog—carry th' dog—get 'is feet wet."

The woman stooped unsteadily, picked up the dog, and they both wavered on again. Ivor walked alongside now, grim and apprehensive. The man seemed to have become aware of him.

"'Mist' Ivor," he said. "Thought so—I'm not tight—can't say better than that, can I?—I'm not writer of books like you—not plutocrat, if you understand my meaning. Want to ask you question: what would you do if you was me?"

There was silence, but for the slip-slippering of the woman's feet behind.

"I don' blame you," said the man, whose speech was getting thicker; "you can't help being a plutothrist. But whash the good of anything for me, except ob-oblivion, if you follow me?"

A faint radiance shone through the mist. The station building loomed suddenly quite close. Ivor steered towards it.

"Goin' up t' London," said the man. "Qui' right!"

He lurched past into the lighted entry, and the woman followed with the dog. Ivor saw them waver through the doorway. And, spinning round, he ran into the mist. 'Perfectly true!' he thought while he was running. Perfectly true! Why had he helped them? What did he care so long as he got rid of man, woman, and dog?

[*1922*]

A MAN OF DEVON

. . . It is quiet here, sleepy, rather—a farm is never quiet; the sea, too, is only a quarter of a mile away, and when it's windy, the sound of it travels up the combe; for distraction, you must go four miles to Brixham or five to Kingswear, and you won't find much then. The farm lies in a sheltered spot, scooped, so to speak, high up the combe side—behind is a rise of fields, and beyond, a sweep of down. You have the feeling of being able to see quite far, which is misleading, as you soon find out if you walk. It is true Devon country—hills, hollows, hedge-banks, lanes dipping down into the earth or going like the sides of houses, coppices, cornfields, and little streams wherever there's a place for one; but the downs along the cliff, all gorse and ferns, are wild. The combe ends in a sandy cove with black rock on one side, pinkish cliffs away to the headland on the other, and a coastguard station. Just now, with the harvest coming on, everything looks its richest, the apples ripening, the trees almost too green. It's very hot, still weather; the country and the sea seem to sleep in the sun. In front of the farm are half-a-dozen pines that look as if they had stepped out of another land, but all round the back is orchard as lush, and gnarled, and orthodox as anyone could wish. The house, a long, white building with three levels of roof, and splashes of brown all over it, looks as if it might be growing down into the earth. It was freshly thatched two years ago—and that's all the newness there is about it; they say the front door, oak, with iron knobs, is three hundred years old at least. You can touch the ceilings with your hand. The windows certainly might be larger—a heavenly old place, though, with a flavour of apples, smoke, sweetbriar, bacon, honeysuckle, and age, all over it.

The owner is a man called John Ford, about seventy, and seventeen stone in weight—very big, on long legs, with a grey, stubbly beard, grey watery eyes, short neck and purplish complexion; he is asthmatic, and has a very courteous, autocratic manner. His clothes are made of Harris tweed—except on Sundays, when he puts on black, a seal ring, and a thick gold cable chain. There's nothing mean or small about John Ford; I suspect him of a warm heart, but he doesn't let you know much about him. He's a north-country man by birth, and has been out in New Zealand all his life. This little Devonshire farm is all he has now. He had a large "station" in the North Island, and was much looked up to, kept open house, did everything, as one would guess, in a narrow-minded, large-handed way. He came to grief suddenly; I don't quite know how. I believe his only son lost money on the turf, and then, unable to face his father, shot himself; if you had seen John Ford, you could imagine that. His wife died, too, that year. He paid up to the last penny, and came home, to live on this farm. He told me the other night that he had only one relation in the world, his granddaughter, who lives here with him. Pasiance Voisey—old spelling for Patience, but they pronounce it Pashyence—is sitting out here with me at this moment on a sort of rustic loggia that opens into the orchard. Her sleeves are rolled up, and she's stripping currants, ready for blackcurrant tea. Now and then she rests her elbows on the table, eats a berry, pouts her lips, and begins again. She has a round little face; a long, slender body; cheeks like poppies; a bushy mass of black-brown hair, and dark-brown, almost black eyes; her nose is snub; her lips quick, red, rather full; all her motions quick and soft. She loves bright colours. She's rather like a little cat; sometimes she seems all sympathy, then in a moment as hard as tortoise-shell. She's all impulse; yet she doesn't like to show her feelings; I sometimes wonder whether she has any. She plays the violin.

It's queer to see these two together, queer and rather sad. The old man has a fierce tenderness for her that strikes into the very roots of him. I see him torn between it and his cold north-country horror of his feelings; his life with her is an unconscious torture to him. She's a restless, chafing thing, demure enough one moment, then flashing out into mocking speeches or hard little laughs. Yet she's fond of him in her fashion; I saw her kiss him once when he was asleep. She obeys him generally—in a way as if she couldn't breathe while he was doing it. She's had a queer sort of education—history, geography, elementary mathematics, and nothing else; never been to school; had a few lessons on the violin, but has taught herself most of what she knows. She is well up in the lore of birds, flowers, and insects; has three cats, who follow her about; and is full of pranks. The other day she called out to me, "I've something for you. Hold out your hand and shut your eyes!" It was a large, black slug! She's the child of the old fellow's only daughter, who was sent home for schooling at Torquay, and made a runaway match with one Richard Voisey, a yeoman farmer, whom she met in the hunting-field. John Ford was furious—his ancestors, it appears, used to lead ruffians on the Cumberland side of the Border—he looked on "Squire" Rick Voisey as a cut below him. He was called "Squire," as far as I can make out, because he used to play cards every evening with a parson in the neighbourhood who went by the name of "Devil" Hawkins. Not that the Voisey stock is to be despised. They have had this farm since it was granted to one Richard Voisey by copy dated 8th September, 13 Henry VIII. Mrs. Hopgood, the wife of the bailiff—a dear, quaint, serene old soul with cheeks like a rosy, withered apple, and an unbounded love of Pasiance—showed me the very document.

"I kape it," she said. "Mr. Ford be tu proud—but other folks be proud tu. 'Tis a pra-aper old fam'ly: all the women is Margery, Pasiance, or Mary; all the men's Richards an' Johns an' Rogers; old as they apple-trees."

Rick Voisey was a rackety, hunting fellow, and "dipped" the old farm up to its thatched roof. John Ford took his revenge by buying up the mortgages, foreclosing, and commanding his daughter and Voisey to go on living here rent free; this they dutifully did until they were both killed in a dog-cart accident, eight years ago. Old Ford's financial smash came a year later, and since then he's lived here with Pasiance. I fancy it's the cross in her blood that makes her so restless, and irresponsible: if she had been all a native she'd have been happy enough here, or all a stranger like John Ford himself, but the two strains struggling for mastery seem to give her no rest. You'll think this a far-fetched theory, but I believe it to be the true one. She'll stand with lips pressed together, her arms folded tight across her narrow chest, staring as if she could see beyond the things round her; then something catches her attention, her eyes will grow laughing, soft, or scornful all in a minute! She's eighteen, perfectly fearless in a boat, but you can't get her to mount a horse—a sore subject with her grandfather, who spends most of his day on a lean, half-bred pony, that carries him like a feather, for all his weight.

They put me up here as a favour to Dan Treffry; there's an arrangement of £ s. d. with Mrs. Hopgood in the background. They aren't at all well off; this is the largest farm about, but it doesn't bring them in much. To look at John Ford, it seems incredible he should be short of money—he's too large.

We have family prayers at eight, then breakfast—after that freedom for writing or anything else till supper and evening prayers. At midday one forages for oneself. On Sundays, two miles to church twice, or you get into John Ford's black books ... Dan Treffry himself is staying at Kingswear. He says he's made his pile; it suits him down here—like a sleep after years of being too wide-awake; he had a rough time in New Zealand, until that mine made his fortune. You'd hardly remember him; he reminds me of his uncle, old Nicholas Treffry; the same slow way of speaking, with a hesitation, and a trick of repeating your name with everything he says; left-handed too, and the same slow twinkle in his eyes. He has a dark, short beard, and red-brown cheeks; is a little bald on the temples, and a bit grey, but hard as iron. He rides over nearly every day, attended by a black spaniel with a wonderful nose and a horror of petticoats. He has told me lots of good stories of John Ford in the early squatter's times; his feats with horses live to this day; and he was through the Maori wars; as Dan says, "a man after Uncle Nic's own heart."

They are very good friends, and respect each other; Dan has a great admiration for the old man, but the attraction is Pasiance. He talks very little when she's in the room, but looks at her in a sidelong, wistful sort of way. Pasiance's conduct to him would be cruel in any one else, but in her one takes it with a pinch of salt. Dan goes off, but turns up again as quiet and dogged as you please.

Last night, for instance, we were sitting in the loggia after supper. Pasiance was fingering the strings of her violin, and suddenly Dan (a bold thing for him) asked her to play.

"What!" she said, "before men? No, thank you!"

"Why not?"

"Because I hate them."

Down came John Ford's hand on the wicker table: "You forget yourself! Go to bed!"

She gave Dan a look, and went; we could hear her playing in her bedroom; it sounded like a dance of spirits; and just when one thought she had finished, out it would break again like a burst of laughter. Presently, John Ford begged our pardons ceremoniously, and stumped off indoors. The violin ceased; we heard his voice growling at her; down he came again. Just as he was settled in his chair there was a soft swish, and something dark came falling through the apple boughs. The violin! You should have seen his face! Dan would have picked the violin up, but the old man stopped him. Later, from my bedroom window, I saw John Ford come out and stand looking at the violin, he raised his foot as if to stamp on it. At last he picked it up, wiped it carefully, and took it in.

My room is next to hers. I kept hearing her laugh, a noise too as if she were dragging things about the room. Then I fell asleep, but woke with a start, and went to the window for a breath of fresh air. Such a black, breathless night! Nothing to be seen but the twisted, blacker branches; not the faintest stir of leaves, no sound but muffled grunting from the cow-house, and now and then a faint sigh. I had the queerest feeling of unrest and fear, the last thing to expect on such a night. There is something here that's disturbing; a sort of suppressed struggle. I've never in my life seen anything so irresponsible as this girl, or so uncompromising as the old man; I keep thinking of the way he wiped that violin. It's just as if a spark would set everything in a blaze. There's a menace of tragedy—or—perhaps it's only the heat, and too much of Mother Hopgood's crame . . .

II

Tuesday

I've made a new acquaintance. I was lying in the orchard, and presently, not seeing me, he came along—a man of middle height, with a singularly good balance, and no lumber—rather old blue clothes, a flannel shirt, a dull red necktie, brown shoes, a cap with a leather peak pushed up on the forehead. Face long and narrow, bronzed with a kind of pale burnt-in brownness; a good forehead. A brown moustache, beard rather pointed, blackening about the cheeks; his chin not visible, but from the beard's growth must be big; mouth I should judge sensuous. Nose straight and blunt; eyes grey, with an upward look, not exactly frank, because defiant; two parallel furrows down each cheek, one from the inner corner of the eye, one from the nostril; age perhaps thirty-five. About the face, attitude, movements, something immensely vital, adaptable, daring, and unprincipled.

He stood in front of the loggia, biting his fingers, a kind of nineteenth-century buccaneer, and I wondered what he was doing in this gallery. They say you can tell a man of Kent or a Somersetshire man; certainly you can tell a Yorkshireman, and this fellow could only have been a man of Devon, one of the two main types found in this county. He whistled; and out came Pasiance in a geranium-coloured dress, looking like some tall poppy—you know the slight droop of a poppy's head, and the way the wind sways its stem. . . . She is a human poppy, her fuzzy dark hair is like a poppy's lustreless black heart, she has a poppy's tantalising attraction and repulsion, something fatal, or rather fateful. She came walking up to my new friend, then caught sight of me, and stopped dead.

"That," she said to me, "is Zachary Pearse. This," she said to him, "is our *lodger*." She said it with a wonderful soft malice. She wanted to scratch me, and she scratched. Half an hour later I was in the yard, when up came this fellow Pearse.

"Glad to know you," he said, looking thoughtfully at the pigs. "You're a writer, aren't you?"

"A sort of one," I said.

"If by any chance," he said suddenly, "you're looking for a job, I could put something in your way. Walk down to the beach with me, and I'll tell you; my boat's at anchor, smartest little craft in these parts."

It was very hot, and I had no desire whatever to go down to the beach—I went, all the same. We had not gone far when John Ford and Dan Treffry came into the lane. Our friend seemed a little disconcerted, but soon recovered himself. We met in the middle of the lane, where there was hardly room to pass. John Ford, who looked very haughty, put on his *pince-nez* and stared at Pearse.

"Good-day!" said Pearse; "fine weather! I've been up to ask Pasiance to come for a sail. Wednesday we thought, weather permitting; this gentleman's coming. Perhaps you'll come too, Mr. Treffry. You've never seen my place. I'll give you lunch, and show you my father. He's worth a couple of hours' sail any day." It was said in such an odd way that one couldn't resent his impudence. John Ford was seized with a fit of wheezing, and seemed on the eve of an explosion; he glanced at me, and checked himself.

"You're very good," he said icily; "my granddaughter has other things to do. You, gentlemen, will please yourselves"; and, with a very slight bow, he went stumping on to the house. Dan looked at me, and I looked at him.

"You'll come?" said Pearse, rather wistfully. Dan stammered: "Thank you, Mr. Pearse; I'm a better man on a horse than in a boat, but—thank you." Cornered in this way, he's a shy, soft-hearted being. Pearse smiled his thanks. "Wednesday, then, at ten o'clock; you shan't regret it."

"Pertinacious beggar!" I heard Dan mutter in his beard; and found myself marching down the lane again by Pearse's side. I asked him what he was good enough to mean by saying I was coming, without having asked me. He answered, unabashed:

"You see, I'm not friends with the old man; but I knew he'd not be impolite to you, so I took the liberty."

He has certainly a knack of turning one's anger to curiosity. We were down in the combe now; the tide was running out, and the sand all little, wet, shining ridges. About a quarter of a mile out lay a cutter, with her tan sail half down, swinging to the swell. The sunlight was making the pink cliffs glow in the most wonderful way and shifting in bright patches over the sea like moving shoals of goldfish. Pearse perched himself on his dinghy, and looked out under his hand. He seemed lost in admiration.

"If we could only net some of those spangles," he said, "an' make gold of 'em! No more work then."

"It's a big job I've got on," he said presently; "I'll tell you about it on Wednesday. I want a journalist."

"But I don't write for the papers," I said; "I do other sort of work. My game is archaeology."

"It doesn't matter," he said, "the more imagination the better. It'd be a thundering good thing for you."

His assurance was amazing, but it was past supper-time, and hunger getting the better of my curiosity, I bade him goodnight. When I looked back, he was still there, on the edge of his boat, gazing at the sea. A queer sort of bird altogether, but attractive somehow.

Nobody mentioned him that evening; but once old Ford, after staring a long time at Pasiance, muttered *à propos* of nothing, "Undutiful children!" She was softer than usual; listening quietly to our talk, and smiling when spoken to. At bedtime she went up to her grandfather, without waiting for the usual command, "Come and kiss me, child."

Dan did not stay to supper, and he has not been here since. This morning I asked Mother Hopgood who Zachary Pearse was. She's a true Devonian; if there's anything she hates, it is to be committed to a definite statement. She ambled round her answer, and at last told me that he was "son of old Cap'en Jan Pearse to Black Mill. 'Tes an old family to Dartymouth an' Plymouth," she went on in a communicative outburst. "They du say Francis Drake tuke five o' they Pearses with 'en to fight the Spaniards. At least that's what I've heard Mr. Zachary zay; Ha-apgood can tell yu." Poor Hopgood, the amount of information she saddles him with in the course of the day! Having given me thus to understand that she had run dry, she at once went on:

"Cap'en Jan Pearse made a dale of ventures. He's old now—they du say nigh an 'undred. Ha-apgood can tell yu."

"But the son, Mrs. Hopgood?"

Her eyes twinkled with sudden shrewdness. She hugged herself placidly.

"An' what would yu take for dinner to-day? There's duck; or yu might like 'toad in the hole,' with an apple tart; or then, there's—Well! we'll see what we can du like." And off she went, without waiting for my answer.

To-morrow is Wednesday. I shan't be sorry to get another look at this fellow Pearse. . . .

III

Friday, 29th July

. . . Why do you ask me so many questions, and egg me on to write about these people instead of minding my business? If you really want to hear, I'll tell you of Wednesday's doings.

It was a splendid morning; and Dan turned up, to my surprise—
though I might have known that when he says a thing, he does it.
John Ford came out to shake hands with him, then, remembering
why he had come, breathed loudly, said nothing, and went in again.
Nothing was to be seen of Pasiance, and we went down to the beach
together.

"I don't like this fellow Pearse, George," Dan said to me on the
way; "I was fool enough to say I'd go, and so I must, but what's he
after? Not the man to do things without a reason, mind you."

I remarked that we should soon know.

"I'm not so sure—queer beggar; I never look at him without
thinking of a pirate."

The cutter lay in the cove as if she had never moved. There too
was Zachary Pearse seated on the edge of his dinghy.

"A five-knot breeze," he said; "I'll run you down in a couple of
hours." He made no inquiry about Pasiance, but put us into his
cockleshell and pulled for the cutter. A lantern-jawed fellow, named
Prawle, with a spiky, prominent beard, long clean-shaven upper lip,
and tanned complexion—a regular hard-weather bird—received
us.

The cutter was beautifully clean; built for a Brixham trawler, she
still had her number—DH 113—uneffaced. We dived into a sort
of cabin, airy, but dark, fitted with two bunks and a small table, on
which stood some bottles of stout; there were lockers, too, and pegs
for clothes. Prawle, who showed us round, seemed very proud of a
steam contrivance for hoisting sails. It was some minutes before we
came on deck again; and there, in the dinghy, being pulled towards
the cutter, sat Pasiance.

"If I'd known this," stammered Dan, getting red. "I wouldn't have
come." She had outwitted us, and there was nothing to be done.

It was a very pleasant sail. The breeze was light from the south-
east, the sun warm, the air soft. Presently Pasiance began singing:

> Columbus is dead and laid in his grave,
> Oh! heigh-ho! and laid in his grave;
> Over his head the apple-trees wave—
> Oh! heigho! the apple-trees wave . . .

> The apples are ripe and ready to fall,
> Oh! heigho! and ready to fall;
> There came an old woman and gathered them all,
> Oh! heigho! and gathered them all. . . .
>
> The apples are gathered, and laid on the shelf,
> Oh! heigho! and laid on the shelf;
> If you want any more, you must sing for yourself,
> Oh! heigho! and sing for yourself.

Her small, high voice came to us in trills and spurts, as the wind let it, like the singing of a skylark lost in the sky. Pearse went up to her and whispered something. I caught a glimpse of her face like a startled wild creature's; shrinking, tossing her hair, laughing, all in the same breath. She wouldn't sing again, but crouched in the bows with her chin on her hands, and the sun falling on one cheek, round, velvety, red as a peach . . .

We passed Dartmouth, and half an hour later put into a little wooded bay. On a low reddish cliff was a house hedged round by pine-trees. A bit of broken jetty ran out from the bottom of the cliff. We hooked on to this, and landed. An ancient, fish-like man came slouching down and took charge of the cutter. Pearse led us towards the house, Pasiance following mortally shy all of a sudden.

The house had a dark, overhanging thatch of the rush reeds that grow in the marshes hereabouts; I remember nothing else remarkable. It was neither old, nor new; neither beautiful, nor exactly ugly; neither clean, nor entirely squalid; it perched there with all its windows over the sea, turning its back contemptuously on the land.

Seated in a kind of porch, beside an immense telescope, was a very old man in a panama hat, with a rattan cane. His pure-white beard and moustache, and almost black eyebrows, gave a very singular, piercing look to his little, restless, dark-grey eyes; all over his mahogany cheeks and neck was a network of fine wrinkles. He sat quite upright, in the full sun, hardly blinking.

"Dad!" said Zachary, "*this* is Pasiance Voisey." The old man turned his eyes on her and muttered, "How do you do, ma'am?" then took no further notice. And Pasiance, who seemed to resent this, soon slipped away and went wandering about amongst the pines. An old woman brought some plates and bottles and laid them casually on a table; and we sat round the figure of old Captain Pearse without a word, as if we were all under a spell.

Before lunch there was a little scene between Zachary Pearse and Dan, as to which of them should summon Pasiance. It ended in both going, and coming back without her. She did not want any lunch, would stay where she was amongst the pines.

For lunch we had chops, wood-pigeons, mushrooms, and mulberry preserve, and drank wonderful Madeira out of common wine-glasses. I asked the old man where he got it; he gave me a queer look, and answered with a little bow:

"Stood me in tu shillin' the bottle, an' the country got nothing out of it, sir. In the early Thirties; tu shillin' the bottle; there's no such wine nowaday; and," he added, looking at Zachary, "no such men."

Zachary smiled and said: "You did nothing so big, dad, as what I'm after, now!"

The old man's eyes had a sort of disdain in them.

"You're going far, then, in the *Pied Witch*, Zack?"

"I am," said Zachary.

"And *where* might yu be goin' in that old trampin' smut factory?"

"Morocco."

"Heu!" said the old man, "there's nothing there; I know that coast, as I know the back o' my hand." He stretched out a hand covered with veins and hair.

Zachary began suddenly to pour out a flood of words:

"Below Mogador—a fellow there—friend of mine—two years ago now. Concessions—trade—gunpowder—cruisers—feuds—money—chiefs—Gatling guns—Sultan—rifles—rebellion—gold."

He detailed a reckless, sordid, bold scheme, which, on the pivot of a trading venture, was intended to spin a whole wheel of political convulsions.

"They'll never let you get there," said old Pearse.

"Won't they?" returned Zachary. "Oh yes, they will, an' when I leave, *there'll be another dynasty, and I'll be a rich man.*"

"Yu'll never leave," answered the old man.

Zachary took out a sheet of paper covered with figures. He had worked the whole thing out. So much—equipment, so much—trade, so much—concessions, so much—emergencies.

"My last mag!" he ended, "a thousand short; the ship's ready, and if I'm not there within a month my chance is as good as gone."

This was the pith of his confidences—an appeal for money, and we all looked as men will when that crops up.

"Mad!" muttered the old man, looking at the sea.

"No," said Zachary. That one word was more eloquent than all the rest of his words put together. This fellow is no visionary. His scheme may be daring, and unprincipled, but—he knows very well what he's about.

"Well!" said old Pearse, "you shall have five hundred of my money, if it's only to learn what yu're made of. Wheel me in!" Zachary wheeled him into the house, but soon came back.

"The old man's cheque for five hundred pounds!" he said, holding it up. "Mr. Treffry, give me another, and you shall have a third of the profits."

I expected Dan to give a point-blank refusal. But he only asked:

"Would that clear you for starting?"

"With that," said Zachary, "I can get to sea in a fortnight."

"Good!" Dan said slowly. "Give me a written promise! To sea in fourteen days and my fair share on the five hundred pounds—no more—no less."

Again I thought Pearse would have jumped at this, but he leaned his chin on his hand, and looked at Dan, and Dan looked at him. While they were staring at each other like this, Pasiance came up with a kitten.

"See!" she said, "isn't it a darling?" The kitten crawled and clawed its way up behind her neck. I saw both men's eyes as they looked at Pasiance, and suddenly understood what they were at. The kitten rubbed itself against Pasiance's cheek, overbalanced, and fell, clawing, down her dress. She caught it up and walked away. Some one, I don't know which of us, sighed, and Pearse cried "Done!"

The bargain had been driven.

"Good-bye, Mr. Pearse," said Dan; "I guess that's all I'm wanted for. I'll find my pony waiting in the village. George, you'll see Pasiance home?"

We heard the hoofs of his pony galloping down the road; Pearse suddenly excused himself, and disappeared.

This venture of his may sound romantic and absurd, but it's matter-of-fact enough. He's after £ s. d.! Shades of Drake, Raleigh, Hawkins, Oxenham! The worm of suspicion gnaws at the rose of romance. What if those fellows, too, were only after £ s. d.?

I strolled into the pine-wood. The earth there was covered like a bee's body with black and gold stripes; there was the blue sea below, and white, sleepy clouds, and bumble-bees booming above the heather; it was all softness, a summer's day in Devon. Suddenly I came on Pearse standing at the edge of the cliff with Pasiance sitting in a little hollow below, looking up at him. I heard him say:

"Pasiance—Pasiance!" The sound of his voice, and the sight of her soft, wondering face made me furious. What business has she with love, at her age? What business have they with each other?

He told me presently that she had started off for home, and drove me to the ferry, behind old grey pony. On the way he came back to his offer of the other day.

"Come with me," he said. "It doesn't do to neglect the Press; you can see the possibilities. It's one of the few countries left. If I once get this business started you don't know where it's going to stop. You'd have free passage everywhere, and whatever you like in reason."

I answered as rudely as I could—but by no means as rudely as I wanted—that his scheme was mad. As a matter of fact, it's much too sane for me; for, whatever the body of a scheme, its soul is the fibre of the schemer.

"Think of it," he urged as if he could see into me. "You can make what you like of it. Press paragraphs, of course. But that's mechanical; why, even I could do it, if I had time. As for the rest, you'll be as free—as free as a man."

There, in five words of one syllable, is the kernel of this fellow Pearse—"As free as a man!" No rule, no law, not even the mysterious shackles that bind men to their own self-respects! "As free as a man!" No ideals; no principles; no fixed star for his worship; no coil he can't slide out of! But the fellow has the tenacity of one of the old Devon mastiffs, too. He wouldn't take "No" for an answer.

"Think of it," he said; "any day will do—I've got a fortnight ... Look! there she is!" I thought that he meant Pasiance; but it was an old steamer, sluggish and black in the blazing sun of mid-stream, with a yellow-and-white funnel, and no sign of life on her decks.

"That's her—the *Pied Witch*! Do her twelve knots; you wouldn't think it! Well! good-evening! You'd better come. A word to me at any time. I'm going aboard now."

As I was being ferried across I saw him lolling in the stern-sheets of a little boat, the sun crowning his straw hat with glory.

I came on Pasiance, about a mile up the road, sitting in the hedge. We walked on together between the banks—Devonshire banks—as high as houses, thick with ivy and ferns, bramble and hazel boughs, and honeysuckle.

"Do you believe in a God?" she said suddenly. "Grandfather's God is simply awful. When I'm playing the fiddle, I can *feel* God; but grandfather's is such a stuffy God—you know what I mean: the sea, the wind, the trees, colours too—they make one *feel*. But I don't believe that life was meant to be 'good' in. Isn't there anything better than being good? When I'm 'good,' I simply feel wicked." She reached up, caught a flower from the hedge, and slowly tore its petals.

"What would you do," she muttered, "if you wanted a thing, but were afraid of it? But I suppose you're never afraid!" she added, mocking me. I admitted that I was some times afraid, and often afraid of being afraid.

"That's nice! I'm not afraid of illness, nor of grandfather, nor of his God; but—I want to be free. If you want a thing badly, you're afraid about it."

I thought of Zachary Pearse's words, "free as a man."

"Why are you looking at me like that?" she said.

I stammered: "What do you mean by freedom?"

"Do you know what I shall do to-night?" she answered. "Get out of my window by the apple-tree, and go to the woods, and play!"

We were going down a steep lane, along the side of a wood, where there's always a smell of sappy leaves, and the breath of the cows that come close to the hedge to get the shade.

There was a cottage in the bottom, and a small boy sat outside playing with a heap of dust.

"Hallo, Johnny!" said Pasiance. "Hold your leg out and show this man your bad place!" The small boy undid a bandage round his bare and dirty little leg, and proudly revealed a sore.

"Isn't it nasty?" cried Pasiance ruefully, tying up the bandage again; "poor little feller! Johnny, see what I've brought you!" She produced

from her pocket a stick of chocolate, the semblance of a soldier
made of sealing-wax and worsted, and a crooked sixpence.

It was a new glimpse of her. All the way home she was telling me
the story of little Johnny's family; when she came to his mother's
death, she burst out: "A beastly shame, wasn't it, and they're so poor;
it might just as well have been somebody else. I like poor people, but
I hate rich ones—stuck-up beasts!'

Mrs. Hopgood was looking over the gate, with her cap on one
side, and one of Pasiance's cats rubbing itself against her skirts. At the
sight of us she hugged herself.

"Where's grandfather?" asked Pasiance. The old lady shook her
head.

"Is it a row?" Mrs. Hopgood wriggled, and wriggled, and out
came:

"Did you get yure tay, my pretty? No? Well, that's a pity; yu'll be
fallin' low-like."

Pasiance tossed her head, snatched up the cat, and ran in doors. I
remained staring at Mrs. Hopgood.

"Dear—dear," she chuckled, "poor lamb. So to spake it's——"
and she blurted out suddenly, "chuckin' full of wra-ath, he is. Well,
there!"

My courage failed that evening. I spent it at the coast-guard
station, where they gave me bread and cheese and some awful cider.
I passed the kitchen as I came back. A fire was still burning there,
and two figures, misty in the darkness, flitted about with stealthy
laughter like spirits afraid of being detected in a carnal meal. They
were Pasiance and Mrs. Hopgood; and so charming was the smell of
eggs and bacon, and they had such an air of tender enjoyment of this
dark revel, that I stifled many pangs, as I crept, hungry up to bed.

In the middle of the night I woke and heard what I thought
was screaming; then it sounded like wind in trees, then like the
distant shaking of a tambourine, with the high singing of a human
voice. Suddenly it stopped—two long notes came wailing out like
sobs—then utter stillness; and though I listened for an hour or more
there was no other sound.

IV

4th August

. . . For three days after I wrote last, nothing at all happened here. I spent the mornings on the cliff reading, and watching the sun-sparks raining on the sea. It's grand up there with the gorse all round, the gulls basking on the rocks, the partridges calling in the corn, and now and then a young hawk overhead.

The afternoons I spent out in the orchard. The usual routine goes on at the farm all the time—cow-milking, bread-baking, John Ford riding in and out, Pasiance in her garden stripping lavender, talking to the farm hands; and the smell of clover, and cows and hay; the sound of hens and pigs and pigeons, the soft drawl of voices, the dull thud of the farm carts; and day by day the apples getting redder. Then, last Monday, Pasiance was away from sunrise till sunset— nobody saw her go—nobody knew where she had gone. It was a wonderful, strange day, a sky of silver-grey and blue, with a drift of wind-clouds, all the trees sighing a little, the sea heaving in a long, low swell, the animals restless, the birds silent, except the gulls with their old man's laughter and kitten's mewing.

A something wild was in the air; it seemed to sweep across the downs and combe, into the very house, like a passionate tune that comes drifting to your ears when you're sleepy. But who would have thought the absence of that girl for a few hours could have wrought such havoc! We were like uneasy spirits; Mrs. Hopgood's apple cheeks seemed positively to wither before one's eyes. I came across a dairymaid and farmhand discussing stolidly with very downcast faces. Even Hopgood, a hard-bitten fellow with immense shoulders, forgot his imperturbability so far as to harness his horse, and depart on what he assured me was "just a wild-goose chaace." It was long before John Ford gave signs of noticing that anything was wrong, but late in the afternoon I found him sitting with his hands on his knees, staring straight before him. He rose heavily when he saw me, and stalked out. In the evening as I was starting for the coastguard station to ask for help to search the cliff, Pasiance appeared, walking as if she could hardly drag one leg after the other. Her cheeks were crimson; she was biting her lips to keep tears of sheer fatigue out of

her eyes. She passed me in the doorway without a word. The anxiety
he had gone through seemed to forbid the old man from speaking.
He just came forward, took her face in his hands, gave it a great
kiss, and walked away. Pasiance dropped on the floor in the dark
passage, and buried her face on her arms. "Leave me alone!" was all
she would say. After a bit she dragged herself upstairs. Presently Mrs.
Hopgood came to me.

"Not a word out of her—an' not a bite will she ate, an' I had a pie
all ready—scrumptious. The good Lord knows the truth—she asked
for brandy; have you any brandy, sir? Ha-apgood 'e don't drink it, an'
Mister Ford 'e don't allaow for anything but caowslip wine."

I had whiskey.

The good soul seized the flask, and went off hugging it. She
returned it to me half empty.

"Lapped it like a kitten laps milk. I misdaoubt it's straong, poor
lamb, it lusened 'er tongue pra-aperly. 'I've a-done it,' she says to me,
'Mums—I've a-done it,' an' she laughed like a mad thing; and then,
sir, she cried, an' kissed me, an' pushed me thru the door. Gude Lard!
What is 't she's a-done?"

It rained all the next day and the day after. About five o'clock
yesterday the rain ceased; I started off to Kingswear on Hopgood's
nag to see Dan Treffry. Every tree, bramble, and fern in the lanes
was dripping water; and every bird singing from the bottom of his
heart. I thought of Pasiance all the time. Her absence that day was
still a mystery; one never ceased asking oneself what she had done.
There are people who never grow up—they have no right to do
things. Actions have consequences—children have no business with
consequences.

Dan was out. I had supper at the hotel, and rode slowly home. In
the twilight stretches of the road, where I could touch either bank
of the lane with my whip, I thought of nothing but Pasiance and her
grandfather; there was something in the half light suited to wonder
and uncertainty. It had fallen dark before I rode into the straw-yard.
Two young bullocks snuffled at me, a sleepy hen got up and ran
off with a tremendous shrieking. I stabled the horse, and walked
round to the back. It was pitch black under the apple-trees and the
windows were all darkened. I stood there a little, everything smelled
so delicious after the rain; Suddenly I had the uncomfortable feeling

that I was being watched. Have you ever felt like that on a dark night? I called out at last: "Is any one there?" Not a sound! I walked to the gate—nothing! The trees still dripped with tiny, soft, hissing sounds, but that was all. I slipped round to the front, went in, barricaded the door, and groped up to bed. But I couldn't sleep. I lay awake a long while; dozed at last, and woke with a jump. A stealthy murmur of smothered voices was going on quite close somewhere. It stopped. A minute passed; suddenly came the soft thud as of something falling. I sprang out of bed and rushed to the window. Nothing—but in the distance something that sounded like footsteps. An owl hooted: then clear as crystal, but quite   low, I heard Pasiance singing in her room:

> The apples were ripe and ready to fall,
> Oh! heigho! and ready to fall.

I ran to her door and knocked.
(Our rooms are like this:—)

"What is it?" she cried.

"Is anything the matter?"

"Matter?"

"Is anything the matter?"

"Ha—ha—ha—ha! Good-night!" then quite low, I heard her catch her breath, hard, sharply. No other answer, no other sound.

I went to bed and lay awake for hours . . .

This evening Dan came; during supper he handed Pasiance a roll of music; he had got it in Torquay. The shopman, he said, had told him that it was a "corker."

It was Bach's "Chaconne." You should have seen her eyes shine, her fingers actually tremble while she turned over the pages. Seems odd to think of her worshipping at the shrine of Bach—as odd as to think of a wild colt running of its free will into the shafts; but that's just it—with her you can never tell.

"Heavenly!" she kept saying.

John Ford put down his knife and fork.

"Heathenish stuff!" he muttered, and suddenly thundered out, "Pasiance!"

She looked up with a start, threw the music from her, and resumed her place.

During evening prayers, which follow every night immediately on food, her face was a study of mutiny. She went to bed early. It was rather late when we broke up—for once old Ford had been talking of his squatter's life. As we came out, Dan held up his hand. A dog was barking. "It's Lass," he said. "She'll wake Pasiance."

The spaniel yelped furiously. Dan ran out to stop her. He was soon back.

"Somebody's been in the orchard, and gone off down to the cove." He ran on down the path. I, too, ran, horribly uneasy. In front, through the darkness, came the spaniel's bark; the lights of the coastguard station faintly showed. I was first on the beach; the dog came to me at once, her tail almost in her mouth from apology. There was the sound of oars working in rowlocks; nothing visible but the feathery edges of the waves. Dan said behind, "No use! He's gone." His voice sounded hoarse, like that of a man choking with passion.

"George," he stammered, "it's that blackguard. I wish I'd put a

bullet in him." Suddenly a light burned up in the darkness on the
sea, seemed to swing gently, and vanished. Without another word
we went back up the hill. John Ford stood at the gate motionless,
indifferent—nothing had dawned on him as yet. I whispered to Dan,
"Let it alone!"

"No," he said, "I'm going to show you." He struck a match, and
slowly hunted the footsteps in the wet grass of the orchard. "Look—
here!"

He stopped under Pasiance's window and swayed the match over
the ground. Clear as daylight were the marks of some one who had
jumped or fallen. Dan held the match over his head.

"And look there!" he said. The bough of an apple-tree below the
window was broken. He blew the match out.

I could see the whites of his eyes, like an angry animal's.

"Drop it, Dan!" I said.

He turned on his heel suddenly, and stammered out, "You're
right."

But he had turned into John Ford's arms.

The old man stood there like some great force, darker than the
darkness, staring up at the window, as though stupefied. We had not
a word to say. He seemed unconscious of our presence. He turned
round and left us standing there.

"Follow him!" said Dan. "Follow him—by God! it's not safe."

We followed. Bending, and treading heavily, he went upstairs. He
struck a blow on Pasiance's door. "Let me in!" he said. I drew Dan
into my bedroom. The key was slowly turned, her door was flung
open, and there she stood in her dressing-gown, a candle in her
hand, her face crimson, and oh! so young, with its short, crisp hair
and round cheeks. The old man—like a giant in front of her—raised
his hands, and laid them on her shoulders.

"What's this? You—you've had a man in your room?"

Her eyes did not drop.

"Yes," she said. Dan gave a groan.

"Who?"

"Zachary Pearse," she answered in a voice like a bell.

He gave her one awful shake, dropped his hands, then raised them
as though to strike her. She looked him in the eyes; his hands dropped,
and he too groaned. As far as I could see, her face never moved.

"I'm married to him," she said; "d'you hear? Married to him. Go out of my room!" She dropped the candle on the floor at his feet, and slammed the door in his face. The old man stood for a minute as though stunned, then groped his way downstairs.

"Dan," I said, "is it true?"

"Ah!" he answered, "it's true; didn't you hear her?"

I was glad I couldn't see his face.

"That ends it," he said at last; "there's the old man to think of."

"What will he do?"

"Go to the fellow this very night." He seemed to have no doubt. Trust one man of action to know another.

I muttered something about being an outsider—wondered if there was anything I could do to help.

"Well," he said slowly, "I don't know that I'm anything but an outsider now; but I'll go along with him, if he'll have me."

He went downstairs. A few minutes later they rode out from the straw-yard. I watched them past the line of hayricks, into the blacker shadows of the pines, then the tramp of hoofs began to fail in the darkness, and at last died away.

I've been sitting here in my bedroom writing to you ever since, till my candle's almost gone. I keep thinking what the end of it is to be; and reproaching myself for doing nothing. And yet, what could I have done? I'm sorry for her—sorrier than I can say. The night is so quiet—I haven't heard a sound; is she asleep, awake, crying, triumphant?

It's four o'clock; I've been asleep.

They're back. Dan is lying on my bed. I'll try and tell you his story as near as I can, in his own words.

"We rode," he said, "round the upper way, keeping out of the lanes, and got to Kingswear by half-past eleven. The horse-ferry had stopped running, and we had a job to find any one to put us over. We hired the fellow to wait for us, and took a carriage at the 'Castle.' Before we got to Black Mill it was nearly one, pitch-dark. With the breeze from the south-east, I made out he should have been in an hour or more. The old man had never spoken to me once: and before we got there I had begun to hope we shouldn't find the fellow after all. We made the driver pull up in the road, and walked round and round, trying to find the door. Then some one cried, 'Who are you?'

"'John Ford.'

"'What do you want?' It was old Pearse.

"'To see Zachary Pearse.'

The long window out of the porch where we sat the other day was open, and in we went. There was a door at the end of the room, and a light coming through. John Ford went towards it; I stayed out in the dark.

"'Who's that with you?'

"'Mr. Treffry.'

"'Let him come in!' I went in. The old fellow was in bed, quite still on his pillows, a candle by his side; to look at him you'd think nothing of him but his eyes were alive. It was queer being there with those two old men.

Dan paused, seemed to listen, then went on doggedly.

"'Sit down, gentlemen,' said old Pearse. 'What may you want to see my son for?' John Ford begged his pardon, he had something to say, he said, that wouldn't wait.

"They were very polite to one another," muttered Dan.

"'Will you leave your message with me?' said Pearse. 'What I have to say to your son is private.'

"'I'm his father.'

"'I'm my girl's grandfather; and her only stand-by.'

"'Ah!' muttered old Pearse, 'Rick Voisey's daughter.'

"'I mean to see your son.'

"Old Pearse smiled. Queer smile he's got, sort of sneering sweet.

"'You can never tell where Zack may be,' he said. 'You think I want to shield him. You're wrong; Zack can take care of himself.'

"'Your son's here!' said John Ford. 'I know.' Old Pearse gave us a very queer look.

"'You come into my house like thieves in the night,' he said, 'and give me the lie, do you?'

"'Your son came to my child's room like a thief in the night; it's for that I want to see him,' and then," said Dan, "there was a long silence. At last Pearse said:

"'I don't understand; has he played the blackguard?'

"John Ford answered, 'He's married her, or, before God, I'd kill him.'

"Old Pearse seemed to think this over, never moving on his

pillows. 'You don't know Zack,' he said; 'I'm sorry for you, and I'm sorry for Rick Voisey's daughter; but you don't know Zack.'

"'Sorry!' groaned out John Ford; 'he's stolen my child, and I'll punish him.'

"'Punish!' cried old Pearse, 'we don't take punishment, not in my family.'

"'Captain Jan Pearse, as sure as I stand here, you and your breed will get your punishment of God.' Old Pearse smiled.

"'Mr. John Ford, that's as may be; but sure as I lie here we won't take it of you. You can't punish unless you make to feel, and that you can't du.'"

And that is truth!

Dan went on again:

"'You won't tell me where your son is!' but old Pearse never blinked.

"'I won't,' he said, 'and now you may get out. I lie here an old man alone, with no use to my legs, night on night, an' the house open; any rapscallion could get in; d'ye think I'm afraid of you?'

"We were beat; and walked out without a word. But that old man; I've thought of him a lot—ninety-two, and lying there. Whatever he's been, and they tell you rum things of him, whatever his son may be, he's a *man*. It's not what he said, nor that there was anything to be afraid of just then, but somehow it's the idea of the old chap lying there. I don't ever wish to see a better plucked one."

We sat silent after that; out of doors the light began to stir among the leaves. There were all kinds of rustling sounds, as if the world were turning over in bed.

Suddenly Dan said:

"He's cheated me. I paid him to clear out and leave her alone. D'you think she's asleep?" He's made no appeal for sympathy, he'd take pity for an insult; but he feels it badly.

"I'm tired as a cat," he said at last, and went to sleep on my bed.

It's broad daylight now; I too am tired as a cat . . .

V

Saturday, 6th August.

I take up my tale where I left off yesterday . . . Dan and I started
as soon as we could get Mrs. Hopgood to give us coffee. The old
lady was more tentative, more undecided, more pouncing, than I had
ever seen her. She was manifestly uneasy: Ha-apgood—who "don't
slape"—don't he, if snores are any criterion—had called out in the
night, "Hark to th' 'arses' oofs!" Had we heard them? And where
might we be going then? 'Twas very earrly to start, an' no breakfast.
Ha-apgood had said it was goin' to shaowerr. Miss Pasiance was not
tu 'er violin yet, an' Mister Ford 'e kept 'is room. Was it?—would
there be—? "Well, an' therr's an 'arvest bug; 'tis some earrly for they!"
Wonderful how she pounces on all such creatures, when I can't
even see them. She pressed it absently between finger and thumb,
and began manoeuvring round another way. Long before she had
reached her point, we had gulped down our coffee, and departed.
But as we rode out she came at a run, holding her skirts high with
either hand, raised her old eyes bright and anxious in their setting of
fine wrinkles, and said:

"'Tidden sorrow for *her*?"

A shrug of the shoulders was all the answer she got. We rode by
the lanes; through sloping farmyards, all mud and pigs, and dirty
straw, and farmers with clean-shaven upper lips and whiskers under
the chin; past fields of corn, where larks were singing. Up or down,
we didn't draw rein till we came to Dan's hotel.

There was the river gleaming before us under a rainbow mist that
hallowed every shape. There seemed affinity between the earth and
the sky. I've never seen that particular soft unity out of Devon. And
every ship, however black or modern, on those pale waters, had the
look of a dream ship. The tall green woods, the red earth, the white
houses, were all melted into one opal haze. It was raining, but the
sun was shining behind. Gulls swooped by us—ghosts of the old
greedy wanderers of the sea.

We had told our two boatmen to pull us out to the *Pied Witch*!
They started with great resolution, then rested on their oars.

"The *Pied Witch*, zurr?" asked one politely; "an' which may her
be?"

That's the West countryman all over! Never say you "nay," never lose an opportunity, never own he doesn't know, or can't do anything—independence, amiability, and an eye to the main chance. We mentioned Pearse's name.

"Capt'n Zach'ry Pearse!" They exchanged a look half-amused, half-admiring.

"The *Zunflaower*, yu mane. That's her. *Zunflaower*, ahoy!" As we mounted the steamer's black side I heard one say:

"*Pied Witch*! A pra-aper name that—a dandy name for her!" They laughed as they made fast.

The mate of the *Sunflower*, or *Pied Witch*, or whatever she was called, met us—a tall young fellow in his shirt-sleeves, tanned to the roots of his hair, with sinewy, tattooed arms, and grey eyes, charred round the rims from staring at weather.

"The skipper is on board," he said. "We're rather busy, as you see. Get on with that, you sea-cooks," he bawled at two fellows who were doing nothing. All over the ship, men were hauling, splicing, and stowing cargo.

"To-day's Friday: we're off on Wednesday with any luck. Will you come this way?" He led us down the companion to a dark hole which he called the saloon. "Names? What! are you Mr. Treffry? Then we're partners!" A schoolboy's glee came on his face.

"Look here!" he said; "I can show you something," and he unlocked the door of a cabin. There appeared to be nothing in it but a huge piece of tarpaulin, which depended, bulging, from the topmost bunk. He pulled it up. The lower bunk had been removed, and in its place was the ugly body of a dismounted Gatling gun.

"Got six of them," he whispered, with unholy mystery, through which his native frankness gaped out. "Worth their weight in gold out there just now, the skipper says. Got a heap of rifles, too, and lots of ammunition. He's given me a share. This is better than the P. and O., and playing deck cricket with the passengers. I'd made up my mind already to chuck that, and go in for plantin' sugar, when I ran across the skipper. Wonderful chap, the skipper! I'll go and tell him. He's been out all night; only came aboard at four bells; having a nap now, but he won't mind that for *you*."

Off he went. I wondered what there was in Zachary Pearse to attract a youngster of this sort; one of the customary twelve children of some country parson, no doubt—burning to shoot a few niggers, and for ever frank and youthful.

He came back with his hands full of bottles.

"What'll you drink? The skipper'll be here in a jiffy. Excuse my goin' on deck. We're so busy."

And in five minutes Zachary Pearse did come. He made no attempt to shake hands, for which I respected him. His face looked worn, and more defiant than usual.

"Well, gentlemen?" he said.

"We've come to ask what you're going to do?" said Dan.

"I don't know," answered Pearse, "that that's any of your business."

Dan's little eyes were like the eyes of an angry pig.

"You've got five hundred pounds of mine," he said; "why do you think I gave it you?"

Zachary bit his fingers.

"That's no concern of mine," he said. "I sail on Wednesday. Your money's safe."

"Do you know what I think of you?" said Dan.

"No, and you'd better not tell me!" Then, with one of his peculiar changes, he smiled: "As you like, though."

Dan's face grew very dark. "Give me a plain answer," he said: "What are you going to do about her?"

Zachary looked up at him from under his brows.

"Nothing."

"Are you cur enough to deny that you've married her?"

Zachary looked at him coolly. "Not at all," he said.

"What in God's name did you do it for?"

"You've no monopoly in the post of husband, Mr. Treffry."

"To put a child in that position! Haven't you the heart of a man? What d'ye come sneaking in at night for? By Gad! Don't you know you've done a beastly thing?"

Zachary's face darkened, he clenched his fists. Then he seemed to shut his anger into himself.

"You wanted me to leave her to you," he sneered. "I gave her my promise that I'd take her out there, and we'd have gone off on Wednesday quietly enough, if you hadn't come and nosed the whole thing out with your infernal dog. The fat's in the fire! There's no reason why I should take her now. I'll come back to her a rich man, or not at all."

"And in the meantime?" I slipped in.

He turned to me, in an ingratiating way.

"I would have taken her to save the fuss—I really would—it's not my fault the thing's come out. I'm on a risky job. To have her with me might ruin the whole thing; it would affect my nerve. It isn't safe for her."

"And what's her position to be," I said, "while you're away? Do you think she'd have married you if she'd known you were going to leave her like this? You ought to give up this business. You stole her. Her life's in your hands; she's only a child!"

A quiver passed over his face; it showed that he was suffering.

"Give it up!" I urged.

"My last farthing's in it," he sighed; "the chance of a lifetime."

He looked at me doubtfully, appealingly, as if for the first time in his life he had been given a glimpse of that dilemma of consequences which his nature never recognises. I thought he was going to give in. Suddenly, to my horror, Dan growled, "Play the man!"

Pearse turned his head. "I don't want your advice anyway," he said; "I'll not be dictated to."

"To your last day," said Dan, "you shall answer to me for the way you treat her."

Zachary smiled.

"Do you see that fly?" he said. "Well—I care for you as little as this," and he flicked the fly off his white trousers. "Good-morning!"

The noble mariners who manned our boat pulled lustily for the shore, but we had hardly shoved off when a storm of rain burst over the ship, and she seemed to vanish, leaving a picture on my eyes of the mate waving his cap above the rail, with his tanned young face bent down at us, smiling, keen, and friendly.

We reached the shore drenched, angry with ourselves, and with each other; I started sulkily for home.

As I rode past an orchard, an apple, loosened by the rain storm, came down with a thud.

> The apples were ripe and ready to fall,
> Oh! heigho! and ready to fall.

I made up my mind to pack, and go away. But there's a strangeness, a sort of haunting fascination in it all. To you, who don't know the people, it may only seem a piece of rather sordid folly. But it isn't the good, the obvious, the useful that puts a spell on us in life. It's the bizarre, the dimly seen, the mysterious for good or evil.

The sun was out again when I rode up to the farm; its yellow thatch shone through the trees as if sheltering a store of gladness and good news. John Ford himself opened the door to me.

He began with an apology, which made me feel more than ever an intruder; then he said:

"I have not spoken to my granddaughter—waited to see Dan Treffry."

He was stern and sad-eyed, like a man with a great weight of grief on his shoulders. He looked as if he had not slept; his dress was out of order, he had not taken his clothes off, I think. He isn't a man whom you can pity. I felt I had taken a liberty in knowing of the matter at all. When I told him where we had been, he said:

"It was good of you to take this trouble. That you should have had to! But since such things have come to pass——" He made a gesture full of horror. He gave one the impression of a man whose pride was struggling against a mortal hurt. Presently he asked:

"You saw him, you say? He admitted this marriage? Did he give an explanation?"

I tried to make Pearse's point of view clear. Before this old man, with his inflexible will and sense of duty, I felt as if I held a brief for Zachary, and must try to do him justice.

"Let me understand," he said at last. "he stole her, you say, to make sure; and deserts her within a fortnight."

"He says he meant to take her—"

"Do you believe that?"

Before I could answer, I saw Pasiance standing at the window. How long she had been there I don't know.

"Is it true that he is going to leave me behind?" she cried out.

I could only nod.

"Did you hear him your own self?"

"Yes."

She stamped her foot. "But he promised! He promised!"

John Ford went towards her.

"Don't touch me, grandfather! I hate every one! Let him do what he likes, I don't care."

John Ford's face turned quite grey.

"Pasiance," he said, "did you want to leave me so much?" She looked straight at us, and said sharply:

"What's the good of telling stories? I can't help its hurting you."

"What did you think you would find away from here?"

She laughed.

"Find? I don't know—nothing; I wouldn't be stifled anyway. Now I suppose you'll shut me up because I'm a weak girl, not strong like *men*!"

"Silence!" said John Ford; "I will make him take you."

"You shan't!" she cried; "I won't let you. He's free to do as he likes. He's free—I tell you all, everybody—free!"

She ran through the window, and vanished.

John Ford made a movement as if the bottom had dropped out of his world. I left him there.

I went to the kitchen, where Hopgood was sitting at the table, eating bread and cheese. He got up on seeing me, and very kindly brought me some cold bacon and a pint of ale.

"I thart I shude be seeing yu, zurr," he said between his bites; "therr's no thart to 'atin 'bout the 'ouse to-day. The old wumman's puzzivantin' over Miss Pasiance. Young girls are skeery critters"—he brushed his sleeve over his broad, hard jaws, and filled a pipe— "specially when it's in the blood of 'em. Squire Rick Voisey werr a dandy; an' Mistress Voisey—well, she werr a nice lady tu, but"— rolling the stem of his pipe from corner to corner of his mouth— "she werr a pra-aper vixen."

Hopgood's a good fellow, and I believe as soft as he looks hard, but he's not quite the sort with whom one chooses to talk over a matter like this. I went upstairs, and began to pack, but after a bit dropped it for a book, and somehow or other fell asleep.

I woke, and looked at my watch; it was five o'clock. I had been asleep four hours. A single sunbeam was slanting across from one of my windows to the other, and there was the cool sound of milk dropping into pails; then, all at once, a stir as of alarm, and heavy footsteps.

I opened my door. Hopgood and a coastguardman were carrying Pasiance slowly up the stairs. She lay in their arms without moving,

her face whiter than her dress, a scratch across the forehead, and two
or three drops there of dried blood. Her hands were clasped, and she
slowly crooked and stiffened out her fingers. When they turned with
her at the stair top, she opened her lips and gasped, "All right, don't
put me down. I can bear it." They passed, and, with a half-smile in
her eyes, she said something to me that I couldn't catch; the door
was shut, and the excited whispering began again below. I waited for
the men to come out, and caught hold of Hopgood. He wiped the
sweat off his forehead.

"Poor young thing!" he said. "She fell—down the cliffs—'tis her
back—coastguard saw her—'twerr they fetched her in. The Lord
'elp her—mebbe she's not broken up much! An' Mister Ford don't
know! I'm gwine for the doctor."

There was an hour or more to wait before he came; a young
fellow; almost a boy. He looked very grave, when he came out of
her room.

"The old woman there—fond of her? nurse her well? . . . Fond
as a dog!—good! Don't know—can't tell for certain! Afraid it's the
spine, must have another opinion! What a plucky girl! Tell Mr. Ford
to have the best man he can get in Torquay—there's C——. I'll be
round the first thing in the morning. Keep her dead quiet. I've left a
sleeping draught; she'll have fever to-night."

John Ford came in at last. Poor old man! What it must have cost
him not to go to her for fear of the excitement! How many times
in the next few hours didn't I hear him come to the bottom of
the stairs; his heavy wheezing, and sighing; and the forlorn tread of
his feet going back! About eleven, just as I was going to bed, Mrs.
Hopgood came to my door.

"Will yu come, sir," she said; "she's asking for yu. Naowt I can zay
but what she will see *yu*; zeems crazy, don't it?" A tear trickled down
the old lady's cheek. "Du 'ee come; 'twill du err' 'arm mebbe, but I
dunno—she'll fret else."

I slipped into the room. Lying back on her pillows, she was
breathing quickly with half-closed eyes. There was nothing to show
that she had wanted me, or even knew that I was there. The wick of
the candles, set by the bedside, had been snuffed too short, and gave
but a faint light; both window and door stood open, still there was
no draught, and the feeble little flame burned quite still, casting a

faint yellow stain on the ceiling like the reflection from a buttercup held beneath a chin. These ceilings are far too low! Across the wide, squat window the apple branches fell in black stripes which never stirred. It was too dark to see things clearly. At the foot of the bed was a chest, and there Mrs. Hopgood had sat down, moving her lips as if in speech. Mingled with the half-musty smell of age, there were other scents, of mignonette, apples, and some sweet-smelling soap. The floor had no carpet, and there was not one single dark object except the violin, hanging from a nail over the bed. A little, round clock ticked solemnly.

"Why won't you give me that stuff, Mums?" Pasiance said in a faint, sharp voice. "I want to sleep."

"Have you much pain?" I asked.

"Of course I have; it's everywhere."

She turned her face towards me.

"You thought I did it on purpose, but you're wrong. If I had, I'd have done it better than this. I wouldn't have this brutal pain." She put her fingers over her eyes. "It's horrible to complain! Only it's so bad! But I won't again—I—promise."

She took the sleeping draught gratefully, making a face, like a child after a powder.

"How long do you think it'll be before I can play again? Oh! I forgot—there are other things to think about." She held out her hand to me. "Look at my ring. Married—isn't it funny? Ha, ha! Nobody will ever understand—that's funny too! Poor Gran! You see, there wasn't any reason—only me. That's the only reason I'm telling you now; Mums is there—but she doesn't count; why don't you count, Mums?"

The fever was fighting against the draught; she had tossed the clothes back from her throat, and now and then raised one thin arm a little, as if it eased her; her eyes had grown large, and innocent like a child's; the candle, too, had flared, and was burning clearly.

"Nobody is to tell him—nobody at all; promise! . . . If I hadn't slipped, it would have been different. What would have happened then? You can't tell; and I can't—that's funny! Do you think I loved him? Nobody marries without love, do they? Not quite without love, I mean. But you see I wanted to be free, he said he'd take me; and now he's left me after all! I won't be left, I can't! When I came to the cliff—

that bit where the ivy grows right down—there was just the sea there, underneath; so I thought I would throw myself over and it would be all quiet; and I climbed on a ledge, it looked easier from there, but it was so high, I wanted to get back; and then my foot slipped; and now it's all pain. You can't think much, when you're in pain."

From her eyes I saw that she was dropping off.

"Nobody can take you away from—yourself. He's not to be told—not even—I don't—want you—to go away, because——" But her eyes closed, and she dropped off to sleep.

They don't seem to know this morning whether she is better or worse . . .

VI

Tuesday, 9th August.

It seems more like three weeks than three days since I wrote. The time passes slowly in a sick house! . . . The doctors were here this morning, they give her forty hours. Not a word of complaint has passed her lips since she knew. To see her you would hardly think her ill; her cheeks have not had time to waste or lose their colour. There is not much pain, but a slow, creeping numbness . . . It was John Ford's wish that she should be told. She just turned her head to the wall and sighed; then to poor old Mrs. Hopgood, who was crying her heart out: "Don't cry, Mums, I don't care."

When they had gone, she asked for her violin. She made them hold it for her, and drew the bow across the strings; but the notes that came out were so trembling and uncertain that she dropped the bow and broke into a passion of sobbing. Since then, no complaint or moan of any kind . . .

But to go back. On Sunday, the day after I wrote, as I was coming from a walk, I met a little boy making mournful sounds on a tin whistle.

"Coom ahn!" he said, "the Miss wahnts t' zee yu."

I went to her room. In the morning she had seemed better, but now looked utterly exhausted. She had a letter in her hand.

"It's this," she said. "I don't seem to understand it. He wants me to do something—but I can't think, and my eyes feel funny. Read it to me, please."

The letter was from Zachary. I read it to her in a low voice, for
Mrs. Hopgood was in the room, her eyes always fixed on Pasiance
above her knitting. When I'd finished, she made me read it again,
and yet again. At first she seemed pleased, almost excited, then came
a weary, scornful look, and before I'd finished the third time she was
asleep. It was a remarkable letter, that seemed to bring the man right
before one's eyes. I slipped it under her fingers on the bed-clothes,
and went out. Fancy took me to the cliff where she had fallen. I
found the point of rock where the cascade of ivy flows down the
cliff; the ledge on which she had climbed was a little to my right—a
mad place. It showed plainly what wild emotions must have been
driving her! Behind was a half-cut cornfield with a fringe of poppies,
and swarms of harvest insects creeping and flying; in the uncut corn
a landrail kept up a continual charring. The sky was blue to the very
horizon, and the sea wonderful, under that black wild cliff stained
here and there with red. Over the dips and hollows of the fields
great white clouds hung low down above the land. There are no
brassy, east-coast skies here; but always sleepy, soft-shaped clouds,
full of subtle stir and change. Passages of Zachary Pearse's letter kept
rising to my lips. After all he's the man that his native place, and life,
and blood have made him. It is useless to expect idealists where the
air is soft and things good to look on (the idealist grows where he
must create beauty or comfort for himself); useless to expect a man
of law and order in one whose fathers have stared at the sea day and
night for a thousand years—the sea, full of its promises of unknown
things, never quite the same, a slave to its own impulses. Man is an
imitative animal . . .

"Life's hard enough," he wrote, "without tying yourself down.
Don't think too hardly of me! Shall I make you happier by taking
you into danger? If I succeed you'll be a rich woman; but I shall
fail if you're with me. To look at you makes me soft. At sea a man
dreams of all the good things on land, he'll dream of the heather, and
honey—you're like that; and he'll dream of the apple-trees, and the
grass of the orchards—you're like that; sometimes he only lies on his
back and wishes—and you're like that, most of all like that . . ."

When I was reading those words I remember a strange, soft, half-
scornful look came over Pasiance's face; and once she said, "But
that's all nonsense, isn't it?"

Then followed a long passage about what he would gain if he succeeded, about all that he was risking, the impossibility of failure, if he kept his wits about him. "It's only a matter of two months or so," he went on; "stay where you are, dear, or go to my Dad. He'll be glad to have you. There's my mother's room. There's no one to say 'No' to your fiddle there; you can play it by the sea; and on dark nights you'll have the stars dancing to you over the waters as thick as bees. I've looked at them often, thinking of you . . ."

Pasiance had whispered to me, "Don't read that bit," and afterwards I left it out . . . Then the sensuous side of him shows up: "When I've brought this off, there's the whole world before us. There are places I can take you to. There's one I know, not too warm and not too cold, where you can sit all day in the shade and watch the creepers, and the cocoa-palms, still as still; nothing to do or care about; all the fruits you can think of; no noise but the parrots and the streams, and a splash when a nigger dives into a water-hole. Pasiance, we'll go there! With an eighty-ton craft there's no sea we couldn't know. The world's a fine place for those who go out to take it; there's lots of unknown stuff in it yet. I'll fill your lap, my pretty, so full of treasures that you shan't know yourself. A man wasn't meant to sit at home . . ."

Throughout this letter—for all its real passion—one could feel how the man was holding to his purpose—the rather sordid purpose of this venture. He's unconscious of it; for he is in love with her; but he must be furthering his own ends. He is vital—horribly vital! I wonder less now that she should have yielded.

What visions hasn't he dangled before her. There was physical attraction, too—I haven't forgotten the look I saw on her face at Black Mill. But when all's said and done, she married him, because she's Pasiance Voisey, who does things and wants "to get back." And she lies there dying; not he nor any other man will ever take her away. It's pitiful to think of him tingling with passion, writing that letter to this doomed girl in that dark hole of a saloon. "I've wanted money," he wrote, "ever since I was a little chap sitting in the fields among the cows . . . I want it for you now, and I mean to have it. I've studied the thing two years; I know what I know . . . The moment this is in the post I leave for London. There are a hundred things to look after still; I can't trust myself within reach of you again till the anchor's weighed. When I rechristened her the *Pied Witch*, I thought of you—you witch to me."

There followed a solemn entreaty to her to be on the path leading to the cove at seven o'clock on Wednesday evening (that is, to-morrow) when he would come ashore and bid her good-bye. It was signed, "Your loving husband, Zachary Pearse."

I lay at the edge of that cornfield a long time; it was very peaceful. The church bells had begun to ring. The long shadows came stealing out from the sheaves; wood-pigeons rose one by one, and flapped off to roost; the western sky was streaked with red, and all the downs and combe bathed in the last sunlight. Perfect harvest weather; but oppressively still; the stillness of suspense . . .

Life at the farm goes on as usual. We have morning and evening prayers. John Ford reads them fiercely, as though he were on the eve of a revolt against his God. Morning and evening he visits her, comes out wheezing heavily, and goes to his own room; I believe, to pray. Since this morning I haven't dared meet him. He is a strong old man—but this will break him up . . .

VII

KINGSWEAR, *Saturday, 13th August.*
It's over—I leave here to-morrow, and go abroad.

A quiet afternoon not a breath up in the churchyard! I was there quite half an hour before they came. Some red cows had strayed into the adjoining orchard, and were rubbing their heads against the railing. While I stood there an old woman came and drove them away; afterwards, she stooped and picked up the apples that had fallen before their time.

> The apples are ripe and ready to fall,
> Oh! heigh-ho! and ready to fall;
> There came an old woman and gathered them all,
> Oh! heigho! and gathered them all.

. . . They brought Pasiance very simply—no hideous funeral trappings, thank God—the farm hands carried her, and there was no one there but John Ford, the Hopgoods, myself, and that young

doctor. They read the services over her grave. I can hear John Ford's
"Amen!" now. When it was over he walked away bareheaded in
the sun, without a word. I went up there again this evening, and
wandered amongst the tombstones. "Richard Voisey," "John, the
son of Richard and Constance Voisey," "Margery Voisey," so many
generations of them in that corner; then "Richard Voisey and Agnes
his wife," and next to it that new mound on which a sparrow was
strutting and the shadows of the apple-trees already hovering. I will
tell you the little left to tell . . .

On Wednesday afternoon she asked for me again.

"It's only till seven," she whispered. "He's certain to come then.
But if I—were to die first—then tell him I'm sorry for him. They
keep saying: 'Don't talk—don't talk!' Isn't it stupid? As if I should
have any other chance! There'll be no more talking after to-night!
Make everybody come, please—I want to see them all. When you're
dying you're freer than any other time—nobody wants you to do
things, nobody cares what you say. . . He promised me I should do
what I liked if I married him—I never believed that really—but
now I *can* do what I like; and say all the things I want to." She lay
back silent; she could not after all speak the inmost thoughts that
are in each of us, so sacred that they melt away at the approach of
words.

I shall remember her like that—with the gleam of a smile in her
half-closed eyes, her red lips parted—such a quaint look of mockery,
pleasure, regret, on her little round, upturned face; the room white,
and fresh with flowers, the breeze fluttering the apple-leaves against
the window. In the night they had unhooked the violin and taken it
away; she had not missed it.

When Dan came, I gave up my place to him. He took her hand
gently in his great paw, without speaking.

"How small my hand looks there," she said, "too small."

Dan put it softly back on the bedclothes and wiped his forehead.

Pasiance cried in a sharp whisper: "Is it so hot in here? I didn't
know." Dan bent down, put his lips to her fingers and left the
room.

The afternoon was long, the longest I've ever spent. Sometimes she
seemed to sleep, sometimes whispered to herself about her mother,
her grandfather, the garden, or her cats—all sorts of inconsequent,

trivial, even ludicrous memories seemed to throng her mind—never once, I think, did she speak of Zachary, but, now and then, she asked the time . . . Each hour she grew visibly weaker. John Ford sat by her without moving, his heavy breathing was often the only sound; sometimes she rubbed her fingers on his hand, without speaking. It was a summary of their lives together. Once he prayed aloud for her in a hoarse voice; then her pitiful, impatient eyes signed to me.

"Quick," she whispered, "I want *him*; it's all so—cold."

I went out and ran down the path towards the cove.

Leaning on a gate stood Zachary, an hour before his time; dressed in the same old blue clothes and leather-peaked cap as on the day when I saw him first. He knew nothing of what had happened. But at a quarter of the truth, I'm sure he divined the whole, though he would not admit it to himself. He kept saying, "It can't be. She'll be well in a few days—a sprain! D'you think the sea-voyage . . . Is she strong enough to be moved now at once?"

It was painful to see his face, so twisted by the struggle between his instinct and his vitality. The sweat poured down his forehead. He turned round as we walked up the path, and pointed out to sea. There was his steamer. "I could get her on board in no time. Impossible! What is it, then? Spine? Good God! The doctors . . . Sometimes they'll do wonders!" It was pitiful to see his efforts to blind himself to the reality.

"It *can't* be, she's too young. We're walking very slow." I told him she was dying.

For a second I thought he was going to run away. Then he jerked up his head, and rushed on towards the house. At the foot of the staircase he gripped me by the shoulder.

"It's not true!" he said; "she'll get better now I'm here. I'll *stay*. Let everything go. I'll stay."

"Now's the time," I said, "to show you loved her. Pull yourself together, man!" He shook all over.

"Yes!" was all he answered. We went into her room. It seemed impossible she was going to die; the colour was bright in her cheeks, her lips trembling and pouted as if she had just been kissed, her eyes gleaming, her hair so dark and crisp, her face so young.

Half an hour later I stole to the open door of her room. She was still and white as the sheets of her bed. John Ford stood at the foot;

and, bowed to the level of the pillows, his head on his clenched fists, sat Zachary. It was utterly quiet. The fluttering of the leaves had ceased. When things have come to a crisis, how little one feels—no fear, no pity, no sorrow, rather the sense, as when a play is over, of anxiety to get away! Suddenly Zachary rose, brushed past me without seeing, and ran downstairs.

Some hours later I went out on the path leading to the cove. It was pitch-black; the riding light of the *Pied Witch* was still there, looking no bigger than a firefly. Then from in front I heard sobbing man's sobs; no sound is quite so dreadful. Zachary Pearse got up out of the bank not ten paces off.

I had no heart to go after him, and sat down in the hedge. There was something subtly akin to her in the fresh darkness of the young night; the soft bank, the scent of honeysuckle, the touch of the ferns and brambles. Death comes to all of us, and when it's over it's over; but this blind business—of those left behind!

A little later the ship whistled twice; her starboard light gleamed faintly—and that was all . . .

VIII

TORQUAY, 30*th October.*
Do you remember the letters I wrote you from Moor Farm nearly three years ago? Today I rode over there. I stopped at Brixham on the way for lunch, and walked down to the quay. There had been a shower—but the sun was out again, shining on the sea, the brown-red sails, and the rampart of slate roofs.

A trawler was lying there, which had evidently been in a collision. The spiky-bearded, thin-lipped fellow in torn blue jersey and sea-boots who was superintending the repairs, said to me a little proudly:

"Bane in collision, zurr; like to zee over her?"

Then suddenly screwing up his little blue eyes, he added:

"Why, I remembers yu. Steered yu along o' the young lady in this yer very craft."

It was Prawle, Zachary Pearse's henchman.

"Yes," he went on, "that's the cutter."

"And Captain Pearse?"

He leant his back against the quay, and spat.

"He was a pra-aper man; I never zane none like 'en."

"Did you do any good out there?"

Prawle gave me a sharp glance.

"Gude? No, 'twas arrm we done, vrom ztart to finish—had trouble all the time. What a man cude du, the skipper did. When yu caan't du right, zome calls it 'Providence'! 'Tis all my eye an' Betty Martin! What I zay es, 'tis these times, there's such a dale o' folk, a dale of puzzivantin' fellers; the world's tu small."

With these words there flashed across me a vision of Drake crushed into our modern life by the shrinkage of the world; Drake caught in the meshes of red tape, electric wires, and all the lofty appliances of our civilization. Does a type survive its age; live on into times that have no room for it? The blood is there—and sometimes there's a throw-back . . . All fancy! Eh?

"So," I said, "you failed!"

Prawle wriggled.

"I wudden' goo for to say that, zurr—'tis an ugly word. Da-am!" he added, staring at his boots, "'twas thru me tu. We were along among the haythen, and I mus' nades goo for to break me leg. The capt'n he wudden' lave me. 'One Devon man,' he says to me, 'don' lave anotherr.' We werr six days where he shuld ha' been tu; when we got back to the ship a——cruiser had got her for gun-runnin'."

"And what has become of Captain Pearse?"

Prawle answered, "Zurr, I belave 'e went to China, 'tis onsartin."

"He's not dead?"

Prawle looked at me with a kind of uneasy anger.

"Yu cudden' kell 'en! 'Tis true, mun'll die zome day. But therr's not a one that'll show better zport than Capt'n Zach'ry Pearse."

I believe that; he will be hard to kill. The vision of him comes up, with his perfect balance, defiant eyes, and sweetish smile; the way the hair of his beard crisped a little, and got blacker on the cheeks; the sort of desperate feeling he gave, that one would never get the better of him, that he would never get the better of himself.

I took leave of Prawle and half a crown. Before I was off the quay I heard him saying to a lady, "Bane in collision, marm! Like to zee over her?"

After lunch I rode on to Moor. The old place looked much the same; but the apple-trees were stripped of fruit, and their leaves beginning to go yellow and fall. One of Pasiance's cats passed me in the orchard hunting a bird, still with a ribbon round its neck. John Ford showed me all his latest improvements, but never, by word or sign alluded to the past. He inquired after Dan, back in New Zealand now, without much interest; his stubbly beard and hair have whitened: he has grown very stout, and I noticed that his legs are not well under control; he often stops to lean on his stick. He was very ill last winter, and sometimes, they say, will go straight off to sleep in the middle of a sentence.

I managed to get a few minutes with the Hopgoods. We talked of Pasiance sitting in the kitchen under a row of plates, with that clinging smell of wood-smoke, bacon, and age bringing up memories, as nothing but scents can. The dear old lady's hair, drawn so nicely down her forehead on each side from the centre of her cap, has a few thin silver lines; and her face is a thought more wrinkled. The tears still come into her eyes when she talks of her "lamb."

Of Zachary I heard nothing, but she told me of old Pearse's death.

"Therr they found 'en, zo to spake, dead—in th' sun; but Haapgood can tell yu," and Hopgood, ever rolling his pipe, muttered something, and smiled his wooden smile.

He came to see me off from the straw-yard. "'Tis like death to the varrm, zurr," he said, putting all the play of his vast shoulders into the buckling of my girths. "Mister Ford—well! And not one of th' old stock to take it wheu 'e's garn . . . Ah! it *werr cruel*; my old woman's never been hersel' since. Tell 'ee what 'tis—don't du t' think tu much."

I went out of my way to pass the churchyard. There were flowers, quite fresh, chrysanthemums and asters; above them the white stone, already stained:

' "PASIANCE,

WIFE OF ZACHARY PEARSE,

'*The Lord hath given, and the Lord hath taken away.*'

The red cows were there too; the sky full of great white clouds, some birds whistling a little mournfully, and in the air the scent of fallen leaves . . .

[*May, 1900*]

THE APPLE TREE

'The Apple-tree, the singing, and the gold.'
MURRAY'S *Hippolytus of Euripides*.

ON their silver-wedding day Ashurst and his wife were motoring
along the outskirts of the moor, intending to crown the festival by
stopping the night at Torquay, where they had first met. This was
the idea of Stella Ashurst, whose character contained a streak of
sentiment. If she had long lost the blue-eyed, flower-like charm,
the cool slim purity of face and form, the apple-blossom colouring,
which had so swiftly and so oddly affected Ashurst twenty-six years
ago, she was still at forty-three a comely and faithful companion,
whose cheeks were faintly mottled, and whose grey-blue eyes had
acquired a certain fullness.

It was she who had stopped the car where the common rose
steeply to the left, and a narrow strip of larch and beech, with here
and there a pine, stretched out towards the valley between the road
and the first long high hill of the full moor. She was looking for a
place where they might lunch, for Ashurst never looked for anything;
and this, between the golden furze and the feathery green larches
smelling of lemons in the last sun of April—this, with a view into
the deep valley and up to the long moor heights, seemed fitting to
the decisive nature of one who sketched in water-colours, and loved
romantic spots. Grasping her paint box, she got out.

"Won't this do, Frank?"

Ashurst, rather like a bearded Schiller, grey in the wings, tall, long-
legged, with large remote grey eyes which sometimes filled with
meaning and became almost beautiful, with nose a little to one side,
and bearded lips just open—Ashurst, forty-eight, and silent, grasped
the luncheon basket, and got out too.

"Oh! Look, Frank! A grave!"

By the side of the road, where the track from the top of the common crossed it at right angles and ran through a gate past the narrow wood, was a thin mound of turf, six feet by one, with a moorstone to the west, and on it someone had thrown a blackthorn spray and a handful of bluebells. Ashurst looked, and the poet in him moved. At cross-roads—a suicide's grave! Poor mortals with their superstitions! Whoever lay there, though, had the best of it, no clammy sepulchre among other hideous graves carved with futilities—just a rough stone, the wide sky, and wayside blessings! And, without comment, for he had learned not to be a philosopher in the bosom of his family, he strode away up on to the common, dropped the luncheon basket under a wall, spread a rug for his wife to sit on—she would turn up from her sketching when she was hungry—and took from his pocket Murray's translation of the "Hippolytus." He had soon finished reading of "The Cyprian" and her revenge, and looked at the sky instead. And watching the white clouds so bright against the intense blue, Ashurst, on his silver-wedding day, longed for—he knew not what. Mal-adjusted to life—man's organism! One's mode of life might be high and scrupulous, but there was always an undercurrent of greediness, a hankering, and sense of waste. Did women have it too? Who could tell? And yet, men who gave vent to their appetites for novelty, their riotous longings for new adventures, new risks, new pleasures, these suffered, no doubt, from the reverse side of starvation, from surfeit. No getting out of it—a mal-adjusted animal, civilised man! There could be no garden of his choosing, of "the Apple-tree, the singing, and the gold," in the words of that lovely Greek chorus, no achievable elysium in life, or lasting haven of happiness for any man with a sense of beauty—nothing which could compare with the captured loveliness in a work of art, set down for ever, so that to look on it or read was always to have the same precious sense of exaltation and restful inebriety. Life no doubt had moments with that quality of beauty, of unbidden flying rapture, but the trouble was, they lasted no longer than the span of a cloud's flight over the sun; impossible to keep them with you, as Art caught beauty and held it fast. They were fleeting as one of the glimmering or golden visions one had of the soul in nature, glimpses of its remote and brooding spirit. Here, with the sun hot on his face, a cuckoo calling from a thorn tree, and in the air the honey savour of gorse—here among the little fronds of the young fern, the starry blackthorn, while the bright clouds drifted by high above the hills and dreamy valleys—here and now was such a glimpse. But in a moment it would pass—as the face of Pan, which looks round the corner of a rock, vanishes at your stare. And suddenly he sat up. Surely there was something familiar about this view, this bit of common, that ribbon of road, the old wall behind him. While they were driving he had not been taking notice—never did; thinking of far things or of nothing—but now he saw! Twenty-six years ago, just at this time of year, from the farmhouse within half a mile of this very spot he had started for that day in Torquay whence it might be said he had never returned. And a sudden ache beset his heart; he had stumbled on just one of those past moments in his life, whose beauty and rapture he had failed to arrest, whose wings had fluttered away into the unknown; he had stumbled on a buried memory, a wild sweet time, swiftly choked and ended. And, turning on his face, he rested his chin on his hands, and stared at the short grass where the little blue milkwort was growing . . .

And this is what he remembered.

I

On the first of May, after their last year together at college, Frank Ashurst and his friend Robert Garton were on a tramp. They had walked that day from Brent, intending to make Chagford, but Ashurst's football knee had given out, and according to their map they had still some seven miles to go. They were sitting on a bank beside the road, where a track crossed alongside a wood, resting the knee and talking of the universe, as young men will. Both were over six feet, and thin as rails; Ashurst pale, idealistic, full of absence; Garton queer, round-the-corner, knotted, curly, like some primeval beast. Both had a literary bent; neither wore a hat. Ashurst's hair was smooth, pale, wavy, and had a way of rising on either side of his brow, as if always being flung back; Garton's was a kind of dark unfathomed mop. They had not met a soul for miles.

"My dear fellow," Garton was saying, "pity's only an effect of self-consciousness; it's a disease of the last five thousand years. The world was happier without."

Ashurst, following the clouds with his eyes, answered:

"It's the pearl in the oyster, anyway."

"My dear chap, all our modern unhappiness comes from pity. Look at animals, and Red Indians, limited to felling their own occasional misfortunes; then look at ourselves—never free from feeling the toothaches of others. Let's get back to feeling for nobody, and have a better time."

"You'll never practise that."

Garton pensively stirred the hotch-potch of his hair.

"To attain full growth, one mustn't be squeamish. To starve oneself emotionally's a mistake. All emotion is to the good—enriches life."

"Yes, and when it runs up against chivalry?"

"Ah! That's so English! If you speak of emotion the English always think you want something physical, and are shocked. They're afraid of passion, but not of lust—oh, no!—so long as they can keep it secret."

Ashurst did not answer; he had plucked a blue floweret, and was twiddling it against the sky. A cuckoo began calling from a thorn tree. The sky, the flowers, the songs of birds! Robert was talking through his hat! And he said:

"Well, let's go on, and find some farm where we can put up." In uttering those words, he was conscious of a girl coming down from the common just above them. She was outlined against the sky, carrying a basket, and you could see that sky through the crook of her arm. And Ashurst, who saw beauty without wondering how it could advantage him, thought: 'How pretty!' The wind, blowing her dark frieze skirt against her legs, lifted her battered peacock tam-o'-shanter; her greyish blouse was worn and old, her shoes were split, her little hands rough and red, her neck browned. Her dark hair waved untidy across her broad forehead, her face was short, her upper lip short, showing a glint of teeth, her brows were straight and dark, her lashes long and dark, her nose straight; but her grey eyes were the wonder—dewy as if opened for the first time that day. She looked at Ashurst—perhaps he struck her as strange, limping along without a hat, with his large eyes on her, and his hair flung back. He could not take off what was not on his head, but put up his hand in a salute, and said:

"Can you tell us if there's a farm near here where we could stay the night? I've gone lame."

"There's only our farm near, sir." She spoke without shyness, in a pretty, soft, crisp voice.

"And where is that?"

"Down here, sir."

"Would you put us up?"

"Oh! I think we would."

"Will you show us the way?"

"Yes, sir."

He limped on, silent, and Garton took up the catechism.

"Are you a Devonshire girl?"

"No, sir."

"What then?"

"From Wales."

"Ah! I *thought* you were a Celt; so it's not your farm?"

"My aunt's, sir."

"And your uncle's?"

"He is dead."

"Who farms it, then?"

"My aunt, and my three cousins."

"But your uncle was a Devonshire man?"

"Yes, sir."

"Have you lived here long?"

"Seven years."

"And how d'you like it after Wales?"

"I don't know, sir."

"I suppose you don't remember?"

"Oh, yes! But it is different."

"I believe you!"

Ashurst broke in suddenly:

"How old are you?"

"Seventeen, sir."

"And what's your name?"

"Megan David."

"This is Robert Garton, and I am Frank Ashurst. We wanted to get on to Chagford."

"It is a pity your leg is hurting you."

Ashurst smiled, and when he smiled his face was rather beautiful.

Descending past the narrow wood, they came on the farm suddenly—a long, low, stone-built dwelling with casement windows, in a farmyard where pigs and fowls and an old mare were straying. A short steep-up grass hill behind was crowned with a few Scotch firs, and in front, an old orchard of apple trees, just breaking into flower, stretched down to a stream and a long wild meadow. A little boy with oblique dark eyes was shepherding a pig, and by the house door stood a woman, who came towards them. The girl said:

"It is Mrs. Narracombe, my aunt."

"Mrs. Narracombe, my aunt" had a quick, dark eye, like a mother wild-duck's, and something of the same snaky turn about her neck.

"We met your niece on the road," said Ashurst; "she thought you might perhaps put us up for the night."

Mrs. Narracombe, taking them in from head to heel, answered:

"Well, I can, if you don't mind one room. Megan, get the spare room ready, and a bowl of cream. You'll be wanting tea, I suppose."

Passing through a sort of porch made by two yew trees and some flowering-currant bushes, the girl disappeared into the house, her peacock tam-o'-shanter bright athwart that rosy-pink and the dark green of the yews.

"Will you come into the parlour and rest your leg? You'll be from college, perhaps?"

"We were, but we've gone down now."

Mrs. Narracombe nodded sagely.

The parlour, brick-floored, with bare table and shiny chairs and sofa stuffed with horsehair, seemed never to have been used, it was so terribly clean. Ashurst sat down at once on the sofa, holding his lame knee between his hands, and Mrs. Narracombe gazed at him. He was the only son of a late professor of chemistry, but people found a certain lordliness in one who was often so sublimely unconscious of them.

"Is there a stream where we could bathe?"

"There's the strame at the bottom of the orchard, but sittin' down you'll not be covered!"

"How deep?"

"Well, 'tis about a foot and a half, maybe."

"Oh! That'll do fine. Which way?"

"Down the lane, through the second gate on the right, an' the pool's by the big apple tree that stands by itself. There's trout there, if you can tickle them."

"They're more likely to tickle us!"

Mrs. Narracombe smiled. "There'll be the tea ready when you come back."

The pool, formed by the damming of a rock, had a sandy bottom; and the big apple tree, lowest in the orchard, grew so close that its boughs almost overhung the water; it was in leaf, and all but in flower—its crimson buds just bursting.

There was not room for more than one at a time in that narrow bath, and Ashurst waited his turn, rubbing his knee and gazing at the wild meadow, all rocks and thorn trees and field flowers, with a grove of beeches beyond, raised up on a flat mound. Every bough was swinging in the wind, every spring bird calling, and a slanting sunlight dappled the grass. He thought of Theocritus, and the river Cherwell, of the moon, and the maiden with the dewy eyes; of so many things that he seemed to think of nothing; and he felt absurdly happy.

II

During a late and sumptuous tea with eggs to it, cream and jam, and thin, fresh cakes touched with saffron, Garton descanted on the Celts. It was about the period of the Celtic awakening, and the discovery that there was Celtic blood about this family had excited one who believed that he was a Celt himself. Sprawling on a horsehair chair, with a hand-made cigarette dribbling from the corner of his curly lips, he had been plunging his cold pin-points of eyes into Ashurst's and praising the refinement of the Welsh. To come out of Wales into England was like the change from china to earthenware! Frank, as a d—d Englishman, had not of course perceived the exquisite refinement and emotional capacity of that Welsh girl! And, delicately stirring in the dark mat of his still wet hair, he explained how exactly she illustrated the writings of the Welsh bard Morgan-ap-Something in the twelfth century.

Ashurst, full length on the horsehair sofa, and jutting far beyond its end, smoked a deeply-coloured pipe, and did not listen, thinking of the girl's face when she brought in a relay of cakes. It had been exactly like looking at a flower, or some other pretty sight in Nature—till, with a funny little shiver, she had lowered her glance and gone out, quiet as a mouse.

"Let's go to the kitchen," said Garton, "and see some more of her."

The kitchen was a white-washed room with rafters, to which were attached smoked hams; there were flower-pots on the window-sill, and guns hanging on nails, queer mugs, china and pewter, and portraits of Queen Victoria. A long, narrow table of plain wood was set with bowls and spoons, under a string of high-hung onions; two sheep-dogs and three cats lay here and there. On one side of the recessed fireplace sat two small boys, idle, and good as gold; on the other sat a stout, light-eyed, red-faced youth with hair and lashes the colour of the tow he was running through the barrel of a gun; between them Mrs. Narracombe dreamily stirred some savoury-scented stew in a large pot. Two other youths, oblique-eyed, dark-haired, rather sly-faced, like the two little boys, were talking together and lolling against the wall; and a short, elderly, clean-shaven man in corduroys, seated in the window, was conning a battered journal. The girl Megan seemed the only active creature—drawing cider and passing with the jugs from cask to table. Seeing them thus about to eat, Garton said:

"Ah! If you'll let us, we'll come back when supper's over," and without waiting for an answer they withdrew again to the parlour. But the colour in the kitchen, the warmth, the scents, and all those faces, heightened the bleakness of their shiny room, and they resumed their seats moodily.

"Regular gipsy type, those boys. There was only one Saxon—the fellow cleaning the gun. That girl is a very subtle study psychologically."

Ashurst's lips twitched. Garton seemed to him an ass just then. Subtle study! She was a wild flower. A creature it did you good to look at. Study!

Garton went on:

"Emotionally she would be wonderful. She wants awakening."

"Are you going to awaken her?"

Garton looked at him and smiled. 'How coarse and English you are!' that curly smile seemed saying.

And Ashurst puffed his pipe. Awaken her! This fool had the best opinion of himself! He threw up the window and leaned out. Dusk had gathered thick. The farm buildings and the wheel-house were all dim and bluish, the apple trees but a blurred wilderness; the air smelled of wood smoke from the kitchen fire. One bird going to bed later than the others was uttering a half-hearted twitter, as though surprised at the darkness. From the stable came the snuffle and stamp of a feeding horse. And away over there was the loom of the moor, and away and away the shy stars which had not as yet full light, pricking white through the deep blue heavens. A quavering owl hooted. Ashurst drew a deep breath. What a night to wander out in! A padding of unshod hoofs came up the lane, and three dim, dark shapes passed—ponies on an evening march. Their heads, black and fuzzy, showed above the gate. At the tap of his pipe, and a shower of little sparks, they shied round and scampered. A bat went fluttering past, uttering its almost inaudible "chip, chip." Ashurst held out his hand; on the upturned palm he could feel the dew. Suddenly from overhead he heard little burring boys' voices, little thumps of boots thrown down, and another voice, crisp and soft—the girl's putting them to bed, no doubt; and nine clear words: "No, Rick, you can't have the cat in bed"; then came a skirmish of giggles and gurgles, a soft slap, a laugh so low and pretty that it made him shiver a little. A blowing sound, and the glim of the candle which was fingering the dusk above, went out; silence reigned. Ashurst withdrew into the room and sat down; his knee pained him, and his soul felt gloomy.

"You go to the kitchen," he said; "I'm going to bed."

III

For Ashurst the wheel of slumber was wont to turn noiseless and slick and swift, but though he seemed sunk in sleep when his companion came up, he was really wide awake; and long after Garton, smothered in the other bed of that low-roofed room, was worshipping darkness with his upturned nose, he heard the owls. Barring the discomfort of his knee, it was not unpleasant—the cares of life did not loom large in night watches for this young man. In fact he had none; just enrolled a barrister, with literary aspirations, the world before him, no father or mother, and four hundred a year of his own. Did it matter where he went, what he did, or when he did it? His bed, too, was hard, and this preserved him from fever. He lay, sniffing the scent of the night which drifted into the low room through the open casement close to his head. Except for a definite irritation with his friend, natural when you have tramped with a man for three days, Ashurst's memories and visions that sleepless night were kindly and wistful and exciting. One vision, specially clear and unreasonable, for he had not even been conscious of noting it, was the face of the youth cleaning the gun; its intent, stolid, yet startled uplook at the kitchen doorway, quickly shifted to the girl carrying the cider jug. This red, blue-eyed, light-lashed, tow-haired face stuck as firmly in his memory as the girl's own face, so dewy and simple. But at last, in the square of darkness through the uncurtained casement, he saw day coming, and heard one hoarse and sleepy caw. Then followed silence, dead as ever, till the song of a blackbird, not properly awake, adventured into the hush. And, from staring at the framed brightening light, Ashurst fell asleep.

Next day his knee was badly swollen; the walking tour was obviously over. Garton, due back in London on the morrow, departed at midday with an ironical smile which left a scar of irritation—healed the moment his loping figure vanished round the corner of the steep lane. All day Ashurst rested his knee, in a green-painted wooden chair on the patch of grass by the yew-tree porch, where the sunlight distilled the scent of stocks and gillyflowers, and a ghost of scent from the flowering-currant bushes. Beatifically he smoked, dreamed, watched.

A farm in spring is all birth—young things coming out of bud and shell, and human beings watching over the process with faint excitement feeding and tending what has been born. So still the young man sat, that a mother-goose, with stately cross-footed waddle, brought her six yellow-necked grey-backed goslings to strop their little beaks against the grass blades at his feet. Now and again Mrs. Narracombe or the girl Megan would come and ask if he wanted anything, and he would smile and say: "Nothing, thanks. It's splendid here." Towards tea-time they came out together, bearing a long poultice of some dark stuff in a bowl, and after a long and solemn scrutiny of his swollen knee, bound it on. When they were gone, he thought of the girl's soft "Oh!"—of her pitying eyes, and the little wrinkle in her brow. And again he felt that unreasoning irritation against his departed friend, who had talked such rot about her. When she brought out his tea, he said:

"How did you like my friend, Megan?"

She forced down her upper lip, as if afraid that to smile was not polite. "He was a funny gentleman; he made us laugh. I think he is very clever."

"What did he say to make you laugh?"

"He said I was a daughter of the bards. What are they?"

"Welsh poets, who lived hundreds of years ago."

"Why am I their daughter, please?"

"He meant that you were the sort of girl they sang about."

She wrinkled her brows. "I think he likes to joke. Am I?"

"Would you believe me, if I told you?"

"Oh, yes."

"Well, I think he was right." She smiled.

And Ashurst thought: 'You *are* a pretty thing!'

"He said, too, that Joe was a Saxon type. What would that be?"

"Which is Joe? With the blue eyes and red face?"

"Yes. My uncle's nephew."

"Not your cousin, then?"

"No."

"Well, he meant that Joe was like the men who came over to England about fourteen hundred years ago, and conquered it."

"Oh! I know about them; but is he?"

"Garton's crazy about that sort of thing; but I must say Joe does look a bit Early Saxon."

"Yes."

That "Yes" tickled Ashurst. It was so crisp and graceful, so conclusive, and politely acquiescent in what was evidently Greek to her.

"He said that all the other boys were regular gipsies. He should not have said that. My aunt laughed, but she didn't like it, of course, and my cousins were angry. Uncle was a farmer—farmers are not gipsies. It is wrong to hurt people."

Ashurst wanted to take her hand and give it a squeeze, but he only answered:

"Quite right, Megan. By the way, I heard you putting the little ones to bed last night."

She flushed a little. "Please to drink your tea—it is getting cold. Shall I get you some fresh?"

"Do you ever have time to do anything for yourself?"

"Oh, yes."

"I've been watching, but I haven't seen it yet."

She wrinkled her brows in a puzzled frown, and her colour deepened.

When she was gone, Ashurst thought: 'Did she think I was chaffing her? I wouldn't for the world!' He was at that age when to some men "Beauty's a flower," as the poet says, and inspires in them the thoughts of chivalry. Never very conscious of his surroundings, it was some time before he was aware that the youth whom Garton had called "a Saxon type" was standing outside the stable door; and a fine bit of colour he made in his soiled brown velvetcords, muddy gaiters, and blue shirt; red-armed, red-faced, the sun turning his hair from tow to flax; immovably stolid, persistent, unsmiling he stood. Then, seeing Ashurst looking at him, he crossed the yard at that gait of the young countryman always ashamed not to be slow and heavy-dwelling on each leg, and disappeared round the end of the house towards the kitchen entrance. A chill came over Ashurst's mood. Clods! With all the good will in the world, how impossible to get on terms with them! And yet—see that girl! Her shoes were split, her hands rough; but—what was it? Was it really her Celtic blood; as Garton had said?—she was a lady born, a jewel, though probably she could do no more than just read and write!

The elderly, clean-shaven man he had seen last night in the kitchen had come into the yard with a dog, driving the cows to their milking. Ashurst saw that he was lame.

"You've got some good ones there!"

The lame man's face brightened. He had the upward look in his eyes which prolonged suffering often brings.

"Yeas; they'm praaper buties; gude milkers tu."

"I bet they are."

"'Ope as yure leg's better, zurr."

"Thank you, it's getting on."

The lame man touched his own: "I know what 'tes, meself; 'tes a main worritin' thing, the knee. I've a 'ad mine bad this ten year."

Ashurst made the sound of sympathy which comes so readily from those who have an independent income, and the lame man smiled again.

"Mustn't complain, though—they mighty near 'ad it off."

"Ho!"

"Yeas; an' compared with what twas, 'tes almost so gude as nu."

"They've put a bandage of splendid stuff on mine."

"The maid she picks et. She'm a gude maid wi' the flowers. There's folks zeem to know the healin' in things. My mother was a rare one for that. 'Ope as yu'll zune be better, zurr. Goo ahn, therr!"

Ashurst smiled. "Wi' the flowers!" A flower herself.

That evening, after his supper of cold duck, junket, and cider, the girl came in.

"Please, auntie says—will you try a piece of our Mayday cake?"

"If I may come to the kitchen for it."

"Oh, yes! You'll be missing your friend."

"Not I. But are you sure no one minds?"

"Who would mind? We shall be very pleased."

Ashurst rose too suddenly for his stiff knee, staggered, and subsided. The girl gave a little gasp, and held out her hands. Ashurst took them, small, rough, brown; checked his impulse to put them to his lips, and let her pull him up. She came close beside him, offering her shoulder. And leaning on her he walked across the room. That shoulder seemed quite the pleasantest thing he had ever touched. But he had presence of mind enough to catch his stick out of the rack, and withdraw his hand before arriving at the kitchen.

That night he slept like a top, and woke with his knee of almost normal size. He again spent the morning in his chair on the grass patch, scribbling down verses; but in the afternoon he wandered about with the two little boys Nick and Rick. It was Saturday, so they were early home from school; quick, shy, dark little rascals of seven and six, soon talkative, for Ashurst had a way with children. By four o'clock they had shown him all their methods of destroying life, except the tickling of trout; and with breeches tucked up, lay on their stomachs over the trout stream, pretending they had this accomplishment also. They tickled nothing, of course, for their giggling and shouting scared every spotted thing away. Ashurst, on a rock at the edge of the beech clump, watched them, and listened to the cuckoos, till Nick, the elder and less persevering, came up and stood beside him.

"The gipsy bogle zets on that stone," he said.

"What gipsy bogle?"

"Dunno; never zeen 'e. Megan zays 'e zets there; an' old Jim zeed 'e once. 'E was zettin' there naight afore our pony kicked-in father's 'ead. 'E plays the viddle."

"What tune does he play?"

"Dunno."

"What's he like?"

"'E's black. Old Jim zays 'e's all over 'air. 'E's a praaper bogle. 'E don' come only at naight." The little boy's oblique dark eyes slid round. "Dy'u think 'e might want to take me away? Megan's feared of 'e."

"Has she seen him?"

"No. She's not afeared o' yu."

"I should think not. Why should she be?"

"She zays a prayer for yu."

"How do you know that, you little rascal?"

"When I was asleep, she said: 'God bless us all, an' Mr. Ashes.' I yeard 'er whisperin'."

"You're a little ruffian to tell what you hear when you're not meant to hear it!"

The little boy was silent. Then he said aggressively:

"I can skin rabbets. Megan, she can't bear skinnin' 'em. I like blood."

"Oh! you do; you little monster!"

"What's that?"

"A creature that likes hurting others."

The little boy scowled. "They'm only dead rabbets, what us eats."

"Quite right, Nick. I beg your pardon."

"I can skin frogs, tu."

But Ashurst had become absent. "God bless us all, and Mr. Ashes!" And puzzled by that sudden inaccessibility, Nick ran back to the stream where the giggling and shouts again uprose at once.

When Megan brought his tea, he said:

"What's the gipsy bogle, Megan?" She looked up, startled.

"He brings bad things."

"Surely you don't believe in ghosts?"

"I hope I will never see him."

"Of course you won't. There aren't such things. What old Jim saw was a pony."

"No! There are bogles in the rocks; they are the men who lived long ago."

"They aren't gipsies, anyway; those old men were dead long before gipsies came."

She said simply: "They are all bad."

"Why? If there are any, they're only wild, like the rabbits. The flowers aren't bad for being wild; the thorn trees were never planted—and you don't mind them. I shall go down at night and look for your bogle, and have a talk with him."

"Oh, no! Oh, no!"

"Oh, yes! I shall go and sit on his rock."

She clasped her hands together: "Oh, please!"

"Why! What does it matter if anything happens to me?"

She did not answer; and in a sort of pet he added:

"Well; I daresay I shan't see him, because I suppose I must be off soon."

"Soon?"

"Your aunt won't want to keep me here."

"Oh, yes! We always let lodgings in summer." Fixing his eyes on her face, he asked:

"Would you like me to stay?"

"Yes."

"I'm going to say a prayer for *you* to-night!"

She flushed crimson, frowned, and went out of the room. He sat cursing himself, till his tea was stewed. It was as if he had tacked with his thick boots at a clump of bluebells. Why had he said such a silly thing? Was he just a towny college ass like Robert Garton, as far from understanding this girl?

IV

Ashurst spent the next week confirming the restoration of his leg, by exploration of the country within easy reach. Spring was a revelation to him this year. In a kind of intoxication he would

watch the pink-white buds of some backward beech tree sprayed
up in the sunlight against the deep blue sky, or the trunks and limbs
of the few Scotch firs, tawny in violent light, or again on the moor,
the gale-bent larches which had such a look of life when the wind
streamed in their young green, above the rusty black underboughs.
Or he would lie on the banks, gazing at the clusters of dog-violets,
or up in the dead bracken, fingering the pink, transparent buds of
the dewberry, while the cuckoos called and yaffles laughed, or a lark,
from very high, dripped its beads of song. It was certainly different
from any spring he had ever known, for spring was within him, not
without. In the daytime he hardly saw the family; and when Megan
brought in his meals she always seemed too busy in the house or
among the young things in the yard to stay talking long. But in the
evenings he installed himself in the window seat in the kitchen,
smoking and chatting with the lame man Jim, or Mrs. Narracombe,
while the girl sewed, or moved about, clearing the supper things
away. And sometimes with the sensation a cat must feel when it
purrs, he would become conscious that Megan's eyes—those dew-
grey eyes—were fixed on him with a sort of lingering soft look
which was strangely flattering.

It was on Sunday week in the evening, when he was lying in the
orchard listening to a blackbird and composing a love poem, that he
heard the gate swing to, and saw the girl come running among the
trees with the red-cheeked, stolid Joe in swift pursuit. About twenty
yards away the chase ended, and the two stood fronting each other,
not noticing the stranger in the grass—the boy pressing on, the girl
fending him off. Ashurst could see her face, angry, disturbed; and
the youth's—who would have thought that red-faced yokel could
look so distraught! And painfully affected by that sight, he jumped
up. They saw him then. Megan dropped her hands, and shrank
behind a tree-trunk; the boy gave an angry grunt, rushed at the
bank, scrambled over and vanished. Ashurst went slowly up to her.
She was standing quite still, biting her lip—very pretty, with her fine,
dark hair blown loose about her face, and her eyes cast down.

"I beg your pardon," he said.

She gave him one upward look, from eyes much dilated; then,
catching her breath, turned away. Ashurst followed.

"Megan!"

But she went on; and taking hold of her arm, he turned her gently round to him.

"Stop and speak to me."

"Why do you beg my pardon? It is not to me you should do that."

"Well, then, to Joe."

"How dare he come after me?"

"In love with you, I suppose."

She stamped her foot.

Ashurst uttered a short laugh. "Would you like me to punch his head?"

She cried with sudden passion:

"You laugh at me—you laugh at us!"

He caught hold of her hands, but she shrank back, till her passionate little face and loose dark hair were caught among the pink clusters of the apple blossom. Ashurst raised one of her imprisoned hands and put his lips to it. He felt how chivalrous he was, and superior to that clod Joe—just brushing that small, rough hand with his mouth! Her shrinking ceased suddenly; she seemed to tremble towards him. A sweet warmth overtook Ashurst from top to toe. This slim maiden, so simple and fine and pretty, was pleased, then, at the touch of his lips! And, yielding to a swift impulse, he put his arms round her, pressed her to him, and kissed her forehead. Then he was frightened—she went so pale, closing her eyes, so that the long, dark lashes lay on her pale cheeks; her hands, too, lay inert at her sides. The touch of her breast sent a shiver through him. "Megan!" he sighed out, and let her go. In the utter silence a blackbird shouted. Then the girl seized his hand, put it to her cheek, her heart, her lips, kissed it passionately, and fled away among the mossy trunks of the apple trees, till they hid her from him.

Ashurst sat down on a twisted old tree growing almost along the ground and, all throbbing and bewildered, gazed vacantly at the blossom which had crowned her hair—those pink buds with one white open apple star. What had he done? How had he let himself be thus stampeded by beauty—or—just the spring! He felt curiously happy, all the same; happy and triumphant, with shivers running through his limbs, and a vague alarm. This was the beginning of—what? The midges bit him, the dancing gnats tried to fly into his mouth, and all the spring around him seemed to grow more lovely and alive; the songs of the cuckoos and the blackbirds, the laughter of the yaffles, the level-slanting sunlight, the apple blossom which had crowned her head—! He got up from the old trunk and strode out of the orchard, wanting space, an open sky, to get on terms with these new sensations. He made for the moor, and from an ash tree in the hedge a magpie flew out to herald him.

Of man—at any age from five years on—who can say he has never been in love? Ashurst had loved his partners at his dancing class; loved his nursery governess; girls in school-holidays; perhaps never been quite out of love, cherishing always some more or less remote admiration. But this was different, not remote at all. Quite a new sensation; terribly delightful, bringing a sense of completed manhood. To be holding in his fingers such a wild flower, to be able to put it to his lips, and feel it tremble with delight against them! What intoxication, and—embarrassment! What to do with it—how meet her next time? His first caress had been cool, pitiful; but the next could not be, now that, by her burning little kiss on his hand, by her pressure of it to her heart, he knew that she loved him. Some natures are coarsened by love bestowed on them; others, like Ashurst's, are swayed and drawn, warmed and softened, almost exhalted, by what they feel to be a sort of miracle.

And up there among the tors he was racked between the passionate desire to revel in this new sensation of spring fulfilled within him, and a vague but very real uneasiness. At one moment he gave himself up completely to his pride at having captured this pretty, trustful, dewy-eyed thing! At the next he thought with factitious solemnity: 'Yes, my boy! But look out what you're doing! You know what comes of it!'

Dusk dropped down without his noticing—dusk on the carved, Assyrian-looking masses of the rocks. And the voice of Nature said: "This is a new world for you!" As when a man gets up at four o'clock and goes out into a summer morning, and beasts, birds, trees stare at him and he feels as if all had been made new.

He stayed up there for hours, till it grew cold, then groped his way down the stones and heather roots to the road, back into the lane, and came again past the wild meadow to the orchard. There he struck a match and looked at his watch. Nearly twelve! It was black and unstirring in there now, very different from the lingering, bird-befriended brightness of six hours ago! And suddenly he saw this idyll of his with the eyes of the outer world—had mental vision of Mrs. Narracombe's snake-like neck turned, her quick dark glance taking it all in, her shrewd face hardening; saw the gipsy-like cousins coarsely mocking and distrustful; Joe stolid and furious; only the lame man, Jim, with the suffering eyes, seemed tolerable to his mind. And the village pub!—the gossiping matrons he passed on his walks; and then—his own friends—Robert Garton's smile when he went off that morning ten days ago; so ironical and knowing! Disgusting! For a minute he literally hated this earthly, cynical world to which one belonged, willy nilly. The gate where he was leaning grew grey, a sort of shimmer passed before him and spread into the bluish darkness. The moon! He could just see it over the bank behind; red, nearly round—a strange moon! And turning away, he went up the lane which smelled of the night and cow-dung and young leaves. In the straw-yard he could see the dark shapes of cattle, broken by the pale sickles of their horns, like so many thin moons, fallen ends-up. He unlatched the farm gate stealthily. All was dark in the house. Muffling his footsteps, he gained the porch, and, blotted against one of the yew trees, looked up at Megan's window. It was open. Was she sleeping, or lying awake perhaps disturbed—unhappy at his absence? An owl hooted while he stood there peering up, and the sound seemed to fill the whole night, so quiet was all else, save for the never-ending murmur of the stream running below the orchard, The cuckoos by day, and now the owls—how wonderfully they voiced this troubled ecstasy within him! And suddenly he saw her at her window, looking out. He moved a little from the yew tree, and whispered: "Megan!" She drew back, vanished, reappeared, leaning far down. He stole forward on the grass patch, hit his shin against the green-painted chair, and held his breath at the sound. The pale blur of her stretched-down arm and face did not stir; he moved the chair, and noiselessly mounted it. By stretching up his arm he could just reach. Her hand held the huge key of the front door, and he clasped that burning hand with the cold key in it. He could just see her face, the glint of teeth between her lips, her tumbled hair. She was still dressed—poor child, sitting up for him, no doubt! "Pretty Megan!" Her hot, roughened fingers clung to his; her face had a strange, lost look. To have been able to reach it—even with his hand! The owl hooted, a scent of sweetbriar crept into his nostrils. Then one of the farm dogs barked; her grasp relaxed, she shrank back.

"Good-night, Megan!"

"Good-night, sir!" She was gone! With a sigh he dropped back to earth, and sitting on that chair, took off his boots. Nothing for it but to creep in and go to bed; yet for a long while he sat unmoving, his feet chilly in the dew, drunk on the memory of her lost, half-smiling face, and the clinging grip of her burning fingers, pressing the cold key into his hand.

V

He awoke feeling as if he had eaten heavily overnight, instead of having eaten nothing. And far off, unreal, seemed yesterday's romance! Yet it was a golden morning. Full spring had burst at last— in one night the "goldiecups," as the little boys called them, seemed to have made the field their own, and from his window he could see apple blossoms covering the orchard as with a rose and white quilt. He went down almost dreading to see Megan; and yet, when not she but Mrs. Narracombe brought in his breakfast, he felt vexed and disappointed. The woman's quick eye and snaky neck seemed to have a new alacrity this morning. Had she noticed?

"So you an' the moon went walkin' last night, Mr. Ashurst. Did ye have your supper anywheres?"

Ashurst shook his head.

"We kept it for you, but I suppose you was too busy in your brain to think o' such a thing as that?"

Was she mocking him, in that voice of hers, which still kept some Welsh crispness against the invading burr of the West Country? If she knew! And at that moment he thought:

'No, no; I'll clear out. I won't put myself in such a beastly false position.'

But, after breakfast, the longing to see Megan began and increased with every minute, together with fear lest something should have been said to her which had spoiled everything. Sinister that she had not appeared, not given him even a glimpse of her! And the love poem, whose manufacture had been so important and absorbing yesterday afternoon under the apple trees, now seemed so paltry that he tore it up and rolled it into pipe spills. What had he known of love, till she seized his hand and kissed it! And now—what did he not know? But to write of it seemed mere insipidity! He went up to his bedroom to get a book, and his heart began to beat violently, for she was in there making the bed. He stood in the doorway watching; and suddenly, with turbulent joy, he saw her stoop and kiss his pillow, just at the hollow made by his head last night. How let her know he had seen that pretty act of devotion? And yet if she heard him stealing away, it would be even worse. She took the pillow up, holding it as if reluctant to shake out the impress of his cheek, dropped it, and turned round.

"Megan!"

She put her hands up to her cheeks, but her eyes seemed to look right into him. He had never before realised the depth and purity and touching faithfulness in those dew-bright eyes, and he stammered:

"It was sweet of you to wait up for me last night."

She still said nothing, and he stammered on:

"I was wandering about on the moor; it was such a jolly night. I—I've just come up for a book."

Then, the kiss he had seen her give the pillow afflicted him with sudden headiness, and he went up to her. Touching her eyes with his lips, he thought with queer excitement: 'I've done it! Yesterday all was sudden—anyhow; but now—I've done it!' The girl let her forehead rest against his lips, which moved downwards till they reached hers. That first real lover's kiss—strange, wonderful, still almost innocent— in which heart did it make the most disturbance?

"Come to the big apple tree to-night, after they've gone to bed. Megan—promise!"

She whispered back: "I promise!"

Then, scared at her white face, scared at everything, he let her go, and went downstairs again. Yes! he had done it now! Accepted her love, declared his own! He went out to the green chair as devoid of a book as ever; and there he sat staring vacantly before him, triumphant and remorseful, while under his nose and behind his back the work of the farm went on. How long he had been sitting in that curious state of vacancy he had no notion when he saw Joe standing a little behind him to the right. The youth had evidently come from hard work in the fields, and stood shifting his feet, breathing loudly, his face coloured like a setting sun, and his arms, below the rolled-up sleeves of his blue shirt, showing the hue and furry sheen of ripe peaches. His red lips were open, his blue eyes with their flaxen lashes stared fixedly at Ashurst, who said ironically:

"Well, Joe, anything I can do for you?"

"Yeas."

"What, then?"

"Yu can goo away from yere. Us don' want yu."

Ashurst's face, never too humble, assumed its most lordly look.

"Very good of you, but, do you know, I prefer the others should speak for themselves."

The youth moved a pace or two nearer, and the scent of his honest heat afflicted Ashurst's nostrils.

"What d'yu stay yere for?"

"Because it pleases me."

"Twon't please yu when I've bashed yure head in!"

"Indeed! When would you like to begin that?"

Joe answered only with the loudness of his breathing, but his eyes looked like those of a young and angry bull. Then a sort of spasm seemed to convulse his face.

"Megan don' want yu."

A rush of jealousy, of contempt, and anger with this thick, loud-breathing rustic got the better of Ashurst's self-possession; he jumped up and pushed back his chair.

"You can go to the devil!"

And as he said those simple words, he saw Megan in the doorway with a tiny brown spaniel puppy in her arms. She came up to him quickly:

"Its eyes are blue!" she said.

Joe turned away; the back of his neck was literally crimson. Ashurst put his finger to the mouth of the little brown bull frog of a creature in her arms. How cosy it looked against her!

"It's fond of you already. Ah! Megan, everything is fond of *you*."

"What was Joe saying to you, please?"

"Telling me to go away, because you didn't want me here."

She stamped her foot; then looked up at Ashurst. At that adoring look he felt his nerves quiver, just as if he had seen a moth scorching its wings.

"To-night!" he said. "Don't forget!"

"No." And smothering her face against the puppy's little fat, brown body, she slipped back into the house.

Ashurst wandered down the lane. At the gate of the wild meadow he came on the lame man and his cows.

"Beautiful day, Jim!"

"Ah! 'Tes brave weather for the grass. The ashes be later than th' oaks this year. 'When th' oak before th' ash——'"

Ashurst said idly: "Where were you standing when you saw the gipsy bogie, Jim?"

"It might be under that big apple tree, as you might say."

"And you really do think it was there?"

The lame man answered cautiously: "I shouldn't like to say rightly that 't *was* there. 'Twas in my mind as 'twas there."

"What do you make of it?"

The lame man lowered his voice.

"They du zay old master, Mist' Narracombe, come o' gipsy stock. But that's tellin'. They'm a wonderful people, yu know, for claimin' their own. Maybe they knu 'e was goin', and sent this feller along for company. That's what I've a-thought about it."

"What was he like?"

"'E 'ad 'air all over 'is face, an' goin' like this, he was, zame as if 'e 'ad a viddle. They zay there's no such thing as bogies, but I've a-zeen the 'air on this dog standin' up of a dark naight, when I couldn' zee nothin' meself."

"Was there a moon?"

"Yeas, very near full, but 'twas on'y just risen, gold-like be'ind them trees."

"And you think a ghost means trouble, do you?"

The lame man pushed his hat up; his aspiring eyes looked at Ashurst more earnestly than ever.

"'Tes not for me to zay that—but 'tes they bein' so unrestin' like. There's things us don' understand, that's zartin, for zure. There's people that zee things, tu, an' others that don't never zee nothin'. Now, our Joe—yu might putt anything under 'is eyes an' 'e'd never see it; and them other boys, tu, they'm rattlin' fellers. But yu take an'

putt our Megan where there's suthin', she'll zee it, an' more tu, or
I'm mistaken."

"She's sensitive, that's why."

"What's that?"

"I mean, she feels everything."

"Ah! She'm very lovin'-'earted."

Ashurst, who felt colour coming into his cheeks, held out his
tobacco pouch.

"Have a fill, Jim?"

"Thank 'ee, sir. She'm one in an 'underd, I think."

"I expect so," said Ashurst shortly, and folding up his pouch,
walked on.

"Lovin'-'earted!" Yes! And what was he doing? What were
his intentions—as they say—towards this loving-hearted girl?
The thought dogged him, wandering through fields bright with
buttercups, where the little red calves were feeding, and the swallows
flying high. Yes, the oaks were before the ashes, brown-gold already;
every tree in different stage and hue. The cuckoos and a thousand
birds were singing; the little streams were very bright. The ancients
believed in a golden age, in the garden of the Hesperides! . . . A
queen wasp settled on his sleeve. Each queen wasp killed meant
two thousand fewer wasps to thieve the apples which would grow
from that blossom in the orchard; but who, with love in his heart,
could kill anything on a day like, this? He entered a field where a
young red bull was feeding. It seemed to Ashurst that he looked like
Joe. But the young bull took no notice of this visitor, a little drunk
himself, perhaps, on the singing and the glamour of the golden
pasture, under his short legs. Ashurst crossed out unchallenged to the
hillside above the stream. From that slope a tor mounted to its crown
of rocks. The ground there was covered with a mist of bluebells,
and nearly a score of crab-apple trees were in full bloom. He threw
himself down on the grass. The change from the buttercup glory and
oak-goldened glamour of the fields to this ethereal beauty under the
grey tor filled him with a sort of wonder; nothing the same, save the
sound of running water and the songs of the cuckoos. He lay there
a long time, watching the sunlight wheel till the crab-trees threw
shadows over the bluebells, his only companions a few wild bees. He
was not quite sane, thinking of that morning's kiss, and of to-night

under the apple tree. In such a spot as this, fauns and dryads surely lived; nymphs, white as the crab-apple blossom, retired within those trees; fauns, brown as the dead bracken, with pointed ears, lay in wait for them. The cuckoos were still calling when he woke, there was the sound of running water; but the sun had couched behind the tor, the hillside was cool, and some rabbits had come out. 'To-night!' he thought. Just as from the earth everything was pushing up, unfolding under the soft insistent fingers of an unseen hand, so were his heart and senses being pushed, unfolded. He got up and broke off a spray from a crab-apple tree. The buds were like Megan—shell-like, rose-pink, wild, and fresh; and so, too, the opening flowers, white, and wild, and touching. He put the spray into his coat. And all the rush of the spring within him escaped in a triumphant sigh. But the rabbits scurried away.

VI

It was nearly eleven that night when Ashurst put down the pocket "Odyssey" which for half an hour he had held in his hands without reading, and slipped through the yard down to the orchard. The moon had just risen, very golden, over the hill, and like a bright, powerful, watching spirit peered through the bars of an ash tree's half-naked boughs. In among the apple trees it was still dark, and he stood making sure of his direction, feeling the rough grass with his feet. A black mass close behind him stirred with a heavy grunting sound, and three large pigs settled down again close to each other, under the wall. He listened. There was no wind, but the stream's burbling whispering chuckle had gained twice its daytime strength. One bird, he could not tell what, cried "Pip—pip," "Pip—pip," with perfect monotony; he could hear a night-jar spinning very far off; an owl hooting. Ashurst moved a step or two, and again halted, aware of a dim living whiteness all round his head. On the dark unstirring trees innumerable flowers and buds all soft and blurred were being bewitched to life by the creeping moonlight. He had the oddest feeling of actual companionship, as if a million white moths or spirits had floated in and settled between dark sky and darker ground, and were opening and shutting their wings on a level with his eyes. In the bewildering, still, scentless beauty of that moment he almost lost memory of why he had come to the orchard. The flying glamour which had clothed the earth all day had not gone now that night had fallen, but only changed into this new form. He moved on through the thicket of stems and boughs covered with that live powdering whiteness, till he reached the big apple tree. No mistaking that, even in the dark, nearly twice the height and size of any other, and leaning out towards the open meadows and the stream. Under the thick branches he stood still again, to listen. The same sounds exactly, and a faint grunting from the sleepy pigs. He put his hands on the dry, almost warm tree trunk, whose rough mossy surface gave forth a peaty scent at his touch. Would she come—would she? And among these quivering, haunted, moon-witched trees he was seized with doubts of everything! All was unearthly here, fit for no earthly lovers; fit only for god and goddess, faun and nymph—not for him and this little country girl. Would it not be almost a relief if she did not come? But all the time he was listening. And still that unknown bird went "Pip—pip," "Pip—pip," and there rose the busy chatter of the little trout stream, whereon the moon was flinging glances through the bars of her tree-prison. The blossom on a level with his eyes seemed to grow more living every moment, seemed with its mysterious white beauty more and more a part of his suspense. He plucked a fragment and held it close—three blossoms. Sacrilege to pluck fruit-tree blossom—soft, sacred, young blossom—and throw it away! Then suddenly he heard the gate close, the pigs stirring again and grunting; and leaning against the trunk, he pressed his hands to its mossy sides behind him, and held his breath. She might have been a spirit threading the trees, for all the noise she made! Then he saw her quite close—her dark form part of a little tree, her white face part of its blossom; so still, and peering towards him. He whispered:

"Megan!" and held out his hands. She ran forward, straight to his breast. When he felt her heart beating against him, Ashurst knew to the full the sensations of chivalry and passion. Because she was not of his world, because she was so simple and young and headlong, adoring and defenceless, how could he be other than her protector, in the dark! Because she was all simple Nature and beauty, as much a part of this spring night as was the living blossom, how should he not take all that she would give him—how not fulfil the spring in her heart and his! And torn between these two emotions he clasped her close, and kissed her hair. How long they stood there without speaking he knew not. The stream went on chattering, the owls hooting, the moon kept stealing up and growing whiter; the blossom all round them and above brightened in suspense of living beauty. Their lips had sought each other's, and they did not speak. The moment speech began all would be unreal! Spring has no speech, nothing but rustling and whispering. Spring has so much more than speech in its unfolding flowers and leaves, and the coursing of its streams, and in its sweet restless seeking! And sometimes spring will come alive, and, like a mysterious Presence, stand, encircling lovers with its arms, laying on them the fingers of enchantment, so that, standing lips to lips, they forget everything but just a kiss. While her heart beat against him, and her lips quivered on his, Ashurst felt nothing but simple rapture—Destiny meant her for his arms, Love could not be flouted! But when their lips parted for breath, division began again at once. Only, passion now was so much the stronger, and he sighed:

"Oh! Megan! Why did you come?"

She looked up, hurt, amazed.

"Sir, you asked me to."

"Don't call me 'sir', my pretty sweet."

"What should I be callin' you?"

"Frank."

"I could not. Oh, no!"

"But you love me—don't you?"

"I could not help lovin' you. I want to be with you—that's all."

"All!"

So faint that he hardly heard, she whispered:

"I shall die if I can't be with you."

Ashurst took a mighty breath.

"Come and be with me, then!"

"Oh!"

Intoxicated by the awe and rapture in that "Oh!" he went on, whispering:

"We'll go to London. I'll show you the world. And I will take care of you, I promise, Megan. I'll never be a brute to you!"

"If I can be with you—that is all."

He stroked her hair, and whispered on:

"To-morrow I'll go to Torquay and get some money, and get you some clothes that won't be noticed, and then we'll steal away. And when we get to London, soon perhaps, if you love me well enough, we'll be married."

He could feel her hair shiver with the shake of her head.

"Oh, no! I could not. I only want to be with you!"

Drunk on his own chivalry, Ashurst went on murmuring:

"It's I who am not good enough for you. Oh! Megan, when did you begin to love me?"

"When I saw you in the road, and you looked at me. The first night I loved you; but I never thought you would want me."

She slipped down suddenly to her knees, trying to kiss his feet.

A shiver of horror went through Ashurst; he lifted her up bodily and held her fast—too upset to speak.

She whispered: "Why won't you let me?"

"It's I who will kiss your feet!"

Her smile brought tears into his eyes. The whiteness of her moonlit face so close to his, the faint pink of her opened lips, had the living unearthly beauty of the apple blossom.

And then, suddenly, her eyes widened and stared past him painfully; she writhed out of his arms, and whispered:

"Look!"

Ashurst saw nothing but the brightened stream, the furze faintly gilded, the beech trees glistening, and behind them all the wide loom of the moonlit hill. Behind him came her frozen whisper: "The gipsy bogle!"

"Where?"

"There—by the stone—under the trees!"

Exasperated, he leapt the stream, and strode towards the beech clump. Prank of the moonlight! Nothing! In and out of the boulders and thorn trees, muttering and cursing, yet with a kind of terror, he rushed and stumbled. Absurd! Silly! Then he went back to the apple-tree. But she was gone; he could hear a rustle, the grunting of the pigs, the sound of a gate closing. Instead of her, only this old apple tree! He flung his arms round the trunk. What a substitute for her soft body; the rough moss against his face—what a substitute for her soft cheek; only the scent, as of the woods, a little the same! And above him, and around, the blossoms, more living, more moonlit than ever, seemed to glow and breathe.

VII

Descending from the train at Torquay station, Ashurst wandered uncertainly along the front, for he did not know this particular queen of English watering places. Having little sense of what he had on, he was quite unconscious of being remarkable among its inhabitants, and strode along in his rough Norfolk jacket, dusty boots, and battered hat, without observing that people gazed at him rather blankly. He was seeking a branch of his London bank, and having found one, found also the first obstacle to his mood. Did he know anyone in Torquay? No. In that case, if he would wire to his bank in London, they would be happy to oblige him on receipt of the reply. That suspicious breath from the matter-of-fact world somewhat tarnished the brightness of his visions. But he sent the telegram.

Nearly opposite to the post office he saw a shop full of ladies' garments, and examined the window with strange sensations. To have to undertake the clothing of his rustic love was more than a little disturbing. He went in. A young woman came forward; she had blue eyes and a faintly puzzled forehead. Ashurst stared at her in silence.

"Yes, sir?"

"I want a dress for a young lady."

The young woman smiled. Ashurst frowned—the peculiarity of his request struck him with sudden force.

The young woman added hastily:

"What style would you like—something modish?"

"No. Simple."

"What figure would the young lady be?"

"I don't know; about two inches shorter than you, I should say."

"Could you give me her waist measurement?"

Megan's waist!

"Oh! anything usual!"

"Quite!"

While she was gone he stood disconsolately eyeing the models in the window, and suddenly it seemed to him incredible that Megan—

his Megan—could ever be dressed save in the rough tweed skirt, coarse blouse, and tam-o'-shanter cap he was wont to see her in. The young woman had come back with several dresses in her arms, and Ashurst eyed her laying them against her own modish figure. There was one whose colour he liked, a dove-grey, but to imagine Megan clothed in it was beyond him. The young woman went away, and brought some more. But on Ashurst there had now come a feeling of paralysis. How choose? She would want a hat too, and shoes, and gloves; and, suppose, when he had got them all, they commonised her, as Sunday clothes always commonised village folk! Why should she not travel as she was? Ah? But conspicuousness would matter; this was a serious elopement. And, staring at the young woman, he thought: 'I wonder if she guesses, and thinks me a blackguard?'

"Do you mind putting aside that grey one for me?" he said desperately at last. "I can't decide now; I'll come in again this afternoon."

The young woman sighed.

"Oh! certainly. It's a very tasteful costume. I don't think you'll get anything that will suit your purpose better."

"I expect not," Ashurst murmured, and went out.

Freed again from the suspicious matter-of-factness of the world, he took a long breath, and went back to visions. In fancy he saw the trustful, pretty creature who was going to join her life to his; saw himself and her stealing forth at night, walking over the moor under the moon, he with his arm round her, and carrying her new garments, till, in some far-off wood, when dawn was coming, she would slip off her old things and put on these, and an early train at a distant station would bear them away on their honeymoon journey, till London swallowed them up, and the dreams of love came true.

"Frank Ashurst! I haven't seen you since Rugby, old chap!"

Ashurst's frown dissolved; the face, close to his own, was blue-eyed suffused with sun—one of those faces where sun from within and without join in a sort of lustre. And he answered:

"Phil Halliday, by Jove!"

"What are you doing here?"

"Oh! nothing. Just looking round, and getting some money. I'm staying on the moor."

"Are you lunching anywhere? Come and lunch with us; I'm here with my young sisters. They've had measles."

Hooked in by that friendly arm Ashurst went along, up a hill, down a hill, away out of the town, while the voice of Halliday, redolent of optimism as his face was of sun, explained how "in this mouldy place the only decent things were the bathing and boating," and so on, till presently they came to a crescent of houses a little above and back from the sea, and into the centre one—an hotel— made their way.

"Come up to my room and have a wash. Lunch'll be ready in a jiffy."

Ashurst contemplated his visage in a looking-glass. After his farmhouse bedroom, the comb and one spare shirt *régime* of the last fortnight, this room littered with clothes and brushes was a sort of Capua; and he thought: 'Queer—one doesn't realise—' But what— he did not quite know.

When he followed Halliday into the sitting-room for lunch, three faces, very fair and blue-eyed, were turned suddenly at the words: "This is Frank Ashurst—my young sisters."

Two were indeed young, about eleven and ten. The third was perhaps seventeen, tall and fair-haired too, with pink-and-white cheeks just touched by the sun, and eyebrows, rather darker than the hair, running a little upwards from her nose to their outer points. The voices of all three were like Halliday's, high and cheerful; they stood up straight, shook hands with a quick movement, looked at Ashurst critically, away again at once, and began to talk of what they were going to do in the afternoon. A regular Diana and attendant nymphs! After the farm this crisp, slangy, eager talk, this cool, clean, off-hand refinement, was queer at first, and then so natural that what he had come from became suddenly remote. The names of the two little ones seemed to be Sabina and Freda; of the eldest, Stella.

Presently the one called Sabina turned to him and said:

"I say, will you come shrimping with us?—it's awful fun!"

Surprised by this unexpected friendliness, Ashurst murmured:

"I'm afraid I've got to get back this afternoon."

"Oh!"

"Can't you put it off?"

Ashurst turned to the new speaker, Stella, shook his head, and smiled. She was very pretty! Sabina said regretfully:

"You might!" Then the talk switched off to caves and swimming.

"Can you swim far?"

"About two miles."

"Oh!"

"I say!"

"How jolly!"

The three pairs of blue eyes, fixed on him, made him conscious of his new importance. The sensation was agreeable. Halliday said:

"I say, you simply must stop and have a bathe. You'd better stay the night."

"Yes, do!"

But again Ashurst smiled and shook his head. Then suddenly he found himself being catechised about his physical achievements. He had rowed—it seemed—in his college boat, played in his college football team, won his college mile and he rose from table a sort of hero. The two little girls insisted that he must see "their" cave, and they set forth chattering like magpies, Ashurst between them, Stella and her brother a little behind. In the cave, damp and darkish like any other cave, the great feature was a pool with possibility of creatures which might be caught and put into bottles. Sabina and Freda, who wore no stockings on their shapely brown legs, exhorted Ashurst to join them in the middle of it, and help sieve the water. He too was soon bootless and sockless. Time goes fast for one who has a sense of beauty, when there are pretty children in a pool and a young Diana on the edge, to receive with wonder anything you can catch! Ashurst never had much sense of time. It was a shock when, pulling out his watch, he saw it was well past three. No cashing his cheque to-day—the bank would be closed before he could get there. Watching his expression, the little girls cried out at once:

"Hurrah! Now you'll have to stay!"

Ashurst did not answer. He was seeing again Megan's face, when at breakfast he had whispered: "I'm going to Torquay, darling, to get everything; I shall be back this evening. If it's fine we can go to-night. Be ready." He was seeing again how she quivered and hung on his words. What would she think? Then he pulled himself together, conscious suddenly of the calm scrutiny of this other young girl, so tall and fair and Diana-like, at the edge of the pool, of her wondering blue eyes under those brows which slanted up a little. If they knew what was in his mind—if they knew that this very night he had meant—! Well, there would be a little sound of disgust, and he would be alone in the cave. And with a curious mixture of anger, chagrin, and shame, he put his watch back into his pocket and said abruptly:

"Yes; I'm dished for to-day."

"Hurrah! Now you can bathe with us."

It was impossible not to succumb a little to the contentment of these pretty children, to the smile on Stella's lips, to Halliday's "Ripping, old chap! I can lend you things for the night!" But again a spasm of longing and remorse throbbed through Ashurst, and he said moodily:

"I must send a wire!"

The attractions of the pool palling, they went back to the hotel. Ashurst sent his wire, addressing it to Mrs. Narracombe:

"Sorry, detained for the night, back to-morrow." Surely Megan would understand that he had too much to do; and his heart grew lighter. It was a lovely afternoon, warm, the sea calm and blue, and swimming his great passion; the favour of these pretty children flattered him, the pleasure of looking at them, at Stella, at Halliday's sunny face; the slight unreality, yet extreme naturalness of it all—as of a last peep at normality before he took this plunge with Megan! He got his borrowed bathing dress, and they all set forth. Halliday and he undressed behind one rock, the three girls behind another. He was first into the sea, and at once swam out with the bravado of justifying his self-given reputation. When he turned he could see Halliday swimming along shore, and the girls flopping and dipping, and riding the little waves, in the way he was accustomed to despise, but now thought pretty and sensible, since it gave him the distinction of the only deep-water fish. But drawing near, he wondered if they would like him, a stranger, to come into their splashing group; he felt shy, approaching that slim nymph. Then Sabina summoned him to teach her to float, and between them the little girls kept him so busy that he had no time even to notice whether Stella was accustomed to his presence, till suddenly he heard a startled sound from her. She was standing submerged to the waist, leaning a little forward, her slim white arms stretched out and pointing, her wet face puckered by the sun and an expression of fear.

"Look at Phil! Is he all right? Oh, look!"

Ashurst saw at once that Phil was not all right. He was splashing and struggling out of his depth, perhaps a hundred yards away; suddenly he gave a cry, threw up his arms, and went down. Ashurst saw the girl launch herself towards him, and crying out: "Go back, Stella! Go back!" he dashed out. He had never swum so fast, and reached Halliday just as he was coming up a second time. It was a case of cramp, but to get him in was not difficult, for he did not struggle. The girl, who had stopped where Ashurst told her to, helped as soon as he was in his depth, and once on the beach they sat down one on each side of him to rub his limbs, while the little ones stood by with scared faces. Halliday was soon smiling. It was—he said—rotten of him, absolutely rotten! If Frank would give him an arm, he could get to his clothes all right now. Ashurst gave him the arm, and as he did so caught sight of Stella's face, wet and flushed and tearful, all broken up out of its calm; and he thought: 'I called her Stella! Wonder if she minded?'

While they were dressing, Halliday said quietly:

"You saved my life, old chap!"

"Rot!"

Clothed, but not quite in their right minds, they went up all together to the hotel and sat down to tea, except Halliday, who was lying down in his room. After some slices of bread and jam, Sabina said:

"I say, you know, you *are* a brick!" And Freda chimed in:

"Rather!"

Ashurst saw Stella looking down; he got up in confusion, and went to the window. From there he heard Sabina mutter:

"I say, let's swear blood bond. Where's your knife, Freda?" and out of the corner of his eye could see each of them solemnly prick herself, squeeze out a drop of blood and dabble on a bit of paper. He turned and made for the door.

"Don't be a stoat! Come back!" His arms were seized; imprisoned between the little girls he was brought back to the table. On it lay a piece of paper with an effigy drawn in blood, and the three names Stella Halliday, Sabina Halliday, Freda Halliday—also in blood, running towards it like the rays of a star. Sabina said:

"That's you. We shall have to kiss you, you know."

And Freda echoed:

"Oh! Blow—Yes!"

Before Ashurst could escape, some wettish hair dangled against his face, something like a bite descended on his nose, he felt his left arm pinched, and other teeth softly searching his cheek. Then he was released, and Freda said:

"Now, Stella."

Ashurst, red and rigid, looked across the table at a red and rigid Stella. Sabina giggled; Freda cried:

"Buck up—it spoils everything!"

A queer, ashamed eagerness shot through Ashurst: then he said quietly:

"Shut up, you little demons!"

Again Sabina giggled.

"Well, then, she can kiss her hand, and you can put it against your nose. It *is* on one side!"

To his amazement the girl did kiss her hand and stretch it out. Solemnly he took that cool, slim hand and laid it to his cheek. The two little girls broke into clapping, and Freda said:

"Now, then, we shall have to save your life at any time; that's settled. Can I have another cup, Stella, not so beastly weak?"

Tea was resumed, and Ashurst, folding up the paper, put it in his pocket. The talk turned on the advantages of measles, tangerine oranges, honey in a spoon, no lessons, and so forth. Ashurst listened, silent, exchanging friendly looks with Stella, whose face was again of its normal sun-touched pink and white. It was soothing to be so taken to the heart of this jolly family, fascinating to watch their faces. And after tea, while the two little girls pressed seaweed, he talked to Stella in the window seat and looked at her water-colour sketches. The whole thing was like a pleasurable dream; time and incident hung up, importance and reality suspended. To-morrow he would go back to Megan, with nothing of all this left save the paper with the blood of these children, in his pocket. Children! Stella was not quite that—as old as Megan! Her talk—quick, rather hard and shy, yet friendly—seemed to flourish on his silences, and about her there was something cool and virginal—a maiden in a bower. At dinner, to which Halliday, who had swallowed too much sea-water, did not come, Sabina said:

"I'm going to call you Frank."

Freda echoed:

"Frank, Frank, Franky."

Ashurst grinned and bowed.

"Every time Stella calls you Mr. Ashurst, she's got to pay a forfeit. It's ridiculous."

Ashurst looked at Stella, who grew slowly red. Sabina giggled; Freda cried:

"She's 'smoking'—'smoking!'—Yah!"

Ashurst reached out to right and left, and grasped some fair hair in each hand.

"Look here," he said, "you two! Leave Stella alone, or I'll tie you together!"

Freda gurgled:

"Ouch! You *are* a beast!"

Sabina murmured cautiously:

"*You* call *her* Stella, you see!"

"Why shouldn't I? It's a jolly name!"

"All right; we give you leave to!"

Ashurst released the hair. Stella! What would she call him—after this? But she called him nothing; till at bedtime he said, deliberately:

"Good-night, Stella!"

"Good-night, Mr. — Good-night, Frank! It *was* jolly of you, you know!"

"Oh—that! Bosh!"

Her quick, straight handshake tightened suddenly, and as suddenly, became slack.

Ashurst stood motionless in the empty sitting-room. Only last night, under the apple tree and the living blossom, he had held Megan to him, kissing her eyes and lips. And he gasped, swept by that rush of remembrance. To-night it should have begun—his life with her who only wanted to be with him! And now, twenty-four hours and more must pass, because—of not looking at his watch! Why had he made friends with this family of innocents just when he was saying good-bye to innocence, and all the rest of it? 'But I mean to marry her,' he thought; 'I told her so!'

He took a candle, lighted it, and went to his bedroom, which was next to Halliday's. His friend's voice called as he was passing:

"Is that you, old chap? I say, come in."

He was sitting up in bed, smoking a pipe and reading.

"Sit down a bit."

Ashurst sat down by the open window.

"I've been thinking about this afternoon, you know," said Halliday rather suddenly. "They say you go through all your past. I didn't. I suppose I wasn't far enough gone."

"What did you think of?"

Halliday was silent for a little, then said quietly:

"Well, I did think of one thing—rather odd—of a girl at Cambridge that I might have—you know; I was glad I hadn't got her on my mind. Anyhow, old chap, I owe it to you that I'm here; I should have been in the big dark by now. No more bed, or baccy; no more anything. I say, what d'you suppose happens to us?"

Ashurst murmured:

"Go out like flames, I expect."

"Phew!"

"We may flicker, and cling about a bit, perhaps?'

"H'm! I think that's rather gloomy. I say, I hope my young sisters have been decent to you?"

"Awfully decent."

Halliday put his pipe down, crossed his hands behind his neck, and turned his face towards the window.

"They're not bad kids!" he said.

Watching his friend, lying there, with that smile, and the candle-light on his face, Ashurst shuddered. Quite true! He might have been lying there with no smile; with all that sunny look gone out for ever! He might not have been lying there at all, but "sanded" at the bottom of the sea, waiting for resurrection on the—ninth day, was it? And that smile of Halliday's seemed to him suddenly something wonderful, as if in it were all the difference between life and death—the little flame—the all! He got up, and said softly:

"Well, you ought to sleep, I expect. Shall I blow out?"

Halliday caught his hand.

"I can't say it, you know; but it must be rotten to be dead. Good-night, old boy!"

Stirred and moved, Ashurst squeezed the hand, and went downstairs. The hall door was still open, and he passed out on to the lawn before the Crescent. The stars were bright in a very dark blue sky, and by their light some lilacs had that mysterious colour of flowers by night which no one can describe. Ashurst pressed his face against a spray; and before his closed eyes Megan started up, with the tiny brown spaniel pup against her breast. "I thought of a girl that I might have—you know. I was glad I hadn't got her on my mind!" He jerked his head away from the lilac, and began pacing up and down over the grass, a grey phantom coming to substance for a moment in the light from the lamp at either end. He was with her again under the living, breathing whiteness of the blossom, the stream chattering by, the moon glinting steel-blue on the bathing-pool; back in the rapture of his kisses on her upturned face of innocence and humble passion, back in the suspense and beauty of that pagan night. He stood still once more in the shadow of the lilacs. Here the sea, not the stream, was Night's voice; the sea with its sigh and rustle; no little bird, no owl, no nightjar called or spun; but a piano tinkled, and the white houses cut the sky with solid curve, and the scent from the lilacs filled the air. A window of the hotel, high up, was lighted; he saw a shadow move across the blind. And most queer sensations stirred within him, a sort of churning, and twining, and turning of a single emotion on itself, as though spring and love, bewildered and confused, seeking the way, were baffled. This girl, who had called him Frank, whose hand had given his that sudden little clutch, this girl so cool and pure—what would *she* think of such wild, unlawful loving? He sank down on the grass, sitting there cross-legged, with his back to the house, motionless as some carved Buddha. Was he really going to break through innocence, and steal? Sniff the scent out of a wild flower, and—perhaps—throw it away? "Of a girl at Cambridge that I might have—you know!" He put his hands to the grass, one on each side, palms downwards, and pressed; it was just warm still—the grass, barely moist, soft and firm and friendly. 'What am I going to do?' he thought. Perhaps Megan was at her window, looking out at the blossom, thinking of him! Poor little Megan! 'Why not?' he thought. 'I love her! But do I—really love her? or do I only want her because she is so pretty, and loves me? What am I going to do?' The piano tinkled on, the stars winked; and Ashurst gazed out before him at the dark sea, as if spell-bound. He got up at last, cramped and rather chilly. There was no longer light in any window. And he went in to bed.

VIII

Out of a deep and dreamless sleep he was awakened by the sound of thumping on the door. A shrill voice called:

"Hi! Breakfast's ready."

He jumped up. Where was he—? Ah!

He found them already eating marmalade, and sat down in the empty place between Stella and Sabina, who, after watching him a little, said:

"I say, do buck up; we're going to start at half-past nine."

"We're going to Berry Head, old chap; you must come!"

Ashurst thought: 'Come! Impossible. I shall be getting things and going back.' He looked at Stella. She said quickly:

"Do come!"

Sabina chimed in:

"It'll be no fun without you."

Freda got up and stood behind his chair.

"You've got to come, or else I'll pull your hair!"

Ashurst thought: 'Well—one day more—to think it over! One day more!' And he said:

"All right! You needn't tweak my mane!"

"Hurrah!"

At the station he wrote a second telegram to the farm, and then—tore it up; he could not have explained why. From Brixham they drove in a very little wagonette. There, squeezed between Sabina and Freda, with his knees touching Stella's, they played "Up Jenkins"; and the gloom he was feeling gave way to frolic. In this one day more to think it over, he did not want to think! They ran races, wrestled, paddled—for to-day nobody wanted to bathe—they sang catches, played games, and ate all they had brought. The little girls fell asleep against him on the way back, and his knees still touched Stella's in the wagonette. It seemed incredible that thirty hours ago he had never set eyes on any of those three flaxen heads. In the train he talked to Stella of poetry, discovering her favourites, and telling her his own with a pleasing sense of superiority; till suddenly she said, rather low:

"Phil says you don't believe in a future life, Frank. I think that's dreadful."

Disconcerted, Ashurst muttered:

"I don't either believe or not believe—I simply don't know."

She said quickly:

"I couldn't bear that. What would be the use of living?"

Watching the frown of those pretty oblique brows, Ashurst answered:

"I don't believe in believing things because one wants to."

"But why should one wish to live again, if one isn't going to?"

And she looked full at him.

He did not want to hurt her, but an itch to dominate pushed him on to say:

"While one's alive one naturally wants to go on living for ever; that's part of being alive. But it probably isn't anything more."

"Don't you believe in the Bible at all, then?"

Ashurst thought: 'Now I shall really hurt her!'

"I believe in the Sermon on the Mount, because it's beautiful and good for all time."

"But don't you believe Christ was divine?"

He shook his head.

She turned her face quickly to the window, and there sprang into his mind Megan's prayer, repeated by little Nick: "God bless us all, and Mr. Ashes!" Who else would ever say a prayer for him, like her who at this moment must be waiting—waiting to see him come down the lane? And he thought suddenly: 'What a scoundrel I am!'

All that evening this thought kept coming back; but, as is not unusual, each time with less poignancy, till it seemed almost a matter of course to be a scoundrel. And—strange!—he did not know whether he was a scoundrel if he meant to go back to Megan, or if he did not mean to go back to her.

They played cards till the children were sent off to bed; then Stella went to the piano. From over on the window seat, where it was nearly dark, Ashurst watched her between the candles—that fair head on the long, white neck bending to the movement of her hands. She played fluently, without much expression; but what a picture she made, the faint golden radiance, a sort of angelic atmosphere—hovering about her! Who could have passionate thoughts or wild desires in the presence of that swaying, white-clothed girl with the seraphic head? She played a thing of Schumann's called "*Warum?*"

Then Halliday brought out a flute, and the spell was broken. After this they made Ashurst sing, Stella playing him accompaniments from a book of Schumann songs, till, in the middle of "*Ich grolle nicht*," two small figures clad in blue dressing-gowns crept in and tried to conceal themselves beneath the piano. The evening broke up in confusion, and what Sabina called "a splendid rag."

That night Ashurst hardly slept at all. He was thinking, tossing and turning. The intense domestic intimacy of these last two days, the strength of this Halliday atmosphere, seemed to ring him round, and make the farm and Megan—even Megan—seem unreal. Had he really made love to her—really promised to take her away to live with him? He must have been bewitched by the spring, the night, the apple blossom! The notion that he was going to make her his mistress—that simple child not yet eighteen—now filled him with a sort of horror, even while it still stung and whipped his blood. He muttered to himself: "It's awful, what I've done—awful!" And the sound of Schumann's music throbbed and mingled with his fevered thoughts, and he saw again Stella's cool, white, fair-haired figure and bending neck, the queer, angelic radiance about her. 'I must have been—I must be—mad!' he thought. 'What came into me? Poor little Megan!' "God bless us all, and Mr. Ashes!" "I want to be with you—only to be with you!" And burying his face in his pillow, he smothered down a fit of sobbing. Not to go back was awful! To go back—more awful still!

Emotion, when you are young, and give real vent to it, loses its power of torture. And he fell asleep, thinking: 'What was it—a few kisses—all forgotten in a month! '

Next morning he got his cheque cashed, but avoided the shop of the dove-grey dress like the plague; and, instead, bought himself some necessaries. He spent the whole day in a queer mood, cherishing a kind of sullenness against himself. Instead of the hankering of the last two days, he felt nothing but a blank—all passionate longing gone, as if quenched in that outburst of tears. After tea Stella put a book down beside him, and said shyly:

"Have you read that, Frank?"

It was Farrar's *Life of Christ*. Ashurst smiled. Her anxiety about his beliefs seemed to him comic, but touching. Infectious, too, perhaps, for he began to have an itch to justify himself, if not to convert her.

And in the evening, when the children and Halliday were mending their shrimping nets, he said:

"At the back of orthodox religion, so far as I can see, there's always the idea of reward—what you can get for being good; a kind of begging for favours. I think it all starts in fear."

She was sitting on the sofa making reefer knots with a bit of string. She looked up quickly:

"I think it's much deeper than that."

Ashurst felt again that wish to dominate.

"You think so," he said; "but wanting the '*quid pro quo*' is about the deepest thing in all of us! It's jolly hard to get to the bottom of it!"

She wrinkled her brows in a puzzled frown.

"I don't think I understand."

He went on obstinately:

"Well, think, and see if the most religious people aren't those who feel that this life doesn't give them all they want. I believe in being good because to be good is good in itself."

"Then you do believe in being good?"

How pretty she looked now—it was easy to be good with her! And he nodded and said:

"I say, show me how to make that knot!"

With her fingers touching his, in manoeuvring the bit of string he felt soothed and happy. And when he went to bed he wilfully kept his thoughts on her, wrapping himself in her fair, cool sisterly radiance, as in some garment of protection.

Next day he found they had arranged to go by train to Totnes, and picnic at Berry Pomeroy Castle. Still in that resolute oblivion of the past, he took his place with them in the landau beside Halliday, back to the horses. And, then, along the sea front, nearly at the turning to the railway station, his heart almost leaped into his mouth. Megan—Megan herself!—was walking on the far pathway, in her old skirt and jacket and her tam-o'-shanter, looking up into the faces of the passers-by. Instinctively he threw his hand up for cover, then made a feint of clearing dust out of his eyes; but between his fingers he could see her still, moving, not with her free country step, but wavering, lost-looking, like some little dog which has missed its master and does not know whether to run on, to run back—where to run. How had she come like this?—what excuse had she found to get away?—what did she hope for? But with every turn of the wheels bearing him away from her, his heart revolted and cried to him to stop them, to get out, and go to her! When the landau turned the corner to the station he could stand it no more, and opening the carriage door, muttered: "I've forgotten something! Go on—don't wait for me! I'll join you at the castle by the next train!" He jumped, stumbled, spun round, recovered his balance, and walked forward, while the carriage with the astonished Hallidays rolled on.

From the corner he could only just see Megan, a long way ahead now. He ran a few steps, checked himself, and dropped into a walk. With each step nearer to her, further from the Hallidays, he walked more and more slowly. How did it alter anything—this sight of her? How make the going to her, and that which must come of it, less ugly? For there was no hiding it—since he had met the Hallidays he had become gradually sure that he would not marry Megan. It would only be a wild love-time, a troubled, remorseful, difficult time—and then—well, then he would get tired, just because she gave him everything, was so simple, and so trustful, so dewy. And dew—wears off! The little spot of faded colour, her tam-o'-shanter cap, wavered on far in front of him; she was looking up into every face, and at the house windows. Had any man ever such a cruel moment to go through? Whatever he did, he felt he would be a beast. And he uttered a groan which made a nursemaid turn and stare. He saw Megan stop and lean against the sea-wall, looking at the sea; and he too stopped. Quite likely she had never seen the sea before, and even in her distress could not resist that sight. 'Yes—she's seen nothing,' he thought; 'everything's before her. And just for a few weeks passion, I shall be cutting her life to ribbons. I'd better go and hang myself rather than do it!' And suddenly he seemed to see Stella's calm eyes looking into his, the wave of fluffy hair on her forehead stirred by the wind. Ah! it would be madness, would mean giving up all that he respected, and his own self-respect. He turned and walked quickly back towards the station. But memory of that poor, bewildered little figure, those anxious eyes searching the passers-by, smote him too hard again, and once more he turned towards the sea. The cap was no longer visible; that little spot of colour had vanished in the stream of the noon promenaders. And impelled by the passion of longing, the dearth which comes on one

when life seems to be whiling something out of reach, he hurried
forward. She was nowhere to be seen; for half an hour he looked for
her; then on the beach flung himself face downward in the sand. To
find her again he knew he had only to go to the station and wait
till she returned from her fruitless quest, to take her train home; or
to take train himself and go back to the farm, so that she found him
there when she returned. But he lay inert in the sand, among the
indifferent groups of children with their spades and buckets. Pity at
her little figure wandering, seeking, was well-nigh merged in the
spring-running of his blood; for it was all wild feeling now—the
chivalrous part, what there had been of it, was gone. He wanted her
again, wanted her kisses, her soft, little body, her abandonment, all
her quick, warm, pagan emotion; wanted the wonderful feeling of
that night under the moon-lit apple boughs; wanted it all with a
horrible intensity, as the faun wants the nymph. The quick chatter
of the little bright trout-stream, the dazzle of the buttercups, the
rocks of the old "wild men"; the calling of the cuckoos and yaffles,
the hooting of the owls; and the red moon peeping out of the velvet
dark at the living whiteness of the blossom; and her face just out of
reach at the window, lost in its love-look; and her heart against his,
her lips answering his, under the apple tree—all this besieged him.
Yet he lay inert. What was it which struggled against pity and this
feverish longing, and kept him there paralysed in the warm sand?
Three flaxen heads—a fair face with friendly blue-grey eyes, a slim
hand pressing his, a quick voice speaking his name—"So you do
believe in being good?" Yes, and a sort of atmosphere as of some old
walled-in English garden, with pinks, and corn-flowers, and roses,
and scents of lavender and lilac—cool and fair, untouched, almost
holy—all that he had been brought up to feel was clean and good.
And suddenly he thought: 'She might come along the front again
and see me!' and he got up and made his way to the rock at the
far end of the beach. There, with the spray biting into his face, he
could think more coolly. To go back to the farm and love Megan
out in the woods, among the rocks, with everything around wild
and fitting—that, he knew, was impossible, utterly. To transplant
her to a great town, to keep, in some little flat or rooms, one who
belonged so wholly to Nature—the poet in him shrank from it. His
passion would be a mere sensuous revel, soon gone; in London, her

very simplicity, her lack of all intellectual quality, would make her his secret plaything—nothing else. The longer he sat on the rock, with his feet dangling over a greenish pool from which the sea was ebbing, the more clearly he saw this; but it was as if her arms and all of her were slipping slowly, slowly down from him, into the pool, to be carried away out to sea; and her face looking up, her lost face with beseeching eyes, and dark, wet hair—possessed, haunted, tortured him! He got up at last, scaled the low rock-cliff, and made his way down into a sheltered cove. Perhaps in the sea he could get back his control—lose this fever! And stripping off his clothes, he swam out. He wanted to tire himself so that nothing mattered, and swam recklessly, fast and far; then suddenly, for no reason, felt afraid. Suppose he could not reach shore again—suppose the current set him out—or he got cramp, like Halliday! He turned to swim in. The red cliffs looked a long way off. If he were drowned they would find his clothes. The Hallidays would know; but Megan perhaps never— they took no newspaper at the farm. And Phil Halliday's words came back to him again: "A girl at Cambridge I might have—Glad I haven't got her on my mind!" And in that moment of unreasoning fear he vowed he would not have her on his mind. Then his fear left him; he swam in easily enough, dried himself in the sun, and put on his clothes. His heart felt sore, but no longer ached; his body cool and refreshed.

When one is as young as Ashurst, pity is not a violent emotion. And, back in the Halliday's sitting-room, eating a ravenous tea, he felt much like a man recovered from fever. Everything seemed new and clear; the tea, the buttered toast and jam tasted absurdly good; tobacco had never smelt so nice. And walking up and down the empty room, he stopped here and there to touch or look. He took up Stella's work-basket, fingered the cotton reels and a gaily-coloured plait of sewing silks, smelt at the little bag filled with woodroffe she kept among them. He sat down at the piano, playing tunes with one finger, thinking: 'To-night she'll play; I shall watch her while she's playing; it does me good to watch her.' He took up the book, which still lay where she had placed it beside him, and tried to read. But Megan's little, sad figure began to come back at once, and he got up and leaned in the window, listening to the thrushes in the Crescent gardens, gazing at the sea, dreamy and blue below the trees. A servant

came in and cleared the tea away, and he still stood, inhaling the
evening air, trying not to think. Then he saw the Hallidays coming
through the gate of the Crescent, Stella a little in front of Phil and
the children, with their baskets, and instinctively he drew back. His
heart, too sore and discomfited, shrank from this encounter, yet
wanted its friendly solace—bore a grudge against this influence, yet
craved its cool innocence, and the pleasure of watching Stella's face.
From against the wall behind the piano he saw her come in and
stand looking a little blank as though disappointed; then she saw
him and smiled, a swift, brilliant smile which warmed yet irritated
Ashurst.

"You never came after us, Frank."

"No; I found I couldn't."

"Look! We picked such lovely late violets!" She held out a bunch.
Ashurst put his nose to them, and there stirred within him vague
longings, chilled instantly by a vision of Megan's anxious face lifted
to the faces of the passers-by.

He said shortly: "How jolly!" and turned away. He went up to his
room, and, avoiding the children, who were coming up the stairs,
threw himself on his bed, and lay there with his arms crossed over
his face. Now that he felt the die really cast, and Megan given up, he
hated himself, and almost hated the Hallidays and their atmosphere
of healthy, happy English homes. Why should they have chanced
here, to drive away first love—to show him that he was going to
be no better than a common seducer? What right had Stella, with
her fair, shy beauty, to make him know for certain that he would
never marry Megan; and, tarnishing it all, bring him such bitterness
of regretful longing and such pity? Megan would be back by now,
worn out by her miserable seeking—poor little thing!— expecting,
perhaps, to find him there when she reached home. Ashurst bit
at his sleeve, to stifle a groan of remorseful longing. He went to
dinner glum and silent, and his mood threw a dinge even over the
children. It was a melancholy, rather ill-tempered evening, for they
were all tired; several times he caught Stella looking at him with a
hurt, puzzled expression, and this pleased his evil mood. He slept
miserably; got up quite early, and wandered out. He went down to
the beach. Alone there with the serene, the blue, the sunlit sea, his
heart relaxed a little. Conceited fool—to think that Megan would

take it so hard! In a week or two she would almost have forgotten! And he—well, he would have the reward of virtue! A good young man! If Stella knew, she would give him her blessing for resisting that devil she believed in; and he uttered a hard laugh. But slowly the peace and beauty of sea and sky, the flight of the lonely seagulls, made him feel ashamed. He bathed, and turned homewards.

In the Crescent gardens Stella herself was sitting on a camp stool, sketching. He stole up close behind. How fair and pretty she was, bent diligently, holding up her brush, measuring, wrinkling her brows.

He said gently:

"Sorry I was such a beast last night, Stella."

She turned round, startled, flushed very pink, and said in her quick way:

"It's all right. I knew there was something. Between friends it doesn't matter, does it?"

Ashurst answered:

"Between friends—and we are, aren't we?"

She looked up at him, nodded vehemently, and her upper teeth gleamed again in that swift, brilliant smile.

Three days later he went back to London, travelling with the Hallidays. He had not written to the farm. What was there he could say?

On the last day of April in the following year he and Stella were married . . .

Such were Ashurst's memories, sitting against the wall among the gorse, on his silver-wedding day. At this very spot, where he had laid out the lunch, Megan must have stood outlined against the sky when he had first caught sight of her. Of all queer coincidences! And there moved in him a longing to go down and see again the farm and the orchard, and the meadow of the gipsy bogle. It would not take long; Stella would be an hour yet, perhaps.

How well he remembered it all—the little crowning group of pine trees, the steep-up grass hill behind! He paused at the farm gate. The low stone house, the yew-tree porch, the flowering currants—not changed a bit; even the old green chair was out there on the grass under the window, where he had reached up to her that night to take the key. Then he turned down the lane, and stood leaning on the orchard gate—grey skeleton of a gate, as then. A black pig even was wandering in there among the trees. Was it true that twenty-six years had passed, or had he dreamed and awakened to find Megan waiting for him by the big apple tree? Unconsciously he put up his hand to his grizzled beard and brought himself back to reality. Opening the gate, he made his way down through the docks and nettles till he came to the edge, and the old apple tree itself. Unchanged! A little more of the grey-green lichen, a dead branch or two, and for the rest it might have been only last night that he had embraced that mossy trunk after Megan's flight and inhaled its woody savour, while above his head the moonlit blossom had seemed to breathe and live. In that early spring a few buds were showing already; the blackbirds shouting their songs, a cuckoo calling, the sunlight bright and warm. Incredibly the same—the chattering trout-stream, the narrow pool he had lain in every morning, splashing the water over his flanks and chest; and out there in the wild meadow the beech clump and the stone where the gipsy bogle was supposed to sit. And an ache for lost youth, a hankering, a sense of wasted love and sweetness, gripped Ashurst by the throat. Surely, on this earth of such wild beauty, one was meant to hold rapture to one's heart, as this earth and sky held it! And yet, one could not!

He went to the edge of the stream, and looking down at the little pool, thought: 'Youth and spring! What has become of them all, I wonder?' And then, in sudden fear of having this memory jarred by human encounter, he went back to the lane, and pensively retraced his steps to the cross-roads.

Beside the car an old, grey-bearded labourer was leaning on a stick, talking to the chauffeur. He broke off at once, as though guilty of disrespect, and touching his hat, prepared to limp on down the lane.

Ashurst pointed to the narrow green mound. "Can you tell me what this is?"

The old fellow stopped; on his face had come a look as though he were thinking: 'You've come to the right shop, mister!'

"'Tes a grave," he said.

"But why out here?"

The old man smiled. "That's a tale, as yu may say. An' not the first time as I've a-told et—there's plenty folks asks 'bout that bit o' turf. 'Maid's Grave' us calls et, 'ereabouts."

Ashurst held out his pouch. "Have a fill?"

The old man touched his hat again, and slowly filled an old clay pipe. His eyes, looking upward out of a mass of wrinkles and hair, were still quite bright.

"If yu don' mind, zurr, I'll zet down—my leg's 'urtin' a bit to-day." And he sat down on the mound of turf.

"There's always a vlower on this grave. An' 'tain't so very lonesome, neither; brave lot o' folks goes by now, in they new motor cars an' things—not as 'twas in th' old days. She've a-got company up 'ere. 'Twas a poor soul killed 'erself."

"I see!" said Ashurst. "Cross-roads burial. I didn't know that custom was kept up."

"Ah! but 'twas a main long time ago. Us 'ad a parson as was very God-fearin' then. Let me see, I've 'ad my pension six year come Michaelmas, an' I were just on fifty when t'appened. There's none livin' knows more about et than what I du. She belonged close 'ere; same farm as where I used to work along o' Mrs. Narracombe—'tes Nick Narracombe's now; I dus a bit for 'im still, odd times."

Ashurst, who was leaning against the gate, lighting his pipe, left his curved hands before his face for long after the flame of the match had gone out.

"Yes?" he said, and to himself his voice sounded hoarse and queer.

"She was one in an 'underd, poor maid! I putts a vlower 'ere every time I passes. Pretty maid an' gude maid she was, though they wouldn't burry 'er up tu th' church, nor where she wanted to be burried neither." The old labourer paused, and put his hairy, twisted hand flat down on the turf beside the bluebells.

"Yes?" said Ashurst.

"In a manner of speakin'," the old man went on, "I think as 'twas a love-story—though there's no one never knu for zartin. Yu can't tell what's in a maid's 'ead—but that's wot I think about it." He drew his hand along the turf. "I was fond o' that maid—don' know as there was anyone as wasn' fond of 'er. But she was tu lovin'-'earted—that's where 'twas, I think." He looked up. And Ashurst, whose lips were trembling in the cover of his beard, murmured again: "Yes?"

"'Twas in the spring, 'bout now as't might be, or a little later—blossom time—an' we 'ad one o' they young college gentlemen stayin' at the farm—nice feller tu, with 'is 'ead in the air. I liked 'e very well, an' I never see nothin' between 'em, but to my thinkin' e' turned the maid's fancy." The old man took the pipe out of his mouth, spat, and went on:

"Yu see, 'e went away sudden one day, an' never come back. They got 'is knapsack and bits o' things down there still. That's what stuck in my mind—'is never sendin' for 'em. 'Is name was Ashes, or somethin' like that."

"Yes?" said Ashurst once more.

The old man licked his lips.

"'Er never said nothin', but from that day 'er went kind of dazed lukin'; didn' seem rightly therr at all. I never knu a 'uman creature so changed in me life—never. There was another young feller at the farm—Joe Biddaford 'is name wer', that was praaperly sweet on 'er, tu; I guess 'e used to plague 'er wi' 'is attentions. She got to luke quite wild. I'd zee her sometimes of an avenin' when I was bringin' up the calves; ther' she'd stand in th' orchard, under the big apple tree, lukin' straight before 'er. 'Well,' I used t'think, 'I dunno what 'tes that's the matter wi' yu, but yu'm lukin' pittiful, that yu be!'"

The old man relit his pipe, and sucked at it reflectively.

"Yes?" said Ashurst.

"I remembers one day I said to 'er; 'What's the matter, Megan?'—'er name was Megan David, she come from Wales same as 'er aunt, ol' Missis Narracombe. 'Yu'm frettin' about something,' I says. 'No, Jim,' she says, 'I'm not frettin'.' 'Yes, yu be!' I says. 'No,' she says, and tu tears cam' rollin' out. 'Yu'm cryin'—what's that, then?' I says. She putts 'er 'and over 'er 'eart: 'It 'urts me,' she says; 'but 'twill sune be better,' she says. 'But if anything shude 'appen to me, Jim, I wants to be burried under this 'ere apple tree.' I laughed. 'What's goin' to 'appen to yu?' I says: 'don't 'ee be fulish.' 'No,' she says, 'I won't be fulish.' Well, I know what maids are, an' I never thought no more about et, till tu days arter that, 'bout six in the avenin' I was comin' up wi' the calves, when I see somethin' dark lyin' in the strame, close to that big apple tree. I says to meself: 'Is that a pig—funny place for a pig to get to!' an' I goes up to et, an' I see what 'twas."

The old man stopped: his eyes, turned upward, had a bright, suffering look.

"'Twas the maid, in a little narrer pool ther' that's made by the stoppin' of a rock—where I see the young gentleman bathin' once or twice. 'Er was lyin' on 'er face in the watter. There was a plant o' goldie-cups growin' out o' the stone just above 'er 'ead. An' when I come to luke at 'er face, 'twas luvly, butiful, so calm's, a baby's— wonderful butiful et was. When the doctor saw 'er, 'e said: "Er culdn' never a-done it in that little bit o' watter ef 'er 'adn't a-been in an extarsy.' Ah! an' judgin' from 'er face, that was just 'ow she was. Et made me cry praaper—butiful et was! 'Twas June then, but she'd a-found a little bit of apple-blossom left over somewheres, and stuck et in 'er 'air. That's why I thinks 'er must a-been in an extarsy, to go to et gay, like that. Why! there wasn't more than a fute and 'arf o' watter. But I tell 'ee one thing—that meadder's 'arnted; I knu et, an' she knu et; an' no one'll persuade me as 'tesn't. I told 'em what she said to me 'bout bein' burried under th' apple tree. But I think that turned 'em—made et luke tu much 's ef she'd 'ad it in 'er mind deliberate; an' so they burried 'er up 'ere. Parson we 'ad then was very particular, 'e was."

Again the old man drew his hand over the turf.

"'Tes wonderful, et seems," he added slowly, "what maids'll du for love. She 'ad a lovin' 'eart; I guess 'twas broken. But us never *knu* nothin'!"

He looked up as if for approval of his story, but Ashurst had walked past him as if he were not there.

Up on the top of the hill, beyond where he had spread the lunch, over, out of sight, he lay down on his face. So had his virtue been rewarded, and "the Cyprian," goddess of love, taken her revenge! And before his eyes, dim with tears, came Megan's face with the sprig of apple blossoms in her dark, wet hair. 'What did I do that was wrong?' he thought. 'What did I do?' But he could not answer. Spring, with its rush of passion, its flowers and song—the spring in his heart and Megan's! Was it just Love seeking a victim! The Greek was right, then—the words of the "Hippolytus" as true to-day!

> For mad is the heart of Love,
> And gold the gleam of his wing;

And all to the spell thereof
Bend when he makes his spring.
All life that is wild and young
In mountain and wave and stream,
All that of earth is sprung,
Or breathes in the red sunbeam;
Yea, and Mankind. O'er all a royal throne
Cyprian, Cyprian, is thine alone!

The Greek was right! over the hill! Megan! Poor little Megan—coming over the hill! Megan under the old apple tree waiting and looking! Megan dead, with beauty printed on her! . . .

A voice said:

"Oh, there you are! Look."

Ashurst rose, took his wife's sketch, and stared at it in silence. "Is the foreground right, Frank?"

"Yes."

"But there's something wanting, isn't there?"

Ashurst nodded. Wanting? The apple tree, the singing, and the gold!

[*1916*]

THE PRISONER

On a fine day of early summer in a London garden, before the birds had lost their spring song, or the trees dropped their last blossoms, our friend said suddenly:

"Why! there's a goldfinch!" Blackbirds there were, and thrushes, and tits in plenty, an owl at night, and a Christopher Columbus of a cuckoo, who solemnly, once a year, mistook this green island of trees for the main lands of Kent and Surrey, but a goldfinch—never!

"I hear it—over there!" he said again, and, getting up, he walked towards the house.

When he came back, our friend sat down again, and observed:

"I didn't know that you kept a cage-bird!" We admitted that our cook had a canary.

"A mule!" he remarked, very shortly.

Some strong feeling had evidently been aroused in him that neither of us could understand.

Suddenly he burst out:

"I can't bear things in cages; animals, birds, or men. I hate to see or think of them." And looking at us angrily, as though we had taken an advantage in drawing from him this confession, he went on quickly:

"I was staying in a German town some years ago, with a friend who was making inquiries into social matters. He asked me one day to go over a prison with him. I had never seen one, then, and I agreed. It was just such a day as this—a perfectly clear sky, and there was that cool, dancing sparkle on everything that you only see in some parts of Germany. This prison, which stood in the middle of the town, was one of those shaped like a star that have been built over there on the plan of Pentonville. The system, they told us, was the same that you might have seen working here many years ago.

The Germans were then, and still, no doubt, are, infatuated with the idea of immuring their prisoners up in complete solitude.

But it was a new toy to them then, and they were enjoying it with that sort of fanatical thoroughness which the Germans give to everything they take up. I don't want to describe this prison, or what we saw in it; as far as an institution run on such dreadful lines can be, it was, I daresay, well managed; the Governor, at all events, impressed me favourably. I'll simply tell you of the one thing which I shall never forget, because it symbolized to me forever the caging of all creatures, animal or human, great or small."

Our friend paused; then, with an added irritation in his voice, as though aware of doing violence to his natural reserve, he went on:

"We had been all over the grizzly place when the Governor asked my friend whether he would like to see one or two of the 'life' prisoners.

"'I will show you one,' he said, 'who has been here twenty-seven years. He is, you will understand'—I remember his very words—'a little worn by his long confinement.' While we were going towards this prisoner's cell, they told us his story. He had been a cabinet-maker's assistant, and when still quite a boy, joined a gang of burglars to rob his own employer. Surprised during the robbery, he had blindly struck out and killed his employer on the spot. He was sentenced to death, but, on the intervention of some Royalty who had been upset by the sight of corpses, I believe at the Battle of Sadowa, his sentence was commuted to imprisonment for life.

"When we entered his cell he was standing perfectly still, gazing at his work. He looked quite sixty, though he could not have been more than forty-six—a bent, trembling ruin of a figure, covered by a drab-coloured apron. His face had the mealy hue and texture of all prisoners' faces. He seemed to have no features; his cheeks were hollow; his eyes large, but, looking back, I can't remember their colour—if, indeed, they had colour in them at all. As we passed in, one by one, through the iron door, he took off his round cap, drab-coloured too, like everything about him, showing his dusty, nearly bald head, with a few short grey hairs on end, and stood in an attitude of 'attention', humbly staring at us. He was like an owl surprised by daylight. Have you ever seen a little child ill for the first time—full of bewilderment at its own suffering? His face was like that, but so extraordinarily gentle! We had seen many of the prisoners, and he was the only one that had that awful *gentleness*. The sound of his voice, too: '*Ja; Herr Direktor—nein, Herr Direktor!*' soft and despairing—I remember it now—there was not a breath of will-power left." Our friend paused, frowning in his effort to re-create the scene. "He held in his hand," he went on presently, "a sheet of stiff paper, on which he had been transcribing the New Testament in letters from a code of writing for the deaf and dumb. When he passed his thin fingers over the type to show us how easily the deaf and dumb could read it, you could see that his hands were dusty like a miller's. There was nothing in the cell to produce that dust, and in my belief it was not dust on his hands, but some excretion from that human plant running to seed. When he held the sheet of paper up, too, it trembled like the wing of an insect. One of us asked who invented the system he was working at, mentioning some name. '*Nein, nein,*' he said, and he stood shivering with eagerness to recollect the right name. At last he dropped his head, and mumbled out: '*Ah, Herr Direktor, ich kann nicht!*' Then all of a sudden the name came bursting from his lips. At that moment, for the first time, he actually looked like a man. I never before then realised the value of freedom; the real meaning of our relations with other human beings; the necessity for the mind's being burnished from minute to minute by sights and sounds, by the need for remembering and using what we remember. This fellow, you see, had no use for memory in his life; he was like a plant placed where no dew can possibly fall on it. To watch that look pass over his face at the mere remembrance of a name was like catching sight of a tiny scrap of green leaf left in the heart of a withered shrub. Man, I tell you, is wonderful—the most enduring creature that has ever been produced!" Our friend rose and began pacing up and down. "His world was not a large one; about fourteen feet by eight. He'd lived in it for twenty-seven years, without a mouse even for a friend. They do things thoroughly in prisons. Think of the tremendous vital force that must go to the making of the human organism, for a man to live through that . . . What do you imagine," he went on, turning to us suddenly, "kept even a remnant of his reason alive?—Well, I'll tell you: While we were still looking at his 'deaf and dumb' writing, he suddenly handed us a piece of wood about the size of a large photograph. It was the picture of a young girl, seated in the very centre of a garden, with bright-coloured flowers in her hand; in the background was a narrow, twisting stream with some rushes, and a queer bird, rather like a raven, standing on the bank. And by the side of the girl a tree with large hanging fruits, strangely symmetrical, unlike any tree that ever grew, yet with something in it that is in all trees—a look as if they had spirits, and were the friends of man. The girl was staring straight at us with perfectly round, blue eyes, and the flowers she held in her hand seemed also to stare at us. The whole picture, it appeared to me, was full of—what shall I say?—a kind of wonder. It had all the crude colour and drawing of an early Italian painting, the same look of difficulty conquered by sheer devotion. One of us asked him if he had learnt to draw before his imprisonment, but the poor fellow misunderstood the question. '*Nein, nein,*' he said, 'the Herr Direktor knows I had no model. It is a fancy picture!' And the smile he gave us would have made a devil weep! He had put into that picture all that his soul longed for—woman, flowers, birds, trees, blue sky, running water; and all the wonder of his spirit that he was cut off from them. He had been at work on it, they said, for eighteen years, destroying and repeating, until he had produced this, the hundredth version. It was a masterpiece. Yes, there he had been for twenty-seven years, condemned for life to this living death—without scent, sight, hearing, or touch of any natural object, without even the memory of them, evolving from his starved soul this vision of a young girl with eyes full of wonder, and flowers in her hand. It's the greatest triumph of the human spirit, and the greatest testimony to the power of Art that I have ever seen."

Our friend uttered a short laugh: "So thick-skinned, however, is a man's mind that I didn't even then grasp the agony of that man's life. But I did later. I happened to see his eyes as he was trying to answer some question of the Governor's about his health. To my dying day I shall never forget them. They were incarnate tragedy—all those eternities of solitude and silence he had lived through, all the eternities he had still to live through before they buried him in the graveyard outside, were staring out of them. They had more sheer pitiful misery in them than all the eyes put together of all the free men I've ever seen. I couldn't stand the sight of them, and hurried out of the cell. I felt then, and ever since, what they say the

Russians feel—for all their lapses into savagery—the sacredness of suffering. I felt that we ought all of us to have bowed down before him; that I, though I was free and righteous, was a charlatan and sinner in the face of that living crucifixion. Whatever crime he had committed—I don't care what it was—that poor lost creature had been so sinned against that I was as dirt beneath his feet. When I think of him—there still, for all I know—I feel a sort of frenzy rising in me against my own kind. I feel the miserable aching of all the caged creatures in the world."

Our friend turned his head away, and for quite a minute did not speak. "On our way back, I remember," he said at last, "we drove through the Stadt Park. There it was free and light enough; every kind of tree—limes, copper beeches, oaks, sycamores, poplars, birches, and apple trees in blossom, were giving out their scent; every branch and leaf was glistening with happiness. The place was full of birds, the symbols of freedom, fluttering about, singing their loudest in the sun. Yes, it was all enchanted ground. And I well remember thinking that in the whole range of Nature only men and spiders torture other creatures in that long-drawn-out kind of way; and only men do it in cold blood to their own species. So far as I know that's a fact of natural history; and I can tell you that to see, once for all, as I did, in that man's eyes, its unutterable misery, is never to feel the same towards your own kind again. That night I sat in a *café* window, listening to the music, the talk, the laughter, watching the people pass in the street—shop-folk, soldiers, merchants, officials, priests, beggars, aristocrats, women of pleasure, and the light streaming out from the windows, and the leaves just moving against the most wonderful, dark blue sky. But I saw and heard nothing of it all. I only saw the gentle, mealy-coloured face of that poor fellow, his eyes, and his dusty, trembling hands, and I saw the picture that he had painted there in hell. I've seen it ever since, whenever I see or hear of any sort of solitary caged creature."

Our friend ceased speaking, and very soon after he rose, excused himself, and went away.

[*1909*]

A SIMPLE TALE

TALKING of anti-Semitism one of those mornings, Ferrand said in his good French: "Yes, *monsieur*, plenty of those gentlemen in these days esteem themselves Christian, but I have only once met a Christian who esteemed himself a Jew. *C'était très drôle—je vais vous conter cela.*

"It was one autumn in London, and, the season being over, I was naturally in poverty, inhabiting a palace in Westminster at fourpence the night. In the next bed to me that time there was an old gentleman, so thin that one might truly say he was made of air. English, Scotch, Irish, Welsh—I shall never learn to distinguish those little differences in your race—but I well think he was English. Very feeble, very frail, white as paper, with a long grey beard, and caves in the cheeks, and speaking always softly, as if to a woman … For me it was an experience to see an individual so gentle in a palace like that. His bed and bowl of broth he gained in sweeping out the kennels of all those sorts of types who come to sleep there every night. There he spent all his day long, going out only at ten hours and a half every night, and returning at midnight less one quarter. Since I had not much to do, it was always a pleasure for me to talk with him; for, though he was certainly a little *toqué*," and Ferrand tapped his temple, "he had great charm of an old man, never thinking of himself no more than a fly that turns in dancing all day beneath a ceiling. If there was something he could do for one of those specimens—to sew on a button, clean a pipe, catch beasts in their clothes, or sit to see they were not stolen, even to give up his place by the fire—he would always do it with his smile so white and gentle; and in his leisure he would read the Holy Book! He inspired in me a sort of affection—there are not too many old men so kind and gentle as that, even when they are 'crackey,' as you call it. Several times I have caught him in washing the feet of one of those sots, or bathing some black eye or other, sure as they often catch—a man of a spiritual refinement really remarkable; in clothes also so refined that one sometimes saw his skin. Though he had never great thing to say, he heard you like an angel, and spoke evil of no one; but, seeing that he had no more vigour than a swallow, it piqued me much how he would go out like that every night in all the weathers at the same hour for so long a promenade of the streets. And when I interrogated him on this, he would only smile his smile of one not there, and did not seem to know very much of what I was talking. I said to myself: 'There is something here to see, if I am not mistaken. One of these good days I shall be your guardian angel while you fly the night.' For I am a connoisseur of strange things, *monsieur*, as you know; though, you may well imagine, being in the streets all day long between two boards of a sacred sandwich does not give you too strong a desire to *flâner* in the evenings. *Eh, bien!* It was a night in late October that I at last pursued him. He was not difficult to follow, seeing he had no more guile than an egg; passing first at his walk of an old shadow into your St. James's Park, along where your military types puff out their chests for the nursemaids to admire. Very slowly he went, leaning on a staff—*une canne de promenade* such as I have never seen, nearly six feet high, with an end like a shepherd's crook or the handle of a sword, a thing truly to make the *gamins* laugh—even me it made to smile, though I am not too well accustomed to mock at age and poverty, to watch him march in leaning on that cane. I remember that night—very beautiful, the sky of a clear dark, the stars as bright as they can ever be in these towns of our high civilisation, and the leaf-shadows of the plane-trees, colour of grapes on the pavement, so that one had not the heart to put foot on them. One of those evenings when the spirit is light, and policemen a little dreamy and well-wishing. Well, as I tell you, my Old marched, never looking behind him, like a man who walks in sleep. By that big church—which, like all those places, had its air of coldness, far and ungrateful among us others, little human creatures who have built it—he passed, into the great Eaton Square, whose houses ought well to be inhabited by people very rich. There he crossed to lean against the railings of the garden in the centre, very tranquil, his long white beard falling over hands joined on his staff, in awaiting what—I could not figure to myself at all. It was the hour when your high *bourgeoisie* return from the theatre in their carriages, whose manikins sit, the arms crossed, above horses fat as snails. And one would see through the window some lady *bercée doucemeut*, with the face of one who has eaten too much and loved too little. And gentlemen passed me, marching for a mouthful of fresh air, *très comme il faut*, their concertina hats pushed up, and nothing at all in their eyes. I remarked my Old, who, making no movement, watched them all as they went by, till presently a carriage stopped at a house nearly opposite. At once, then, he began to cross the road quickly, carrying his great stick. I observed the lackey pulling the bell and opening the carriage door, and three people coming forth—a man, a woman, a young man. Very high *bourgeoisie*, some judge, knight, mayor—what do I know?—with his wife and son, mounting under the porch. My Old had come to the bottom of the steps, and spoke, in bending himself forward, as if supplicating. At once those three turned their faces, very astonished. Although I was very intrigued, I could not hear what he was saying, for, if I came nearer, I feared he would see me spying on him. Only the sound of his voice I heard, gentle as always; and his hand I saw wiping his forehead, as though he had carried something heavy from very far. Then the lady spoke to her husband, and went into the house, and the young son followed in lighting a cigarette. There rested only that good father of the family, with his grey whiskers and nose a little bent, carrying an expression as if my Old were making him ridiculous. He made a quick gesture, as though he said, 'Go!' then he too fled softly. The door was shut. At once the lackey mounted, the carriage drove away, and all was as if it had never been, except that my Old was standing there, quite still. But soon he came returning, carrying his staff as if it burdened him. And recoiling in a porch to see him pass I saw his visage full of dolour, of one overwhelmed with fatigue and grief; so that I felt my heart squeeze me. I must well confess, *monsieur*, I was a little shocked to see this old sainted father asking, as it seemed, for alms. That is a thing I myself have never done, not even in the greatest poverty—one is not like your 'gentlemen'—one does always some little thing for the money he receives, if it is only to show a drunken man where he lives. And I returned in meditating deeply over this problem, which well seemed to me fit for the angels to examine; and knowing what time my Old was always re-entering, I took care to be in my bed before him. He came in as ever, treading softly so as not to wake us others, and his face had again its serenity, a little 'crackey.' As you may well have remarked, *monsieur*, I am not one of those individuals who let everything grow under the nose without pulling them up to see how they are made. For me the greatest pleasure is to lift the skirts of life, to unveil what there is under the surface of things which are not always what they seem, as says your good little poet. For that one must have philosophy, and a certain industry, lacking to all those gentlemen who think they alone are industrious because they sit in chairs and blow into the telephone all day, in filling their pockets with money. Myself, I coin knowledge of the heart—it is the only gold they cannot take from you. So that night I lay awake. I was not content with what I had seen; for I could not imagine why this old man, so unselfish, so like a saint in thinking ever of others, should go thus every night to beg, when he had always in this palace his bed, and that with which to keep his soul within his rags. Certainly we all have our vices, and gentlemen the most revered do, in secret, things they would cough to see others doing; but that business of begging seemed scarcely in his character of an old altruist—for in my experience, *monsieur*, beggars are not less egoist than millionaires. As I say, it piqued me much, and I resolved to follow him again. The second night was of the most different. There was a great wind, and white clouds flying in the moonlight. He commenced his pilgrimage in passing by your House of Commons, as if toward the river. I like much that great river of yours. There is in its career something of very grand; it ought to know many things, although it is so silent, and gives to no one the secrets which are confided to it. He had for objective, it seemed, that long row of houses very respectable, which gives on the Embankment, before you arrive at Chelsea. It was painful to see the poor Old, bending almost double against that great wind coming from the west. Not too many carriages down here, and few people—a true wilderness, lighted by tall lamps which threw no shadows, so clear was the moon. He took his part soon, as of the other night, standing on the far side of the road, watching for the return of some lion to his den. And presently I saw one coming, accompanied by three lionesses, all taller than himself. This one was bearded, and carried spectacles—a real head of learning; walking, too, with the step of a man who knows his world. Some professor—

I said to myself—with his harem. They gained their house at fifty
paces from my Old; and, while this learned one was opening the
door, the three ladies lifted their noses in looking at the moon. A
little of aesthetic, a little of science—as always with that type there!
At once I had perceived my Old coming across, blown by the wind
like a grey stalk of thistle; and his face, with its expression of infinite
pain as if carrying the sufferings of the world. At the moment they
see him those three ladies drop their noses and fly within the house
as if he were the pestilence, in crying, 'Henry!' And out comes my
monsieur again, in his beard and spectacles. For me, I would freely
have given my ears to hear, but I saw that this good Henry had his
eye on me, and I did not budge, for fear to seem in conspiracy. I
heard him only say: 'Impossible! Impossible! Go to the proper place!'
and he shut the door. My Old remained, with his long staff resting
on a shoulder bent as if that stick were of lead. And presently he
commenced to march again whence he had come, curved and
trembling, the very shadow of a man, passing me, too, as if I were the
air. That time also I regained my bed before him, in meditating very
deeply, still more uncertain of the psychology of this affair, and
resolved once again to follow him, saying to myself: 'This time I shall
run all risks to hear.' There are two kinds of men in this world,
monsieur—one who will not rest content till he has become master
of all the toys that make a fat existence—in never looking to see of
what they are made; and the other, for whom life is tobacco and a
crust of bread, and liberty to take all to pieces, so that his spirit may
feel good within him. Frankly, I am of that kind. I rest never till I
have found out why this is that; for me mystery is the salt of life, and
I must well eat of it. I put myself again, then, to following him the
next night. This time he traversed those little dirty streets of your
great Westminster where all is mixed in a true pudding of lords and
poor wretches at two sous the dozen; of cats and policemen; kerosene
flames, abbeys, and the odour of fried fish. Ah! truly it is frightful to
see your low streets in London; that gives me a conviction of
hopelessness such as I have never caught elsewhere; piquant, too, to
find them so near to that great House which sets example of good
government to all the world. There is an irony so ferocious there,
monsieur, that one can well hear the good God of your *bourgeois*
laugh in every wheel that rolls, and the cry of each cabbage that is

sold; and see him smile in the smoky light of every flare, and in the candles of your cathedral, in saying to himself: 'I have well made this world. Is there not variety here?—*en voilà une bonne soupe!*' This time, however, I attended my Old like his very shadow, and could hear him sighing as he marched, as if he also found the atmosphere of those streets too strong. But all of a sudden he turned a corner, and we were in the most quiet, most beautiful little street I have seen in all your London. It was of small, old houses, very regular, which made as if they inclined themselves in their two rows before a great church at the end, grey in the moonlight, like a mother. There was no one in the street, and no more cover than hair on the head of a pope. But I had some confidence now that my Old would not remark me standing there so close, since in these pilgrimages he seemed to remark nothing. Leaning on his staff, I tell you he had the air of an old bird in a desert, reposing on one leg by a dry pool, his soul looking for water. It gave me that notion one has sometimes in watching the rare spectacles of life—that sentiment which, according to me, pricks artists to their work. We had not stayed there too long before I saw a couple marching from the end of the street, and thought: 'Here they come to their nest.' Vigorous and gay they were, young married ones, eager to get home; one could see the white neck of the young wife, the white shirt of the young man, gleaming under their cloaks. I know them well, those young couples in great cities, without a care, taking all things, the world before them, *très amoreux*, without, as yet, children; jolly and pathetic, having life still to learn—which, believe me, *monsieur*, is a sad enough affair for nine rabbits out of ten. They stopped at the house next to where I stood; and, since my Old was coming fast as always to the feast, I put myself at once to the appearance of ringing the bell of the house before me. This time I had well the chance of hearing. I could see, too, the faces of all three, because I have by now the habit of seeing out of the back hair. The pigeons were so anxious to get to their nest that my Old had only time to speak, as they were in train to vanish. 'Sir, let me rest in your doorway!' *Monsieur*, I have never seen a face so hopeless, so cribbled with fatigue, yet so full of a gentle dignity as that of my Old while he spoke those words. It was as if something looked from his visage surpassing what belongs to us others, so mortal and so cynic as human life must well render all who dwell in this earthly paradise. He held his long staff upon one shoulder, and I had the idea, sinister enough, that it was crushing his body of a spectre down into the pavement. I know not how the impression came, but it seemed to me that this devil of a stick had the nature of a heavy cross reposing on his shoulder; I had pain to prevent myself turning, to find if in truth 'I had them,' as your drunkards say. Then the young man called out: 'Here's a shilling for you, my friend!' But my Old did not budge, answering always: 'Sir, let me rest in your doorway!' As you may well imagine, *monsieur*, we were all in the silence of astonishment, I pulling away at my bell next door, which was not ringing, seeing I took care it did not; and those two young people regarding my Old with eyes round as moons, out of their pigeon-house, which I could well see was prettily feathered. Their hearts were making seesaw, I could tell; for at that age one is still impressionable. Then the girl put herself to whispering, and her husband said those two words of your young 'gentlemen,' 'Awfully sorry!' and put out his hand, which held now a coin large as a saucer. But again my Old only said: 'Sir, let me rest in your doorway!' And the young man drew back his hand quickly as if he were ashamed, and saying again, 'Sorry!' he shut the door. I have heard many sighs in my time—they are the good little accompaniments to the song we sing, we others who are in poverty; but the sigh my Old pushed then—how can I tell you?—had an accent as if it came from Her, the faithful companion, who marches in holding the hands of men and women so that they may never make the grand mistake to imagine themselves for a moment the good God. Yes, monsieur, it was as if pushed by Suffering herself, that bird of the night, never tired of flying in this world where they talk always of cutting her wings. Then I took my resolution, and, coming gently from behind, said:

'My Old—what is it? Can I do anything for you?' Without looking at me, he spoke as to himself: 'I shall never find one who will let me rest in his doorway. For my sin I shall wander for ever!' At this moment, *monsieur*, there came to me an inspiration so clear that I marvelled I had not already had it a long time before. He thought himself the Wandering Jew! I had well found it. This was certainly his fixed idea, of a cracked old man! And I said: 'My Jew, do you know this? In doing what you do, you have become as Christ, in a world of wandering Jews!' But he did not seem to hear me, and only just as we arrived at our palace became again that old gentle being, thinking never of himself."

Behind the smoke of his cigarette a smile curled Ferrand's red lips under his long nose a little on one side.

"And, if you think of it, *monsieur*, it is well like that. Provided there exists always that good man of a Wandering Jew, he will certainly have become as Christ, in all these centuries of being refused from door to door. Yes, yes, he must well have acquired charity the most profound that this world has ever seen, in watching the crushing virtue of others. All those gentry, of whom he asks night by night to let him rest in their doorways, they tell him where to go, how to *ménager* his life, even offer him money, as I had seen; but, to let him rest, to trust him in their houses—this strange old man—as a fellow, a brother voyager—that they will not; it is hardly in the character of good citizens in a Christian country. And, as I have indicated to you, this Old of mine, cracked as he was, thinking himself that Jew who refused rest to the good Christ, had become, in being refused for ever, the most Christ-like man I have ever encountered on this earth, which, according to me, is composed almost entirely of those who have themselves the character of the Wandering Jew."

Puffing out a sigh of smoke, Ferrand added: "I do not know whether he continued to pursue his idea, for I myself took the road next morning, and I have never seen him since."

[*1914*]

THE CONSUMMATION

ABOUT 1889 there lived in London a man named Harrison, of an amiable and perverse disposition. One morning, at Charing Cross Station, a lady in whom he was interested said to him:

"But Mr. Harrison, why don't you *write*? You are just the person!"

Harrison saw that he was, and at the end of two years had produced eleven short stories, with two of which he was not particularly pleased, but as he naturally did not like to waste them, he put them with the others and sent them all to a publisher. In the course of time he received from the publisher a letter saying that for a certain consideration or commission he would be prepared to undertake the risk of publishing these stories upon Harrison's incurring all the expenses. This pleased Harrison, who, feeling that no time should be wasted in making his "work" public, wrote desiring the publisher to put the matter in hand. The publisher replied to this with an estimate and an agreement, to which Harrison responded with a cheque. The publisher answered at once with a polite letter, suggesting that for Harrison's advantage a certain additional sum should be spent on advertisements. Harrison saw the point of this directly, and replied with another cheque—knowing that between gentlemen there could be no question of money.

In due time the book appeared. It was called "In the Track of the Stars," by Cuthbert Harrison; and within a fortnight Harrison began to receive reviews. He read them with an extraordinary pleasure, for they were full of discriminating flattery. One asked if he were a "Lancelot in disguise." Two Liberal papers described the stories as masterpieces; one compared them to the best things in Poe and de Maupassant; and another called him a second Rudyard Kipling. He was greatly encouraged, but, being by nature modest, he merely wrote to the publisher inquiring what he thought of a second edition. His publisher replied with an estimate, mentioning casually that he had already sold about four hundred copies. Harrison, referred to his cheque-book and saw that the first edition had been a thousand copies. He replied, therefore, that he would wait. He waited, and at the end of six months wrote again. The publisher replied that he had now sold four hundred and three copies, but that, as Mr. Harrison had at present an unknown name, he did not advise a second edition: there was no market for short stories. These had, however, been so well received that he recommended Mr. Harrison to write a long story. The book was without doubt a success, so far as a book of short stories could ever be a success . . . He sent Harrison a small cheque, and a large number of reviews which Harrison had already received.

Harrison decided not to have a second edition, but to rest upon his *succés d'estime*. All his relations were extremely pleased, and almost immediately he started writing his long story. Now it happened that among Harrison's friends was a man of genius, who sent Harrison a letter.

"I had no idea," he said, "that you could write like this; of course my dear fellow, the stories are not 'done'; there is no doubt about it, they are not 'done.' But you have plenty of time; you are young, and I see that you can do things. Come down here and let us have a talk, about what you are at now."

On receiving this Harrison wasted no time, but went down. The man of genius, over a jug of claret-cup, on a summer's afternoon, pointed out how the stories were not "done."

"They show a feeling for outside drama," said he, "there is none of the real drama of psychology."

Harrison showed him his reviews. He left the man of genius on the following day with a certain sensation of soreness. In the course of a few weeks, however, the soreness wore off, and the words of the man of genius began to bear fruit, and at the end of two months Harrison wrote:

"You are quite right—the stories were not 'done.' I think, however, that I am now on the right path."

At the end of another year, after submitting it once or twice to the man of genius, he finished his second book, and called it "John

Endacott." About this time he left off alluding to his "work" and began to call his writings "stuff."

He sent it to the publisher with the request that he would consider its publication on a royalty. In rather more than the ordinary course of time the publisher replied, that in his opinion (a lay one) "John Endacott" didn't quite fulfil the remarkable promise of Mr. Harrison's first book; and, to show Harrison his perfect honesty, he enclosed an extract from the "reader's" opinion, which stated that Mr. Harrison had "fallen between the stools of art and the British public." Much against the publisher's personal feelings, therefore, the publisher considered that he could only undertake the risk in the then bad condition of trade—if Mr. Harrison would guarantee the expenses.

Harrison hardened his heart, and replied that he was not prepared to guarantee the expenses. Upon which the publisher returned his manuscript, saying that in his opinion (a lay one) Mr. Harrison was taking the wrong turning, which he (the publisher) greatly regretted, for he had much appreciated the pleasant relations which had always existed between them.

Harrison sent the book to a younger publisher, who accepted it on a postponed royalty. It appeared.

At the end of three weeks Harrison began to receive reviews. They were mixed. One complained that there was not enough plot; another, fortunately by the same post, that there was too much plot. The general tendency was to regret that the author of "In the Track of the Stars" had not fulfilled the hopes raised by his first book, in which he had shown such promise of completely hitting the public taste. This might have depressed Harrison had he not received a letter from the man of genius couched in these terms:

"My dear fellow, I am more pleased than I can say. I am now more than ever convinced that you can do things."

Harrison at once began a third book.

Owing to the unfortunate postponement of his royalty he did not receive anything from his second book. The publisher sold three hundred copies. During the period (eighteen months) that he was writing his third book the man of genius introduced Harrison to a critic, with the words: "You may rely on his judgment; the beggar is infallible."

While to the critic he said: "I tell you, this fellow can do things."

The critic was good to Harrison, who, as before said, was of an amiable disposition.

When he had finished his third book he dedicated it to the man of genius and called it "Summer."

"My dear fellow," wrote the man of genius, when he received his copy, "It is good! There is no more to be said about it; it is good! I read it with indescribable pleasure."

On the same day Harrison received a letter from the critic which contained the following: "Yes, it's undoubtedly an advance. It's not quite Art, but it's a great advance!"

Harrison was considerably encouraged. The same publisher brought out the book, and sold quite two hundred copies; but he wrote rather dolefully to Harrison, saying that the public demand seemed "almost exhausted." Recognising the fact that comparisons are odious, Harrison refrained from comparing the sale of the book with that of "In the Track of the Stars," in which he had shown such promise of "completely hitting the public taste." Indeed, about this time he began to have dreams of abandoning the sources of his private income and living the true literary life. He had not many reviews, and began his fourth book.

He was two years writing this "work," which he called "A Lost Man," and dedicated to the critic. He sent a presentation copy to the man of genius, from whom he received an almost immediate reply:

"My dear fellow, it is amazing, really amazing how you progress! Who would ever imagine you were the same man that wrote 'In the Track of the Stars'! Yet I pique myself on the fact that even in your first book I spotted that you could do things. Oh!—I wish I could write like you! 'A Lost Man' is wonderfully good."

The man of genius was quite sincere in these remarks, which he wrote after perusing the first six chapters. He never, indeed, actually finished reading the book—he felt so tired, as if Harrison had exhausted him—but he always alluded to it as "wonderfully good," just as if he really had finished it.

Harrison sent another copy to the critic, who wrote a genuine warm letter, saying that he, Harrison, had "achieved" it at last. "This," he said, "is *art*. I doubt if you will ever do anything better than this . . . I crown you."

Harrison at once commenced his fifth book.

He was more than three years upon this new "work," and called it "A Pilgrimage." There was a good deal of difficulty in getting it published. Two days after it appeared, however, the critic wrote to Harrison: "I cannot tell you," he said, "how very good I think your new book. It is perhaps stronger than 'A Lost Man,' perhaps more original. If anything it is too——I have not finished it yet, but I've written off at once to let you know."

As a matter of fact, he never finished the book. He could not—it was too——! "It's wonderfully good," he said, however, to his wife, and he made *her* read it.

Meanwhile, the man of genius wired saying: "Am going to write to you about your book. Positively am, but have lumbago and cannot hold pen."

Harrison never received any letter, but the critic received one saying: "Can you read it? I *can't*. Altogether over 'done.'"

Harrison was elated. His new publisher was not. He wrote in a peevish strain, saying there was *absolutely no sale*. Mr. Harrison must take care what he was doing or he would exhaust his public, and enclosing a solitary review, which said amongst other things: "This book may be very fine art, too fine altogether. We found it dull."

Harrison went abroad, and began his sixth book. He named it "The Consummation," and worked at it in hermit-like solitude; in it, for the first time, he satisfied himself. He wrote, as it were, with his heart's blood, with an almost bitter delight. And he often smiled to himself as he thought how with his first book he had so nearly hit the public taste; and how of his fourth the critic had said: "This is art. I doubt if you will ever do anything better than this." How far away they seemed! Ah! this book was indeed the "consummation" devoutly to be wished.

In the course of time he returned to England and took a cottage at Hampstead, and there he finished the book. The day after it was finished he took the manuscript and, going to a secluded spot on the top of the Heath, lay down on the grass to read it quietly through. He read three chapters, and, putting the remainder down, sat with his head buried in his hands.

"Yes," he thought, "I *have* done it at last. *It is good*, wonderfully good!" and for two hours he sat like that, with his head in his hands.

He had indeed exhausted his public. It was too good—*he could not read it himself!*

Returning to his cottage, he placed the manuscript in a drawer. He never wrote another word.

[*1904*]

ACME

IN these days no man of genius need starve. The following story of my friend Bruce may be taken as proof of this assertion. Nearly sixty when I first knew him, he must have written already some fifteen books, which had earned him the reputation of "a genius" with the few who know. He used to live in York Street, Adelphi, where he had two rooms up the very shaky staircase of a house chiefly remarkable for the fact that its front door seemed always open. I suppose there never was a writer more indifferent to what people thought of him. He profoundly neglected the Press—not with one of those neglects which grow on writers from reading reviews of their own works—he seemed never to read criticism, but with the basic neglect of "an original," a nomadic spirit, a stranger in modern civilisation, who would leave his attics for long months of wandering, and come back there to hibernate and write a book. He was a tall, thin man, with a face rather like Mark Twain's, black eyebrows which bristled and shot up, a bitten drooping grey moustache, and fuzzy grey hair; but his eyes were like owl's eyes, piercing, melancholy, dark brown, and gave to his rugged face an extraordinary expression of a spirit remote from the flesh which had captured it. He was a bachelor, who seemed to avoid women; perhaps they had "learned" him that; for he must have been very attractive to them.

The year of which I write had been to my friend Bruce the devil, monetarily speaking. With his passion for writing that for which his Age had no taste—what could he expect? His last book had been a complete frost. He had undergone, too, an operation which had cost him much money and left him very weak. When I went to see him that October, I found him stretched out on two chairs, smoking the Brazilian cigarettes which he affected—and which always affected me, so black and strong they were, in their yellow maize-leaf coverings. He had a writing-pad on his knee, and sheets of paper scattered all around. The room had a very meagre look. I had not seen him for a year and more, but he looked up at me as if I'd been in yesterday.

"Hallo!" he said; "I went into a thing they call a cinema last night. Have you ever been?"

"Ever been? Do you know how long the cinema has been going? Since about 1900."

"Well! What a thing! I'm writing a skit on it!"

"How—a skit?"

"Parody—wildest yarn you ever read."

He took up a sheet of paper and began chuckling to himself.

"My heroine," he said, "is an Octoroon. Her eyes swim, and her lovely bosom heaves. Everybody wants her, and she's more virtuous than words can say. The situations she doesn't succumb to would freeze your blood; they'd roast your marrow. She has a perfect devil of a brother, with whom she was brought up, and who knows her deep dark secret and wants to trade her off to a millionaire who also has a deep dark secret. Altogether there are four deep dark secrets in my yarn. It's a corker."

"What a waste of your time!" I said.

"My time!" he answered fiercely. "What's the use of my time? Nobody buys my books."

"Who's attending you?"

"Doctors! They take your money, that's all. I've got no money. Don't talk about me!" Again he took up a sheet of manuscript and chuckled.

"Last night—at that place—they had—good God!—a race between a train and a motor-car. Well, I've got one between a train, a motor-car, a flying machine, and a horse."

I sat up.

"May I have a look at your skit," I said, "when you've finished it?"

"It is finished. Wrote it straight off. D'you think I could stop and then go on again with a thing like that?" He gathered the sheets and held them out to me. "Take the thing—it's amused me to do it. The heroine's secret is that she isn't an Octoroon at all she's a De La

Casse—purest Creole blood of the South; and her villainous brother isn't her brother; and the bad millionaire isn't a millionaire; and her penniless lover is. It's rich, I tell you!"

"Thanks," I said drily, and took the sheets.

I went away concerned about my friend, his illness, and his poverty, especially his poverty, for I saw no end to it.

After dinner that evening I began languidly to read his skit. I had not read two pages of the thirty-five before I started up, sat down again, and feverishly read on. Skit! By George! He had written a perfect scenario—or, rather, that which wanted the merest professional touching-up to be perfect. I was excited. It was a little gold-mine if properly handled. Any good film company, I felt convinced, would catch at it. Yes! But how to handle it? Bruce was such an unaccountable creature, such a wild old bird! Imagine his having only just realised the cinema! If I told him his skit was a serious film, he would say: "Good God!" and put it in the fire, priceless though it was. And yet, how could I market it without *carte blanche*, and how get *carte blanche* without giving my discovery away? I was deathly keen on getting some money for him; and this thing, properly worked, might almost make him independent. I felt as if I had a priceless museum piece which a single stumble might shatter to fragments. The tone of his voice when he spoke of the cinema—"What a *thing*!" kept coming back to me. He was prickly proud, too—very difficult about money. Could I work it without telling him anything? I knew he never looked at a newspaper. But should I be justified in taking advantage of that—in getting the thing accepted and produced without his knowing? I revolved the question for hours, and went to see him again next day.

He was reading.

"Hallo! You again? What do you think of this theory—that the Egyptians derive from a Saharan civilisation?"

"I don't think," I said.

"It's nonsense. This fellow——" I interrupted him.

"Do you want that skit back, or can I keep it?"

"Skit? What skit?"

"The thing you gave me yesterday."

"That! Light your fire with it. This fellow——"

"Yes," I said; "I'll light a fire with it. I see you're busy."

"Oh, no! I'm not," he said. "I've nothing to do. What's the good of my writing? I earn less and less with every book that comes out. I'm dying of poverty."

"That's because you won't consider the public."

"How can I consider the public when I don't know what they want?"

"Because you won't take the trouble to find out. If I suggested a way to you of pleasing the public and making money, you'd kick me out of the room."

And the words: "For instance, I've got a little gold-mine of yours in my pocket," were on the tip of my tongue, but I choked them back. 'Daren't risk it!' I thought. 'He's given you the thing. *Carte blanche—cartes serrés!*'

I took the gold-mine away and promptly rough-shaped it for the film. It was perfectly easy, without any alteration of the story. Then I was faced with the temptation to put his name to it. The point was this: If I took it to a film company as an authorless scenario, I should only get authorless terms; whereas, if I put his name to it, with a little talking I could double the terms at least. The film public didn't know his name, of course, but the inner literary public did, and it's wonderful how you can impress the market with the word "genius" judiciously used. It was too dangerous, however; and at last I hit on a middle course. I would take it to them with no name attached, but tell them it was by "a genius," and suggest that they could make capital out of the incognito. I knew they would feel it *was* by a genius.

I took it to an excellent company next day, with a covering note saying: "The author, a man of recognised literary genius, for certain reasons prefers to remain unknown." They took a fortnight in which to rise, but they rose. They had to. The thing was too good in itself. For a week I played them over terms. Twice I delivered an ultimatum—twice they surrendered; they knew too well what they had got. I could have made a contract with £2,000 down which would have brought at least another £2,000 before the contract term closed; but I compounded for one that gave me £3,000 down, as likely to lead to less difficulty with Bruce. The terms were not a whit too good for what was really the "acme" of scenarios. If I could have been quite open, I could certainly have done better.

Finally, however, I signed the contract, delivered the manuscript, and received a cheque for the price. I was elated, and at the same time knew that my troubles were just beginning. With Bruce's feeling about the film, how the deuce should I get him to take the money? Could I go to his publishers, and conspire with them to trickle it out to him gradually, as if it came from his books? That meant letting them into the secret; besides, he was too used to receiving practically nothing from his books; it would lead him to make enquiry, and the secret was bound to come out. Could I get a lawyer to spring an inheritance on him? That would mean no end of lying and elaboration, even if a lawyer would consent. Should I send him the money in Bank of England notes, with the words: "From a lifelong admirer of your genius"? I was afraid he would suspect a trick, or stolen notes, and go to the police to trace them. Or should I just go, put the cheque on the table, and tell him the truth?

The question worried me terribly, for I didn't feel entitled to consult others who knew him. It was the sort of thing that, if talked over, would certainly leak out. It was not desirable, however, to delay cashing a big cheque like that. Besides, they had started on the production. It happened to be a slack time, with a dearth of good films, so that they were rushing it on. And, in the meantime there was Bruce—starved of everything he wanted, unable to get away for want of money, depressed about his health and his future. And yet so completely had he always seemed to me different, strange, superior to this civilisation of ours, that the idea of going to him and saying simply:

"This is yours, for the film you wrote," scared me. I could hear his: "I? Write for the cinema? What do you mean?"

When I came to think of it, I had surely taken an extravagant liberty in marketing the thing without consulting him. I felt he would never forgive that, and my feeling towards him was so affectionate, even reverential, that I simply hated the idea of being cast out of his affections. At last I hit on a way that by introducing my own interest might break my fall. I cashed the cheque, lodged the money at my bank, drew my own cheque on it for the full amount, and armed with that and the contract, went to see him.

He was lying on two chairs, smoking his Brazilians, and playing with a stray cat which had attached itself to him. He seemed rather less prickly than usual, and after beating about the bushes of his health and other matters, I began:

"I've got a confession to make, Bruce."

"Confession!" he said. "What confession?"

"You remember that skit on the film you wrote, and gave me, about six weeks ago?"

"No."

"Yes, you do—about an Octoroon."

He chuckled. "Oh! Ah! That!"

I took a deep breath, and went on:

"Well, I sold it; and the price of course belongs to you."

"What? Who'd print a thing like that?"

"It isn't printed. It's been made into a film—superfilm, they call it."

His hand came to a pause on the cat's back, and he glared at me. I hastened on:

"I ought to have told you what I was doing, but you're so prickly, and you've got such confounded superior notions. I thought if I did, you'd be biting off your nose to spite your own face. The fact is, it made a marvellous scenario. Here's the contract, and here's a cheque on my bank for the price—£3,000. If you like to treat me as your agent, you owe me £300. I don't expect it, but I'm not proud, like you, and I shan't sneeze."

"Good God!" he said.

"Yes, I know. But it's all nonsense, Bruce. You can carry scruples to altogether too great length. Tainted source! Everything's tainted, if you come to that. The film's a quite justified expression of modern civilisation—a natural outcome of the Age. It gives amusement; it affords pleasure. It may be vulgar, it may be cheap, but we *are* vulgar, and we are cheap, and it's no use pretending we're not—not you, of course, Bruce, but people at large. A vulgar Age wants vulgar amusement, and if we can give it that amusement, we ought to; life's not too cheery, anyway."

The glare in his eyes was almost paralysing me, but I managed to stammer on:

"You live out of the world—you don't realise what humdrum people want; something to balance the greyness, the—the banality of their lives. They want blood, thrill, sensation of all sorts. You didn't mean to give it them, but you have, you've done them a benefit, whether you wish to or not, and the money's yours and you've got to take it."

The cat suddenly jumped down. I waited for the storm to burst.

"I know," I dashed on, "that you hate and despise the film——"

Suddenly his voice boomed out:

"Bosh! What are you talking about? Film! I go there every other night."

It was my turn to say: 'Good God!'" And, ramming contract and cheque into his empty hand, I bolted, closely followed by the cat.

[*1923*]

DEFEAT

SHE had been standing there on the pavement a quarter of an hour or so after her shilling's worth of concert. Women of her profession are not supposed to have redeeming points, especially when—like May Belinski, as she now preferred to dub herself—they are German; but this woman certainly had music in her soul. She often gave herself these "music baths" when the Promenade Concerts were on, and had just spent half her total wealth in listening to some Mozart and a Beethoven symphony.

She was feeling almost elated, full of divine sound, and of the summer moonlight that was filing the whole dark town. Women "of a certain type" have, at all events, emotions—and what a comfort that is, even to themselves! To stand just there had become rather a habit of hers. One could seem to be waiting for somebody coming out of the concert, not yet over—which, of course, was precisely what she was doing. One need not forever be stealthily glancing and perpetually moving on in that peculiar way, which, while it satisfied the police and Mrs. Grundy, must not quite deceive others as to her business in life. She had only "been at it" long enough to have acquired a nervous dread of almost everything—not long enough to have passed through that dread to callousness. Some women take so much longer than others. And even for a woman "of a certain type" her position was exceptionally nerve-racking in war-time, going as she did by a false name. Indeed, in all England there could hardly be a greater pariah than was this German woman of the night.

She idled outside a book-shop humming a little, pretending to read the titles of the books by moonlight, taking off and putting on one of her stained yellow gloves. Now and again she would move up as far as the posters outside the hall, scrutinising them as if interested in the future, then stroll back again. In her worn and

discreet dark dress, and her small hat, she had nothing about her to
rouse suspicion, unless it were the trail of violet powder she left on
the moonlight.

For the moonlight this evening was almost solid, seeming with
its cool still vibration to replace the very air; in it the war-time
precautions against light seemed fantastic, like shading candles in
a room still full of daylight. What lights there were had the effect
of strokes and stipples of dim colour laid by a painter's brush on
a background of ghostly whitish-blue. The dreamlike quality of
the town was perhaps enhanced for her eyes by the veil she was
wearing—in daytime no longer white. As the music died out of her,
elation also ebbed. Somebody had passed her, speaking German, and
she was overwhelmed by a rush of nostalgia. On this moonlit night
by the banks of the Rhine—whence she came—the orchards would
be heavy with apples; there would be murmurs and sweet scents; the
old castle would stand out clear, high over the woods and the chalky-
white river. There would be singing far away, and the churning of
a distant steamer's screw; and perhaps on the water a log raft still
drifting down in the blue light. There would be German voices
talking. And suddenly tears oozed up in her eyes, and crept down
through the powder on her cheeks. She raised her veil and dabbed
at her face with a little, not-too-clean handkerchief, screwed up in
her yellow-gloved hand. But the more she dabbed the more those
treacherous tears ran. Then she became aware that a tall young man
in khaki was also standing before the shop-window, not looking at
the titles of the books, but eyeing her askance. His face was fresh and
open, with a sort of kindly eagerness in his blue eyes. Mechanically
she drooped her wet lashes, raised them obliquely, drooped them
again, and uttered a little sob . . .

This young man, captain in a certain regiment, and discharged
from hospital at six o'clock that evening, had entered Queen's Hall
at half-past-seven. Still rather brittle and sore from his wound, he had
treated himself to a seat in the grand circle, and there had sat, very
still and dreamy, the whole concert through. It had been like eating
after a long fast—something of the sensation Polar explorers must
experience when they return to their first full meal. For he was of
the New Army, and before the war had actually believed in music, art,
and all that sort of thing. With a month's leave before him, he could

afford to feel that life was extraordinarily joyful, his own experiences particularly wonderful; and, coming out into the moonlight, he had taken what can only be described as a great gulp of it, for he was a young man with a sense of beauty. When one has been long in the trenches, lain out wounded in a shell-hole twenty-four hours, and spent three months in hospital, beauty has such an edge of novelty, such a sharp sweetness, that it almost gives pain. And London at night is very beautiful. He strolled slowly towards the Circus, still drawing the moonlight deep into his lungs, his cap tilted up a little on his forehead in that moment of unmilitary abandonment; and whether he stopped before the book-shop window because the girl's figure was in some sort a part of beauty, or because he saw that she was crying, he could not have made clear to anyone.

Then something—perhaps the scent of powder, perhaps the yellow glove, or the oblique flutter of the eyelids—told him that he was making what he would have called "a blooming error," unless he wished for company, which had not been in his thoughts. But her sob affected him, and he said:

"What's the matter?"

Again her eyelids fluttered sideways, and she stammered:

"Not'ing. The beautiful evening—that's why!"

That a woman of what he now clearly saw to be "a certain type" should perceive what he himself had just been perceiving, struck him forcibly, and he said:

"Cheer up."

She looked up again swiftly. "All right! But you are not lonelee like me."

For one of that sort she looked somehow honest; her tear-streaked face was rather pretty, and he murmured:

"Well, let's walk a bit and talk it over."

They turned the corner and walked east, along streets empty and beautiful, with their dulled orange-glowing lamps, and here and there the glint of some blue or violet light. He found it queer and rather exciting—for an adventure of just this kind he had never had. And he said doubtfully:

"How did you get into this? Isn't it an awfully hopeless life?"

"Ye-es, it ees—" her voice had a queer soft emphasis. "You are limping—haf you been wounded?"

"Just out of hospital."

"The horrible war—all the misery is because of the war. When will it end?"

He looked at her, and said:

"I say—what nationality are you?"

"Rooshian."

"Really! I never met a Russian girl."

He was conscious that she looked at him, then very quickly down. And he said suddenly:

"Is it as bad as they make out?"

She slipped her yellow-gloved hand through his arm.

"Not when I haf anyone as nice as you; I never haf yet, though;" she smiled—and her smile was like her speech, slow, confiding. "You stopped because I was sad; others stop because I am gay. I am not fond of men at all. When you know, you are not fond of them."

"Well! You hardly know them at their best, do you? You should see them at the front. By George! they're simply splendid—officers and men, every blessed soul. There's never been anything like it—just one long bit of jolly fine self-sacrifice; it's perfectly amazing."

Turning her blue-grey eyes on him, she answered:

"I expect you are not the last at that. You see in them what you haf in yourself, I think."

"Oh! not a bit—you're quite out. I assure you when we made the attack where I got wounded there wasn't a single man in my regiment who wasn't an absolute hero. The way they went in—never thinking of themselves—it was simply superb!"

Her teeth came down on her lower lip, and she answered in a queer voice: "It is the same too, perhaps, with—the enemy."

"Oh, yes, I know that."

"Ah! You are not a mean man. How I hate mean men!"

"Oh! they're not mean really—they simply don't understand."

"Oh! you are a baby—a good baby, aren't you?"

He did not quite like being called a baby, and frowned; but was at once touched by the disconcertion in her powdered face. How quickly she was scared!

She said clingingly:

"But I li-ike you for it. It is so good to find a ni-ice man."

This was worse, and he said abruptly:

"About being lonely? Haven't you any Russian friends?"

"Rooshian! No! The town is so beeg! Haf you been in the concert?"

"Yes."

"I, too—I love music."

"I suppose all Russians do."

She looked up at his face again, and seemed to struggle to keep silent; then she said quietly:

"I go there always when I haf the money."

"What! Are you so on the rocks?"

"Well, I have just one shilling now." And she laughed.

The sound of that little laugh upset him—she had a way of making him feel sorry for her every time she spoke.

They had come by now to a narrow square, east of Gower Street.

"This is where I lif," she said. "Come in!"

He had one long moment of violent hesitation, then yielded to the soft tugging of her hand, and followed. The passage-hall was dimly lighted, and they went upstairs into a front room, where the curtains were drawn, and the gas turned very low. Opposite the window were other curtains dividing off the rest of the apartment. As soon as the door was shut she put up her face and kissed him—evidently formula. What a room! Its green and beetroot colouring and the prevalence of cheap plush disagreeably affected him. Everything in it had that callous look of rooms which seem to be saying to their occupants: "You're here to-day and you'll be gone to-morrow." Everything except one little plant, in a common pot, of maidenhair fern, fresh and green, looking as if it had been watered within the hour; in this room it had just the same unexpected touchingness that peeped out of the girl's matter-of-fact cynicism.

Taking off her hat, she went towards the gas, but he said quickly:

"No, don't turn it up; let's have the window open and the moonlight in." He had a sudden dread of seeing anything plainly—it was stuffy, too, and, pulling the curtains apart, he threw up the window. The girl had come obediently from the hearth, and sat down opposite him, leaning her arm on the window-sill and her chin on her hand. The moonlight caught her cheek where she had just renewed the powder, and her fair crinkly hair; it caught the plush of the furniture, and his own khaki, giving them all a touch of unreality.

"What's your name?" he said.

"May. Well, I call myself that. It's no good askin' yours."

"You're a distrustful little soul, aren't you?"

"I haf reason to be, don't you think?"

"Yes, I suppose you're bound to think us all brutes?"

"Well, I haf a lot of reasons to be afraid all my time. I am dreadfully nervous now; I am not trusting anybody. I suppose you haf been killing lots of Germans?"

He laughed.

"We never know, unless it happens to be hand to hand. I haven't come in for that yet."

"But you would be very glad if you had killed some?"

"Glad? I don't think so. We're all in the same boat so far as that's concerned. We're not glad to kill each other. We do our job—that's all."

"Oh! it is frightful. I expect I haf my broders killed."

"Don't you get any news ever?"

"News! No indeed, no news of anybody in my country. I might not haf a country; all that I ever knew is gone—fader, moder, sisters, broders, all—never any more I shall see them, I suppose, now. The war it breaks and breaks—it breaks hearts." Her little teeth fastened again on her lower lip in that sort of pretty snarl. "Do you know what I was thinkin' when you came up? I was thinkin' of my native town and the river there in the moonlight. If I could see it again I would be glad. Were you ever homeseek?"

"Yes, I have been—in the trenches; but one's ashamed, with all the others."

"Ah! ye-es!" It came from her with a hiss. "Ye-es! You are all comrades there. What is it like for me here, do you think, where everybody hates and despises me, and would catch me, and put me in prison, perhaps?"

He could see her breast heaving with a quick breathing painful to listen to. He leaned forward, patting her knee, and murmuring: "So sorry."

She said in a smothered voice:

"You are the first who has been kind to me for so long! I will tell you the truth—I am not Rooshian at all—I am German."

Hearing that half-choked confession, his thought was: "Does she really think we fight against women?" And he said:

"My dear girl, who cares?"

Her eyes seemed to search right into him. She said slowly:

"Another man said that to me. But he was thinkin' of other things. You are a veree ni-ice boy. I am so glad I met you. You see the good in people, don't you? That is the first thing in the world—because there is really not much good in people, you know."

He said, smiling:

"You're a dreadful little cynic!" Then thought: 'Well—of course!'

"Cyneec? How long do you think I would live if I was not a cyneec? I should drown myself to-morrow. Perhaps there are good people, but, you see, I don't know them."

"I know lots."

She leaned forward eagerly.

"Well now—see, ni-ice boy—you haf never been in a hole, haf you?"

"I suppose not a real hole."

"No, I should think not, with your face. Well, suppose I am still a good girl, as I was once, you know, and you took me to some of your good people, and said: 'Here is a little German girl that has no work, and no money, and no friends.' Your good people they will say: 'Oh! how sad! A German girl!' and they will go and wash their hands."

Silence fell on him. He saw his mother, his sister, others—good people, he would swear! And yet——! He heard their voices, frank and clear; and they seemed to be talking of the Germans. If only she were not German as well!

"You see!" he heard her say, and could only mutter:

"I'm sure there *are* people."

"No. They would not take a German, even if she was good. Besides, I don't want to be good any more—I am not a humbug—I have learned to be bad. Aren't you going to kees me, ni-ice boy?"

She put her face close to his. Her eyes troubled him, but he drew back. He thought she would be offended or persistent, but she was neither; just looked at him fixedly with a curious inquiring stare; and he leaned against the window, deeply disturbed. It was as if all clear and simple enthusiasm had been suddenly knocked endways; as if a certain splendour of life that he had felt and seen of late had been dipped in cloud. Out there at the front, over here in hospital, life had been seeming so—as it were—heroic; and yet it held such mean and murky depths as well! The voices of his men, whom he had come to love like brothers, crude burring voices, cheery in trouble, making nothing of it; the voices of doctors and nurses, patient, quiet, reassuring voices; even his own, voice, infected by it all, kept sounding in his ears. All wonderful somehow, and simple; and nothing mean about it anywhere! And now so suddenly to have lighted upon this, and all that was behind it—this scared girl, this base, dark, thoughtless use of her! And the thought came to him: 'I suppose my fellows wouldn't think twice about taking her on! Why, I'm not even certain of myself, if she insists!' And he turned his face and stared out at the moonlight. He heard her voice:

"Eesn't it light? No air-raid to-night. When the Zepps burned— what a horrible death! And all the people cheered—it is natural. Do you hate us veree much?"

He turned round and said sharply:

"Hate? I don't know."

"I don't hate even the English—I despise them. I despise my people too—perhaps more, because they began this war. Oh, yes! I know that. I despise all the peoples. Why haf they made the world so miserable— why haf they killed all our lives—hundreds and thousands and millions of lives—all for not'ing? They haf made a bad world—everybody hating, and looking for the worst everywhere. They haf made me bad, I know. I believe no more in anything. What is there to believe in? Is there a God? No! Once I was teaching little English children their prayers—isn't that funnee? I was reading to them about Christ and love. I believed all those things. Now I believe not'ing at all—no one who is not a fool or a liar can believe. I would like to work in a hospital; I would like to go and help poor boys like you. Because I am a German they would throw me out a hundred times, even if I was good. It is the same in Germany and France and Russia—everywhere. But do you think I will believe in love and Christ and a God and all that—not I! I think we are animals—that's all. Oh! yes—you fancy it is because my life has spoiled me. It is not that at all—that's not the worst thing in life. These men are not ni-ice, like you, but it's their nature, and," she laughed, "they help me to live, which is something for me, anyway. No, it is the men who think themselves great and good, and make the war with their talk and their hate, killing us all—killing all the boys like you, and keeping poor people in prison, and telling us to go on hating; and all those dreadful cold blooded creatures who write in the papers—the same in my country, just the same; it is because of all them that I think we are only animals."

He got up, acutely miserable. He could see her following him with her eyes, and knew she was afraid she had driven him away. She said coaxingly: "Don't mind me talking, ni-ice boy. I don't know anyone to talk to. If you don't like it, I can be quiet as a mouse."

He muttered:

"Oh! go on, talk away. I'm not obliged to believe you, and I don't."

She was on her feet now, leaning against the wall, her dark dress and white face just touched by the slanting moonlight; and her voice came again, slow and soft and bitter:

"Well, look here, ni-ice boy, what sort of a world is it, where millions are being tortured—horribly tortured, for no fault of theirs at all? A beautiful world, isn't it? 'Umbug! silly rot, as you boys call it. You say it is all 'Comrade!' and braveness out there at the front, and people don't think of themselves. Well, I don't think of myself veree much. What does it matter?—I am lost now, anyway; but I think of my people at home, how they suffer and grieve. I think of all the poor people there and here who lose those they love, and all the poor prisoners. Am I not to think of them? And if I do, how am I to believe it a beautiful world, ni-ice boy?"

He stood very still, biting his lips.

"Look here! We haf one life each, and soon it is over. Well, I think that is lucky."

He said resentfully:

"No! there's more than that."

"Ah!" she went on softly, "you think the war is fought for the future; you are giving your lives for a better world, aren't you?"

"We must fight till we win," he said between his teeth.

"Till you win. My people think that, too. All the peoples think that if they win the world will be better. But it will not, you know; it will be much worse, anyway."

He turned away from her and caught up his cap; but her voice followed him.

"I don't care which wins, I despise them all—animals—animals! Ah! Don't go, ni-ice boy—I will be quiet now."

He took some notes from his tunic pocket, put them on the table, and went up to her.

"Good-night."

She said plaintively:

"Are you really going? Don't you like me enough?"

"Yes, I like you."

"It is because I am German, then?"

"No."

"Then why won't you stay?"

He wanted to answer: "Because you upset me so," but he just shrugged his shoulders.

"Won't you kees me once?"

He bent, and put his lips to her forehead; but as he took them away she threw her head back, pressed her mouth to his and clung to him.

He sat down suddenly, and said:

"Don't! I don't want to feel a brute."

She laughed. "You are a funny boy, but you are veree good. Talk to me a little, then. No one talks to me. I would much rather talk, anyway. Tell me, haf you seen many German Prisoners?"

He sighed—from relief, or was it from regret?

"A good many."

"Any from the Rhine?"

"Yes, I think so."

"Were they very sad?"

"Some were—some were quite glad to be taken."

"Did you ever see the Rhine? Isn't it beautiful? It will be wonderful to-night. The moonlight will be the same here as there; in Rooshia too, and France, everywhere; and the trees will look the same as here, and people will meet under them and make love just as here. Oh! isn't it stupid, the war?—as if it was not good to be alive."

He wanted to say: "You can't tell how good it is to be alive till you're facing death, because you don't live till then. And when a whole lot of you feel like that—and are ready to give their lives for each other, it's worth all the rest of life put together." But he couldn't get it out to this girl who believed in nothing.

"How were you wounded, ni-ice boy?"

"Attacking across open ground—four machine-gun bullets got me at one go off."

"Weren't you veree frightened when they ordered you to attack?" No, he had not been frightened just then! And he shook his head and laughed.

"It was great. We did laugh that morning. They got me much too soon, though—a swindle!"

She stared at him.

"You laughed?"

"Yes, and what do you think was the first thing I was conscious of next morning—my old colonel bending over me and giving me a squeeze of lemon. If you knew my colonel, you'd still believe in things. There is something, you know, behind all this evil. After all, you can only die once, and if it's for your country all the better."

Her face, with intent eyes just touched with dark, had in the moonlight a most strange, other-world look. Her lips moved:

"No, I believe in nothing. My heart is dead."

"You think so, but it isn't, you know, or you wouldn't have been crying when I met you."

"If it were not dead, do you think I could live my life—walking the streets every night, pretending to like strange men—never hearing a kind word—never talking, for fear I will be known for a German. Soon I shall take to drinking, then I shall be '*kaput*' very quick. You see, I am practical; I see things clear. To-night I am a little emotional; the moon is funny, you know. But I live for myself only now. I don't care for anything or anybody."

"All the same, just now you were pitying your people, and prisoners, and that."

"Yes, because they suffer. Those who suffer are like me—I pity myself, that's all; I am different from your English women. I see what I am doing; I do not let my mind become a turnip just because I am no longer moral."

"Nor your heart either."

"Ni-ice boy, you are veree obstinate. But all that about love is 'umbug. We love ourselves, nothing more."

Again, at that intense soft bitterness in her voice, he felt stifled and got up, leaning on the window sill. The air out there was free from the smell of dust and stale perfume. He felt her fingers

slip between his own, and stay unmoving. If she was so hard and
cynical, why should he pity her? Yet he did. The touch of that hand
within his own roused his protective instinct. She had poured out
her heart to him—a perfect stranger! He pressed it a little, and felt
her fingers crisp in answer. Poor little devil! This was a friendlier
moment than she had known for years! And after all, fellow-feeling
was bigger than principalities and powers! Fellow-feeling was all-
pervading as this moonlight, which she had said would be the
same in Germany—as this white ghostly glamour wrapping the
trees, making the orange lamps so quaint and decoratively useless
out in the narrow square, where emptiness and silence reigned. He
looked round into her face—in spite of kohl and powder, and the
red salve on her lips, it had a queer, unholy, touching beauty. And
he had suddenly the strangest feeling, as if they stood there—the
two of them—proving that kindness and human fellowship were
stronger than lust, stronger than hate; proving it against meanness
and brutality, and the sudden shouting of newspaper boys in some
neighbouring streets, whose cries, passionately vehement, clashed
into each other, and obscured the words—what was it they were
calling? His head went up to listen; he felt her hand rigid within his
arm—she too was listening. The cries came nearer, hoarser, more
shrill and clamorous; the empty moonlight seemed of a sudden
crowded with figures, footsteps, voices, and a fierce distant cheering.
"Great victory—great victory! Official! British! Severe defeat of the
'Uns! Many thousand prisoners!" So it sped by, intoxicating, filling
him with a fearful joy; and leaning far out, he waved his cap and
cheered like a madman; and the whole night seemed to him to
flutter and vibrate and answer. Then he turned to rush down into
the street, struck against something soft, and recoiled. The girl! She
stood with hands clenched, her face convulsed, panting, and even in
the madness of his joy he felt for her. To hear this—in the midst of
enemies! All confused with the desire to do something, he stooped
to take her hand; and the dusty reek of the table cloth clung to his
nostrils. She snatched away her fingers, swept up the notes he had
put down, and held them out to him.

"Take them—I will not haf your English money—take them."
And suddenly she tore them across twice, three times, let the bits
flutter to the floor, and turned her back to him. He stood looking

at her leaning against the plush-covered table which smelled of dust, her head down, a dark figure in a dark room with the moonlight sharpening her outline—hardly a moment he stayed, then made for the door . . .

When he was gone, she still stood there, her chin on her breast—she who cared for nothing, believed in nothing—with the sound in her ears of cheering, of hurrying feet, and voices; stood in the centre of a pattern made by fragments of the torn-up notes, staring out into the moonlight, seeing, not this hated room and the hated square outside, but a German orchard, and herself, a little girl, plucking apples, a big dog beside her; a hundred other pictures, too, such as the drowning see. Her heart swelled; she sank down on the floor, laid her forehead on the dusty carpet, and pressed her body to it.

She who did not care—who despised all peoples, even her own—began, mechanically, to sweep together the scattered fragments of the notes, assembling them with the dust into a little pile, as of fallen leaves, and dabbling in it with her fingers, while the tears ran down her cheeks. For her country she had torn them, her country in defeat! She, who had just one shilling in this great town of enemies, who wrung her stealthy living out of the embraces of her foes! And suddenly in the moonlight she sat up and began to sing with all her might—"*Die Wacht am Rhein.*"

[*1916*]

VIRTUE

HAROLD Mellesh, minor clerk in an Accident Assurance Society, having occasion to be present at a certain Police Court to give evidence in the matter of a smashed car, stood riveted by manifestations of the law entirely new to him. His eyes, blue and rather like those of a baby, were opened very widely, his ingenuous forehead wrinkled, his curly hair was moving on his scalp, his fists involuntarily clenching his straw hat. He had seen four ladies of the town dealt with—three "jugged," and one fined—before his sensations reached their climax. Perhaps she was prettier than the others, certainly younger, and she was crying.

"First time you've been here—two pounds, and ten shillings costs."

"But I haven't any money, sir."

"Very well—fourteen days."

Tears streaking the remains of powder—a queer little sound, and the sensations within young Mellesh simmered like a kettle coming to the boil. He touched a blue sleeve in front of him.

"Here," he said, "I'll pay her fine."

He felt the glance of the policeman running over him like a chilly insect.

"Friend of yours?"

"No."

"I shouldn't, then. She'll be here again within the month."

The girl was passing, he saw the swallowing movement of her throat and said with desperation:

"I don't care. I'll pay it."

The policeman's glance crept about him clammily.

"Come with me, then."

Young Mellesh followed him out.

"Here," said his policeman to the one in charge of the girl, "this gentleman'll pay the fine."

Conscious of a confusion of glances, of his own cheeks reddening furiously, young Mellesh brought out his money—just two pounds fifteen; and, handing over the two pounds ten, he thought: 'My hat! What would Alice say?'

He heard the girl's gasped out: "Ow! Thank you!" his policeman's muttered: "Waste o' money! Still, it was a kind action," and passed out into the street. Now that his feelings had given off that two pound ten's worth of steam he felt chilly and dazed, as if virtue had gone out of him. A voice behind him said:

"Thank you ever so much—it *was* kind of you."

Raising his straw hat he stood uncomfortably to let her pass.

She pushed a card into his hand. "Any time you're passing, I'll be glad to see you; I'm very grateful."

"Not at all!" With a smile, confused like her own, he turned off towards his office.

All day, among his accidents, he felt uncertain. Had he been a fool; had he been a hero? Sometimes he thought:

'What brutes they are to those girls!' and sometimes 'Don't know; suppose they must do something about it.' And he avoided considering how to explain the absence of two pounds ten shillings on which Alice had been reckoning. His soul was simple like the expression on his face.

He reached home at the usual hour—six-thirty. His home was grey and small and had a little bit of green up Chalk Farm way, where the Tube made all things possible.

His wife, who had just put their baby daughter to bed, was sitting in the parlour darning his socks. She looked up—surely her forehead was rather like a knee!

"You wear your socks properly, Harold," she said; "it's all I can do to mend this pair." Her eyes were china-blue, round like saucers; her voice had the monotony of one brought up to minimise emotion. A farmer's daughter, young Mellesh had become engaged to her during a holiday in Somerset. Pale himself, from office and the heat, he thought how pale she looked.

"The heat's dreadful, isn't it?" she said. "Sometimes I wish we'd never had baby. It does tie you in the evenings. I *am* looking forward to Whitsuntide, that I am."

Young Mellesh, tall and straggly, bent over and kissed her forehead. How on earth to let her know that he had "blewed" their holiday? He was realising that he had done an awful thing. Perhaps—oh! surely she would understand how he couldn't sit and see that girl "jugged" before his eyes for want of it! But not until the end of their small supper did he say abruptly:

"I got quite upset this morning, Alice. Had to go down to the Police Court about that car smash I told you of, and afterwards I saw them run in a lot of those Piccadilly girls. It fair sickened me to see the way they treat them."

His wife looked up; her face was childlike.

"Why, what do they do to them?"

"Quod them for speakin' to men in the street."

"I s'pose they're up to no good."

Irritated by the matter-of-factness in her voice, he went on:

"They speak to 'em as if they were dirt."

"Well, aren't they?"

"They may be a loose lot, but so are men."

"Men wouldn't be so loose if they weren't there."

"I suppose it's what you call a vicious circle;" and, pleased with his play on words, he added: "One or two of them were pretty."

His wife smiled; her smile had a natural teasing quality.

"They treat *them* better, I suppose?"

That was jolly cynical! and he blurted out:

"One, quite young, never there before, they gave her a fortnight just because she hadn't any money—I couldn't stick it; I paid her fine."

There was sweat on his forehead. His wife's face had gone quite pink.

"You paid? How much?"

He was on the point of saying: "Ten shillings." But something in his soul revolted. "Regular pill—two pound ten;" and he thought glumly: 'Oh! what a fool I've been!'

He did wish Alice wouldn't open her mouth like that, when nothing was coming out—made her look so silly! Her face puckered suddenly, then became quite blank; he was moved as if he had hit or pinched her.

"Awfully sorry, Alice," he muttered. "Never meant to—she—she cried."

"Course she cried! You fool, Harold!"

He got up, very much disturbed.

"Well, and what would *you* have done?"

"Me? Let her stew in her own juice, of course. It wasn't your affair."

She too had risen. He thrust his fingers through his hair. The girl's face, tear-streaked, confusedly pretty, had come up before him, her soft common grateful voice tickled his ears again. His wife turned her back. So! he was in for a fit of sulks. Well! No doubt he had deserved it.

"I dare say I was a fool," he muttered, "but I did think you'd understand how I felt when I saw her cry. Suppose it had been you!" From the toss of her head, he knew he had said something pretty fatal.

"Oh! So that's what you think of me!"

He grasped her shoulder.

"Of course I don't, Alice, don't be so silly!"

She shook off his hand.

"Whose money was it? Now baby and me'll get no holiday. And all because you see a slut crying."

Before he could answer she was gone. He had an awful sense of having outraged justice. Given away her holiday—given his wife's holiday to a girl of the streets! Still, it was his own holiday, too; besides, he earned the money! He'd never wanted to give it to the girl; hadn't got anything for it! Suppose he'd put it into the offertory bag, would Alice have been in such a temper even if it was their holiday? He didn't see much difference. He sat down with knees apart, and elbows planted on them, staring at the peonies on the Brussels carpet paid for on the hire system. And all those feelings that rise in people who live together, when they don't agree, swirled in his curly head, and troubled his eyes, candid like a baby's. If they *would* treat the wretched girls like dirt! If only she hadn't cried! She hadn't meant to cry; he could tell that by the sound of it. And who was the magistrate—he didn't look too like a saint; who was any man to treat her like that? Alice oughtn't—No! But suddenly he saw Alice again bending over his socks—pale and tired with the heat—doing things for him or baby—and he had given away her holiday! No denying that! Compunction flooded him. He must go up and find her and try and make his peace—he would pawn his bicycle—she should have her holiday—oh! yes!

He opened the door and listened. The little house was ominously quiet—only the outside evening sounds from buses passing in the main road, from children playing on the doorsteps of the side street, from a man with a barrow of bananas. She must be up in the bedroom with baby! He mounted the steep whitewashed stairway. It wanted a carpet, and fresh paint; ah! and a lot of other things Alice wanted—you couldn't have everything at once on four pound ten a week—with the price of living what it was. But she ought to have remembered there were things he wanted too—yes, precious bad, and never thought of getting. The door of their bedroom was locked; he rattled the handle. She opened suddenly, and stood facing him on the little landing.

"I don't want you up here."

"Look here, Alice—this is rotten."

She closed the door behind her.

"It is! You go down again, I don't want you. Think I believe that about crying! I'd be ashamed, if I were you!"

Ashamed! He might have been too soft, but why ashamed?

"Think I don't know what men are like? You can just go to your rotten girl, if she's so pretty!" She stood hard and stiff against the door, with red spots in her cheeks. She almost made him feel a villain—such conviction in her body.

"Alice! Good Lord! You must be crazy! I've done nothing!"

"But you'd like to. Go along! I don't want you!"

The stabbing stare of her blue eyes, the muffled energy of her voice, the bitterness about her mouth all made a fellow feel—well, that he knew nothing about anything—coming from one's wife like that! He leaned back against the wall.

"Well, I'm damned!" was all he could get out.

"D'you mean to say she didn't ask you?"

The insides of his hands grew wet. The girl's card in his pocket!

"Well, if you like to be a cat I can't help it. What d'you take me for?"

"Giving your own child's money to a dirty slut! You owed it— that's the truth—or will. Go on with you; don't stand there!"

He had a nasty longing to smite her on the mouth—it looked so bitter. "Well," he said slowly, "now I understand."

What was it that he understood? That she was all of a piece with something, with that Police Court, with the tone of the men's voices, with something unsparing, hard and righteous, which came down sharp on people?

"I thought—I think you might——" he stammered.

"Ugh!" The sound exasperated him so, that he turned to go downstairs.

"You whited sepulchre!"

The door clicked before he could answer the odd insult; he heard the key turned. Idiotic! The little landing seemed too small to hold his feelings. Would he ever have said a word to Alice, if he *had* done it? Why! He had never even thought of doing anything!

Giddy from chagrin he ran downstairs, and, clawing his straw hat from the rack, went out. The streets were malodorous from London fog, fried fish, petrol, hot dirty people; he strode along troubled, his eyes very rueful. So this was what he was really married to—this—this! It was like being married to that Police Court! It wasn't human—no, it wasn't—to be so suspicious and virtuous as all that! What was the use of being decent and straight, if this was all you got for it? Someone touched him on the shoulder.

"Mister, you're all white behind; let me brush you."

He stood still confusedly, while a stout fair man smote his back up and down with a large flat hand. Whited sepulchre! A bubble of rage rose to his lips. All right! She should see! He felt for the girl's card, and was suddenly amazed to find that he had no need to look at it—he remembered the address. Not far off, on the other side of the Euston Road! That was funny—had he been looking at it without realising? They said you had a subconscious mind. Well, what about it? No, it was his conscious mind that was going to serve Alice out! He had reached the Euston Road. Crossing it, he began to feel a queer pleasurable weakness in the legs. By this he knew that he was going to do wrong. He was not going to visit the girl just to serve his wife out, but because the prospect was——! That was bad—bad: it would put Alice in the right! He stood still at the corner of a narrow square, with a strip of garden, and railings round it. He leaned against those railings, his eyes searching the trees. He had always been quite straight with his wife—it was she who had put the idea into his head. And yet his legs being pleasurably weak seemed in an odd way to excuse her. It was like his doubt whether they hadn't to do something about it at the Police Court. Barring Alice—barring the Police Court—where would he—would any man be? Without virtue, entirely without virtue. A pigeon in the garden cooed. "Any time you're passing, I'll be glad to see you."

It had sounded genuine—really grateful. And the girl had looked— not worse than anybody else! If Alice had been sympathetic about it he would never have thought of the girl again; that is—well——! The doubt set his legs in motion. He was a married man, and that was all about it. But he looked across at the numbers on the houses. Twenty-seven! Yes, there it was! A bloom of lilac brushed his face. The scent jerked him suddenly back to the farm in Somerset and he and Alice courting. Alice—not the Alice on the landing! He scrutinised the shabby house, and suddenly went hot all over. Suppose he went in there—what would that girl think? That he had paid her fine because——! But that wasn't it at all—oh! no—he wasn't a squirt like that! He turned his face away, and walked on fast and far.

The signs were lit above the theatres; traffic was scanty, the streets a long dawdle of what vehicles and humans were about. He came to Leicester Square and sat down on a bench. The lights all round him brightened slowly under the dusk—theatre lights, street lamps. And the pity of things smote him, sitting there. So much of everything; and one got so little of anything! Adding figures up all day, going home to Alice—that was life! Well; it wasn't so bad when Alice was nice to him. But—Crikey!—what one missed! That book about the South Sea Islands—places, peoples, sights, sounds, scents, all over the world! Four pound ten a week, a wife, a baby! Well, you couldn't have things both ways—but had he got them either way? Not with the Alice on the landing!

Ah! Well! Poor Alice; jolly hard on her to miss her holiday! But she might have given him the chance to tell her that he would pawn his bicycle. Or was it all a bad dream? Had he ever really been in that Police Court, seen them herding those girls to prison—girls who did what they did because—well, like himself, they had missed too much. They'd catch a fresh lot to-night. What a fool he'd been to pay that fine!

'Glad I didn't go into that girl's house, anyway,' he thought. 'I would have felt a scum!' The only decent thing about it all had

been her look when she said: "Ow! thank you!" That gave him a
little feeling of warmth even now; and then—it, too, chilled away.
Nothing for it! When he had done sitting there, he must go home!
If Alice had thought him a wrong-un before, what would she think
when he returned? Well, there it was! The milk was spilt! But he did
wish she hadn't got such a virtue on her.

The sky deepened and darkened, the lights stared white; the
Square Garden with its flower-beds seemed all cut out and stiff, like
scenery on a stage. Must go back and "stick" it! No good to worry!

He got up from the bench and gave himself a shake. His eyes,
turned towards the lights of the Alhambra, were round, candid,
decent, like the eyes of a baby.

[*1922*]

THE NEIGHBOURS

In the remote country, Nature, at first sight so serene, so simple, will soon intrude on her observer a strange discomfort; a feeling that some familiar spirit haunts the old lanes, rocks, wasteland, and trees, and has the power to twist all living things around into some special shape befitting its genius.

When moonlight floods the patch of moorland about the centre of the triangle between the little towns of Hartland, Torrington, and Holsworthy, a pagan spirit steals forth through the wan gorse; gliding round the stems of the lonely, gibbet-like fir trees, peeping out amongst the reeds of the white marsh. That spirit has the eyes of a borderer, who perceives in every man a possible foe. And, in fact, this high corner of the land has remained border to this day, where the masterful, acquisitive invader from the North dwells side by side with the unstable, proud, quick-blooded Celt-Iberian.

In two cottages crowning some fallow land two families used to live side by side. That long white dwelling seemed all one, till the eye, peering through the sweet-brier which smothered the right-hand half, perceived the rude, weather-beaten presentment of a Running Horse, denoting the presence of intoxicating liquors; and in a window of the left-hand half, that strange conglomeration of edibles and shoe-leather which proclaims the one shop of a primitive hamlet.

These married couples were by name Sandford at the eastern and Leman at the western end; and he who saw them for the first time thought: "What splendid-looking people!"

They were all four above the average height, and all four as straight as darts. The innkeeper, Sandford, was a massive man, stolid, grave, light-eyed, with big fair moustaches, who might have stepped straight out of some Norseman's galley. Leman was lean and lathy, a regular Celt, with an amiable, shadowy, humorous face. The two women were as different as the men. Mrs. Sandford's fair, almost transparent cheeks coloured easily, her eyes were grey, her hair pale brown; Mrs. Leman's hair was of a lustreless jet-black, her eyes the colour of a peaty stream, and her cheeks had the close creamy texture of old ivory.

Those accustomed to their appearance soon noted the qualifications of their splendour. In Sandford, whom neither sun nor wind ever tanned, there was a look as if nothing would ever turn him from acquisition of what he had set his heart on; his eyes had the idealism of the worshipper of property, ever marching towards a heaven of great possessions. Followed by his cowering spaniel, he walked to his fields (for he farmed as well as kept the inn) with a tread that seemed to shake the lanes, disengaging an air of such heavy and complete insulation that even the birds were still. He rarely spoke. He was not popular. He was feared—no one quite knew why.

On Mrs. Sandford, for all her pink and white, sometimes girlish look, he had set the mark of his slow, heavy domination. Her voice was seldom heard. Once in a while, however, her reserve would yield to garrulity, as of water flowing through a broken dam. In these outbursts she usually spoke of her neighbours the Lemans, deploring the state of their marital relations. "A woman," she would say, "must give way to a man sometimes; I've had to give way to Sandford myself, I have." Her lips, from long compression, had become thin as the edge of a teacup; all her character seemed to have been driven down below the surface of her long, china-white face. She had not broken, but she had chipped; her edges had become jagged, sharp. The consciousness that she herself had been beaten to the earth seemed to inspire in her that waspish feeling towards Mrs. Leman—"a woman with a proud temper," as she would say in her almost lady-like voice; "a woman who's never bowed down to a man—that's what she'll tell you herself. 'Tisn't the drink that makes Leman behave so mad, 'tis because she won't give way to him. We're glad to sell drink to anyone we can, of course; but 'tisn't that what's makin' Leman so queer. 'Tis her."

Leman, whose long figure was often to be seen seated on the wooden bench of his neighbour's stone-flagged little inn, had, indeed, begun to have the soaked look and scent of a man never quite drunk, and hardly ever sober. He spoke slowly, his tongue seemed thickening; he no longer worked; his humorous, amiable face had grown hangdog and clouded. All the village knew of his passionate outbreaks and bursts of desperate weeping; and of two occasions when Sandford had been compelled to wrest a razor from him. People took a morbid interest in this rapid deterioration, speaking of it with misgiving and relish, unanimous in their opinion that—summat'd 'appen about that; the drink wer duin' for George Leman, *that* it wer, praaperly!

But Sandford—that blond, ashy-looking Teuton—was not easy of approach, and no one cared to remonstrate with him; his taciturnity was too impressive, too impenetrable. Mrs. Leman, too, never complained. To see this black-haired woman, with her stoical, alluring face, come out for a breath of air, and stand in the sunlight, her baby in her arms, was to have looked on a very woman of the Britons. In conquering races the men, they say, are superior to the women; in conquered races, the women to the men. She was certainly superior to Leman. That woman might be bent and mangled, she could not be broken; her pride was too simple, too much a physical part of her. No one ever saw a word pass between her and Sandford. It was almost as if the old racial feelings of this borderland were pursuing in these two their unending conflict. For there they lived, side by side under the long, thatched roof, this great primitive, invading male, and that black-haired, lithe-limbed woman of older race, avoiding each other, never speaking—as much too much for their own mates as they were, perhaps, worthy of each other.

In this lonely parish, houses stood far apart, yet news travelled down the May-scented lanes and over the whin-covered moor with a strange speed; blown perhaps by the west wind, whispered by the pagan genius of the place in his wanderings, or conveyed by small boys on large farm horses.

On Whit-Monday it was known that Leman had been drinking all Sunday; for he had been heard on Sunday night shouting out that his wife had robbed him, and that her children were not his. All next day he was seen sitting in the bar of the inn soaking steadily. Yet on Tuesday morning Mrs. Leman was serving in her shop as usual—a really noble figure, with that lustreless black hair of hers—very silent, and ever sweetening her eyes to her customers. Mrs. Sandford, in one of her bursts of garrulity, complained bitterly of the way her neighbours had "gone on" the night before. But unmoved, ashy, stolid as ever, Sandford worked in the most stony of his fields.

That hot, magnificent day wore to its end; a night of extraordinary beauty fell. In the gold moonlight the shadows of the lime-tree leaves lay, blacker than any velvet, piled one on the other at the foot of the little green. It was very warm. A cuckoo called on till nearly midnight. A great number of little moths were out; and the two broad meadows which fell away from the hamlet down to the stream were clothed in a glamorous haze of their own moonlit buttercups. Where that marvellous moonlight spread out across the moor it was all pale witchery; only the three pine-trees had strength to resist the wan gold of their fair visitor, and brooded over the scene like the ghosts of three great gallows. The long white dwelling of "the neighbours," bathed in that vibrating glow, seemed to be exuding a refulgence of its own. Beyond the stream a night-jar hunted, whose fluttering harsh call tore the garment of the scent-laden still air. It was long before sleep folded her wings.

A little past twelve o'clock there was the sound of a double shot. By five o'clock the next morning the news had already travelled far; and before seven quite a concourse had gathered to watch two mounted constables take Leman on Sandford's pony to Bideford Gaol. The dead bodies of Sandford and Mrs. Leman lay—so report ran—in the locked bedroom at Leman's end of the neighbours' house. Mrs. Sandford, in a state of collapse, was being nursed at a neighbouring cottage. The Leman children had been taken to the Rectory. Alone of the dwellers in those two cottages, Sandford's spaniel sat in a gleam of early sunlight under the eastern porch, with her nose fixed to the crack beneath the door.

It was vaguely known that Leman had "done for 'em"; of the how, the why, the when, all was conjecture. Nor was it till the assizes that the story of that night was made plain, from Leman's own evidence, read from a dirty piece of paper:

"I, George Leman, make this confession—so help me, God! When I came up to bed that evening, I was far gone in liquor and so had been for two days off and on, which Sandford knows. My wife was in bed. I went up, and I said to her: 'Get up!' I said; 'do what I tell you for once!' 'I will not!' she said. So I pulled the bedclothes off her.

When I saw her all white like that, with her black hair, it turned me queer, and I ran downstairs and got my gun, and loaded it. When I came upstairs again, she was against the door. I pushed, and she pushed back. She didn't call out, or say one word—but pushed; she was never one to be afraid. I was the stronger, and I pushed in the door. She stood up against the bed, defying me with her mouth tight shut, the way she had; and I put up my gun to shoot her. It was then that Sandford came running up the stairs and knocked the gun out of my hand with his stick. He hit me a blow over the heart with his fist, and I fell down against the wall and couldn't move. And he said: 'Keep quiet!' he said, 'you dog!' Then he looked at her. 'And as for you,' he said, 'you bring it on yourself! You can't bow down, can't you? *I'll* bow you down for once!' And he took and raised his stick. But he didn't strike her; he just looked at her in her nightdress, which was torn at the shoulders, and her black hair ragged. She never said a word, but smiled at him. Then he caught hold of her by the arms, and they stood there. I saw her eyes; they were black as two sloes. He seemed to go all weak of a sudden, and white as the wall. It was like as they were struggling which was the better of them, meaning to come on to one another at the end. I saw what was in them as clear as I see this paper. I got up and crept round, and I took the gun and pointed it, and pulled the triggers one after the other, and they fell dead, first him, then her; they fell quietly, neither of them made a noise. I went out and lay down on the grass. They found me there when they came to take me. This is all I have to write, but it is true that I was far gone in liquor, which I had of him . . ."

[*1909*]

STROKE OF LIGHTNING

THIS was before the war, and conditions were such that the tragedies and comedies of our private lives seemed still to have importance.

I had not seen my friend Frank Weymouth for some years, before coming across him and his wife that Christmas at the big hotel in Heliopolis. He was always a sunny fellow with a spilt-wine look about him, which not even a house-mastership at a Public School had been able to overcome: his wife, whom I had only met twice before, surprised me a little. I remembered a quiet, rather dark, little person with a doubting eye; but this was a very kitten of a woman, brimful of mischief and chaff, and always on the go—reaction, no doubt, from the enforced decorum of a house where she was foster-mother of forty boys, in an atmosphere of being under glass, and the scrutiny of intensive propriety. In our Egyptian hotel, with its soft, clever Berberine servants, its huge hall, palm-garden and cosmopolitan guests, its golf-course with little dark, scurrying Arab caddies, and the desert at its doors, Jessie Weymouth frolicked and rolled her large dark eyes, scratched and caressed us with her little paws. Life had suddenly got into her, and left its tail outside for her to chase. She dragged us all along in her gay pursuit of it; and Weymouth roused my admiration by his smiling acquiescence in her outrageous "goings-on." He knew, I suppose, that she was devoted to him, and her bark no bite. His "term" had been a hard one; he was in a mood of lying-back, physically run down, mentally flattened out. To soak in idleness and the sun was all he seemed to care about.

I forget who first conceived our desert trip, but it was Jessie Weymouth who fostered it. The Weymouths were not rich, and a desert trip costs money. They, myself, and a certain Breconridge couple had agreed to combine, when the Breconridges were suddenly summoned home by their daughter's illness. Jessie Weymouth danced with disappointment. "I shall die if we don't go now," she cried; "we simply must scare up somebody."

We scared up the Radolins—an Austrian couple in our hotel whom we had been meeting casually after dinner. He was a Count, in a bank at Constantinople, and she, I think, the daughter of a Viennese painter. They used to interest me from being so very much the antithesis of the Weymouths. He was making the most of his holiday, dancing, playing golf, riding; while she seemed extraordinarily listless, pale, and, as it were, dragged along by her lively husband. I would notice her lounging alone in the gorgeous hall, gazing apparently at nothing. I could not make up my mind about her looks. Her figure was admirable, so were her eyes—ice-green, with dark lashes. But that air of tired indifference seemed to spoil her face. I remember doubting whether it were not going to spoil our trip. But Jessie Weymouth could not be denied, and Radolin, we all admitted, was good company.

We started, then, from Mena House, like all desert excursionists on New Year's Day. We had only a fortnight before us, for the Weymouths were due back in England on the twentieth.

Our dragoman was a merry scoundrel by disposition and an Algerian Bedouin by race. Besides him we had twelve Arabs, a Greek cook, seven camels, four donkeys, and five tents. We took the usual route for the Fayoum. I remember our start so well. In front, Jessie Weymouth on a silver-grey donkey, and our scoundrel on his pet camel. Then Radolin, Weymouth and I on the other three donkeys, and Hélène Radolin perched up, remote and swaying, on the other riding camel. The pack camels had gone on ahead. All day we dawdled along, following the river towards Samara, where we camped that night at a due distance from the evil-smelling village. I had the middle tent, Weymouths to my right, Radolins to my left. Everything was well done by our merry scoundrel, and dinner, thanks to him, Jessie Weymouth and Radolin, a lively enough feast. Still, these first three days, skirting cultivation, were disappointing. But on the fourth we were well out on the lonely sands, and the desert air had begun to go to our heads. That night we camped among bare hills under a wonderful starry sky, cold and clear as crystal. Our scoundrel surpassed himself at dinner; Jessie Weymouth and Radolin were like madcaps, Weymouth his old sunny self. Only

Hélène Radolin preserved her languor, not offensively, but as though she had lost the habit of gaiety.

That night I made up my mind, however, that she really was a beautiful woman. The long days in the sun had given her colour, taken the tired look out of her face; and at least twice during the evening I caught Weymouth's eyes fixed on her as if he, too, had made that discovery.

The pranks of Jessie Weymouth and Radolin reached their limit at dinner, and they finished by rushing out into the night to the top of a neighbouring hillock.

Sitting in my tent doorway, counting the stars, I was joined by our scoundrel. The fellow had been in England and knew about Western freedom and the manners of our women.

"She certainly is a good one, Mrs. Weymut," he said to me. "Mr. Weymut a very quiet man. I think he will be tired of her flirts, but he never say nothing—too bloody gentle. The Count he is a good one too, but the Countess—ah! she made of ice! We get some fresh fruit to-morrow at the Fayoum." He went on to his men, two hundred yards away among the camels.

It was wonderfully silent. The light from stars and a half moon powdered the sands; no wind at all, yet deliciously cold—the desert in good mood; no influence quite so thrilling to pulses, yet so cooling to fevers; no sound, no movement in all the night!

"Isn't it heavenly? Good-night!"

Hélène Radolin was passing me in her fur. The look on her face, the movement of her body, seemed to belong to the lonely silence. She went into her tent. I sat on, smoking. And presently, outside the dining tent, I saw Weymouth, his head thrown back, drawing in deep breaths. By the light of the lantern over the tent door, he had a look as if inspired by a curious happy wonder. Then he too went to his tent. Ten minutes later the madcaps returned, Mrs. Weymouth in front, very quiet; her face, indeed, wore a rather mortified expression, as if she had fallen a little in her own estimation. They went into their tents, and I heard voices a moment, to left and right; then the stillness and the powdering light enveloped all.

Next day, bored with donkey-riding, I walked with the Arabs and saw little of my companions. Weymouth and the Countess, I think, were on the two riding camels, Radolin and Mrs. Weymouth

on their donkeys. We came to the edge of the Fayoum about five
o'clock. That camping ground was narrow. In tents, when jammed
together, one can't avoid hearing at least the tone of neighbouring
talk, and I was struck by a certain acrimony in the Weymouth tent.
Jessie Weymouth seemed complaining that Frank hadn't spoken to
her all day.

"I suppose," she said, "you didn't like my running out with
Countie last night?"

Weymouth's voice, quite good-humoured, answered:

"Oh! not a bit; why should I mind?"

By the ensuing silence I seemed to realise that Jessie Weymouth
was disappointed. Perhaps I hadn't really a feeling of suspense that
evening, but, in reminiscence, it seems to me I had. Dinner was
certainly a disharmonic feast: little Mrs. Weymouth audacious and
rueful; Weymouth and the Countess subdued, Radolin artificial;
our scoundrel and myself had to make the running. That fellow was
needle-sharp, though not always correct in his conclusions.

"Mrs. Weymut got a fly in her little eye," he said to me as I
was turning in. "I make it all right to-morrow; I get a dancer at
Sennourès. Oho, she, is a good one! She make the married couples
'appy. We get some fresh eggs too."

Severe silence in the tents to right and left that night!

A whole day's travelling through the crops of the Fayoum brought
us to the camping ground outside Sennourès, among a grove of
palm trees—charming spot, but lacking the clear, cold spirituality of
the desert night.

The dancer was certainly "a good one." What a baggage—all lithe,
supple enticement, and jangle of shivering beads! The excitement
of the Arabs, the shocked goggling eyes of Jessie Weymouth—
quite a little Puritan when it came to the point!—the laughter of
our scoundrel, Hélène Radolin's aloofness, which kept even that
daughter of Egypt in her place, were what impressed me during the
performance.

Towards the end the Egyptian made a dead set at Weymouth, and,
getting nothing out of him except his smile, became quite cross.
Leaning down to our scoundrel and slinking her eyes round at
the Countess, she murmured something malicious. Our laughing
scoundrel patted her, and we broke up. In ten minutes our camp was

empty—dancer, Arabs, all had gone off to the village. I went out and stood in darkness among the palm trees, listening to the shivering of their leaves.

Inside the dining tent Radolin was playing the guitar. The sound was soothing after the vibrant Arab music. Presently I saw Weymouth come out of the tent. He stood under the lamp at the entrance, looking back; his face was fully lighted for me, but invisible, I think, to those within. I shall never forget the look on it. Adoration incarnate!

'Hallo!' I thought, 'what's this?' And just then Hélène Radolin came out too. She passed him quietly; he did not attempt to speak or follow; but she saw. Oh! yes, she saw; then vanished into her tent. And Weymouth stood, rooted, as if struck by lightning, while, on and on, behind him rose the thrum of that guitar and all around us the shivering of the palm leaves in a gusty breeze.

Quite the custom, I believe, in these days to laugh at this sort of thing—at such sudden leaps of an irresponsible force; to suggest that they are old-fashioned, overrated—literary, in fact. The equality of the sexes—they say—the tendency of women towards brains and trousers, have diminished Venus; and yet, I fancy what happened to my friend Weymouth may still happen to young gentlemen who talk as if love had no fevers and no proprietary instincts; as if, when you burn for a woman, you are willing to leave her to another, or share her with him without fuss. Of course there are men who have no blood in their veins; but my friend Weymouth unfortunately had; not for nothing was the sunny, spilt-wine look about his hair and cheeks and dark-blue eyes.

For the rest of our desert trip the situation hopelessly promoted that adoration. Little Jessie Weymouth certainly did her best to help. She was the only one of us blind to what had happened. Her perceptions, you see, were blunted by the life of strenuous duty which she and Weymouth led in term time, and by the customary exhaustion of her husband during the holidays. She could not imagine him otherwise than sober. But now—if ever a man were drunk! The thing became so patent that it was quite painful to see her continued blindness. Not till sunset of the second day, with the Fayoum behind us, in our high camp on the desert's edge, did she sense her tragedy. *Those two* were sitting in camp-chairs close together, watching the sun go down. Our

Arabs, presented with a ram to soothe their grief at abandoning the joys of the Fayoum, were noisily preparing the animal to the idea of being eaten. Our scoundrel and Radolin were absent; I was sketching; Jessie Weymouth lying down in her tent. Those two were alone—their faces turned towards each other, their hands, perhaps, touching. A strange violet was in the light over the bare hills: how much they saw of it, I know not, nor what they were saying to each other, when Jessie Weymouth came out of her tent, stretching and yawning, and, like the kitten she was, went stealing up behind to startle them. Three yards away, unseen, unheard, I saw her stop. Her lips opened, her eyes went wide with amazement. Suddenly she covered them with her hands, turned round and stole back into her tent.

Five minutes later out she came again, with bright, hard spots of colour in her cheeks. I saw her run up to them, her feverish attempts at gaiety; and that to those two she simply did not exist. We none of us existed for them. They had found a world of their own, and we were shadows in the unreal world which they had left. You know the pink-flowered daphne, the scent of whose blossoms is very sweet, heavy, and slightly poisonous; sniff it too much and a kind of feverish fire will seize on you. Those two had sniffed the daphne!

Walls have a singular value for civilised beings. In my thin tent between the thin tents of those two couples, prevented by lack of walls from any outlet to their feelings, I seemed to hear the smothered reproaches, the smothered longings. It was the silence of those two suddenly stricken lovers that was so impressive: I, literally, did not dare to speak to Weymouth while we were all mixed up like that. This English schoolmaster had lost, as if by magic, all power of seeing himself as others saw him. Not that those two "carried on"—nothing so normal; they just seemed to have stepped into quiet oblivion of everything but each other.

Even our scoundrel was puzzled. "In my house, when my wife behave bad, I beat her," he said to me; "when I behave bad she scratch my face." But there it was—we had no walls; Hélène Radolin could not be beaten, Weymouth could not have his face scratched. It was most awkward.

Things come to an end, and I never breathed more freely than when Mena House delivered us from that frightful close companionship.

As if by common consent, we dined at separate tables. After dinner

I said to Weymouth:

"Come up and see the Sphinx by moonlight."

He came, still in his dream. We reached the Sphinx in silence, and sat down over against her on the sand. At last I said:

"What are you going to do now, old man?"

"I can't leave her." It was as if we had discussed the thing a dozen times already.

"But you have to be back on the twentieth?"

"I know."

"My dear fellow, it's ruination. And Jessie?"

"She must do what she likes."

"This is madness, Frank!"

"Perhaps. I can't go; that's all."

"What about *her*?"

"I don't know. I only know that where she goes I must."

I just sat staring at the blunt shadow of the Sphinx's broken profile on the moonlit sand. The strange actionless, desert love-dream was at an end indeed! Something definite—horrible, perhaps—must happen now! And I stammered out:

"For God's sake, old boy, think of your wife, your work, yourself— be reasonable! It isn't worth it, really!"

"Perhaps not. This has nothing to do with reason." From a master at an English Public School the remark appeared to me fantastic. And, suddenly, he got up, as if he had been bitten. He was realising suddenly the difference that walls make. His face had a tortured look. The woman he loved, walled up with the man she had married! Behind us the desert, hundreds of miles of clean, savage sand, and in it we humans—tame and spiritual! Before us walls, and we humans—savage, carnal again! Queer! I doubt if he saw the irony; but he left me sitting there and went hurrying back to the hotel.

I stayed on a little with the riddle of the Ages, feeling it simple compared with this riddle of the moment. Then I followed him down. Would it resolve itself in terms of L.S.D.? After all, these four people had to live—could they afford to play fast and loose with the realities? Hélène Radolin had no money, I knew; Weymouth his mastership and a few hundreds saved; Jessie Weymouth a retired Colonel for a father; Radolin his banking partnership.

A night of walls had its effect. Radolin took his wife back to

Heliopolis next day. The Weymouths remained at Mena House: in three days they were due to sail.

I well remember thinking: 'There, you see, it doesn't do to exaggerate. This was a desert mirage and will pass like one. People are *not* struck by lightning!' But in a mood of morbid curiosity I went out to Heliopolis.

In the traincar on the way I felt a sort of disappointment— Hélène Radolin was a Roman Catholic, Frank Weymouth an English gentleman. The two facts put such a stopper on what I wanted stopped. And we all have a sneaking love for the romantic, or—shall we say?—dramatic.

Well! The Radolins were gone. They had started that morning for Constantinople. In the Oriental hall where all this had begun, I sat, browsing over my Turkish coffee, seeing again my friend Weymouth, languid and inert; his little wife's flirtatious liveliness; Radolin so *debonair*; Hélène Radolin, silent, her ice-green eyes slightly reddened in the lids as if she had been crying. The white-garbed Berberines slipped by; Greek gentlemen entertained their dubious ladies; Germans raised a guttural racket; the orchestra twanged out the latest tango. Nothing was changed but those figures of my vision. And suddenly one of them materialised—Weymouth was standing as if lost, where the lobby opened into the hall. From his face it was clear to me that he knew they were gone; before I could join him he went out hastily. I am sorry now that I did not follow.

That evening at Mena House I was just beginning to undress when Jessie Weymouth tapped on my door.

"Have you seen Frank?"

I told her where I had seen him in the afternoon.

"That woman!" she cried. "He's not come back."

I assured her that the Radolins were gone away home. She stared at me and began to cry. She cried and cried, and I did not try to stop her. She was not only desolate and miserable, but bitter and angry. 'So long as she can be angry,' I thought, 'she'll get over it. One is not angry under a death blow.'

At last she had cried her misery out, but not her anger or dismay. What was she to do? I tried to persuade her that Frank would turn up in time for them to start to-morrow evening. He was probably trying to work the thing out of his system; she must look on it as a fever, a kind of illness. She laughed wildly, scornfully, and went out.

Weymouth did not turn up, but the morning brought me a letter, enclosing a cheque for £300, a note to his wife, and a sealed envelope addressed to the headmaster of his Public School.

The letter to me ran as follows: —

"Old man, I admit that I am behaving like a cad but it's either this or the sweet waters of oblivion; and there's less scandal this way. I have made up some story for my chief; please post it. The cheque is for all my substance except some fifty pounds. Take care of it for my wife; she'll get another five hundred, about, out of the turnover of our house. She will go to her father, no doubt, and forget me, I hope. Do, please, like a good fellow, see her safely on board. It's not likely that I shall ever come back to England. The future is quite dark, but where *she* is there I must be. Poste restante Constantinople will find me, so far as I know at present. Good bye and bless you.

"Your affectionate,
"F. W."

I did see Jessie Weymouth on board her ship, and a precious job it was.

A week later I, too, started for Constantinople, partly because I had promised Mrs. Weymouth, partly because I could not reconcile myself to the vision of my friend in the grip of his passion, without a job, almost without money.

The Radolins inhabited an old house on the far shore almost opposite the Rumeli Hissar. I called on them without warning, and found Hélène Radolin alone. In a room all Turkish stuffs and shadowy lights, she looked very different from her desert self. She had regained her pale languor, but her face had a definite spirit, lacking when I first saw her. She spoke quite freely.

"I love him; but it is madness. I have tried to send him away; but he will not go. You see, I am a Catholic; my religion means much to me. I must not go away with him. Take him back to England with you; I cannot bear to see him ruin his life like this for me."

I confess to looking at her with the wonder whether it was religion or the lack of L.S.D.

"Ah!" she said. "You don't understand; you think I am afraid of poverty with him. No! I am afraid of losing my soul, and his."

The way she said that was extraordinarily impressive. I asked her if she saw him.

"Yes; he comes. I have to let him. I cannot bear the look on his face when I say 'No.'" She gave me his address.

He had a garret in a little Greek hotel just above Galata—a ramshackle place, chosen for its cheapness. He did not seem surprised to see me. But I was startled. His face, shrunken and lined, had a bitter, burnt-up look, which deepened the set and colour of his eyes till they looked almost black. A long bout of disease will produce just that effect.

"If she didn't love me," he said, "I could bear it. But she does. Well! So long as I can see her, I shall stand it; and she'll come—she'll come to me at last."

I repeated her words to me; I spoke of his wife, of England—no memory, no allusion, no appeal touched him.

I stayed a month and saw him nearly every day; I did not move him by one jot. At the end of that month I should never have known him for the Frank Weymouth who had started out with us from Mena House on New Year's Day. Changed! He was! I had managed to get him a teaching job through a man I knew at the Embassy—a poor enough job—a bare subsistence. And watching my friend day by day, I began to have a feeling of hatred for that woman. Yet I knew that her refusal to indulge their passion was truly religious. She really did see her lost soul and his, whirling entwined through purgatory like the souls of Paolo and Francesca in Watts' picture. Call it superstition, or what you will, her scruples were entirely genuine, and, from a certain point of view, quite laudable.

As for Radolin, he took it all precisely as if there were nothing to take; smooth and debonair as ever—a little harder about the mouth and eyes, and that was all.

The morning before I went home it made my way once more up the evil-smelling stairs to my friend's garret. He was standing at the window, looking down over the bridge—that tragic bridge at Galata where unfortunates used to trade, perhaps still trade, the sight of their misfortunes. We stood there side by side.

"Frank," I said, "do you ever look at yourself in the glass? This can't go on."

No smile can be so bitter as a smile that used to be sunny.

"So long as I can see her, I shall last out."

"You surely don't want a woman to feel she's lost her soul, and is making you lose yours? She's perfectly sincere, in that."

"I know. I've given up asking. So long as I can see her, that's all."

It was mania!

That afternoon I took a boat over to the Radolins'. It was April— the first real day of spring, balmy and warm. The Judas trees of the Rumeli Hissar were budding, the sun laying on the water the tints of opal; and all the strange city of mosques and minarets, Western commerce and Oriental beggary, was wonderfully living under that first spring sun. I brought my boat up to the Radolins' landing stage, and got out. I mounted the steps, greened over by the wash of the water, and entered their little garden courtyard. I had never come this way before, and stood for a moment looking through the mimosas and bougainvilleas for a door that would satisfy formality. There was a grille to the left, but to reach it I would have to pass in front of the wide ground-floor window, whence I had sometimes looked out over the water to the Rumeli Hissar. My shoes made no noise on the marble path, but what I saw in the room stopped me from trying to pass.

Hélène Radolin was sitting perfectly still in a low chair sideways to the window, her hands on her lap, her eyes fixed on the tiled floor, where a streak of sunlight fell. In the curve of her grand piano, resting his elbows on it, Weymouth was leaning back, equally still, gazing down at her. That was all. But the impression I received of life arrested, of frozen lava, was in a way terrible. I stole back down the steps into my boat, and out on to the opal-tinted waters.

I have nothing more to tell you of this business. The war came down on us all soon after. Rumours I have heard, but know nothing, as they say, of my own knowledge. Yet it has seemed to me worth while to set down this record of a "stroke of lightning," in days when people laugh at such absurdities.

[*1921*]